# KEEPERS OF THE CAUSEWAY

**By**

**Ken Scott**

Fortis
Publishing Services

First Edition 2022 Fortis Publishing



ISBN 978-1-913822-51-4

Fortis Publishing
Kemp House
160 City Road
London
EC1V 2NX

For Tommy and Irene, resting in peace, together once again.

## Acknowledgements

To the incredible team at Fortis, especially to Joan the 'Ed' and Dan, Dan, the cover man.

To the beautiful people of Holy Island and the crew at The Ship Inn. I spent a wonderful week there during the final rewrite of this book.

And a special mention to Pete Saunders, who persuaded me that this story was worthy of a second chance.

## Authors Note

This book is a revamped, new version of my third work of fiction 'The Sun Will Still Shine Tomorrow' which went out of print five years ago.

www.kenscottbooks.com

# Prologue

"Quickly, just go now. Go before they come after you."

"But the causeway, it's already covering with water. I'll never make it."

"You will. It's only three miles to the mainland; if you run hard, you'll be there in less than thirty minutes."

The youth looked across the broad expanse of sand and water. He had a decision to make. He'd felt the fists and boots of the locals a few hours ago and didn't fancy a second beating…or worse. "Will I see you again?"

"Of course you will, but please hurry."

He peered out again into the pitch-darkness and it sent a shiver up his spine. He'd known his latest girlfriend for a matter of weeks and had really been taken with her. And the few stolennights of passion in the small bedroom above the public house. Pleasant memories.

He'd enjoyed his first and probably his last visit to Holy Island. And that body. She was certainly something special.

She stood in front of him, pleading. "Just go, you're wasting time. Please!"

Tears now. Tears falling onto those beautiful cheeks, cascading downwards towards those wonderful-tasting lips. And a strange feeling inside. Who knows? He'd never felt it before; this was special, very special. He would come back to the island. He had to. He had to stand his corner, fight for the woman he loved, so to speak.

Why on earth did he have to interfere, the man in the suit, so cocksure of himself? He'd accused him of offering drugs to the islanders, said he was going to call the police. He had been frightened. The man had said they'd searched his bedroom, found them. And then the locals seemed to gang up on him; then it was like something out of a Hammer House of Horror. A good kicking outside and then waking up in chains in a dungeon. Jesus… he thought it was a bad dream. A dungeon, a cell. This was 2008, for Christ's sake, it just wasn't for real.

And then the vision.

The beautiful Claire mopping his brow as he came to. Telling him she'd come to rescue him; he had to escape. And she'd produced a key and told him to be quick. Jeez… his head hurt as he stood up. But that kiss, that embrace, her smell and the taste.

Heaven.

"Are you listening to me? Go now. Please – across the causeway."

She looked at her watch, peered out across the darkened sands stretching out like a black lake. "Please go."

She looked behind her, a worried look on her face, and then she turned to face him. More tears, the bottom lip trembling. "They've killed before."

"They've what?"

"Killed. Took the poor half-unconscious lad out into the North Sea in January and threw him overboard."

"But the police? Why?"

"Just go, don't argue."

She turned round, looked back in the village's direction. "I can hear them coming; go now."

And he looked into those frightened eyes, those piercing, beautiful blue eyes and her copper-coloured hair, wet now and darkened from the light rain beginning to fall. And she did look scared. She looked terrified as she glanced back at the village and then back across the causeway. "Please, just go."

He took her hands. He too could now hear the voices growing ever closer. He could see a torch, its penetrating beam seeking him out. He looked out to the causeway. "You're sure it's safe?" The sea had begun to lap against the causeway road, an odd puddle now covering the tarmac.

"Of course I am. I was born here, remember? But you have to hurry. Please hurry, you're wasting time." Her voice had an air of desperation. She reached into her pocket. "Take this."

A torch.

He took it from her, felt for the on/off switch.

"No," she cried, almost shouting at him, "no time, just go." She leaned forward and brushed his lips with hers.

"I love you," she whispered. "Go!"

It was the most wonderful sound he'd heard in his life. He wanted to reply, wanted to tell her he loved her too. But the voices were growing louder. "I'll call you tomorrow, Claire, I promise."

He turned and ran across to the causeway, cursing as he splashed through the puddles. He set off, jogging lightly, aware that he wasn't as fit as he used to be, but convinced he could run the distance across to the mainland, especially as his life depended on it.

He remembered reading the stories in the Newcastle Chronicle of the poor bastards who'd been caught out on the causeway and had to be rescued or, worse, had to spend a night atop the safety tower in the middle of the causeway. All alone in the pitch-black, with only the sound of the roaring sea below for company. No mobile phones worked on Holy Island, no phone box in the safety tower, no way of contacting the emergency authorities.

A strange geographical, sea-level location, with Cheviot Hills on the mainland a few miles to the west blocking all signals. And the stubborn islanders blocking all attempts to erect a communication mast anywhere near their beloved community. And then there were the few that hadn't even made it to the safety tower. Their bodies washed up several days later along the coast. And something gnawed at him. Something Claire said about murder.

Sure enough, the first mile or so was a breeze as the road stretched out before him. He felt invigorated but wished he'd visited the gym a little more the previous month as his breathing pattern increased. The second mile. Not so good; a few nagging doubts crept into his head and his leg muscles began to burn.

Damn! The sea water had all but covered the causeway now; it lapped around the soles of his battered Nike trainers and made the running difficult. Every couple of minutes, a surge of water seemed to sweep in from the open sea, almost like a mini tidal wave. He could just make out the white lines along the centre of the road. He looked up. The half-moon shone across the sea, illuminating his route to safety. Thank God for that.

He slowed to a forced walk and cursed as a thick cloud drifted across the moon, plunging the route into darkness. And he remembered the torch. He stopped, tried to remember where he'd put it. He looked up, could just make out the lights from the small cottages on the mainland. He felt the hard shape of the torch in his inside jacket pocket.

"Claire," he whispered and raised a smile with little effort. He thought about the weekend and the good times ahead. He thought about their future and how he'd take her away from this damned island. He'd rescue her. His damsel in distress.

He pulled the torch from his pocket, located and flicked the switch upwards. It flickered into life but immediately dimmed. He lifted the beam to his eyes. A silly thing to do as it powered into life again, giving him a moment of temporary blindness. He stopped again, rubbing at his eyes. Too many stops, too many delays. Claire stood on the island, straining to pick out the form of her lover. She was frantic now; she could just pick out the beam of the torch and his progress was woefully slow. Just what the hell was he playing at?

And then the torch went out, plunging the causeway into darkness.

He tried it again and again and still it was useless. He cursed as he threw it into the sea. And now he felt fear. He walked on slowly, wary of each step, struggling to pick out the white lines. The safety tower, he thought. Where was it? He remembered seeing one when he came onto the island. He couldn't remember passing it. Surely he couldn't have missed it. He looked at the distant lights of the mainland. They were close – he'd make it; he was sure he could even swim it from here. The safety tower, he'd reach the safety tower, climb up, do a quick recce and go for it. The sea water was halfway up his ankles now and his walking had turned into a slow shuffle. He couldn't believe how quickly the water was rising, almost an inch or two every minute and he cursed himself for dawdling earlier.

The safety tower.

He looked up ahead and convinced himself he could make out a faint shadow. Yes. It was definitely something. He looked down at his legs. The water was halfway up his shins. Shit! He couldn't see the white lines. Where were the edges of the causeway? Was there a drop to the sand below? He couldn't remember. He looked back. Could he make it back to the island? Did he want to make it back to the island? A few figures stood together at the island end of the causeway, silhouetted against the faint glow of the streetlamps. Torches, their beams trained on the causeway, trained on him. He couldn't go back, not now.

The safety tower. His last hope.

He strained his eyes into the blackness of the night. He could make out the frame of the tower now. He allowed himself a smile, only about twenty feet away. It loomed up large as he approached it. The freezing cold North Sea numbed his legs now, the water up to his knees making it difficult to set one leg in front of the other. He spotted the ladder and reached out for it. He didn't notice the abnormally large wave surging towards the causeway from the south side, a wave that would ultimately add another few feet to the depth of the water, a wave that would sweep him from the causeway into the freezing perilous waters and fast flowing undercurrents of the North Sea.

"How do you convince them, Claire?"

She feigned a smile. "Oh, I have my ways."

"Think he'll make it?"

She lied. "I doubt it. If he'd been Linford Christie, perhaps. But not him; he was out of condition, a bit flabby across the middle." He was fit enough, she thought, and he'd had a torch. He'd pick the white road lines out, no problem. He might be up to his waist in water at the end of the causeway, but he'd make it.

"Think he'll make the tower?"

Claire shrugged her shoulders. "Doesn't matter if he does. You can pick him up first thing and give him a short boat ride."

Father Thompson stretched out a hand, squeezed her shoulder gently.

“You’ve done a good job again, Claire; the brotherhood appreciates it. Your father would be proud of you. God bless you,child.”

“My father. Yes.” My great protector, she thought to herself; itwas he who’d battered her *uncle* Jake senseless when she’d told him what happened. Only he wasn’t her *uncle*, just a very good family friend whom she had called *uncle* since childhood. Why did her parents have to die? Why had it been *uncle* Jake who’d broken the news and why had it been *uncle* Jake and his wife who’d formally adopted her at fourteen? There was no protector then, no one to stop his advances each time his wife left the house.

The girl turned towards the village, pulled up her collar to protect herself against the elements, and walked towards home, praying she’d get a phone call very soon.

# Chapter 1

Ashley Clarke had never liked the first name his parents had christened him with. He cringed every time he heard his mother's voice using it, be it in the confines of his small, terraced home, outside, or worse, as her tones echoed on the wind as she screeched in her 'come home now' pitch from the scullery door.

Yeah, that was definitely the worst. He'd be in the middle of a game as darkness descended over the east end of Newcastle when in the distance he could hear that terrible sound.

Ma never came looking, never bothered to walk the twenty-five yards to the Heaton Junky that was the unofficial and strictly off-limits playground of every latchkey kid in Heaton. Perhaps it was just as well she didn't come looking, he thought to himself. Nevertheless, he still hated that sound… "Aaaashleeeeey." And, of course, as soon as he'd heard the voice, he'd turn round and head for home.

Two reasons really. First, he couldn't take the chance that his mother would dare to come looking for him. She'd warn him every day to stay away from '*The Junction*'.

The British Rail fencing had been breached yet again. (By Ashley and his friends.) The fencing that was supposed to keep Ashley and his gang and others like them away. But what a playground it was. Stationary coal wagons and disused buildings and warehouses left over from an era when coal was definitely king.

Heaton Junction had been the intersection for just about every coal train, cement and steel wagon from the North of England. Train after train had pulled in and dragged their cargoes to and from the junction. And, of course, the yard had prospered and grown and adjusted accordingly, giving Ash and his pals the greatest adventure playground in the world.

The wagons were pushed away into the holding yards adjacent to the back streets of Spencer Street, Cleghorn Street, Richardson Street and Ebor Street. They were mostly deserted during the hours of daylight as the goods were generally moved at night, leaving the tracks free during the day for the passengerson the main East Coast line.

Occasionally, a member of the British Transport Police or a British Rail labourer patrolled the rough land. What was the point Ashley thought; not one member of his gang had ever been caught. The boys were used to the terrain, knew every conceivable escape route and had even built a few themselves. One game involved creeping up to the workers' makeshift canteen, housed in an old steel container, braying on the sides with a tin shovel as many times as the individual dared risk, giving a just sufficient head start to escape the furious workmen as they sprinted from within. Two or three seconds elapsed as they ran out, determined to catch the ruffian that had disturbed a pleasant lunch break or even forty winks before the next part of their shift began.

Ashley and his pals had laughed and cheered, sitting on top of the twelve-foot boundary wall, ready to shin down before scurrying into the warren of back lanes. But then his pals' ridicule as the sound reverberated through the streets or across the junction yard: "Aaaashleeeeey."

He was always 'Clarkey' or 'Ash'. The Ebor Street gang he ran with preferred 'Ash' whilst his school pals stuck to 'Clarkey'. He didn't mind either. What he did mind however was his mates' reaction to the correct form of his name. "It's a flippin' lassie's name, man," Millsa (Alan Mills) cried out as Ashley frowned and turned for home. Millsa mimicked a girl by placing a hand on his hip and his other one high in the air whilst the rest of the gang laughed. Darky Dowsa (on account of Graeme Dowson's jet-black hair) squealed with delight as he joined in the fun. Why not Bob or Kev, perhaps Derek or Steven, Jimmy even, Ashley thought, as he pushed his cold hands into his pockets and headed off up the gloomy street.

"It's just not fair," he mumbled as he turned the back lane into Ebor Street and gave his mother a token smile and a wave as he caught sight of her cotton floral apron fluttering on the breeze as she stood at the back gate.

"C'mon, wor Ashley, your dinner's getting cold."

"Can't you call me Ash, Ma?" he asked in desperation, knowing his mother's reply as always.

"Of course I can't, Ashley. That's your name and I like it. It's a lovely name, the name the priest christened you with. And anyway, why would I call you after something that's discarded into a dirty old ashtray?"

A few days later, a policeman had knocked at all the doors of the terraced streets. All the doors, that is, where the old copper knew a boy lived between the ages of six and twelve years old. Ma quite naturally had invited him in, offered him a cup of tea. And Dad? What was it with his dad? He'd stood up the whole time the policeman had sat in the scullery drinking from the best mug in the house, exactly like he did whenever Father O'Leary called. A strange respect, agreeing with everything the policeman had said. Officer this and officer that; yes, officer, no, officer, can I kiss your arse, officer.

And at that moment, the very moment that Dad had offered to take the law into his own hands, to help the 'officer' deal with the troublemakers at the junction in any way he could, Ashley Clarke knew... just knew... that when he grew up, when he entered the big adult world of work, there would be no shipyard, no mineshaft, no job at British Rail. No. There was only one profession he wanted to follow.

Ashley Clarke had been accepted into the police force two weeks after his eighteenth birthday. He walked into the kitchen and immediately noticed the tears on his mother's cheeks. He wasn't sure if she was happy or sad. She looked sad. She handed him the letter. "It's from the police, Ashley. You've been accepted. Your training starts in ten days' time."

Then why are you so sad? Ashley thought to himself. He grabbed at the letter and felt a big smile pull across his face. Why aren't you feeling the way I am? Why aren't you proud? He read the letter and then realised why. Sure, he'd been accepted, why not? He'd stuck it at school, passed his A levels with flying colours and taken care to stay out of trouble in his teenage years. Not such an easy task in the backstreets he'd grown up in. Already, two of his best pals had ended up in borstal.

He'd focused on sport, turned his attention to the school football team and even managed to get a place in the squad of the famous Wallsend Boys' Club when they'd set up a trial at the school. Latterly, he'd turned to boxing, joined Whitley Bay Boxing Club.

He'd been determined to turn the tide in the all too regular fights he'd been involved in. Part and parcel of the culture and environment he had grown up in. And yes, having a girl's name didn't exactly help. All in all, a perfect candidate for Northumbria Police.

So why then were they offering him a place in the Metropolitan Police in London? The recruitment officer had suggested he apply for both and he'd been only too happy to do just as the friendly sergeant had suggested. But then again, if he'd said jump off the Tyne Bridge, Ashley would have agreed without so much as a question. And now he knew why Ma was upset. A little proud. Of course. And a little sad.

Sad, because she knew that even if the letter had instructed him to join the force of the Outer Mongolia police based in an undiscovered jungle, her son Ashley Clarke wouldn't have hesitated to ask what time the next train left.

He read on. Not enough vacancies in the Northumbria force, Durham Constabulary was oversubscribed too. An all-expenses-paid weekend and a return train ticket to Kings Cross. Lodgings at the Met College in Hendon. It was everything he'd dreamed of since he was eleven years of age. And as he drifted off to sleep that evening, he realised that he'd never even been past York, never mind to London.

# Chapter 2

The pressure was off.

Although Ashley didn't have his results, he knew in his heart that he had done well. He'd kept his nose clean, applied himself and had tried his hardest. The end result was that feeling of quiet satisfaction, the same feeling that he'd had two years earlier when he had passed his O levels; he knew he had doneit. He hadn't been the brightest kid in the class, but he'd studied until the tears of boredom ran down his cheeks. And still he'd studied more.

Now it was time to chill. It was going to be the best summer ever. Everything was shaping up the right way. He'd receive the results and hopefully a start date before September. The feeling of self-fulfilment was oozing from within Ash, but for now, the immediate goal was to make the most of the summer ahead. The summer had been just as he had imagined it would be. The four pals had rolled on from one party to another, staying over at different friends' houses, trips to the beach, Monsters of Rock Festival at Donnington, a last-minute trip to France on a Transalpine rail ticket. They'd thought about it one day and headed off the next, the intrepid four setting foot on foreign soil for the first time in their lives, a daunting prospect. Off to LaRochelle on the west coast of France with not even a tent or a sleeping bag between them, but "Hey, what the hell, let's do it; this is how empires were built," Tom had said. He had it all sussed; it seemed like he had done this sort of thing a thousand times before.

The summer had gone according to plan, just the way Ash had hoped, but something was lingering within him and he knew the time would come.

He hadn't mentioned anything to any of his pals but he knew he would have to before long, because the little trip that he had made to London would soon yield its result.

The weekend trip to Holy Island on that scorching August bank holiday weekend was quite simply the icing on the cake, with a succulent glazed cherry on top. A full turnout. The whole gang was there, and even the girls managed to invent the right excuses to their parents. Everyone camped on the beach. It was like living in the hip early 1970s with BBQs, music, campfires, cool beers, lots of laughter, and all of this off the north-eastcoast of England.

Ash just wished he could bottle this atmosphere and keep it with him forever. Sadly, the weekend had to come to an end, and when the forlorn figure arrived home on that Tuesday morning in late August, he took one look at the brown A4 envelope addressed to him lying on the kitchen table and he knew the time had come. Reality sank in. His life was about to change.

The rail network seemed like life's blood: a huge twisting and turning pattern spreading like veins and arteries throughout the length and breadth of the land. Ash had never realised the significance of them before, but it dawned on him that it was an ever-present theme in his life from his father's employment as a train driver for British Rail, the junky playground as a mischievous child, the means of escape and of course the freedom of travelling through France weeks earlier.

And now it was the link between his roots in the north to his new life in '*The Smoke*', the big city.

The sixteen weeks at Hendon training school flew past with a familiar outcome: a successful course and a good pass mark. This wasn't natural, and there was no arrogance on Ash's part. He was not a natural academic and, as a consequence he knew that he would have to work harder than most of his fellow recruits. Now only a few days remained at training school, getting prepared for the real world. And, finally, a meeting with the top man of the college, Inspector Lawson. Butterflies in the stomach and yet a strange feeling of confidence.

"So then, have you given much thought to your posting, Clarke? Where can you see yourself on the beat?"

A strange question, thought Ash, and one that was a hot topic of conversation between Ash and his fellow recruits. It was the very last thing they would find out at training school on the last day. The suspense was consuming everyone; nobody wanted to end up with a bad posting.

"I like the sound of 'C' Division, Vine Street, Sir."

In the short time that Ash had been in London, he had realised that the West End was the place for him. He had been told by a number of sources that Vine Street was the station to be at. Anyway, it wasn't likely to happen, the odds were stacked against him. He knew he could end up anywhere from Brixton to Heathrow.

"Mmm, interesting, the bright lights of the West End. Well, like I say, once again, well done, Clarke. Enjoy the next thirty years. It will fly past. It has done for me. That's all, Clarke, on your way."

The whole intake sat in the conference hall on the last day. The room was filled with nervous anticipation; everyone was waitingwith bated breath to hear their fate, all that is except for Ash. He was only nineteen years of age, younger than most of his fellow recruits, but he sat there with a familiar feeling. He had wondered what had been the purpose of his meeting with Inspector Lawson, but his suspicions would soon be confirmed. The commander of the training school stood at the lectern, and one by one the recruits learned their fate. The booming voice from the imposing persona of Commander Penrose dealt up surprise, disappointment and, in Ash's case, confirmation. "PC Ashley Clarke, you are posted to Vine Street Police Station."

A wry smile came across Ash's face and the supportive comments of his mates accompanied this warm feeling of satisfaction: *"Nice one, Ash"* and *"Go on, Geordie"*. Yes, it was all coming together rather nicely.

The real world would soon descend on Ash, the comfort and sanctity of his learning environments at school and the police college quickly becoming a distant memory, as would the thoughts of the previous summer when he felt so young and carefree. His desire to pursue his chosen profession would soon unearth a murky world of drugs, prostitution, death and despair, all of which would test his resolve. '*Make me or break me*' was his self-invented motto. That's the way Ash looked at things, but deep inside, he knew it was the job for him.

Two years of pounding the beat around the streets of the West End, from the rags of the Soho beats to the riches of Mayfair and St James's, every square inch of Vine Street's patch had its attractions and a deep history, and Ashley made the most of it. From the nights spent sitting on top of various vantage points in the depths of Mayfair, his eyes straining in the dimly lit night in the hope of catching an old-time cat burglar in the act, to the drug addicts and prostitutes that loitered in the backstreets of Soho. This was all part of the learning curve. It was Ash's bread and butter. Every day another incident, another experience and, from time to time, his beat duties were interspersed with direct involvement in some high-profile situations that opened his eyes even further.

Ash had been on the front line at a number of demonstrations around the city and was well used to the abuse by now. He'd been covered in paint, phlegm, milk, eggs, you name it, in the running battles that generally broke out. In Trafalgar Square during the anti-apartheid demonstrations, he'd even had the delights of a sanitary towel slapped across his face whilst standing outside South Africa House.

By now he had also seen his fair share of death from the carnage of the IRA bombings in central London to the almost daily discovery of an overdosed drug addict lying slumped in the doorways behind Charing Cross Road or an old vagrant who had just slipped away in the middle of a freezing cold night.

He would never forget that fateful day on Tuesday April the 17th, 1984 when his Bow Street colleague Janet Bakewell had been shot and killed outside an embassy building in St James's Square. Cut down in a hail of bullets that came from the third-floor window of the embassy.

The memory of that sunny spring morning was etched in his brain. The cherry blossom had been in full bloom within the square. Ash was already in pain, but his pain was minor; it was from the blisters caused by a brand-new pair of shoes having their first outing. This pain would pale into insignificance compared to the pain that would be felt by Janet's family, her friends and colleagues. By the time Ash had finished his tour of duty that day, his socks were soaked by the fluid from his weeping blisters. At least he could take his shoes off; he didn't dare to think about his pain. Like most of his colleagues that night, the only answer was to stick together in their social groups and drink until the small hours, trying to make some sense out of what had happened.

The John Snow public house on the corner of Broadwick Street was the appropriate venue for Ash and his colleagues in their sombre mood.

After they had sunk the required amount and numbed their brains, they drifted off one by one. Ash retired to the nearby section house that was his home.

He stood in his room for a while, staring out of the fifth-floor window across the rooftops of Soho. It was never really dark there; even in the dead of the night the sodium lighting gave the city no rest and, as he stared out from behind his mirrored wall, a tear rolled down his cheek for his departed colleague. The section house was a gloomy depressing place to be that night; the echoes of laughter that usually rang out around the corridors were replaced with an eerie silence. He crashed onto his pillow in a semi-drunken, exhausted haze.

And later, the 1984 miners' strike, yet another week on the picket line. Ash's tenth visit to the Yorkshire coalfields, each time having to stay for a week at a time in a converted gym on an army base sleeping up to one hundred cops at a time. Not that there was much sleep to be had: the working day would start around 2 am with a hearty cooked breakfast in the army canteen. To forsake this mountainous plateful for an extra half-hour in bed was plain foolish. Neither Ash nor his colleagues were particularly hungry at this unearthly juncture, considering they had only finished their last pint about two hours earlier, but a long day lay in store for them and they would need to draw on the reserves of their 2 am feast. An essential piece of equipment during the day was the pillow that would help them nod off again against the coach window whilst being driven to whichever coalfield needed the police resources on site. Then it was out onto the line face to face with the striking miners, face to face with working-class men and boys just like him.

After standing around for a few hours, a welcome reprieve would arrive in the form of a power nap back on the bus whilst being herded to the site where the blue line would be deployed, and so it went on, finally finishing around teatime. Then it was back to the cramped makeshift digs, a quick shower and hot meal at the canteen, then out to the local for a decent swill.

It was during these evenings in the local pubs that Ash detected the overwhelming sense of hostility from the struggling communities. The tills in the bar would normally have been ringing with the proceeds of the miners' earnings, but it was a different story now. The penniless miners were at home whilst hordes of cops from all over the country had descended upon their territory, filling the bars and lavishly spending their overtime pay in view of everyone.

This didn't rest easy with Ash; his humble origins in the east end of Newcastle had instilled in him morals and a respect for anyone trying to earn a decent living. He had total sympathy for the community that was being torn apart by a government policy. During the conflict, Ash openly attempted to converse with any miner that stood opposite him on the picket line and nine times out of ten there was an open dialogue, a conversation, some kind of mutual understanding. Ash lowered the barrier and the veil that was his uniform and attempted to show some respect for his fellow human who just wanted to earn a decent crust. But just when Ash's efforts had fallen on a sympathetic ear it would all come crashing down. The line would jostle and everyone would be moved along a space or two and now Ash's new acquaintance would be face to face with another Met copper. This one was from the Home Counties, perhaps a leafy suburb in Surrey. And in a deliberate attempt to get a reaction, a sly derogatory comment.

"Was that your bird in the Red Lion last night? Nice girl, very friendly, if you know what I mean." Then the copper would reach into his pocket and pull out a wad of ten-pound notes and start to count them in the face of the penniless miner. And a reaction from the miner as sure as eggs were eggs: a curse, a flailing fist directed at the provoker and then a quickly executed arm lock and a grin.

"You're all the fucking same, you're fucking scum, the lot of you, fuck off back to London."

Only seconds earlier Ash had been in the kind of conversation that would have been commonplace between two pals, and now this troubled soul was being frog-marched away to the nearest police van, carrying with him a renewed hatred towards the police. Ash felt sick to the pit of his stomach; he'd seen this before in isolated incidents, the arrogance and lack of respect that some of his fellow officers had towards some individuals was beyond his comprehension. It was at times like this that Ash was ashamed to be wearing the uniform that he had been so proud to earn.

A year the strike had lasted. A whole year…

Ashley was back on his familiar Soho beat on his favourite shift, the night shift, quietly moving through the back lanes that connected Wardour Street, Dean Street, Greek Street and the surrounding area. Doc Martens were his chosen night shift shoe. The cushion sole allowed the stealth approach to the next quiet back lane, alleyway or courtyard where he happened upon his prey: a drug deal going down, a thief rummaging through the contents of a stolen bag before dumping it, a prostitute and her punter. There were rich pickings to be had if you were hungry enough to put yourself around like the young enthusiastic Ash.

Tonight was one of those nights that not even Ash could do much about, all quiet on the western front. He'd covered the ground over and over again, but there was nothing doing. For a moment his thoughts strayed back to the picket line and the attitude of some of his uniform colleagues that were starting to piss him off. He knew he couldn't spend the rest of career pounding the beat; it was time to start weighing up his options. As he turned the corner into Greek Street, he couldn't help but notice the tramp lying in the recesses of the doorway; he was just a shadow cowering in the dark corner, long greasy hair, beard, an assortment of rags surrounding him. He'd seen him around before over the recent weeks but hadn't taken much notice of him. Tramps would come and go, some had been around for years sleeping in their regular pitch, some would even die where they lay.

"You all right?" Ash enquired, as he stood over the wretched soul.

"Go away," came the voice from behind the greasy beard. It was only two words, but Ash instantly recognised the dulcet tones.

"Well, there's no need to be like that is there, especially to a fellow Geordie?"

At that point a grubby hand emerged from within the ragged coat, the palm opened outwards revealing a silver badge identical to the one Ash was carrying in his back pocket, the one that he had been so proud to receive from Commander Penrose over two years ago.

"Listen, pal, I'm on surveillance. Will you just fuck off before you blow the job out? And another thing, stop being so keen, get out of here for the night, put your feet up and grab a cup of tea somewhere."

Ash disappeared into the black night, but a light had switched on in his head. From that moment, he knew where his future lay.He had a newfound purpose, he had to start planning. His mind was working overtime. He couldn't do much about it until the following week, when he was back on day shift.

The news that the divisional crime squad were not going to recruit any new members for the next twelve months came asa bitter blow to Ash. His plan was in tatters; there was no way he could wait that long and, if this was not depressing enough, his gloom was compounded even further when the news filtered through about the crime squad's latest success.

They had raided the address on Greek Street where his Geordie counterpart had been keeping watch. Ten kilos of high-grade coke, four section one firearms, two thousand rounds of .38 calibre ammunition and three of Soho's highest profile Maltese hierarchy had all been taken out. All in all, a huge feather in the cap for the West End Crime Squad. The excitement was too much. Ash knew what he wanted and he wanted it now. He racked his brain. He had to act. There must be something he could do. He couldn't contemplate the prospect of pounding the beat for another twelve months. He began to think about his brief meeting with Inspector Lawson at training school.

The third floor of Vine Street Police Station was home to the senior officers and sitting in prime place was the office of Chief Superintendent Mike McCaffrey, a man who was nearing the end of his distinguished police career. He was immensely respected throughout the Met. He had been a first-class operator in his day and had achieved legendary status. He'd been the Vine Street Commander for just over twelve months. The first time that Ash had heard about his arrival at Vine Street was whilst he was on sick leave, nursing a broken leg. Ash hobbled down the stairs of the section house to pick up his mail from the office. He opened the small brown envelope that was addressed to him. It read:

Dear Ashley,

As you may know, I have recently been posted to Vine Street asthe Chief Superintendent. I am conscious I have not met you yet and was sorry to hear of the unfortunate injury to your leg.

I hope your recovery is going well but please do not rush back to work too early. If there is anything you need in the meantime (except money!!) please do not hesitate to contact me. When you do return please come and see me.

Yours sincerely,

Mike McCaffrey

Upon his return to work, Ash had responded to McCaffrey's request. Ash was always wary of a new boss. However, he felt instantly at ease with his new chief. He was a true gentleman, a career detective. It hadn't escaped McCaffrey's notice that the hours that Ash had spent pounding the beat had earned him the highest number of crime arrests at the station.

Over the next twelve months, McCaffrey acknowledged Ash every time they met, which would invariably be in the charge room while Ash was booking in another arrest.

"Morning, Geordie. Busy again, keep up the good work."

Austin Reed was a well-known store on Regent Street, just up from the Man in the Moon passage which led into Vine Street.On the lower level was the gentleman's barber shop, which was normally reserved for the city gent types to have themselvesgroomed for a princely sum.

Ash knew that it opened at 8 am and today he would be the first customer, because this wasn't just any old haircut, it wasn't the normal trim he would settle for at Pete the Barber's in the dingy basement on Wardour Street. If he was about to do something radical, the preparation and state of mind had to be right. His uniform had never been so immaculate and he could just about make out his reflection in the toecaps of the shoes that had just about crippled him months earlier.

He knew exactly what time he would carry out his operation. He had walked past the office often enough on route to the admin department and he knew that by about 9.30 am McCaffrey would have had his daily briefings and updates by his underlings and would be just about to settle down to the business at hand.

As he reached the landing of the third floor, he took a deep breath. His heart was practically jumping out of his chest. *No going back now,* he thought to himself. Ash reached the open doorway, stood still and knocked on the heavily gloss-panelled door. McCaffrey looked up from the heavy oak deskand peered at Ash through his bi-focals.

"Ah, Geordie, come in, have a seat."

"I'd rather not, Sir. What I've got to say won't take long, if Icould have a minute of your time."

McCaffrey smiled, removed his glasses and rested them on the table.

"Very well. What is it you want to say?"

Ashley walked further into the massive office and stood in front of McCaffrey's' desk

"Sir, I just want you to know that I wish to be considered for the CID."

He felt a lump in his throat; he paused as if about to deliver a best man's speech. "And I want to work on the divisional crime team; I know that is where my future is."

McCaffrey rearranged a few papers on his enormous oak desk, raked his fingers through his hair and exhaled.

"That's all very well, Clarke, but there's a process in place for that and we won't be advertising for vacancies for another twelve months".

"I know, Sir. I just wanted to bring it to your attention, that's all."

"I see. Well, thanks for letting me know. Just keep up the graft, keep your nose clean and we'll see how things work out for you next year."

"Thank you, Sir."

"Is that everything, Clarke?"

"Yes, Sir.Thank you, Sir."

McCaffrey had never called Ashley by his surname. He'd always thought being called Geordie by such a senior officer was a term of endearment. He'd always thought he'd been on the right side of McCaffrey, but in the space of less than a minute he'd managed to blow everything. That sort of approach was unheard of. The audacity of walking into the Chief Superintendent's office proclaiming one's desires was the stuff of fiction.

"Okay then… on your way."

Ashley turned to walk out as McCaffrey's head lowered and focused on the mound of paperwork requiring his attention, and, as Ash took the last few steps towards the doorway, the voice from behind the heavy Victorian desk slowed his pace. "By the way, Geordie, you've got some fucking nerve, haven't you?"

The softly spoken, unassuming Irish accent of the gentleman that was McCaffrey washed over Ash with a warm glow, and in that instant, he knew he had done the right thing. A familiar feeling of quiet satisfaction came upon him and as he walked from the office, his reply was simple.

"I want it that badly, Sir."

The familiar roll-call played out once more in the basement parade room as Ashley and his fellow shift colleagues stood to attention.

"Appointments."

This was the familiar regimental order called out by the parade sergeant with the uniform shift inspector standing by his side. Everyone responded by producing pocket notebook, truncheon and whistle for inspection. The parade consisted of formal instructions and notifying each officer which beat they would patrol that day.

A brief update on local intelligence rounded up the parade briefing whilst any internal mail and correspondence was dished out. Ashley was handed a small brown envelope.

PC A. CLARKE, A Relief.

The letter within it took the wind out of Ashley Clarke's sail. It had been less than a week since his audacious manoeuvre in the office of Chief Superintendent McCaffrey.

The letter was brief, to the point and so very sweet.

PC Clarke has been selected for interview for a position with the Divisional Crime Squad. The interview will take place this coming Thursday at 2pm. The interview will be conducted by Chief Superintendent McCaffrey and Detective Chief Inspector Belcher.

The elegance and refinement of Savile Row to the west of Regent Street seemed at odds with the bland, modern structure of the West End Central Police Station. 'C' Division Crime Squad was located deep within its bowels.

For Ashley, it was just like starting all over again; he was the new boy, the tea boy, the sprog. Call it what you want. It didn't matter to Ashley because this is where he wanted to be. He was more than happy to put up with any short-term nonsense, and he was expecting his fair share of flak. Being a copper was tough; being in 'C' division was harder still. He would get stick for his accent, and his place of birth; he would be a Geordie bastard until he was accepted into the team and get the raw end of any deal again and again. A big nose, slightly thinning hair, a slight speech impediment, everything that could… would be picked up on. It was life in the police, a necessary part of creating that thick layer of skin, the wide shoulders that were necessary to handle the job. What galled Ashley more than anything were the policemen and women who ran to their superiors crying foul, taking millions out of the system because they couldn't hack the job. It was survival of the fittest, end of story; what chance did a copper have on the streets if he or she couldn't take a gentle ribbing or an occasional offensive remark? He had had plenty of warning about some of the characters that made up this squad, and he knew that the hard core of hand-picked detectives that made up the team stood and fell by their results which, as they stood in the current climate, were pretty impressive.

This was the dirty end of policing, the pro-active undercover nature of their work required a unique bond and sense of humour; if you didn't fit in you were on your way in no time at all. Everyone had to pull together. It was a far cry from the main office detectives who came to work in their smart suits and investigated the routine enquiries. They didn't look out of place walking along Savile Row. However, their counterparts on the crime squad often looked like they had just been released from a cell block at the back of West End Central.

"Welcome onboard, Ash." A friendly voice greeted him with a familiar accent. "Andy Gibbons, we've met once before." Although Ash was pretty good at putting a name to a face, he was lost on this occasion.

"I'm sorry. When was that?"

The clean-shaven northerner replied, "When I told you to fuck off in Greek Street a couple of months ago. You nearly blew the job out, man."

He laughed out loud.

"Only kidding, mate. You weren't to know. It doesn't matter now, we still got a cracking result on that job. We've heard a lot about you, Ash, and we're glad you're here. You'll fit in just fine." Ash was lost for words. He looked at Andy Gibbons closely, trying to visualize him as the dirty tramp he'd seen in the doorway a couple of months ago.

Days to weeks, weeks to months, months to years, one good job after another, time was skipping by. Ash and Andy had become inseparable. They had become a formidable partnership and had been at the hub of every decent job that had been pulled off by the crime squad. But Ash knew that things were likely to change. Andy had been mentioning it more and more of late, and it came as no surprise when he dropped the bombshell. Ash understood. He had thought that he would more than likely do the same thing if he was in Andy's shoes, but for Andy, it was here and now. Both of his parents were in poor health and their only other child, Andy's sister, lived in New Zealand. He knew he would have to transfer to his native north-east to be closer to his parents and nobody could criticise him for that. This was a bitter blow for Ash. He was losing his work partner, soul mate, best friend, and there was only one way Ash would cope, and that was to totally immerse himself in the job.

After fifteen years, this had become Ash's town; he'd seen the whole spectrum of the underworld, he'd eaten, slept and shit the job year after year. He'd seen all there was to see in the undercover world and had been seconded from time to time with various Scotland Yard squads.

Being an undercover cop had brought Ash all the excitement and variety that he could have imagined, and more. He'd never considered promotion at all; he'd seen all the halfwits and yes men jumping up the ladder over the years and he didn't want to be part of the same circus. He wasn't in it for the extra money or credence of rank; he was on a decent wage and, with years of selling his soul to the job, he had earned a small fortune in overtime which he had invested wisely in the purchase of a splendid apartment in Belsize Park. He had latched onto the apartment when property was affordable, before the property boom of the late 80s. All in all, he was in a very healthy financial position; he wanted for nothing except the love of a good woman. Unfortunately, with this line of work, any woman would have to have the patience of a saint to put up with all that went with it.

And Alexis had put up with it. She did have the patience of a saint, but then again there was only so much a girl could put up with. Alexis... why? Everything was beginning to take its toll; he'd lived in a dirty world for a long time. He'd worked hard, but played hard too. All too often. He was still a fit man and when he got the time in between working and drinking he would take his aggression out on the punchbag in the basement gym at Trenchard section house.

He would pound away for what seemed like an eternity, his thoughts drifting back to his youth at Whitley Bay Boxing Club as the sweat cascaded from him in the hot stuffy basement. And as the frustration and aggression evaporated through his pores, his thoughts would wander back to Alexis.

Yes, he still felt fit… fighting fit, but he also knew that nearly twenty years of hard drinking with his workmates had done him no favours.

The Smithfield Tavern at Smithfield Market saw the more extreme version of a quick pint after work, for it was here that cops from all over the Met would descend after finishing the night shift at 6am for a handy eight-to-ten-pint session. The only patrons within the establishment that had a special licence to open at that hour for the market traders would be the night shift cops and a handful of vagrants that would invariably end up having their drinks bought for them from pissed-up, off-duty cops. The same cops that would probably arrest them for begging, if both parties were on the other side of the pub threshold.

Ash always kept an eye on the impending premiership fixtures as he knew when he was likely to get the phone call, a very welcome call at that. Andy was welcome at any time, but the visit of the black ’n whites for a key fixture in the capital always seemed the perfect way to stay in touch. Andy more or less had a room for himself at Ash’s apartment.

They would reminisce about the good times they’d had many years ago. And after a few beers Andy would inevitably try to persuade Ash to jack it all in and move back up north.

"Start afresh, take your feet off the gas a bit," he'd say. "There's more to life than the fucking job."

"There's no way you will catch me going back into uniform."

The mere thought sent a shiver up Ash's spine.

"I wouldn't know where to start. I'd be completely out of my depth. It's been nearly thirteen years since I wore a uniform."

"It's not that bad up there, you know. We've even got computers and radios. Look at me, I've even managed to get promoted. I had some good times when I transferred back. There're some good lads up there; you'll slot in no problem." Ash had lost count of the times they'd had this conversation, but the minute Andy was heading back north on the train, it was forgotten about.

The incident had prayed on his mind for six weeks now; the demons and the gremlins in his head he'd tried to fight had won. Whichever way he looked at it, deep down, he knew he could have prevented the carnage. After the first explosion, he'd been one of the first on the scene. It was like something out of a First World War movie scene. Body parts, limbs, fragments of bone and charred, blackened flesh lay everywhere. Slaughter of the innocents: the working men and women of London, students, children, British, African, German, American, Muslim, Christian, Hindu, Buddhist. It didn't matter.

The suicide bombers had bombed in the name of their god. The platform was thick with black acrid smoke and dust, but was gradually beginning to clear. Several fires raged on what wasonce a City of London tube train, now a twisted, burning mass of steel and roasted blackened flesh.

He stood frozen on number two platform wishing he could have turned the clock back twenty minutes. A young Asian woman looked up at him as she lay on the platform. She mouthed the word *help*.

She lay in a bloodied heap in her tattered underclothes, exposing a bloody breast. The blast from the bomb had blown most of her clothes away and, with it, death's dignity. Ashley knelt down, held her hand and wiped a trickle of blood from her eye. Her hand was icy. Ashley felt for a pulse but found none. She gazed into his eyes, smiled a last smile at the undercover cop, then closed her eyes forever. He could have stopped it, should have stopped it.

Never break your cover, he'd been told, whatever the circumstances. And he'd sat inside the entrance of Kings Cross station as he'd watched the four men embrace. It was a long embrace, very emotional and two of them shed tears. Ashley had watched their outburst of emotion and figured that one or two of them were on their way to Heathrow or Gatwick for a long trip back home, maybe never to return.

That was the only explanation. Men didn't hug and cry like that over a week's holiday or a day at the office. They were off on a long, long journey.

Then it happened.

They walked into the station together. They didn't part.

Ashley stood. Why? They hadn't parted, why the great show of emotion? He thought back to the twin towers in New York. No, surely not.

"DCI Gibbons, can I help?"

"It's me, Ash."

DCI Andy Gibbons recognised the significance of the call."I think it's time, Andy. Can you help me?"

Andy had been waiting many years to hear his old mucker Ashley utter those words. The timing couldn't have been better and yet, his friend's voice wasn't full of the optimism and enthusiasm of old. Andy detected it straight away.

"What is it, Ash? You don't sound so good."

Ashley never answered the question, and such was their almost telepathic understanding of each other that Andy Gibbons let it drop. Ashley would come out with the reason when the time was right.

Andy Gibbons was in the perfect position. In the ten years thathe had been in Northumbria police he had become a well- respected senior detective and was able to pull a few strings. It would be a complete waste of such an experienced undercover officer to have him pounding the beat again, as was the normal protocol for anyone transferring forces. Andy had been kidding Ash when he had told him on numerous occasions that it wasn't that bad, for he remembered that when he came back ten years ago, he'd hated pounding the beat after the excitement of undercover work.

Fortunately for Andy, he was in the right place at the right time. He had recruited a snout that was heavily involved in an armed blagging crew. He knew the lad from his school days and he was eating out of the palm of Andy's hand.

This soon flagged up at the Force intelligence department. Andy was summoned to the Newcastle CID headquarters and was immediately seconded onto the investigation into the armed blaggings that had been going on throughout Tyneside and was assigned to his new partner, DC John Markwell, who would become a close friend.

Andy's uniform was consigned to the loft once again.

Andy sat at his desk feeling quite pleased with himself. In the twenty years he had been in the job he'd had the privilege towork with two first-rate detectives at the opposite ends of the country, and now, with the privilege of rank and a quick phone call to John Markwell, the plan had been hatched. John Markwell would soon have a new partner on the Newcastle crime team.

It would be a perfect match.

# Chapter 3

Ashley Clarke stepped off the train at Newcastle Central Station. He'd decided some months back that nearly twenty years in the Met was long enough for anyone. Besides, the force had changed. Policing had changed. The inspectors and superintendents had changed too.

Too much political correctness, too much paperwork, not enough hours 'real policing'.

He walked out of the old Victorian concourse and into Neville Street and hoped… prayed… that perhaps the Northumbrian Force had somehow managed to escape the winds of change. As he ordered his first beer in the Sour Grapes, opposite Newcastle Central Station, he resigned himself to the fact that it probably hadn't.

His new partner introduced himself as DC John Markwell. "Nice to meet you, Ashley. I get called Johnny down here, sometimes Holy John."

"Down here? I don't understand," replied Ashley. "And why Holy John?"

DC Markham laughed. "I come from Holy Island, up byBerwick upon—"

Ashley held up a hand.

"Don't worry, Holy John, I know where you come from. St Cuthbert's Island, the Holy Island of Lindisfarne. I spent time there as a teenager, a very pleasant evening with a girl called Marie Cherrie from Dunbar."

"You don't say."

"I took a group of youths on a fifty-three-mile walk there in my early twenties; we camped out overnight once we made it. I loved the place, even managed to get back there a couple of times since."

DC John Markwell beamed. "You did?"

"You sound surprised."

"It's just that… oh well, never mind. It's just that we islanders are quite protective of the place. It seems that someone is always having a go at us, you know, wanting us to embrace change, move on, that sort of thing. It's just such a special place and even in somewhere as close by as Newcastle people say holy where?"

Ashley Clarke grinned, already warming to his new colleague. "What do you expect, John? I mean, you buggers cut yourself off from the outside world twice every day."

DC John Markwell smiled. "Yeah, I'm afraid there's nothing we can do about nature and the big man in the sky, I'm afraid. But there again, it goes to make the place a little different, a little special."

Ashley dropped his Nike sports bag on DC John Markwell's desk.

“So where do I make my pitch, Holy John? What side of the desk do I take?”

DC John Markwell looked a little sheepish.

“I’m afraid you don’t. We don’t have a personal desk in Northumbria Police, just a locker in the basement. You can use this desk any time you want, the phone, and of course the computer. But then again, so can another twelve DCs.”

Ashley shook his head.

“We’ll get by, Ashley, don’t you worry about—"

“Ash! I’d prefer if you called me Ash. Let’s start off on the right foot.”

“Ash it is then.”

The two newly acquainted partners shook hands warmly, John Markwell placing his left hand on the back of Ashley’s right and squeezing gently as if they were long-lost buddies from way back.

“I’m sure we’re gonna get along just fine, Ash… just fine.”

They kicked off their first shift at six the following morning. DC Markwell had suggested an *intelligence day* taking Ashley through the police computer files and offloading the information held and the hearsay on the local villains.

Newcastle, like other big inner cities, was trying to stem the tide of drugs and control several warring factions vying to rule the roost. It was a never-ending battle, one the Northumbria Force seemed to be losing.

“There was a bit of a shoot-out two weeks ago, Ash. Sixteen of the fuckers met up in Leazes Park in broad daylight. It was supposed to be a battle of the hard men. But, as per usual, the side that were losing at the time pulled out some shooters. The other side responded and two of the poor bastards ended up in the morgue."

Ashley shook his head. "I thought that only happened in The Smoke, occasionally on Moss Side in Manchester or Croxteth in Liverpool."

DC Markwell drained the last of his coffee dregs.

"'Fraid not, Ash, it's happening here on Tyneside these days; five times last year, in fact. I can't say I lost too much sleep over the bastards on the slab, but I was sorry to say there'd be another two to replace them by the end of the same week."

It was true.

Ashley Clarke had seen the same thing happen all too often in London. Two families, sometimes three, occasionally four, all wanting to be top dog… king of the castle. Reputation was all-important, the fear factor reigned supreme. It had been going on for centuries, glorified by the Krays and the Richardsons, portrayed on the silver screen as a glamorous occupation.

And that's how they viewed it. An occupation. The Newcastle villains were no different. They viewed themselves as businessmen and couldn't really see what it was they were doing wrong. Protection, drugs and prostitution were their mainstay and it was certainly very lucrative. They turned a blind eye to the misery and heartache they caused threatening violence and death to anyone and everyone who stood in their way. They never wanted to notice the suicide of a failed businessman paying exorbitant fees for *protection* whose loans to the bank and tax payments could no longer be met. They never noticed the premature ageing of the teenage girls and boys they offered up for prostitution or the junkies they created at the drop of a hat.

Only last night, the front page of the Evening Chronicle had announced yet another drugged up twenty-year-old and a teenager murdered for a five quid wrap. They just turned the other cheek: the villains, the gangsters, the hard men.

Their ill-gotten gains from the seedier side of their work fronted up legitimate shops, garages and fast food restaurants and any other business they could buy into for a knock-down price.

It was DCs Clarke's and Markwell's responsibility to infiltrate those businesses and prove that they were there solely for the purpose of money laundering: turning dirty money into clean. A month into the job and there was a breakthrough: the two partners had been tipped off. One of the city firms had been offering up crack cocaine at a quid a go. Worse still, it was being offered outside an East End school to the pupils.

The economics were straightforward; it was what was known as a 'loss-leader'. The villains were prepared to forego the immediate profit on the sale at this early stage. They were creating an unlimited supply of future addicts who would stop at nothing to get future fixes. Crack cocaine is one of the most addictive drugs on the market, creating an incredibly intense high. The faster the absorption, the more intense the high. The effects are short-lived and, once the drug has left the brain, the user experiences a coke 'crash', generally depression, irritability and an overpowering urge to get the next fix as quickly as possible.

Ashley Clarke had seen it destroy whole communities all around London. It was an evil tide he was determined to turn away from Newcastle.

The villain at the top, Billy Graham, ran a fleet of legitimate, supposedly successful businesses, but anybody and everybodyknew they were being propped up by the income from drugs. Ashley had been briefed about him, given chapter and verse over the course of the last few weeks.

The two partners had been undercover for just over a week. Ashley had been placed on the street outside the school disguised as a road sweeper. He'd taken the role to heart and hadn't washed or shaved for a fortnight prior. He wore an old baseball cap that could literally walk home of its own accord and the standard issue orange overalls from Cityworks.

And he'd swept the two-mile long road from top to bottom for nine days now, so much so that it almost shined. DC Markwell had the slightly more pleasant job of sales assistant in the newsagent across the street that offered up a perfect view of the front of the school.

It also allowed a skilful listener to take in the conversations of the children coming and going several times a day. DC Markwell had heard enough of the dialogue to know that his intelligence reports were good. Nine days with a hard, cold-handled brush and DC Ashley Clarke wasn't so convinced.

He whispered yet another car number plate into the handle of his brush that contained the microphone, back to the temporary operation room situated in a disused three-storey flat a hundred yards from the school. And he received the same reply he had heard for nine days: "It's clean, Ash, belongs to a Mark

Pickering from Longbenton. Outstanding parking fine and D & D in his youth."

Ashley sighed, scratched furiously at his facial stubble, and wondered why the hell any man actually grew a beard. It was one of life's unanswered questions, he thought.

He turned around at the top of the street to begin yet another long walk back towards the school. His feet ached now, as well as his hands, and his back cried out for mercy.

The black BMW X5 slowly came to a halt outside Four Lane Ends Metro Station. A thickset gorilla climbed from the passenger side, walked around the front of the car as if holding two imaginary medicine balls under each arm and began a conversation with the driver.

He flicked a casual glance at the streets around the concourse and Ashley whispered the details of the car number plate back to base.

The battered old Walkman earphone crackled into life. "Villain, Ash. Big time."

"Who?" he asked as he dragged his hand slowly across the bottom of his nose, wiping away the not so imaginary snot and grime.

"The BMW belongs to Bulldog Billy Graham, recognised Godfather of the North Side. Two convictions for armed robbery, four for GBH. Served a total of sixteen years inside. He's more astute these days and richer. Doesn't get his hands dirty anymore."

An interruption and Ashley recognised his partner's dulcet tones.

"Ash, it's me, John. Where is the car? Can you describe the driver? What do the occupants look like? What—"

"Whoa, John. Steady on, one question at a time."

"Sorry, Ash, probably not Bulldog driving anyway. If they really are about to do some dealing, he wouldn't be that stupid to get involved. A car's on its way."

Ashley spoke. "A gorilla is opening the back door. Three youths have jumped out, two white guys and an Asian."

Ashley manoeuvred the dustcart around, checked on the position of the video camera inside, and pressed record. Another voice interrupted his train of thought through his earpiece.

"Positive ID. We see him. I don't believe it. What's he playing at? It's Bulldog."

"You're kidding me?" The hairs rose on the back of Ashley's neck. He could almost smell the tension from his new partner in the newsagent's and the back-up squad in the flat. Ashley remembered his Met training, took a deep breath.

"The youths are talking to the driver now. It's three twenty-five.The school will be out in five minutes."

The silence in the patrol room deafened Ashley as he continued.

"The BMW is pulling away. Driver only. Gorilla walking over to the Metro entrance and the three youths are walking in the direction of the school."

Ashley's earpiece crackled into life.

"Positive ID on the gorilla team. Steve Macintosh, goes by the name of Mad Mac. Known as Bulldog's right-hand man and has a reputation in a scrap to chew flesh if he isn't getting his own way. He bit off a rugby player's nose on Gosforth High Street a few years ago. He got away with it. Bulldog pulled six witnesses from the street, claimed the rugby player attacked Macintosh first."

Then an instruction Ashley Clarke didn't want to hear.

"You stick to him, DC Clarke. We've a car following Bulldog and a team on the youths. As soon as they start and deal, we'll let you know. That's your cue to take Mad Mac. For Christ's sake, don't let him get on that Metro."

*Thanks a fucking bunch,* Ash thought to himself, *don't I get any help?*

Ashley reluctantly pushed his cart over towards the Metro and studied the small screen hidden deep within. He applied the brake and waited. More information through his earpiece told him the youths were all under video surveillance.

The BMW had been pulled over by the traffic police. The driver informed he'd strayed four miles over the speed limit, the two cops instructed to make him wait.

Ashley checked his watch and looked on as a few stray pupils walked up to the Metro. Four agonising minutes passed and then the command he was waiting for.

"Two youths dealing, Asian youth approaching a pupil as we speak. Go, team, go," came the command from the excited team leader.

"DC Clarke, arrest Macintosh. Squad car 47, assist traffic police at Haddricks Mill Road immediately."

Ashley Clarke took a deep breath and walked towards the gorilla leaning against the advertising hoarding at the entrance of the Four Lane Ends Metro. It was as if he'd sensed the scruffy specimen standing staring at him wasn't really the man he pretended to be.

"What the fuck are you looking at?"

Ashley composed himself, took a deep breath and willed himself to be just that little more intimidating.

It often worked: a confident demeanour and aggressive speech generally caused an opponent to back down, but this time, he wasn't so sure it would.

"I never really believed the rumours that Mad Stevey Mac was that ugly but, sure enough, it's true."

Mac hesitated, took a nervous step forward."Who are you, you cheeky cunt?"

Ashley stepped back. "Whoa... and, Jesus, your breath smells like you've been licking your dog's arse for a week."

Macintosh, not so sure now, looked around for some support. Where was Bulldog? Were the lads carrying out their instructions? He felt in his pocket for his mobile. Checked it. No missed calls. Everything was okay. He took another step forward as Ashley stood his ground.

"Who are you? How do you know who I am?"

"Everyone knows who Bulldog's arse bandit is."

The penny dropped.

"You're filth, aren't you?"

"Bright." Ashley smiled. "Let me guess, the customary nine O levels, sixth form and on to uni."

Ashley pulled out his warrant card, thrust it at arm's length in the direction of the astonished thug.

"Shit for brains, Macintosh, you're fucking nicked. You have the right to remain silent, though I doubt you probably will, given the size of your ugly pig-shaped mouth. Anything you say maybe used against you in a court of law. You have the right to talk to a lawyer and have a lawyer present with you during questioning. If you cannot afford a lawyer, one will be appointed for you. You underworld types call them your brief, I believe. So, shit for brains, you're fucking nicked. That's your rights read. Do you wish to say anything?"

Macintosh stepped forward, made a grab for the warrant card with his left hand while swinging a wild punch with his right. Ashley turned slightly to the left and rammed his right fist into his aggressor's solar plexus. Macintosh winced, staggered as Ashley swept through his standing foot. Nineteen stone of thug crashed to the concourse floor as Ash leapt on his back, pulling out the plastic restraints, securing them onto a flailing hand. "You fucking bastard, you're hiding behind your pissing uniform."

Ashley couldn't help but laugh. "Cityworks, you mean? I'm hiding behind a Cityworks uniform."

The irony was lost on the injured man but, just as Ashley reached for the free wrist, the air was forced from his lungs. Another gorilla, not much smaller than Macintosh, had headbutted him in the back and lay slightly dazed on the ground wishing he'd held back just a little.

"You okay, Mac?" he gasped, pleased to have assisted his criminal colleague. Macintosh smiled, regained his composure and got up onto his knees.

"A golden rule, copper. One you've chosen to ignore. Always post a back-up, a little muscle to help you out if things aren't going your way."

Ashley tried to answer, tried to respond with a witty, confident-sounding comment. The words froze in his throat. Mac, on his feet now, delivered a sharp kick to the ribs. The normal commuters and people going about their business looked on but did not come to his assistance.

Ashley curled up in an involuntary ball and Mac dropped his nineteen-stone frame into his ribcage. Ashley wanted to scream, to cry out in pain, but still the sound wouldn't come. Mac leant over him, his sour breath inches from Ashley's face. "And now, copper, my party trick... my Hannibal Lecter special."

A hideous laugh, Mac's open mouth coming ever closer to his face. Hot breath... his teeth splitting the skin of his nose and the all too familiar taste of his own blood trickling into his mouth.

And then, respite.

A familiar voice, Macintosh's head snapping back over and daylight and the sweet smell of oxygen.

Ashley groaned.

"Holy John. Thank Christ."

John Markham grinned at Ashley who was still lying prone on the ground.

"Thought you might need some help, buddy – I sprinted up from the school, sorted him out." He pointed over to the wall where Macintosh's unconscious tag partner lay. "And managed to get to you before Mad Mac got the salt and pepper out."

Back at the station, the team were debriefed and congratulated by Chief Superintendent Roddam.

"It seems we're due a few beers tonight, lads. Two hundred thousand pounds worth of crack cocaine recovered from Bulldog's BMW and the whole of his little exercise filmed forprosperity. He's wriggled his way out of many a tight hole in the past, but this time he's quaking in his boots."

Holy John squeezed Ashley's shoulder, beaming like a Cheshire cat.

"No beer for you, partner. You're on a fast track to the RVI to get those ribs checked out."

And although Ashley Clarke tried to convince his new partner that there wasn't any treatment for broken ribs, John Markwell insisted on driving him to hospital personally and sitting for two hours in the waiting area adjacent to the consulting rooms. Afterwards, he dropped the car off at the station in Market Street and hailed a taxi outside. Within fifteen minutes, they were sitting in a small room at the rear of the Osborne Hotel in Jesmond, toasting their good fortune with their already well-oiled colleagues.

Andy Gibbons stood at the bar grinning, overseeing his successful team, ready to deliver the debrief.

# Chapter 4

The following morning, Ashley eased himself from his bed. Never before had he experienced such pain. Every breath, every cough, the slightest change in any direction caused a shooting dagger-like sensation to bury itself deep in his ribcage. Each stab felt as if his lungs would collapse at any minute.

Filled up with an overdose of Ibuprofen, he walked gingerly into the station at Market Street. John Markwell looked up from the desk.

"Jesus H, Ash, you look like shit."

Ashley didn't respond, knowing that even the slightest effort of speech would cause extreme discomfort. Instead, he nodded in agreement. Somehow, John Markwell seemed to understand. Ash looked around the station. It was still buzzing from yesterday's success. Chief Superintendent Roddam was hanging around, trying to be one of the boys again even though he'd been behind his Canadian maple desk during the entire operation. He was talking to *a suit* that Ashley hadn't seen before. Ashley didn't like the look of him.

"It went like clockwork. My team were magnificent; we'd been after Billy Graham for years."

Ashley had seen it all before. The team had carried off the perfect operation. Everyone and everything had fallen perfectly into place. First-class policing from every member of the team. And then the suits arrived and a man not involved at any stage of the wonderfully executed operation stood at the front of the line in the backslapping queue.

Roddam continued.

"We had a bit of a celebration last night. Some of the boys are a bit rough this morning." He shot a disapproving glance at Ashley, who by now really did feel like shit.

Ashley eased into the chair beside Markwell.

"John. I didn't get a chance to thank you yesterday. I—"

Markwell held up his hand.

"There's no need, Ash… partners, remember? I didn't mind the rough stuff, quite enjoyed it if the truth be told. It was that bloody half-mile sprint to get there that was the hard bit." Ashley laughed and regretted it instantly as the knife rasped up the inside of his lungs once again.

DC Rob Shanks chipped in. "Jesus, Ash, are you gonna be up for the interviews?"

Ash wheezed a reply. "No problem, Shanksy, just try and stop me.That's the best bit."

Rob Shanks had been leading the unit, staking out the dealers. He'd been patient and meticulous and timed the hits flawlessly, leaving the dealers just enough time to commit their offences. Intent to supply was the lesser charge; Rob Shanks wanted the cream from the top of the milk.

All three youths had offloaded the crack cocaine to at least one pupil from the school. Everything had been filmed for good measure.

Afterwards, Shanks had sent the uniforms with the victims to their home addresses.

The uniforms had read the riot act out in front of the children's parents, but the children had escaped with a caution and hopefully had received the biggest fright of their short lives. "Interviews start at ten, Ash. Should be fairly routine, but we need at least one of the dealers to implicate Bulldog as the main man."

"No problem, Shanksy. I looked in on them last night. They all look pretty scared."

DC Rob Shanks walked over to the desk and picked up a file. "Two seventeen-year-olds from Cowgate: John Potts and Marcus Appleby. Both addicts I'm afraid, a bit of previous for shoplifting and thieving. And a Pakistani kid with nothing at all on his card. A bit weird really, not the sort of kid who'd be working for Bulldog."

Shanks rubbed his chin, shook his head. "Which one do you want to have a go at first?"

Ashley Clarke prised himself from the desk and at the same time dropped yet another painkiller in his mouth and swilled it down with a mouthful of lukewarm sweet tea. He turned the file around, studied the profiles of the three dealers caught red-handed.

"I'll try the Paki kid first. My guess is that he's terrified, never seen the inside of a cell before."

Within two hours of interviewing Rafi Patel, Ashley Clarke had a confession with more or less everything the Northumbria Police wanted. The other two dealers, when confronted with this information, yielded too and admitted that the notorious Billy Graham had supplied them with crack cocaine to sell, for which they received a very handsome hourly rate of pay.

No income tax, no national insurance deductions.

Ashley Clarke wandered back to the cell where the frightened Pakistani youth now sat with his solicitor and the statement that Ashley wanted signed.

Ashley spoke. "Can we talk off the record?"

He looked in the direction of the solicitor, a twenty-something youth not much older than his client. The solicitor shot a glance at his client who shrugged his shoulders. Ashley continued, assuming the gesture as a positive.

"How did you get mixed up with that lot?"

Silence.

"I mean, you hardly fit the profile of your two colleagues, do you? They've been in trouble with the law since they came out of nappies. They're both addicts and ideal candidates for Graham and his henchmen to manipulate."

Ashley sat down at the table, placed his elbows in front of the youth and rested his chin on his fists.

"But not you, Rafi, right?"

A twenty-second pause elapsed.

"You're from a respectable business family; your father has fourshops."

"Five." The youth answered with an obvious hint of pride at his father's business acumen.

"Sorry, Rafi... five."

At last, a breakthrough, thought Ashley. The guard was slipping. "From what I'm led to believe, Rafi, you've been working those shops a hundred hours a week. Your old man's ill now, isn't he? Can't manage the hours he once could. You're running the show now, aren't you?"

For the first time the Pakistani youth made eye contact with Ashley. The fear in his eyes had vanished now and instead it was replaced with a realisation.

"So who's gonna run the empire when you're in Durham, Rafi?"

Matthewson the solicitor jumped to his feet. "Whooaa... just a second. We're off the record here. Let's keep it nice, no threats or I call it a day. You've had your confession, he's admitted what you wanted him to admit, end of story."

Ashley turned away to face the solicitor.

"No threats?" he shouted at the young solicitor. "No threats! Are you kidding me, Matthewson, or are you missing the big picture? This kid has been threatened and bullied by Graham and his gang to stoop so low as to create a whole generation of crack addicts before they can legally vote. What sort of threats do you think it would take to make a decent kid stoop that low?"

Ashley pointed to Matthewson's client.

"He's in the gutter, Mr Solicitor. He's in there with the rats and pieces of shit and used johnnies and for the first time in my life, I'm getting sympathetic vibes for a dealer."

He looked at Rafi Patel's frightened and confused state and the tears gently welling in his eyes. Rafi glanced at his solicitor for help. Matthewson averted his gaze, looked down at the table at his notes, pawed through them with no real purpose, no real direction. It was as if he too wanted his client to speak. And he did.

"This is off the record, right?"

Ashley nodded his head. The solicitor shrugged his shoulders and cast his eyes in the direction of the frozen tape recorder.

It was Matthewson's turn to hold up a hand. "I'm not so sure this is—"

Rafi interrupted. "It started about four years ago. I knew nothing about it, of course, I was just a kid. Father explained itto me when the real trouble started about six months ago."

"Real trouble?" Matthewson asked.

Rafi ignored him, didn't even acknowledge him with a glance. "And what I'm about to tell you, I will never ever repeat outside this station, let alone a courtroom. You don't realise how evil these men are."

Ashley and the solicitor inched ever closer.

"Father had noticed the trouble had been getting steadily worse. Sure we'd had an odd break-in and some shoplifting, the sort of thing you'd kind of expect in the not too salubrious areas of Newcastle but really nothing out of the ordinary."

He hesitated, paused for a second. Ashley noticed his hands trembling as he pressed them into the table.

"But then things escalated out of all proportion. We were getting almost daily reports of incidents from the shops. Bricks were hurled through the plate glass windows every other night. We installed shutters in all the shops but stolen cars and vans ram-raided them before they were even bloody paid for."

He reached over for the cigarette packet Ashley had slid across the table. The youth nodded his appreciation and, as Ashley struck a match, he bent his head down, cigarette at the ready. He stretched back, took a long pull and blew the smoke high into the air. The nicotine fix hit instantly. He seemed to relax... ready to go again.

"The insurance companies refused to cover us. We were finding it hard to stock the shelves and the takings were dropping almost daily. And then..."

He took another long drag on the cigarette and laughed. "And then our saviour arrived."

"Billy Graham," said Ashley.

The youth nodded. "Correct... He turned up to see Father dressed in a suit and tie. Father said he looked ever the part of a successful businessman."

Matthewson shook his head, reached for Ashley's cigarettes and added to the pollution in the small interview room.

"Said he could help, said he'd heard we'd been having trouble but it would stop overnight if we could meet his 'expenses' as he called them."

"Protection money," Ashley whispered gently.

Rafi shrugged his shoulders, took another pull on the cigarette before exhaling.

"Only it was never called that. Father said that the man claimed he had certain contacts and the perpetrators of these crimes would be taken to one side and warned of the consequences should they shit on the doorstep of the Patel shops."

Rafi Patel looked at Ash. "He refused. Father knew it was a racket and didn't want any part of it."

"So he turned nasty, pulled in the heavies."

Rafi shook his head. He continued.

"Quite the opposite. Mr Graham couldn't have been nicer. He shook Father's hand, thanked him for his time, even left a business card. But as he left, he told Father he would implementa month's trial regardless, at no cost."

Rafi Patel stood up, stubbed his cigarette out in the ashtray and turned to look up at the barred window two feet above him. "And, surprise, surprise, during the month of February 2001 not as much as a single packet of chewing gum was robbed from any of the five Patel shops." He turned round to face Ashley and the solicitor.

"A minor miracle, gentleman. And, of course, Father was delighted. The staff were happy again, takings were up and towards the end of the month we even had a phone call from an insurer offering to quote us again."

It was old hat to Ashley Clarke. Time and time again he'd seen the same thing happen in Hammersmith and Tottenham and Kilburn and just about every district he'd ever worked in London.

In they'd come: the gangsters, the hard men, Neanderthal Man. Without the intelligence or know-how or confidence or ability to attempt to start a business of their own. They'd latch on like a parasite to an already successful well-established operation and bleed it dry.

Why be judged on their own efforts? Why take a risk to earn a crust? No! Let's just sink our shit-ridden claws into somebody that has already succeeded. Let's tell him we want some of his profit. Tell him that if he doesn't agree we'll ruin him anyway and hurt him and his kin into the bargain. It's a no-brainer, a sure-fire winner.

Ashley felt sick to the core… knew exactly how the poor kid's story would end.

"Father called his number from the business card. Told Mr Graham he'd like to talk. He arrived suited up the following day and they agreed on a figure amounting to a few hundred pounds a month." Rafi sighed.

"Father figured it was a fair price to pay."

"So what went wrong?" Matthewson enquired.

Rafi sighed, glared at Matthewson then turned back to face Ashley.

"What happened?" asked Ashley, already knowing what the answer would be.

"The payments, Mr Clarke. Everything skipped along just fine. But then after a few months, Mr Graham pushed up the payments. He doubled them overnight. Within two months he'd increased them again and Father just couldn't afford it." Rafi wiped at a tear in the corner of his eye.

"He missed a payment. Mr Graham visited the shop and Father told him that their arrangement was finished. It was too expensive. Father said Mr Graham just laughed. Mr Graham said he'd be back begging for his security services within the week. That's what his business card said, Mr Clarke: *William Graham, Security Consultant*."

Matthewson got up from the table. "I think you've said enough, Mr Patel. DC Clarke gets the picture I really—"

Rafi ignored him.

"Within two hours our shop in Byker had been petrol- bombed. That evening two of our shops were burgled. They left disgusting, filthy messages on the counters."

"I'm calling this discussion to a close, DC Clarke." Matthewson stood up, gathered up some papers and made as if getting ready to leave.

Rafi Patel looked up from his chair, glared at his solicitor with a look of disgust.

"You're fired, Mr Matthewson. I don't want you to represent me anymore."

The solicitor froze, open-mouthed, for once speechless. "You're as bad as him. You and your firm represent him. You run after him like little sewer rats. Every time he picks the phone up, you look out your running shoes."

Ashley spoke. "I'm not surprised. He's one of their best customers, Rafi. If it's not Billy Graham in the dock, it's one of his little lackeys."

Rafi nodded. "And when you do represent us, Matthewson, you try to make sure we distance ourselves from him. Only this time he's screwed up. Big time. And still you wanted me to say he was only the driver and didn't supply us with the drugs. Only when you found out it was his car and he was the driver and his prints were all over the bags did it eventually sink in. He screwed up, Mr Matthewson; even you can't help him this time." He took another drag on his cigarette, inhaled deeply. "But don't worry, this is off the record. Tell Mr Graham he's safe on the protection racket charges at least. My guess is he'll get enough time anyway without me risking my life." He turned back to face Ashley. "As much as I'd love to add a few more years onto his sentence, I can't put my family at risk. His network is big and dangerous and Mr Graham would still send out his orders from his prison cell."

Ashley looked into the eyes of the prisoner: a mixture of fear, determination.

Rafi Patel turned to his solicitor.

"Didn't you hear me, Mr Matthewson? I said you're sacked, so please leave me."

The solicitor remained motionless.

Ashley spoke. "The door is the brown wooden thing in the wall, Mr Matthewson."

Matthewson rose to his feet, annoyed, defeated, bitter at the injection of humour by the policeman. His best client had screwed up and this time he couldn't help him, couldn't fight his corner, couldn't shift the blame to anyone else, nor could he get him off on a technicality. Ashley Clarke watched his every step as he left the room. Rafi was the first to speak.

"Mr Graham tries to pretend he's helping us when we're in trouble. Sends in the big lawyer, flash suit, Armani briefcase, and money no object. And it dawned on me during the first interview with Matthewson. He isn't interested in saving our backsides, just saving Billy Graham's. Why not? He pays the bills after all. The lawyer comes in, paints a bleak picture and tells us Billy Graham will move heaven and earth to help us."

Ashley stood up, walked around the table. "I've seen it a million times before, Rafi, but what I want to know is how you ended up dealing crack to kids."

The remark brought the youngster back to reality. His two-minute tirade had left him feeling sorry for himself, and now Ashley Clarke had brought back the guilt trip. A full minute elapsed in which Ashley stood in a forced silence. He would speak, Ash knew; just stay quiet.

"Father contacted him again. Within the hour, Graham was in Dad's office. Father said he seemed sympathetic, understood that retail profits were being squeezed. Graham announced a six-month payment holiday. And again, the trouble stopped. Father turned the shops round yet again."

The youngster fingered the mug of lukewarm tea. Ashley remained quiet.

"Graham didn't show up again for nearly nine months. Apologised, said he'd been busy. He hit Dad with a bill for over twenty thousand pounds, the missing monthly payments plus a ridiculously large, accrued interest figure."

Ashley sighed… spoke. "And you had to start working for him to clear the debt."

Rafi broke down. The tears he'd been fighting since his arrest eventually came and he sobbed like a child.

# Chapter 5

Ashley was a little concerned as he walked into Roddam's office five minutes after his shift began.

He'd been summoned, as Holy John had called it, almost as soon as he'd walked into the station.

"Take a seat, Ashley." Roddam smiled as he walked into the Chief's office. A bad sign, he thought.

Roddam dispensed with any niceties, came straight to the point.

"There's been an allegation, Ashley; an allegation of racism, I'm afraid." Ashley's mouth gaped open. There may have been one or two things that people could have said about Ashley Clarke's police career since he'd stepped off that train at Kings Cross all those years ago. One or two mistakes he'd made along the way. Occasionally, he could have been accused of being overly physical during an arrest. A couple of times he'd been more than keen when carrying out a dawn raid on a known dealer and occasionally he'd accepted the odd free drink at a public house on his beat. But racism? Definitely not.

Ashley stayed composed; he wanted to jump in and tell Roddam there had been some sort of mistake, but he bit his lip and let him continue.

"It was during the visit by Chief Superintendent Harrison last week."

Ashley shook his head. "I'm not with you, Sir, I've never met a Chief Superintendent Harrison."

"You didn't exactly meet him. He was with me last week prior to the interviews. He's from West Mercia, working on some new-fangled management project. He was in the suit, remember?"

"Yes, Sir. I remember now, but what does that have to do with me and where does the racism accusation fit in?"

Roddam pawed at a four- or five-page report on his desk. He adjusted his glasses and read.

"It was at nine fifteen exactly when the officer, later identified as DC Ashley Clarke, made an offensive racist statement directed at the prisoner Rafi Patel."

Ashley took a step forward. "No, Sir, not me; he's mistaken me for someone else. He's made a mistake."

Roddam smiled. A strange smile, maybe even sympathetic and he removed his glasses.

"I'm afraid he wasn't, Ashley. I was there too. I heard you."

"No, Sir… No, I'm not a—"

Roddam held up a hand. "Calm down, Ashley. What you said was an off-the-cuff remark. Certainly not racist, not in my book anyway."

Ashley's head was still in turmoil. He hadn't said anything racist. What on earth was Roddam talking about? He must have mentioned Rafi Patel. They'd picked him up wrong, misheard a word or a phrase perhaps.

"You must have still mistaken me, Sir. I—"

"It's here in black and white, Ashley, and I know what I heard. You called the prisoner a Paki."

Ashley thought back to the exact incident. Roddam spoke."Remember now?"

Ashley nodded. "I remember saying I was going to interview the Paki kid."

"So you aren't denying it?"

"That's the offence, Sir? Me saying I was going to interview the Paki kid."

Roddam nodded. Ashley's mouth opened wide. He shook his head in disbelief.

"This isn't happening, Sir. Tell me this isn't happening. It can't be. It wasn't racist. If it had been a Glaswegian kid down there, Iwould have called him a Scots kid or if he'd been from Czechoslovakia, he would have been the Czech kid."

Roddam stood up, walked over to where Ashley stood. He leant back and sat on the desk.

"Calling someone a Paki just isn't done these days, surely you know that?"

"I was shortening the country of his birth, Sir. You're the one being racist if you're treating him different to someone else." As soon as he heard the sentence escape from his mouth, Ashley knew he was in trouble. As soon as he saw the angerin Roddam's eyes, he just knew. What he didn't know or expect was what Roddam said next.

"I'm sorry, DC Clarke, you're suspended."

No, thought Ashley… no.

"Leave the station just as soon as you have got your things together."

Ashley grinned. He didn't know why. He almost laughed out loud. This was surely some sort of practical joke. The Chief was in on the ploy. The lads were hiding behind the cupboard, ready to jump out at any minute.

"You have to be joking me, Sir?" Ashley asked, dumbfounded. This just didn't happen in real life, right?

"I never joke, Ashley."

First-name terms again, bad vibes back. "I have no choice. Harrison's filed a complaint, and you've just admitted to his accusation."

Ashley's temper simmered. He felt a growing rage. Nearly twenty years dedicating his life to the job, twenty years battling against the type of scum normal people only read about in the papers. He'd taken two knifes, more beatings than he cared to remember.

He blamed the job for the break-up in his relationship with Alexis. Three years he'd been engaged to her and most of that time she'd been trying to fix a date for the wedding. He'd been putting it off ever since he'd gone undercover for the Met. Didn't really know why and couldn't really explain it to her. He guessed it was the danger, didn't want her to find out just what the job entailed.

He was mixing with and infiltrating the most dangerous drug dealing gangs in London and if he made one slip-up and they found out that the *addict* they were selling drugs to was really a cop, Alexis would have been a young widow. That was why he had been putting it off. That was the reason. He'd crack this job then return home to Newcastle, his beautiful fiancée on his arm and they'd set a date.

*He lived his role as a drug addict to the full. For four weeks, he'd effectively disappeared off the face of Alexis's earth. He'd been living in a dirty squat with rats and cockroaches and other junkies and addicts. He'd been running with the gangs and begging on the street for the price of his next hit.*

*And he couldn't take the chance of calling anyone, let alone Alexis, as he got nearer and nearer to the gang lords at the top. He'd dumped his mobile phone in the Thames at Fulham. Oh, how he'd wanted to call during that month-long period. The station had calledher each week, explained he was okay. They couldn't be sure though. He hadn't made contact with them either.*

*He'd passed her on the street one day. Thank God, she hadn't recognised him. She wouldn't have.*

*His hair hadn't even been combed, let alone washed, for a month. He'd grown a short, dark, unkempt beard and he had a black swollen eye following an altercation with one of his housemates. He'd deliberately lost the fight, taken the kicking. It wouldn't have looked good if his Met police self-defence training had kicked it.*

*He'd dressed in clothes one step up from a tramp. She had given him a cursory glance as she'd passed, almost looked a bit apprehensive. A little worried. Why not? He'd played the part well. A junkie, just the type to snatch a handbag for the price of the next fix. Easier still, a punch to the face of the victim to snuff out any resistance, maybe a blade. She'd pulled her shoulder bag tightly into her body, taken a firm grip of the strap and then... she was gone.*

"Don't worry, Ashley, I'll back you up on this one. It's the PC brigade again. I know you didn't mean what he's suggesting, and I'll get this suspension overturned in days. DCI Gibbons says you and him go back a long way, says you're a good cop." Roddam's words of comfort never registered.

*And eventually he'd cracked the job. His information had secured the arrests that would eventually result in convictions and long sentences. Ashley was on a high; he positively glowed when he'd returned to the station to receive the adulation of his team. And he'd taken his time and showered like he'd never showered before, washing the filth and the human scum from his body.*

*And when he'd showered and dried off, he'd showered again, and then twice more. And as he stood and looked in the mirror as he shaved, he delighted in getting acquainted with his old, familiar face once again. A splash of after-shave and a walk through the station backroom dressed in only a towel. The lads in the station had chipped in by way of a thank you and a brand new pair of Levi 501s together with a starched, crisp white granddad shirt, hung on two separate hangers in the locker room. He opened his locker and hauled out his battered beige deck shoes and a new pack of boxers.*

*He felt good as he walked down the Kings Road in Chelsea in bright summer sunshine. He'd called in to a Costa Coffee shop, treated himself to a large latte and a smoked salmon and cream cheese baguette. He'd been eating shit for weeks, it seemed.*

*It was six thirty in the evening. Alexis would be in by now. Surely? He'd stopped at a flower shop, picked up a ridiculously expensive bouquet of flowers, and wondered why he was delaying the meeting.*

"I'll tell them you'll take a wrap at divisional level, a black mark on your record and back on duty as quick as possible. I'm behind you one hundred percent."

*There'd never been anyone like her before or since. He'd realized just how much he loved her the instant he'd discovered the note.*

"DC Clarke… speak to me. At least acknowledge me."

*Her words blamed the job. She couldn't go on, couldn't take any more. 'The last straw.' 'Not knowing whether you were alive or dead.' And it continued as Ashley's tears dropped onto the paper. It told of a promotion and how the company Alexis worked for had offered her a year-long post in New York. The posting was several weeks away, but she felt it best if she left now, didn't want him to contact her.*

"The job, Sir."

"Yes, yes, Ashley. I'll get you back on the job just as soon as—"

"It fucking stinks, doesn't it?"

Roddam fell back in his seat, astounded that a lower-ranking officer had dared to utter the F-word in his inner sanctum. Roddam wanted to lecture, wanted to lay down the law, but by the time he'd regained the ability to speak again Ashley Clarke had gone.

Ashley didn't bother with an explanation for his colleagues. He pulled a few personal items from his locker and climbed the stairs from the station into the gloom of the Newcastle day. He was in a daze, this couldn't be happening.

Alexis. Alexis again. Why did she always come back to him in the bleak periods of his life? She would be halfway through her contract now. At first he'd tried to call her but every time he'd rung her mobile he'd been cut off. Eventually, after a few days, it didn't even ring out, an obvious sign that she'd replaced the phone.

He'd tried to see her anywhere and everywhere. He'd been to her office, *away on a training course,* they'd said, but refused to tell him where. And her mother's house in Chiswick. Four times, he'd been, and four times her parents had stood on the step and refused him entry. Her mother stood with tears in her eyes, swore blind she hadn't moved back to the family home and yet… something… something didn't ring true. Joanna Brody was hiding something. And why had she looked so sad when Ashley turned away?

"Take care, Ash," she had shouted after him as he reluctantly made his way down the red gravel driveway to the road. Each step felt like he was placing a million miles between himself and Alexis.

He had lost her.

As he reached the bottom of the drive, he just knew he had lost her.

His mobile phone rang. The name Holy John flashed up on thedisplay.

"Ash? Where the hell are you?" Ashley pressed *end* and turned right towards the central motorway and cursed the draconian licensing laws of England. He walked and walked. He walked the familiar streets of Jesmond, through Armstrong Park and down into

Heaton and Byker. He stood at the top of Walker Road and watched the huge cranes of Swan Hunter shipyard. The day heleft school, a quarter of his classmates made the short trip across town and began their working lives there. It was a job for life, the careers officer had said, and his father had tried oh so hard to make Ash stay at home.

"A good job at the shipyards. London's streets aren't paved with gold," he'd said. "Stay where you belong, son."

The sight of the cranes had depressed him then just as much as they did now. He pulled up the collar of his coat, cast an eye up to the ever-darkening sky and picked up the pace.

At eleven o'clock, he watched as the tiny double doors of the Queens Arms in Shieldfield opened. He took a quick look around him, then headed for the opening. He wanted to think that the Queens hadn't changed, but it had. In his early twenties, he'd return home to Newcastle at every opportunity and, more often than not, the hours were spent in this small welcoming hostelry, a stone's throw from Newcastle city centre.

At one thirty-seven, a familiar face sat down at his table.

"I've heard the bad news, Ash," John Markham said with a voice that reeked of sympathy. "Roddam came down before lunchtime and briefed the team."

Ashley nodded a hello in his direction and shrugged his shoulders as if to say who cares. But he did care.

"I put out a call to the uniforms; a few of them had spotted you over Heaton, then walking along Byker

Bridge. I figured you'd need a drink or two, heard this place was an old haunt of yours."

Ashley smiled. The beer had begun to kick in; so too had the Talisker single malt. He gave a prayer of thanks to Bacchus. He felt at ease with the world, as if nothing really mattered. He hadn't thought about what tomorrow might bring or the day after.

"Roddam's a good guy, Ash; reckons he'll have you back within a week or two. He's backing you all the way." John Markham laughed. "He had a quiet word with me, reckons you were a bit out of order up there. Won't take it any further though."

John Markham sat with Ashley for another two hours and made no attempt to persuade him to leave. Each time he asked for another drink, Markham obeyed his command.

Ashley's speech was now slurred and on what was to be his final trip to the toilet he needed a chair for support and two walls to make it there safely. As he staggered back to the table Markham offered him a lift home. He was only too happy to accept it. Ash knew when he'd had enough. The alcohol had served its purpose. Markham poured him into the back of the unmarked car and drove him the short distance to his rented flat in Fenham.

At eight the next morning, Ashley awoke with a start. He looked at his watch. He'd crawled into bed just after five the previous afternoon. Fifteen hours of uninterrupted sleep. *Jesus*, who was hammering the door down at this time of the morning?

Holy John stood grinning on the step, two Styrofoam cartons in his hand.

"I thought a good English breakfast might cure those hangover blues. The deli on Acorn Road does the best in town, opens real early. Not as good as a Holy Island special, mind, but definitely the best in town."

"What the hell are you up to this early on a Sunday morning, John?"

"I've been to the early morning service, Ash, never miss a Sunday."

Ashley rubbed at his heavy eyelids, screwed them up tightly asa ray of early morning sunshine shot over John Markham's shoulder blade.

"Church?"

John smiled. "Church and a good breakfast, praise the Lord."

"Praise the Lord, John... yeah...praise the Lord."

Ashley wanted to dive into an atheist argument and ask Holy John how come the scriptures tell us the world was created a few thousand years ago and yet the Natural History Museum in London houses some dinosaur bones three million years old. He wanted to, he really did, but the moment passed.

John wafted the cartons in front of Ashley's face. The smell of the bacon and sausage and fried eggs and black pudding tugged at his taste buds and if it had been Charles Manson with a machete between his teeth, he still would have allowed him in. Ash shuffled along the narrow, woodblock hallway in his boxers. He pointed to the right.

"Kitchen's over there, grab a couple of plates and put the kettle on. I need to take a piss."

Ashley sat opposite John Markham as they attacked the heart attack special. Ashley was comfortable in his company. He'd warmed to the man who, only a few weeks ago, had been a complete stranger. Markham had come to his rescue not once but twice now in such a short period of time.

"Getting pissed out of your brain won't help things, y'know, Ash," John Markham mumbled with a half-eaten sausage in his mouth.

Ashley looked up, swirled the warm tea around the cup, smiled at his colleague.

"You're wrong, John. Getting hammered always helps."

"Don't be stupid, Ash, you—"

Ashley nodded his head. "It does, John, it helps. I had a great time yesterday afternoon feeling sorry for myself. It gave me time to think."

"About what?"

"About what sort of shit job we are both doing, about what's happening to the world, about having to think long and hard before we say something in case someone else interprets them totally differently. What right has anyone got to call me a racist?"

"Look, Ash, it ain't that bad—"

"John, I'm suspended, for fuck's sake. How bad can it get? I'm hanging onto my career by the skin of my teeth."

John Markham stood up, walked around the table, and placed a comforting hand on his pal's shoulder.

"Remember yesterday, Ash? Remember I was telling you about Roddam?"

Ashley scratched his head, couldn't remember anything abouta conversation involving Roddam. John continued.

"Roddam's a good guy. He likes you. He's spoken with the suit who reported you." John Markham turned to face Ashley, threw a smile that said you owe me one.

"Roddam has pulled rank. As soon as you issue an apology, you're back on the job!"

"A what?"

"An apology. A little black mark on your record admitting you were out of order, you made a bad choice of words, an error of judgement the politicians call it. The suit has his little victory but a good cop still keeps his job."

Ashley looked up. "No disciplinary hearing?"

"Just a routine interview."

John Markham was now grinning. He pulled out a sheet of paper from his hip pocket.

"Roddam's even drafted it out for you. Of course it needs to be in your handwriting but have a read."

Ashley took the A4 sheet of paper and began to read.

# Chapter 6

It was a familiar name, but one he couldn't place straightaway. She sounded familiar too, and by the tone of her voice, she obviously knew him. And then it clicked.

"Jesus…" he whispered under his breath as the blast from the past came back to him. He'd been in the same class as her son, Tommy Wilkinson. Of course, how could he forget?

Tom had been one of his gang in secondary school. He'd spoken to him only a few months ago when Tom had been travelling. Kate, his mother, had been one of the youngest and, yeah, sexiest mothers at the school gates. She'd had Tom at about fifteen years of age. Ashley figured out the maths: she'd be in her mid-forties now.

"Jesus," Ashley whispered quietly as his hand covered the telephone receiver, remembering how good she'd looked all those years ago.

Lost in his thoughts, he became aware of a nervous voice, a sad voice on the other end of the phone. Kate exchanged the usual pleasantries, said she'd heard he was back in Newcastle. "How's Tom doing then?" Ashley asked. "What's he up to these days?"

A split second or two of silence, a sigh, then Kate Wilkinson dropped the bombshell.

"You don't know, Ashley, do you? Tom's been missing for nearly two months."

It was Ashley's turn to take a deep breath. "He's what?"

"Missing, Ashley. He's bummed around ever since he left school, travelled the world, only ever kept a job long enough to save up enough money for his next jaunt. I'd like you to try to find out what happened to him."

"He's missing?"

"Missing, Ashley. The police don't want to know; quoted some crazy figure about the number of people that disappear each year."

"But me? Why have you chosen to call me?" An uncomfortable couple of seconds' delay ensued. It seemed like an eternity. "Two reasons, Ashley. The first is fairly obvious. You knew Tom, knew him very well. I'd like to think you cared for him, cared enough to want to find him."

Ashley couldn't argue with that; he found himself thinking back to the good times Tom Wilkinson and he'd had together, the scrapes they'd got into. He was no angel, a bit of a risk-taker. Ashley had liked that. He answered almost instinctively.

"Sure, Mrs Wilkinson, sure. And the second reason?"

"I'd... heard... errr, you might have a little time on your hands."

The sentence hit Ashley like a hammer. He paused… took a deep breath.

"Bad news travels fast. Who spilled the beans?"

"I'd rather not say, Ashley. And one other thing."

"Yeah?"

"Call me Kate. You're not fourteen anymore."

Ashley chuckled. "I suppose it's habit. I guess I'm thinking back to those days again. You'll always be Tom's mother, I suppose." Tom's mother, he thought to himself. Jesus, he'd had such a crush on her. Occasionally he'd read stories in the newspapers about frustrated housewives who now and then took a schoolboy lover, and he'd prayed that Kate Wilkinson, Tom's mother, would do it to him. Of course, it wasn't to be. No such bloody luck. And why had the dozy fifteen- and sixteen-year-olds complained or spilled the beans to their parents? Were they crazy? His greatest sexual fantasy of his teenage years: Ashley Clarke and Mrs Wilkinson. Tom's Ma teaching him the tricks of the trade.

"Can we meet up, Ashley? Soon?"

Ashley couldn't get the picture of his best pal out of his head. That cheeky grin, the couldn't-give-a-shit frown, the shrug of the shoulders when things went wrong. His favourite expression, *the sun will still shine tomorrow,* he'd say, whatever kick in the teeth life had dealt him. A girlfriend running off with someone else, sacked from a job, always: *the sun will still shine tomorrow*. Ashley answered. "I'm sorry, Mrs… sorry, Kate. The thing is, you've heard wrong. It was a misunderstanding. I'll be back at work in a few days. I won't have time."

Kate Wilkinson resorted to pleading, explained she was in a good position to pay expenses. He could work on his days off, he'd have access to the police computer and records of the disappearance.

"Look, Kate, I can make a few discreet enquiries with whoever it was who investigated the disappearance, but that's it. You've been watching too many TV cop shows. That sort of thing doesn't happen; it's not allowed."

Ashley heard his old friend's mother sobbing now.

"That's what's wrong nowadays, Ashley. Nothing's allowed. You're telling me the police wouldn't step in if a copper was trying to find a friend in his own time?"

Ashley couldn't answer; he wanted to help but thought of the professional consequences. Some bastard would object, that was for sure, and goodness knows what would happen if a police officer was found looking up anything that they weren't officially working on. It happened in the old days.

An unsolved crime, a copper with a little time on his hands, and a few different questions to a few different individuals and, more often than not, a breakthrough. Ashley found himself defending the system he now realised he hated.

"We just can't have individuals interfering with every unsolved case. The computer system just couldn't cope; it would crash." Ashley smelt the bullshit as he spoke.

Kate Wilkinson said she understood, said she was sorry for bothering him. Her voice dropped to barely a whisper and she ended the call.

Ashley Clarke had been summonsed for eight-thirty on Wednesday morning that week. As he walked into Market Street Station, the first individual to greet him was John Markham.

"Alright, Ash, you got your statement?"

Ashley reached into his pocket and pulled out the envelope that contained the written statement his commanding officer had prepared. Ashley hadn't altered one word, moved one comma, changed one sentence, but the two paragraphs had still taken him the best part of a day to write out.

He'd sat for over an hour before the pen even touched the paper. And he'd cringed as he'd read and copied the statement verbatim. He wanted to tear it to shreds as he read '*an error of judgement*' and he'd wanted to punch the next person he met, as he'd handwritten the politically correct garbage word for word.

"Best get it over with, Ash. The suit's up there too."Ashley looked puzzled.

"Yeah, the suit's there, Ash. Wants his moment of glory. C'mon."

The suit, the one who had started this debacle, this waste of time and effort, not to mention the good old British taxpayers' hard-earned cash. Markham took him by the shoulder and steered him in the direction of the door that led to the stairs. DC Roddam's office was on the third floor. As they walked up together, Ashley asked a question.

"What are you doing here, John? You're not coming in, are you?"

"I'm afraid so, mate. I'm your personal representative."

Ashley shrugged his shoulders, couldn't believe it. Four police officers off the street.

"The suit, John. What the fuck is he here for?"

"Procedure, Ash. He made the complaint, he reads you the riot act, tells you how you've let your colleagues down and what a dirty little dog turd you are, and how lucky you are to keep your job."

Ashley shook his head. John Markham continued.

"Roddam has a go, too. He's your superior officer, so he ostracises you. Don't take it personally though. Roddam rang me at the weekend, told me to tell you that."

They turned into the corridor on the third floor. Roddam's office faced them at the far end.

"You and Roddam seem quite close, Holy John."

Markham smiled. "You could say that. He's a decent bloke, is old Roddam and, like he says, don't take it personally." Markham knocked on the door twice, waited for acknowledgement from within, opened it and walked in.

"Stay there a minute, Ash. I'll make sure they're ready for you." A minute later, the door opened and Markham beckoned Ashley to move forward. Roddam sat behind the enormous desk with the suit sitting three or four feet away at the side. Neither smiled. Neither stood up.

Roddam spoke.

"DC Clarke, this is Chief Superintendent Harrison from West Mercia." Ashley nodded.

"Take a seat."

Roddam motioned to the seat on the opposite side of the desk. Ashley pulled the seat out, dragged it several feet away from the desk, and sat down.

Roddam looked at him with a look of dismay and Chief Superintendent Harrison gave a confident smirk. The look said bow down to me, respect me, do as I ask. I can make or break your career. The suit spoke.

"You know why you are here, DC Clarke. Do you have your written statement?"

He thrust the envelope onto the desk in front of him. It was a rebellious move. Ashley remembered his pal's favourite saying about the sun still shining. He didn't want to be here, he shouldn't be here, this wasn't happening.

Roddam read the statement and passed it across the desk to Chief Superintendent Harrison who studied the text in detail. When he had finished, he looked up and nodded to Roddam. Roddam began his verbal assault. Nothing personal, Holy John had said. Just as well, really. It lasted a full five minutes, but Ashley never heard a word. He was in the mountains, his favourite mountains in the Lake District or the highlands of Scotland; it didn't matter. But he was there. He had always had the ability to beam himself wherever he wanted, Star Trek style and blank out the moment.

And Tom Wilkinson, he was there too. Two pals on a day's jaunt across the fells, then dropping down to an old inn for a traditional meal and half a dozen beers, a toast to Bacchus. A taxi back into town, a nightcap and a near unconscious ten-hour sleep in a local B and B.

The sudden silence brought him back. Chief Superintendent Harrison spoke.

"You don't seem too concerned about what your superior officer has just said, Mr Clarke."

Ashley spoke. "I wasn't listening."

Three words, but by the look on both superintendents' faces, you'd think a judge had just passed a death sentence on both of them. Chief Superintendent Harrison composed himself first. "I beg your pardon?"

"I wasn't listening. I was walking along the edge of Ben Lawyers in the Trossachs."

The two superintendents looked at each other in amazement... puzzlement... Ashley wasn't quite sure which. He became aware of a movement behind him. John Markham stepped in.

"Excuse me, Sir." He directed a question to Roddam. "Could we have a five-minute break?"

Roddam pulled at his tie, loosened it a little. "I think that might be a good idea, Markham. I don't think Mr Clarke realises the seriousness of the situation."

The suit jumped up.

"That's not in the rule book, I'm afraid. I want this sorted out now. I haven't got time to—"

"Yes, you have," interrupted Roddam. "You're staying overnight. Give the man a break. He's not thinking straight." Roddam rose to his feet, nodded at John Markham and flicked a glance towards the door.

John Markham physically lifted Ashley Clarke from the chair and guided him out of the room before the suit could lodge another objection.

"What the fuck are you playing at?" he snarled at Ashley once they were outside in the corridor.

"Do you know how much power those two have between them? They could finish you on the spot. Just play the game, Ashley, play the fucking game, man."

Ashley smiled at John Markham. He paused for a second.

"A game, Holy John. A game, is that what it is? We're playing a game?"

"Of course it's a game. The suit wants his victory, wants to go back down South and say to the boys he sorted the Geordie racist out. Made him eat humble pie, stopped his future advancement in the force."

Markham was whispering now. His voice sounded soft… convincing.

"So what we're gonna do is go back in there with an apology and play their little game, Ash, because if you don't they win."

"They win, John?"

"They win."

Markham's breathing had returned to normal, his red face had regained its normal colouring. Ashley Clarke needed the job, needed the money, and needed the buzz on a daily basis. He needed the thrill of dealing with the bad boys. Childhood games, good against evil at its rawest, Cowboys and Indians, Japs and Commandos, the good guys always coming out on top.

And on the other side of the door, Ashley wondered, good guys or bad guys?

He looked at Markham.

"Who are the good guys, Holy John?" Markham furrowed his brow, then smiled.

"You and me, Ash, we're the good guys. Now let's get in there and get this out of the way. Then we can go and fight the baddies, the undesirables, clean the streets up."

Ashley Clarke nodded.

"Let's do it, John, let's go and fight the bad guys." Markham grinned broadly.

"That's my partner, the bad guys. Let's go and get them." Ashley took his seat once again.

John Markham resumed his position under the window. Ashley looked at Roddam who raised his eyebrows as if to say, 'are you ready' and Chief Superintendent Harrison looked at him with a look that said he was spoiling for a fight.

"So, Ashley," Roddam started, "are you feeling a little better now?"

"Down from the hilltops now," smirked Chief Superintendent Harrison.

*The bad guy... he's the bad guy.*

"Yes, Sir, a lot better. I must apologise for my actions before." He glanced across at Chief Superintendent Harrison. "I was out of order. I've been under a lot of pressure lately, what with the move and things."

"Is that your excuse for those racist remarks, officer?" Chief Superintendent Harrison taunted.

"What racist remarks would that be, Sir?"

Chief Superintendent Harrison hauled off his glasses quickly, ina deliberate gesture, a gesture that said, 'don't push me'.

"I'm beginning to lose my patience with you, DC Clarke. You know why you're here. The only reason you're not in the dole queue right now is because you have the full support of your commanding officer. DCI Gibbons speaks very highly of you too."

"You want me out of the job, Chief Superintendent Harrison. Is that what you are saying?"

Ashley wanted to be back there, in the job, be enthusiastic just like in the old days but his heart just wasn't in it anymore. He was fighting for his career, his livelihood and he was on the ropes with his gumshield on the floor, legs like lead.

The Chief Superintendent stood up. He peered down at Ashley.

"I don't want racists in the force, Clarke."

The comment grated on Ashley. He clenched his fists, took a deep breath.

"I'm not a racist, Chief Superintendent Harrison. Never have been, never will be. I'm not a racist and I never meant the comment in a racist way. If you want to interpret it that way then it's your problem, not mine. My remark simply shortened the country of a person's birth. A Pakistani will always be called a Paki, A Scotsman a Scot, an Irishman a paddy."

"Well, they shouldn't be, officer. People should think before they call an Irishman a paddy. They should think before they speak, think how distressing it is for the person concerned." Ashley smiled.

"Distressing, Sir? The kid wasn't even there, for God's sake, how could he get distressed?"

Ashley's voice had risen a decibel or two; it was trembling, beginning to croak. This interview was getting sillier and sillier. "It makes no difference, officer. If you use it behind his back or not, it can still cause distress."

"I was called Geordie in the Met for nearly fifteen years, told I was a Scotsman with his brains kicked out. I didn't exactly like it, but I wouldn't say it stressed me out. My partner was called Taffy, no guesses where he came from. Are you saying I was racially abused? Are you saying that John Evans suffered emotional traumas? And what about Andrej Bojke? His father was an immigrant from Poland. Everyone called Andy the Pole. Everyone from the cleaners up over. He was Andy the Pole."

"Has he been racially abused for all those years? Does he have a case against the Met for racial harassment throughout his career?"

Chief Superintendent Harrison looked confused, angry that Ashley had dared to defend his remark.

"No, of course not. That's different."

"No, it's not, Sir. It's exactly the same. We had a lad from Glasgow called the sweaty, he hated the name. Imagine going through life called a sweaty sock, how bad is that?"

"Look, Officer Clarke, this conversation has gone far enough. We're not here to discuss nicknames from the past we're here to address a serious racist incident."

"And what about Bob the Fish?"

"What?"

"Bob the Fish, a copper in my unit. He had two huge protruding eyes and got Bob the Fish."

Superintendent Harrison resembled Bob the Fish now. Big bulging eyes, puffed up around the gills. Ashley was surprised steam wasn't coming from his ears.

Roddam shook his head, held it in his hands. John Markham gave Ashley a stiff finger in the ribs as if to say drop it. But hewouldn't, his hackles were well and truly standing on end. "Everyone has to be born somewhere, Sir. Everyone is taunted or teased about where they are born, it's part of life. Take the North-East; what Newcastle man hasn't been called a Geordie bastard at some time in their lives and what about the Mackems and the Smoggies? What about the poor buggers from Hartlepool?"

Harrison removed his glasses.

"If you must know, Clarke, I was born in Hartlepool. What's wrong with that?"

Ashley grinned.

"My father served in the Navy. He was stationed there, but what has that—"

"You're a monkey hanger," he laughed, "a fucking monkey hanger. Do the lads at your station down south know that?" Chief Superintendent Harrison fell back into his seat. Roddam's mouth gaped open in amazement; the second time Ashley Clarke had dared to utter the F-word. John Markham's hand covered his eyes and he shook his head in disbelief. It was all over, no going back now.

"That's racism, Sir." Ashley grinned, felt composed. "During the Napoleonic war, your ancestors hung a monkey because they thought it was a French spy. And they have the nerve to call the Irish stupid."

He turned slightly as he looked and smiled at his superintendent. Then back to the suit. John Markham dropped his head in his hands and started groaning.

"Dozy bastards." He was laughing now. "The fucking monkey couldn't speak to answer the charges, so they hung it. You're a monkey hanger, Sir. Harrison, the monkey hanger. Got a bit of a ring to it, don't you think?"

Ashley exhaled deeply, took another deep breath. "Is that good enough for you or do you need some physical violence too? Verbal racism is a little harder to prove, I believe."

Ashley leant forward, took the Chief Superintendent by the lapels.

"H'angus the monkey Harrison."

He pulled his fist back and took aim at the bridge of his nose. John Markham sprang forward and held him in a bear hug before he could dispatch the blow. Roddam dived across the desk too, his huge clumsy frame upending it, spilling the neatly stacked paperwork onto the floor. The desktop computer slid across the shiny surface and crashed to the floor. The screen smashed into a thousand fragments with a bang.

And suddenly, as Ashley lay on the floor with two of his colleagues restraining him, he calmed down. He smiled and closed his eyes and felt the anxieties and frustrations that had built up over fifteen years simply float away.

# Chapter 7

Ashley looked up at the old brass sign that read 'Milburn House'.

It was like something from a bygone era. As he walked throughthe door, the feeling didn't disappear.

"The building time forgot," he muttered to himself. "Jesus, it even smells old."

But not an unpleasant smell, he thought to himself as he checked out the nameplates and found the office name he was looking for: *Just Flirting*, a dating agency. He stole a quick look behind him just to make sure no one was looking at him as he fingered the sign.

He made his way up to the fourth floor and sauntered along the gloomy passage with no real urgency to get there. What would he say when he walked in? He lingered at the huge glass door and gave it a half-hearted push. To his dismay, it swung open effortlessly and he was greeted with a beaming, shiny white smile from a twenty-something brunette.

"Can I help you, Sir?"

"Erm, yes, I'm looking for a lady."

“Then you’ve come to the right place. Can I take your name?”

“No… I mean, yes… Ashley Clarke.”

“Okay, Ashley, take a seat and we’ll get some details.”

“No, you misunderstand. I’m looking for Kate Wilkinson; she’s the boss here, isn’t she?”

The girl flicked Ashley a disapproving look.

“Ms Wilkinson. Yes, I’ll just get her. She’s the owner, not the boss. We like to work as a team here.”

Ashley walked over to the seating area adjacent to the receptionist’s desk. He pawed at a magazine, *Vogue,* and then he picked up a *Tatler*. Pretty people graced the front covers and he wondered just how many of *Just Flirting*’s client base fell into that category.

Within two minutes, Kate Wilkinson breezed into reception. “Aaashleey….”

The sight took Ashley’s breath away. She could have passed for a lady ten years younger. She hugged him tightly and held him for an uncomfortable length of time. The receptionist over his shoulder clearly disapproved. He broke the grip. She kissed him on the lips, brushed a tear away from her eyes.

“Oh, Ashley, it’s so nice to see you again. It must be ten years.”

“All of that, Kate. You look, errr… stunning.”

And she did. She wore a tight-fitting, burgundy-coloured business suit with a brilliant white gentleman’s open-neck shirt. Her figure wouldn’t have looked out of place on a teenage catwalk model and she wore just enough make-up to accentuate her high cheekbones and delicate features. "Thanks, Ash, you don't look so bad yourself."

Ashley blushed, not because of her comment. It was the sort of blush he had had whenever he had called at Tom's door all those years ago. And those feelings, those sexual yearnings flowed back through his body again.

"Come through. Come through to my office." She took his hand and led him away.

"Hold all calls for me would you, Sandie. Say for the next half an hour or so."

The girl on reception nodded and ludicrously made a note onher desk pad. Ashley walked past a temporary dividing wall and into the main office. Four very attractive girls sat at workstations, all deep in conversation on the sort of headphones you find in a modern call centre. Kate Wilkinson pointed at a large oak-panelled door in the far corner.

"My office is over there, Ash. Go take a seat, I'll arrange some coffee. How do you take it, Ashley?"

"Black, Kate, please, a sprinkling of sugar."

"Looking after that figure, Ash, huh? Me too; once you hit the mid-thirties you've got to be a bit more careful, hit the gym, cut down on the wine."

Ashley wanted to tell her that he hadn't quite got to that stage yet. In fact he'd never *hit the gym* yet, as she called it and he was probably drinking more now than he had at nineteen or twenty. He'd need to do something about it soon. He was slipping into an all too familiar routine: a couple of beers at lunchtime, maybe a couple of glasses of wine in the evening. And yes… he'd noticed the old jeans and T-shirts were a little bit tighter these days.

He wanted to tell her that her gym routine had obviously worked a treat and maybe he could join her one day, but she had disappeared over the other side of the office talking to one of the girls.

As instructed, he meandered into Kate Wilkinson's huge and rather impressive office. He stole a quick look at her personal effects. Those could tell an on-the-ball policeman an awful lot about someone.

Pictures of Tom.

Only Tom. Pictures when he was a baby and the more familiar-looking pictures as a teenager, the teenager Ashley knew and loved. And a recent picture, in the middle of her desk, maybe only a year or two old of Tom on a beach somewhere. Somewhere hot by the looks of it. Maybe Thailand, New Zealand, somewhere like that.

He picked it up. That grin, that devil-may-care attitude. *The sun will still shine tomorrow.* Kate caught him unawares, placed a cup in front of him.

"Eighteen months ago, Ash. The last photograph of him I have, the same one Northumbria police got." She sighed, walked around the desk and sat down. Took a long drink from her cup, shook her head. "Not that they ever seemed interested." Ashley looked away from the photograph and into the sea-green, hypnotic eyes of Kate Wilkinson. They were just how he remembered.

"No offence to you, Ash, but I never even received the courtesy of one lousy phone call. It was me that did all the running, me that kept ringing HQ at Ponteland. And all I got wasthat it was being investigated, we're doing our best, Mrs Wilkinson, or a sympathetic female civilian explaining the statistics of missing persons, how they'd sometimes turn up at the family home years later as if nothing had happened."

She continued.

"Once I even marched right in there, demanded to see the man at the top. I was crying, in a right state. He'd been missing a fortnight. I was frantic with worry."

"A fortnight isn't long, Kate. You can't blame them."

"You're right, Ash. A fortnight isn't long for a son not to call his mother but as much as Tom was unreliable and took off every now and again on a whim, he would religiously call me wherever he was in the world… every few days. Call it Mother's intuition if you like. I knew something was wrong. I wanted to get a hold of those policemen and shake some sense into them. I must have rung his mobile phone two or three hundred times."

Ashley wanted to say he understood. He stayed silent.

"I had a call from him, said he was going up to Holy Island."

"Holy Island?"

"Yeah, up near Berwick, you know it?"

Ash nodded.

"He'd just packed the latest job in. They'd kept it open for himwhile he'd been on his latest venture but felt he wanted to move on." She smiled at Ashley, took another sip from the cup. "I don't need to tell you what he's like, Ashley. You know him better than most. I remember it well because he called from a payphone, said his mobile didn't receive on the island." Kate Wilkinson's hands were trembling now. The tears were clearly visible in those beautiful green eyes that Ashley couldn't break away from. He wanted to reach across the desk and comfort her. He wanted to say something profound, and something that reassured her that her son was alive and well. "He said he wanted a few days away, somewhere quiet, somewhere to chill out. He told me not to worry. Not to worry, Ash. Can you believe it? He'd booked into a small inn, 'The Ship' on the island."

A slight smile, another gulp at the coffee, then a sigh.

"Said he'd met a nice girl, Clara. He said she was called, though I'm not too sure. I might be wrong. That's where she was from, Holy Island."

Ashley reached in his pocket, pulled out a notepad and a pen. "Guess I'd better get some details, The Ship Inn, you said."

Kate Wilkinson looked up from her cup, gulping at the hot liquid in her mouth. She placed the cup on the desk without really looking where she was putting it. It tipped over as it cameto rest unevenly on a thick desk diary, spilling coffee on some papers before she grasped at the cup and managed to right it. She didn't seem at all concerned.

"You mean you'll find out what happened to him, Ashley?" Without giving him time to answer, Kate Wilkinson was on her feet and around Ashley's side of the desk throwing her arms around him. She released her grip, composed herself and smoothed her skirt down flat against her hips as she straightened up once again.

"Oh thanks, Ashley, thank you so much. I'm so grateful… so, so grateful. It means so much to me."

And then a look. A look that Ashley recognised so well. It was a look of resignatio caught the look every time a criminal had realised that he or she had been caught in the trap. No escape. No get out of jail card, no pass go, no collect two hundred pounds.

The look that said, 'Okay, you got me'.

And the tears, those tears beginning to form again, distorting her vision. Another few seconds and the first one would fall. "You don't believe we'll find him alive, Kate, do you?"

A different look. Be sympathetic. Help me.

"Like I said, Ashley, mother's intuition." She walked slowly around the desk and sat down in the oversized black leather chair. She reached for the cup of coffee but, before it reached her lips, thought better of it and returned it to the desk.

"I sensed something a couple of days after that phone call. He sounded fine on the phone, said he would call by the weekend. Even before then, the Thursday it was, around eight or nine in the evening, I experienced a feeling like I'd never had before." She stood up, turned her back on Ashley and stared deep into the photograph of Tom hanging there. He couldn't have been more than five years old, that cheeky grin evident even at that early age.

She turned around.

"I tell a lie, Ashley, I had experienced it before." She hesitated. "Once or twice as a teenager. Remember falling in love, Ashley? Remember the feeling when the person you were dating was the most important creature in the world; remember thinking they were even more special than your parents?"

The inevitable tear trickled onto her delicate and beautifully formed cheek. The mascara followed a split second later.

"And remember the phone call that said it was over? Worse even, your best pal ringing up to say they'd been seen with someone else."

Ashley remembered.

A vision of Alexis appeared at that exact moment and he knew precisely the feeling Kate Wilkinson was describing.

That night. The thoughts flying around his head, the knot in his stomach, the feeling that the world as he knew it could never be the same again. That feeling. So powerful. So strong.

"On that Thursday evening… that's what I felt like, Ashley, only a hundred times worse and it stayed with me until the early hours of Friday morning."

And slowly, as if in slow motion, she sank back and moulded herself into her seat again.

"I knew, Ashley. I knew then he was dead. I know he's dead."

"Don't be silly, Kate, you can't possibly know that."

Kate Wilkinson didn't reply to the statement.

"I went up to Holy Island, Ashley, when I realised that the police weren't taking me seriously. I booked into The Ship. As soon as the receptionist clapped eyes on the credit card with the name Wilkinson on, I swear the entire community clammed up. It was as if everyone knew, Ashley."

"What do you mean, Kate? Knew what?"

"Knew why I was there, knew I was looking for him."

"Is that what they said?"

Kate shook her head, climbed from her chair yet again, obviously uncomfortable relaying the story. She began a slow walk away from the desk behind Ashley. He turned around on the seat, watched her pause by the door. He expected her to turn round and face him. She didn't. She stood for what seemed like an eternity, staring at the door that led out into the main office.

"To a man, woman and child, Ashley, they said they'd never seen hide nor hair of him. Never heard the name, never seen the face when I showed them the photograph. In fact, Ashley, I swear some people never even looked properly at the photograph before replying they'd never seen him before. I'd show them, hold up the photograph and they'd look right through it. It's as if..."

"Go on. Tell me what you think."

"It was as if the entire island was hiding something."

Ashley fingered the handle on his coffee cup as a shiver ran up his back.

"The receptionist at The Ship looked through the bookings, said no one by the name of Wilkinson had reserved a room there. And yet, Ashley, he didn't say he was going to book a room. He definitely said he'd booked one, even told me how reasonable it was."

Ashley pushed his pen into his pocket. "I'll make some enquiries back at the station, call in a few favours, see wherethey got to with the investigation."

"I want to know, Ash. I just want to know. That's not too much for a mother to ask, is it?"

Ashley shook his head.

"I want to lay him to rest, Ashley. I want his body back. Backhere in Newcastle, where he belongs, and a proper funeral."

Ashley shrugged his shoulders. "There might be a simp -"

"A simple explanation, Ashley. Go on then, tell me; tell me what the simple explanation is. Take a guess. Tell me your hunch at this precise moment in time. Believe me, I've thought of them all. I've lain awake until daylight has come and I still haven't thought up or dreamt up anything that makes sense. I don't know of any reason why my son couldn't find a telephone and make that call to tell me he was okay."

She was convinced he was dead. There wasn't a glimmer of hope in those beautiful, sad eyes.

He'd read of mothers and fathers who clung to a silk thread of hope that their children would pull back from an impossible medical illness. He'd heard of the stories of plane crashes with no survivors, yet parents, brothers and sisters, husbands and wives would be convinced that someone would be found a mile or two from the wreckage, alive. Or a shipwreck, and for ten years those parents would hope, hope the impossible and imagine a way, create a ridiculous story in their heads of how *their loved one* had defied the odds and swam to a desert islandand would miraculously flag down the next passing ship.

But not Kate Wilkinson. "One other thing, Ashley."

"Go on."

"I checked out the electoral role of the island."

"Yeah."

"There was no Clara. No record of any girl called Clara on the island. I don't know. Perhaps the islanders may have been telling the truth after all. Perhaps he never got there."

# Chapter 8

A buzzer sounded as he opened the door to the small convenience store at the top of Richardson Road in Fenham. On the whole, the area was quite pleasant, predominantly private housing, businesses and plenty of green areas nestling in the shadow of St James's Park.

But the buzzer on the door indicated an underlying problem with certain individuals not too keen to carry out an old- fashioned trade where money is generally exchanged for goods. Ashley remembered the old corner shop of long ago on Rothbury Terrace in Heaton, with a bell on a spring to warn old Mrs White that a customer had come into the shop and needed serving. Mrs White could hear the bell from anywhere in the upstairs flat that was home, the upstairs flat above the corner shop and, wherever she was in that upstairs flat, she would be down to serve the customer in less than a minute. Nowadays, if the shopkeeper disappeared for a minute, half his stock would have walked out the door by the time he returned. Ashley lingered in the doorway observing

Rafi Patel serving a youngster cigarettes. His police instinct kicked in and he wondered if the boy was sixteen. He probably was… just.

Ashley didn't care. If the kid wanted to smoke despite all the health warnings, then he was just plain stupid. And if Rafi refused to allow the purchase, then the kid would just get one of his older mates to make it. Or worse, the shop would be robbed in the hours of darkness.

Rafi smiled as he handed the customer the change. He looked up, spotted Ashley and gave a sort of half-hearted wave.

"Mr Clarke, how's it going, Sir?"

Ashley leaned over the counter and offered his hand."Good, Rafi. And you?"

Rafi sighed.

"Oh, not too bad, Mr Clarke?"

Ashley held up a hand.

"Please, Rafi, we aren't in the station now. Call me Ashley…errr, I mean Ash. Ash, I prefer Ash."

Rafi looked a little taken aback, perhaps a little untrusting."So you're not on duty."

Ashley laughed a little. "No, not on duty, Rafi, just here to see how the shops are doing. You're a hard-working kid, Rafi. Are you making plenty of money, my friend?"

"Just a minute," Rafi replied.

He picked up a telephone handset from beneath the counter, punched in three or four digits and broke into his native tongue. A couple of minutes later an older man appeared from a doorway that Ashley guessed led to upstairs. The old man was clearly Rafi's father, the same soft features and facial expressions. Even the way he walked over towards Ashley mirrored his son's gait.

"Officer, very nice to meet you. I'm Sidney Patel. You may call me Sid."

Ashley puzzled at the western forename.

"Yes, Sidney's an unusual name for a Pakistani gentleman, isn't it? My father thought it would help me progress in your country. Rafi is the third generation of our family to have lived in England. So many better opportunities than in Pakistan. We are very proud of our adopted country and of our city's football team." Mr Patel pointed at the huge Newcastle United crest hanging in a frame above the counter.

"Rafi and I are season ticket holders, never miss a game." Ashley took the old man's hand and shook it warmly. A leathery hand, a hand that bore testament to over forty years' hard labour.

"Me too… in the old Gallowgate End, Mr Patel, and you?"

"The Milburn Stand, officer, about ten feet from the halfway line. We are almost on speaking terms with the manager."

Ashley and the two shopkeepers broke out into smiles, but almost immediately the old man's face straightened. "Officer… I'm sorry, I know you aren't here to talk football. I'm forgetting my manners. Rafi tells me you need to talk to him. I normally take a little nap about now. I open the shop up at six in the morning, you see, so my customers can buy a paper on their way to work. I'll look after the shop while you two go upstairs."

Rafi's head tilted and he flicked his eyes over in the direction of the doorway his father had come through.

Ashley started walking over. As he brushed past Mr Patel, the old man gripped his arm lightly. He whispered gently in Ashley's ear. "He's a good boy, officer. He was forced into it, you know. They take money from me, eat into my profits. I have overdrafts and loans with the banks just to make ends meet. He's a good boy, Rafi's a goodboy."

Ashley placed a hand on his shoulder.

"I know, Mr Patel. I know he's a good boy."

A worried look came across the old man's face now, his voice stuttering a little, his bottom lip trembling.

"Then you'll help him, officer?"

Ashley sighed. "I don't know if I can, Mr Patel."

"He won't survive prison, you know that? He's not the type that can look after himself. They forced him, officer, they forced him."

Ashley squeezed the old man's shoulder, nodded his head and walked slowly towards Rafi, who held the door ajar. Ashley wanted to help. That's why he was here.

"It's been quiet since they were all arrested… err… we were all arrested. Graham's team are keeping a low profile until the court case. I am being told that he's still running the operation from his prison cell."

Rafi rubbed at his tired eyes, paused for a second or two. Ashley wondered whether the youth trusted him, whether he wanted to divulge the next bit of information. But he did.

"I've heard there's a bit of a power struggle going on too."

Ashley nodded. "You're right. The other two big gangs in the city are waging a mini-war. They figure

Bulldog is looking at a ten-year stretch. They're trying to move in on some of his business activities, particularly the protection."

Rafi sat on an old leather sofa, crouched forward, his body rigid and tense, his hands steepled together tightly.

"Have any of the gangs moved in here?"

Rafi unsteepled his hands, dragged one of them through his thick mane of jet-black hair. He was a handsome young man, Ashley thought, soft, almost feminine features. His father was right, prison would be hell.

"Not yet, Mr Clarke."

"Ash, remember?"

"Yes, sorry, Ash." The youth forced a smile. "Not yet, Ashley. I've only had one visit from a member of Graham's gang. He said there wouldn't be any collections for a few months but made it clear that the payments would mount up."

Ashley frowned in disappointment. "So the fact that Bulldog has been banged up on remand hasn't made a blind bit of difference?"

The Pakistani youth shook his head and wiped a tissue in the corner of his eye. He spoke in a soft tone.

"I'll be banged up too, as you call it, in a little over a month."

"When's the date of the trial?"

"October 15th. I won't survive prison, you know that." A tear trickled down the side of his face.

"I was locked up for six hours once in a cell at Market Street, mistaken identity." He forced a smile. "You white guys think we all look the same."

Ashley smiled, shrugged his shoulders by way of an apology.

"It was the worst six hours of my life. I was sharing a cell with an old tramp who was actually enjoying a roof over his head and some regular food, and a hardened criminal who had a swastika tattooed on his right arm. He threatened me the whole time, called me the vilest names you could imagine. There was one toilet in the corner of the cell, no privacy and, of course, no toilet seat. How can people live like that? How can these people survive months, years, living like that? Even an animal in a zoo has better conditions than that."

Ashley spoke. "Because that's what most of them are, Rafi… animals. They don't think of the consequences before they plunge a knife into someone or stamp on someone's head so hard they kill him. It's beyond their logic to think that far ahead."

"Well, I've thought about it, Ash. My solicitor reckons I'm looking at a few years in prison; dealing to kids is the worst and perhaps I do deserve it."

"Stop beating yourself up, Rafi, you were forced into it." Rafi seemed to ignore Ashley.

"Perhaps it's God's way. I have good insurance. A man called Mr Hunter deals with our community, calls round a couple oftimes a year. Last year he persuaded me to sign up for a big policy."

Ashley realised what the poor kid was getting at.

"Two hundred thousand pounds will go to my father if I die. He could pay off our debts and still have enough to retire, sell a couple of the shops or rent them out."

"You're not thinking straight, Rafi. It doesn't need to come to that."

Rafi stared straight ahead, looking right through Ashley, focusing on nothing in particular.

"Allah will provide."

"What if you don't go to prison?"

"God is good. He works out everything in the end. He sent me a message through a dream. I dreamt I was hanging from a light fitting, a torn bed sheet around my neck."

He focused on Ashley, the youth was smiling. "God sent me that message, Ashley." Ashley decided that now was not the time to express his atheist views.

"What if the judge is sympathetic, Rafi? He'll know all about Bulldog. Jesus, everybody in the city knows about him, he'll know how he works. Tell him about the protection racket, tell him about the debt, tell him how he forced your hand."

Rafi climbed from the seat, walked over to the far side of the small lounge. He turned and faced Ashley.

"I've already been advised what will happen if I disclose that tothe courts. I can't deny I was dealing for him. I had to admit it. That's bad enough, but Graham cocked up, not me, and he isn't holding the confession against me. But if I disclose to the courts that he forced my hand, then he's looking at another five years."Rafi wiped a handkerchief across his nose. "Five years of hell for my family. His monkeys have been into the shop, warnedwhat will happen to the shops and…"

He paused. So much emotion, so much terror. "And my little brother."

Ashley wanted to speak, wanted to find the words.

“I’ve to take whatever the courts throw at me, Ashley. I’ve made my confession, it’s been signed and I mustn’t deviate from it in any way. Anything I say will add a year or two, maybe more, to Bulldog’s sentence and he’s made it clear that just wouldn’t do.”

“Do you have your solicitor’s number, Rafi?”

“Yes.”

“Then give it to me.”

“Why? You’re on the other side, so to speak.”

“No, I’m not. I’m not on the force anymore, I’ve resigned. And I’m on your side and you aren’t going to prison.”

“How… Why?”

“I’ll explain everything once I’ve spoken to your solicitor.”

“But Billy Graham, Ashley, his gang. I’m scared, my brother, the shops, I can’t—”

“I’ll take care of that, Rafi, now go and get the bloody number.”

Ashley opened the door to the shop as he folded the piece of paper and slipped it into his Levi’s pocket.

“One last question, Rafi.” Ashley paused by the door. Rafi Patel raised an eyebrow. “What?”

“Would it offend you if I called you a Paki?”

Rafi Patel thought it a strange question. A half grin crept acrosshis face.

“It depends on what context, Mr Clarke. If you called me a Paki bastard as I know some people do, then yes, I would be offended. But if you said you were going to the Paki shop, then no, I wouldn’t lose any sleep over it.”

Rafi laughed.

"I know some of my favourite customers use that term. They don't mean to offend. Why do you ask?"

Ashley shook his head. "No reason, Rafi. No reason really." He looked over at the counter. Mr Patel was serving two elderly women and was deep in conversation with them. He thought about waiting to say goodbye. He ambled over to the shop doorway and pulled the door towards him. The buzzer. Mr Patel looked up.

Ashley shouted over. "Mr Patel, Rafi's a good boy. Don't you forget it."

Mr Patel gave a little wave, smiled and Ashley walked out into the bright sunshine.

# Chapter 9

A phone call to John Markham seemed like a good place to start. John had been good to Ashley as always. Even after his outburst with the Chief Superintendent of West Mercia Police. He'd let the team down, Markham had said, let Roddam down who'd backed him all the way. But, most of all, the PC brigade had won. Another little victory, Holy John had described it, another good cop off the streets. He'd let Markham down alright, left his partner in the lurch. Ashley hadn't regretted his decision, but just couldn't shake the guilt where John Markham was concerned.

Holy John had taken him out for a few drinks round Newcastle the night after he'd officially penned his resignation letter. He'd been advised to write this quickly before the suit managed to get back to Birmingham and to start formal proceedings for dismissal.

During their drunken night out ending up in a lap dancing club, Markham had suggested to Ashley that he let the bastards have it in his resignation letter.

"Tell the fuckers how it really is, Ash. Let them have it. Tell them what's wrong with the force, tell them about the twats at the top. Give them it straight, three or four pages, maybe more, and make sure the letter finds its way to all and sundry in every division you've ever been involved with."

Ashley, who pondered over the letter for most of the night, took it in to Roddam at eight-thirty sharp the next day. Roddam opened it. It read: *'I resign.'*

That was it.

Ashley thanked Roddam for his support, turned and walked out the door, leaving behind a speechless superintendent. "How's it going, Holy John, still upset with me?" John Markham smiled on the other end of the phone. Of course, Ashley couldn't see him, but something about the way he sounded told Ashley the man just couldn't get upset with him; he was smiling, glad to hear his pal's voice.

"I'm upset with you, you stubborn bastard, because Northumbria police have lost a good cop. You fancy another night on the tiles?"

"No, Holy John, I'm not sure I can handle another night out with you. What the hell do they wean you buggers on up on Holy Island? Raw alcohol?"

John Markham laughed. "It's you toonies, man! Think you come from the big hard city and can drink for England. You're even worse, Ash, because you've been softened up with all those years down south."

"I can't argue with that, John. Fancy a beer at dinner time? I've got a favour to ask you."

Ashley sat in the Monkey Bar on Pilgrim Street. Only it wasn't called the Monkey Bar. Never had been, never would be. It was just known as the Monkey Bar twenty years ago. John Markham walked in fifteen minutes late. He looked around the bar, spotted Ashley in the corner. Ashley gave a wave. John Markham spotted him, acknowledged the wave and walked over.

"The Monkey Bar, Ash? The fucking Monkey Bar? What century are you in, for Christ's sake? I've been up and down Pilgrim Street four times looking for the bloody Monkey Bar."

"So you found it, John. What's the problem?"

"What's the problem? I had to ring the lads at Market Street in the end, and one of the guys nearing the pension explained where it is."

"Sit down, Holy Man; I'll get you a beer."

Ashley stood up and wandered over to the bar. He could still hear John Markham muttering about 'the fucking Monkey Bar,' as he reached the counter.

He returned with a refill for himself and placed a glass on the table beside his ex-partner. John Markham took a long drink, drained half the glass with his first mouthful.

"Thirsty, John?"

"You could say that, Ash. Had a shit of a morning. What about you, what you been doing with yourself?"

Ashley took a purposely slow drink of his beer, unsure how to approach the question he'd wanted to ask John Markham ever since he'd left Kate Wilkinson.

"C'mon, Ash, spit it out. I know when an ex-cop is after a favour. What do you want?"

Ashley laughed. "It's as obvious as that, is it?"

"'Fraid so, Toon Boy. 'Fraid so!"

"Okay, bear with me. I need to tell you a story about a good pal of mine and his gorgeous, gorgeous mother."

It took Ashley about thirty minutes to explain the facts, as Kate Wilkinson had relayed them in her office. He explained why he'd called John Markham and figured that he had a foot in both camps, so to speak. If anyone could find out about a missing man last spotted on Holy Island, surely John Markham, Holy John, could.

"Only he wasn't spotted, Ash, was he?"

"Well no, but—"

"Just a phone call from the lad telling his mother he was on the island."

"Okay, I take your point, but why would he want to say he wason Holy Island when he wasn't? It doesn't make any sense, John."

John Markham looked up, caught the barmaid's eye and signified two more drinks in the universal language of the invisible glass in a quivering hand as his other hand signalled two… the polite way.

"I don't know, Ash. I really don't know. But you're saying this lady, the lady whose hips you wanna dislocate—"

Ashley held up a hand. "Whoa, John, I didn't say that. I just saidhow attractive she was all those years ago."

"Is, Ash, you said is."

"Okay, John, I said is… but look, man, we're getting distracted here."

It was Holy John's turn to hold a hand up.

"Sorry, Ash. Sorry. I know I'm changing the subject." John Markham looked at his watch.

"I'll make some enquiries. Search around a little in the files. See if I can find out about your pal. But from here it looks as if he hasn't even been to the island. We've an emotionally disturbed mother who's convinced her son telephoned from there. But might he have said he's going there perhaps? Planning a trip, maybe? Your lady, the one you wanna lay."

"John… please."

Another hand raised in the air by way of an apology, a mischievous grin.

"Okay, okay…" Another token sip from his glass, then another question. "The islanders, Ash, how come they all said they'd never seen him? It doesn't make any sense other than…" He paused, drew breath, took a drink from his glass and returned it to the table. Ashley Clarke hung on his words. "… No sense at all, Ashley. I know those islanders, they'd want to help. My guess is that Tom Wilkinson has never ever been to Holy Island. My guess is that he never ever made it."

John Markham left the Monkey Bar a little after two thirty. Ashley had convinced him to help. He'd agreed he would poke around a little in the old files of the investigation and even said he'd take a trip up to the island and *nose around.*

Good old Holy John, not many like him these days.

Three days after the meeting in the Monkey Bar, Ashley's mobile rang and the name *Holy John* flashed on the display.

"Holy John, how's it going, buddy? How's life treating those at the top?"

For once, John Markham dispensed with all niceties and preambles.

"I've some news, Ash."

"Go on."

"Not the news you want to hear."

Silence… for a split second, a hollow feeling and a knot beginning to form in the pit of Ashley's stomach.

"A body's been washed up on Redcar beach. A young male, thirty to forty years of age. I'm sorry, Ashley."

Ashley held his breath, took a bite at his bottom lip and held it there for a minute, not enjoying the silence at the other end of the phone.

"No, John, no. It can't be Tom. I mean, surely if it was Tom, the body would have been washed up long ago? It must be over two months."

"It's not unusual, Ash. The currents of the North Sea don't really follow a pattern. That body could have been to Norway and back, and at two or three miles an hour, how long do you think that would take? Some bodies get pulled out a few hundred yards and then get caught up on an inshore current. They can be washed onto a beach in twenty-four hours." He sighed. "Some take much, much longer."

Ashley thought again. He didn't want to hear this news. He looked for excuses.

"Probably just coincidence, Redcar must be a hundred miles away from Holy Island. Surely bodies don't travel that far. It can't be Tom. I mean, bodies just can't float that far and how do you know it's him? The body must be dropping to bits if it's been in the sea that long and—"

Markham jumped in. Ashley knew why, his voice mellow, his voice soothing, sympathetic even, prolonging the inevitable. "Firstly, Ashley, we don't even know if he's been to the island, he may have fallen into the sea off Redcar Pier, for all we know but, yes, bodies can travel that far. In fact it's not an unusual occurrence."

Ashley spoke. "But, John, it's—"

John Markham interrupted again. "I went up to the island. Roddam allowed me a couple of days to investigate, figured if anybody was suited to that job then I was. I found out Jack Shit, Ash. Nobody has ever heard of Tom Wilkinson and there are no records of him staying anywhere on the island. I've checked the visitors' books of every place with a bed on the island, even the hotels and bed and breakfasts and campsites on the mainland. No one called Tom Wilkinson has visited the island or anywhere near it within the last year. No credit card receipts, no restaurant bills, nothing. I checked the gift shops, the post office, even the boats in the harbour doing the pleasure cruises."

"But he would never leave a credit card receipt, John. He was strictly a cash man, didn't believe in cards or cheques."

"But if he stayed over there'd be a record in a guesthouse or a hotel, Ash."

"Yeah, John, okay but the body, surely you can't—"

"The body is remarkably well preserved, Ash. The North Sea is a cold place even in August. Sure the fish have had a go at him and I have been told by the Cleveland lads to try and persuade the mother not to take a look. He ain't a pretty sight."

"But ID, John, surely the mother will need to ID him?"

The silence at the other end of the phone told Ashley Clarke the answer he was dreading.

Almost a whisper now. John Markham was finding it difficult. He'd been trying to let Ashley down gently.

"Dental records, Ash. I'm sorry. We've had a positive ID." Another pause and an audible sharp intake of breath on the other end of the phone.

"Tom Wilkinson is dead, Ashley. The body in the morgue at Middlesbrough Central is Tom Wilkinson."

*The sun will still shine tomorrow.*

He remembered his old pal's favourite saying. Ashley composed himself, tried to get practical, fighting the tears and the hurt and a feeling deep in his chest he'd never felt before. Not the separation from Alexis, not the death of his grandfather. His bottom lip quivered. He remembered how hard everyone thought he was, wouldn't be appropriate for a tough northern copper to shed a tear. He thought of Kate. The feelings deep inside wouldn't subside.

"Who tells his mother, John? Who breaks the bad news?"

"I hadn't even thought of that, Ash. Roddam would have my balls if he knew I'd delivered the news to you first. He doesn't even know. I'm on my way up to his office now, just as soon as I hang up."

"Can I tell her, John? It would be better coming from me."

A pause at the other end of the line. John Markham contemplating, John Markham wondering how he could bend the rules just a little more for the benefit of his friend.

"I'll see what I can do."

"Thanks, John, thanks. I really appreciate it."

"I take it you'd rather tell her than a uniform gatecrash wherever it is she works. Does she work, Ashley?"

"Yeah, yeah, an office in Milburn House, Just Flirting, a dating agency. She's the boss. Try to speak to Roddam, John. Tell him I've known the family for thirty-odd years. I'll jump in the car now. I can be with her in less than half an hour."

John Markham hung up and promised he'd try his best. He'd pushed the risk boat out again for Ashley. The paybacks were building by the day.

Ashley Clarke made the journey from his apartment in Fenham to Newcastle city centre in less than twenty minutes. He cursed the lack of parking spaces in the city centre but neverthelessmanaged to find a space at the bottom of Dean Street and literally ran up the hill in the direction of Milburn House.

As he entered the foyer of the massive building, he slowed down. He realised that, in fact, he didn't really want to get there that quickly after all. The death march, his colleagues in the Met had called it. The worst job in policing. Telling a mother her child was dead. Far worse than being first on the scene of a fatal car crash, a murder or a suicide. Ashley had witnessed some horrific incidents in his police career, but none came anywhere near telling a parent about the death of their child.

He remembered the first time; he'd never forget it. He didn't even have to say anything; the mother just knew. The look on the policeman's and policewoman's faces and the uniform and that familiar conversation.

"Mrs Johnson.""Yes."

"PC Clarke, my colleague, WPC Brown."

"What is it?"

"May we come in?"

"What's wrong? Where is he?"

"May we come in, please?"

... and then realisation, the realisation that her son wasn't in trouble, wasn't in a hospital bed. The realisation at that precise moment that her son would never be back home again.

Sixteen years old. Knifed in the street in broad daylight.

Why on earth had he volunteered? Sandie, the receptionist, wasn't smiling today. Something was wrong. Before he had a chance to ask her, she spoke.

"She's in her office. The police are with her. She's in a hellish state. I suppose you know?"

Ashley nodded. Without asking, he walked through the main office towards the private quarters of Kate Wilkinson. His mobile rang just as he reached her doorway. John Markham. He answered it, didn't speak.

"Ash, I'm sorry. Roddam wouldn't have it, told me it needed to be official. He sent two policewomen round to her office within ten minutes."

"I know, John, I'm there now."

"How's she taking it?"

"I'll let you know soon, John. I'm about to walk into her office.I have to go."

"Ash, I'm sorry, mate, I did try."

"I know, John. I know you did."

He pressed end and slipped the phone into his baggy Levi's pocket. He didn't bother to knock, the door was slightly ajar. He gave it a gentle push and made a deliberate movement so that Kate would see him and speak first. A coward's way out, he thought, but he could live with it for the time being.

The policewomen sat opposite the distraught woman. He recognised the younger, dark-haired girl to his left: Paula. He'd noticed her in the station a few times; she seemed quite friendly,a popular member of the team, attractive. The older policewoman had a look on her face that said she'd seen it all before and wanted to get back to the station.

She spoke first.

"Hi, I take it you're Ashley Clarke?" Ashley nodded.

"Officer Markham said you'd be on your way."

Kate stood up. Her whole body shook. It looked as if her legs would give way as she walked towards Ashley.

"I knew this moment would come, Ashley, but it doesn't make it any easier."

She fell into his open arms and he held her tight. Paula tugged at the sleeve of her colleague and two or three quick eye signals between the two policewomen and the ex-policeman confirmed that his ex-colleague's task had been completed and the grieving mother would prefer to be left in the company of a friend without a uniform.

# Chapter 10

Ashley Clarke stayed with Kate Wilkinson for the rest of the day and drove her home in her car just after six.

He'd pick his own car up in the morning; his car and, likely, a couple of parking tickets. Kate mentioned her address as they left the city centre: Darras Hall Estate, near Ponteland. Land of the rich and famous, he'd called it before he left for London all those years ago. This dating business must pay, he thought to himself.

They sat in an awkward silence for most of the journey, save for an occasional sniff from Kate or a dab of the eyes with a paper tissue. Twice Ashley tried to make small talk, comfort her, but quickly gave up. He figured she was better left alone with her thoughts during the thirty-minute drive north.

The streets at Darras Hall were as impressive as he remembered as a youngster, and Kate Wilkinson's house in a small exclusive cul-de-sac at the end of Runnymede Road was simply breathtaking. The house stood in its own grounds and the elegant electronic gates eased gently open after Kate had managed to locate the remote control.

"Park the car over there." She pointed at the triple garage in the far corner. An elderly gardener pottered around with a wheelbarrow at the bottom of a beautifully manicured lawn, the size of a small football pitch in front of the house. "Would you like a cup of tea..." she hesitated, "or something stronger?"

He wanted something stronger... sure. But figured the time, the place and the company weren't quite right. He cast his eye over the façade of the house.

"No, Kate, I need to get back. I've a few things to do."

He made his apologies and left. He stopped off at the Blackbird public house on the edge of the estate for something stronger and called a cab.

* * *

Ashley, as arranged, turned up at the rented flat on Chillingham Road, Heaton, to assist Kate with the unenviable task of 'breaking up' her son's home, as she put it. Ashley stood outside Number 320 for a good fifteen minutes before Kate arrived, apologising profusely, blaming the city traffic.

"So sorry, Ash, getting through Jesmond at this time of day is just impossible."

It was eleven in the morning. Rush hour had long gone and Ashley looked over Kate's shoulder down Chillingham Road, which was almost deserted. She'd been putting the grim task off. Who could blame her, who could blame a mother for not rushing to her dead son's house to dismantle his belongings?

"The funeral's on Friday, Ash," she said, as she handed Ashley the front door key and beckoned him with a rapid eye movement and a tilt of the head to open the door.

"We need to get it over with and then I can put it all behind me.The funeral and, er… this."

Ashley didn't answer. He inserted the key in the door and gave a gentle push. Two months of junk mail, advertising flyers for pizza houses, joiners and new businesses as well as normal post blocked his path. He kicked the pile to one side and eased open the door. Kate sighed as she seemed to look through the pile of papers.

"To tell you the truth, Ash, I've done most of my mourning over the last two months. I knew he was dead, just knew a few days after he hadn't called. It was an awful feeling… just awful and yet a feeling I can't describe. I remember ringing the police one night at midnight, begging them to take me seriously. I just knew something awful was happening to him. The feeling persisted for around four hours. I never slept a wink."

She picked up a handful of papers, took a quick look and then cast them into the corner of the small passageway.

"And then the feeling passed… as quickly as it came… and then I knew."

Ashley knew exactly what she meant. He'd read about these extraordinary moments many times: a sibling on the other side of the world predicting the exact time and circumstances of the death of a brother or sister. He'd experienced a similar event when at twenty-one years of age he broke a leg playing football. His twin sister had called their mother within minutes of the accident and complained of pains in her right leg. The same leg that Ashley had shattered. A compound fracture of the tibia and fibula.

The inexplicable.

He knelt down and sifted through a few papers.

"Bills mostly, Kate. Bills and bank statements and of course all the usual junk stuff." He held up some free papers and a brown envelope with Northern Electric emblazoned across the front. "They all have to be written to, I'm afraid, and settled. A person's debt doesn't die with them, contrary to popular opinion."

Kate frowned. "No?"

"I'm afraid not. The estate becomes liable."

Kate knelt down, made eye contact with Ashley.

"That's the least of my problems, Ashley. I'll sort it. The dating game pays well, you know."

Ashley thought back to the previous day and her house at Darras Hall.

"We've over four thousand members now, all paying between twenty-five and fifty pounds a month, depending on their activity."

Ashley did the calculations quickly in his head.

"We cover the whole of the North of England and some of Scotland too."

She took the Northern Electric envelope from him. "So the likes of this isn't a problem."

Ashley sifted through a few more.

"Nevertheless they still have to be paid and written to." He started separating the important-looking documentation from the junk mail and began placing the brown and white envelopes on the first stair in a neat pile. "I'll take care of this if you want, Kate. You've enough to worry about organising the funeral. I'll have it sorted by the end of the week. I'll come over and tell you what cheques need to be written."

She reached for his hand. "Oh, Ash, would you? That would be great."

Ashley nodded. "No problem. I'll see if I can find a couple of carrier bags."

He began climbing the stairs to the upper flat. He looked back down at Kate who stared up at him like a lost puppy with big, sad, damp eyes.

"You'll need to go through his personal things, I'm afraid, Kate. Take what you want home with you and I'll take care of the rest."

"Thanks, Ash." She turned away. "I've an old suitcase in the car. I'll go and get it."

Within an hour, Ashley had filled three bags with rubbish and had a pile of letters, four inches high, neatly stacked on the small dining room table which sat in a corner of the living room. A few minutes later Kate appeared carrying the suitcase. She looked a little guilty as she announced, "This sounds so cold right now, but I really do want to get out of here." She patted the side of the case. "I've everything I want right here. The rest can go. Here's his laptop computer, Ash. I don't know if it's of any use to you, but you might as well have it." Ashley reached up and took hold of the computer case, placed it on the floor beside him.

The first tear fell.

Kate wandered over to the dining table. Ashley stood up. He had an overwhelming urge to comfort her, to take her in his arms. Why couldn't he? What was stopping him? For a brief second, they stared at each other and then Kate took a step forward. He felt an almost gravitational pull towards her, something he couldn't fight.

She sobbed for a full three minutes as Ashley held her close, perversely enjoying the moment. Her smell, each movement, each tiny spasm of her body. It was delicious. He didn't want to let her go.

And then she composed herself. Her grip on him slackened and she pulled away. She stood at arm's length, looking up at him. Her mascara had run down both cheeks and she made a vain attempt to tidy herself up with an already damp tissue. "Thanks, Ashley, thanks. I don't know what I'd do without you." She leant forward to give him a token kiss, a sign of her appreciation. Ashley leaned forward, their eyes fixed. Those eyes, those gorgeous, deep emerald pools. And her breath, the heady, sweet smell of her breath as her mouth opened to meet him. He inched closer, as if in slow motion, a puzzled look in her eyes now. Those eyes. But no resistance as their lips met. It lasted a split second, half a second at the most; he wanted to stay there longer, he wanted to open his mouth, move his lips the way lovers do, probe gently with his tongue, but by magical mutual consent and exact timing, they parted. Half a second, that's all. Half a second of bliss. She bent down, reached for the suitcase and made her excuses to go. And he noticed that the tears had subsided and a gentle smile had returned to her lips and a sparkle had returned to *those* eyes.

No time like the present, he thought, ignoring his lifelong motto of 'always putting off tomorrow what can be achieved today'. He picked up the first letter from his kitchen table: a Vodaphone mobile phone bill £37.61. He checked the last few entries. Nearly all mobile numbers, a few 0191 Newcastle numbers and one or two London numbers too. Conspicuousby its absence was the 01289 code of Holy Island. Perhaps Markham had been right all along. After all, if he'd booked in at the island, he'd need to call wherever it was he was staying.

He jotted the amount and the recipient together with the address of Vodaphone on an A4 piece of paper he would present to Kate when his task was complete. After he'd typed out a five-line letter to the company on his laptop, he walked through to the combined fax and photocopier in the lounge and photocopied the bill. He returned and sat back down at the table. He sighed… only another twenty-nine to go.

Three hours later he picked up the final documentation. A bank statement: Barclays Haymarket Branch. He copied and pasted the now familiar reply and placed the name *Mrs K Wilkinson* at the bottom of the page. He picked up the statement, walked through to the photocopier again. He checked the balance: £2,701 in credit. No other bank account, no building society book or any other form of savings. Not much to show for twenty years, Ashley thought to himself. He smiled. That was Tom though.

He lived life in easy street. He'd pull a few quid together, packa bag and set off on his travels. England, Scotland, Europe, the Far East, New Zealand, it didn't really matter. Tom had seen more of the world in his all too short existence than the nextman if he lived to be a hundred. Bizarrely Ash was jealous. Fifteen years in London, a couple of trips to Ibiza and a few European games with Newcastle United. Jealous of a dead man. He opened the cover and placed the statement face down, pressed *copy*. The machine whirred into action and when it stopped he lifted the cover to remove the document. His task was complete. He checked the entries on the statement as he wandered back through to the kitchen. Tom had been backpacking the Silk Road for three months before returning home to Northumberland the final two weeks of his life. He smiled as he looked at the cash withdrawals from around the world and remembered a telephone conversation with Tom on his mobile as he bivouacked in the Taklimakan Desert.

The Silk Road. The ancient trade route between East and West. He'd promised to meet up with Ashley as soon as he returned home, tell him about the great adventure. He'd hiked and hitch-hiked along the route for nearly three months and,despite his great friend lying in his coffin, Ashley couldn't help but envy him.

He fingered the statements. His heart skipped a beat. *Jesus, a cash withdrawal in Tehran. How dangerous was that?* And further down, several Chinese towns and cities, some of which Ashley had never heard of: Xian, Jiayuguan and Turpan.

But it was the entry at the very bottom of the page that hit Ashley like a prize-fighter's finest shot. Not a cash withdrawal in a potentially volatile, political Third World country or a war-torn Middle Eastern state. No. It was the final entry. The cash withdrawal long after he'd climbed aboard the Boeing 737 for that twelve-hour flight back home. The cash withdrawal back home in his home county. The hundred-pound withdrawal from Barclays Bank in Marygate, Holy Island.

# Chapter 11

The display read 'Holy John'. He pressed call. "We need to talk."

"What is it, Ash?"

"I'll tell you soon enough. Depends when you can get away, John. I've got all the time in the world, remember?"

John Markham walked into the Monkey Bar precisely ten minutes after his six till two shift finished at Market Street Police Station.

"You don't look so happy, Ash," he announced, with a half-hearted smile etched across his face.

Ashley stood up, shook his ex-partner's hand warmly.

"I'm fine, John. It's just something I found in Tom's flat. I think you should see it."

"Tom's flat, do you have keys or something?"

"No. I was helping his mother empty it. It's rented. We needed to clear it, said I'd deal with the paperwork and stuff."

Ashley handed the folded document across. "A bank statement. I don't understand—"

"Look at the last entry, John."

Ashley watched as Markham's eyes traced the entries at the bottom of the page. His eyes came to rest in a hypnotic-type stare. The colour drained from John Markham's cheeks.

"Fuck me."

"My words exactly, John." Ashley smiled. "I don't suppose anything's amiss, but I just can't believe no one on Holy Island has ever seen or spoken to Tom Wilkinson."

John Markham didn't answer. He just nodded in the direction of Ashley and sat in silence for a few seconds contemplating... thinking... still holding the statement. He looked at it again as if not believing his eyes the first time round.

"It won't go away, John. It's there in black 'n white."

Ashley got up from his seat and walked over to the barmaid, ordered and collected two beers and sat back down. He placed the two beers down on the table.

"Help me here, Holy John, help me."

Markham reached across for the glass, didn't say anything, instead took a drink from the glass.

"He was my mate, John, my best mate at school. You understand I need to get to the bottom of this. I need to do it for his mother. You know what they say: a mother can't get on with her life unless she can tie up all the loose ends, no matter how nasty they are."

"What makes you think there's a nasty ending?" John Markham asked, as he placed his beer on the table. It was a token effort at a drink, a nervous effort. Ashley watched carefully, staring into his ex-colleague's eyes. He waited. Waited for what seemed likean eternity, determined not to speak. His patience paid off.

"I'll go up again, Ash, square it with Roddam. If anything dodgy is going on up there, then I want to know about it. I'll show him the bank account statement."

John Markham pawed at his glass, looked as if he would take another drink, but the moment passed. He reached across and Ashley placed the statement in Markham's hand.

"Thanks, John, thanks, I really appreciate it and we can go up together and maybe?"

Markham held up a hand. "Whoa, Ashley… don't even go there. I'm in your head already and you ain't going up there."

"But it's not as if I've—"

"… anything to do. I know. Like I said, I'm in your head, buddy, and there's no way are you getting into any more trouble. I shouldn't even be in here with you; you're tarnished, mate. You're bad news, and what if Roddam found out we were carrying out a nice, cosy, joint investigation? Where do you think that would leave me? I tell you where it would leave me: on the scrap heap, buddy, that's where."

Ashley realised it was futile, realised that what John Markham was saying was right. Jesus, why hadn't he thought about it? Here was Markham offering to help him yet again and he hadn't even thought the plan through.

"Sorry, John, I hadn't thought about that." Ashley placed a hand on his friend's shoulder.

"You know, John, the only thing I regret about finishing with the force is not getting the opportunity to work with you longer. I don't miss the job. It's changed, you know that, everybody knows that, but we got off on the right foot. I regret not being able to repay you for what you did with Bulldog's numpty." John Markham reached for his glass, blushed a little as he raised it to his lips.

"You're a great mate, John, and a good cop. You've stuck your neck out for me on more than one occasion. It must—"

"Stop slavering, you big southern mongrel poof."

Ashley leapt from his seat and locked Markham's head in a playful stranglehold.

"Calling me a poof, you bloody island inbred redneck?"

Markham swept a gentle leg under Ashley and the two of them crashed to the floor in a fit of laughter. The noise was enough to bring the barmaid scurrying from behind the counter.

"Stop it now," she screamed, unaware the two men were only playing. "I'll call the police."

Markham whipped his warrant card out from his back pocket, laughing.

"It's okay, darling, they're here already." Ashley collapsed in a fit of laughter. He thought about pulling his warrant card out too and fumbled in his back pocket as he remembered he hadn'thanded it into the station as instructed. He brushed the smooth leather of the holder and eased it from his pocket about an inch. But Ashley figured the card might just come in handy a little later on and pushed it back down into the pocket.The barmaid placed her hands on her hips and tilted her head to one side, patting her chest sarcastically.

"The country is in safe hands, eh? Our boys are the best in the world. Bloody grown men acting like kids." She cursed as she grabbed the two pint pots and walked away. "You can come back in when you start acting like adults. You're lucky I don't pick the phone up and ring Market Street, tell them there are two of their lads acting like twats."

Markham called Ashley the following day. He explained that Roddam wouldn't entertain yet another investigation.

They needed to get the crime figures down, an instruction from the suits above. Why open up a crime that stood very little chance of getting solved, assuming a crime had been committed that is. Why create a damn new crime, he'd said by way of an explanation.

John Markham had relayed the story to Ash and explained that Roddam had sent the uniforms out that morning to target motorists using mobile phones.

"An easy nick," Ashley said, "not like they can deny it."

"Exactly, Ash, and a one hundred per cent crime-detected and crime-solved rate. That's all they're bloody interested in these days. Zero tolerance to the poor bastard going thirty-four in a thirty zone, a crime detected and a crime solved."

"So that's it, John, case closed."

"I'm afraid so, Ash."

"But what did he say about the bank statement?"

A pause at the other end of the phone line and then a deep breath.

"He said there could have been a dozen reasons."

"Like?"

"Like he could have gone on a day trip there, maybe spent acouple of hours, had a pub lunch then returned to the mainland. That would explain why nobody remembered him."

"Okay, I accept that's possible. What else?"

"The card could have been stolen or even lent to his new girl. Clara, I think you said she was called."

"Yeah Clara, that's right, John, only there's no Claras on the island, is there?"

A deep sigh from Markham. "How do you know?"

"The electoral roll, John, it wasn't too difficult. There's only a few hundred people living there at any one time."

Ashley detected a slight hostility in John Markham's voice now, a man concerned.

"Jesus, Ash, have you been poking around? I told you?"

"Not me, John, Kate Wilkinson. She checked it out. No Clara on the island, at least not over the age of eighteen anyway."

Markham changed tune, laughed a little. "So he got a hold of a seventeen-year-old. They have the nicest arses, remember?" Ashley smiled. He remembered being on duty with Markham a few weeks before he'd resigned. They'd been undercover in Newcastle city centre casing out a joint frequented by some local villains. They'd been there over seven hours and still the villains hadn't shown up.

They'd resorted to silly games and nonsense talk to try and relieve the monotony. They'd asked why you never see a baby pigeon, counted the cars coming into the city and debated why the most popular colour was white. It was a hot day; the city centre was full of girls and young women shopping. They'd had a debate on what age the average female of the species had the perfect figure or, more particularly, the perfect backside.

They'd spent the next hour debating the issue and both agreed it was seventeen.

John Markham interrupted his pleasant thoughts. "Or maybe she wasn't an islander after all."

"No, his mum definitely said she was from the island, John."

"Possibly. But maybe she was just someone working there. We get dozens of girls every season working in the pubs and hotels, the gift shops and they don't appear on the electoral roll."

Ashley hadn't thought of that. Perhaps there was a Clara after all.

"My advice is to just leave it, Ash. The mother wanted a body, wanted to lay him to rest. What good will it do her, bringing everything back again? By the way, Ash, there was another possible sighting of your pal in Whitburn near Sunderland. The timeframe fits in with his disappearance."

"Go on."

"A young girl walking her dogs along the clifftop path claims she saw a young man fall from the cliffs. It was a piss poor foggyday, visibility down to about fifty metres. Anyway, this girl phoned the police from her mobile and the local plod contacted the coastguard. A helicopter was scrambled from RAF Boulmer, but the search found nothing. As no one had been reported missing at the time, it was assumed the girl must have been mistaken. We contacted the girl again only last week. Roddam himself went down to Sunderland Nick to question her."

"A chief super went to interview her?"

"Yeah, Ash, that's what I said. Anyway, he did, and he also persuaded her to try to describe the man she saw falling."

"And you're gonna tell me now it could have been Tom."

"It's right there in the statement, Ash... I'm sorry."

"I'm sorry too, John. At first you say visibility was poor and now she gives a detailed description of the body. The police dismissed her story at first and now, when it suits them, she has the fucking eyes of an eagle."

There was a pause at the other end of the phone and again Ashley regretted putting his voice into gear before engaging his brain.

"I'm sorry, John, I'm not getting at you. It's just?"

"No offence taken, Ash, but, like I say, I suggest you let it lie... it's for the best. That's my advice, friend to friend, so to speak." Another pause and Ashley once again struggled for any words to thank his friend for his understanding. As he opened his mouth to speak, John beat him to it.

"When does the coroner sit? When's the funeral?"

"The coroner sits next Tuesday, John. Kate will arrange the funeral as soon as they release the body. What do you think he'll record?"

"I dunno, Ash, my guess is accidental death or possibly an open verdict, more likely an open verdict because of the marks on the body. We—"

"Whoa, John, just hold it there a minute. What did you say about marks on the body?"

"A few marks on the body, Ash, maybe consistent with a fall into the sea."

"And maybe not."

Markham sighed. "Maybe not, Ash, but we'll find out soon enough. Either way, it's time for everyone to move on. Another door closed, no happy ending, but no nasty one either. Another hurdle overcome. She can then face up to the funeral, Ash. You'll be there to support her, I take it?"

"Of course."

"And then she gets on with the rest of her life, Ash. That's how it happens. That's what she needs."

"The rest of her life," Ashley muttered into the phone. Yeah… the rest of her life.

# Chapter 12

Kate Wilkinson sat with Ashley in Middlesbrough Crown Court as the coroner deliberated over proceedings. It was a sombre affair with the usual people in attendance. Curiosity seekers, a smattering of journalists, law students and people with nothing better to do.

A middle-aged PC sat opposite the public gallery, just slightly to the left of John Roddam. Ashley was curious as to why Roddam had made the hour-long trip down the A19. There were more uniformed police officers sitting with Roddam; two or three were vaguely familiar. He assumed they were his former colleagues from Northumbria Police, though couldn't be sure.

After John Markham's brief lecture, Ashley had agreed that the accidental verdict would be best all round even if there were a few small loose ends.

He wanted to reassure Kate and tell her it was over. He wanted to help with the funeral arrangements and get on with his own life, and so she could get on with hers.

An open verdict. That would be a little trickier. Never mind; Kate had no knowledge of the law and none whatsoever of what a coroner's verdict actually meant. If an open verdict was the outcome, he'd reassure her that it was normal when the exact nature of the cause of death hadn't been clearly established. The first verdict came after about thirty-five minutes of mundane bureaucratic procedures and formalities.

Death by drowning.

No surprise there. A policeman from Berwick-upon-Tweed, PC John Renton, then went on to describe how he'd carried out an investigation to establish where Tom Wilkinson had fallen in the water. It had been mentioned that Northumbria Police had been asked to establish if a connection had been made between Holy Island and the deceased. He went on to explain that the mother of the deceased had intimated that the last phone call suggested he intended to visit the island.

The coroner, Dr Douglas, a large, bespectacled, no-nonsense type, addressed the policeman.

"So, Police Constable Renton, what conclusion did you arrive at? Had the deceased ever been to Holy Island and was thereany evidence to suggest where he entered the water?"

PC Renton examined his notes, took a deep breath.

"Well, Sir, I followed several lines of enquiries. As you know, a small amount of alcohol was found in the body of the deceased. I figured a good place to start would be the pubs on the island. I interviewed all of the regulars over a three-day period. The island population is just over three hundred and during the course of my investigation, I interviewed just about every person over the age of eighteen. I showed them the latest photograph supplied by the deceased's mother."

The coroner removed his glasses, peered down from the dock.

"And, constable?"

"Not one person can recall seeing the deceased, Sir."

The coroner replaced his spectacles and began making notes in a large book on the desk.

After a few minutes, he looked up.

"That will be all, constable."

PC Renton nodded and, as he sat down, cast a glance in Ashley's direction. It ruffled Ashley; was that a grin or a slight smirk? Or had he just imagined it?

Next up was the pathologist, Dr Alex Morgan, who had carried out the autopsy.

No real surprises as he read out the technicalities and medical names associated with drowning. Anoxic brain damage and saltwater drowning.

"Brain damage, you say, Dr Morgan?"

"Anoxic brain damage, Sir. It means lack of oxygen, not the sort of brain damage caused by a blow, a punch or a kick. Mr Wilkinson's lungs were three times their normal weight from the amount of water they'd taken in."

Kate Wilkinson reached for Ashley's hand and gripped it tightly. He looked across; her eyes, focused on the policeman in the dock, welled up with tears.

"Ah, I see, Dr Morgan," the coroner replied as he turned a few pages in his book. Again he removed his glasses before speaking to the pathologist. "But I understand the deceased had a few abrasions on and around his face and a broken rib?"

"Yes, Sir," the pathologist replied.

The coroner once again consulted his notes.

"The sort of injuries that could have been attributed to a fall perhaps... say from a cliff or a harbour wall."

"Yes, Sir," the pathologist answered politely.

The coroner stood up, closed his book and spoke.

"I think I've heard all I need to know. We'll adjourn for lunch and I'll deliver my verdict later this afternoon."

Ashley looked across at the Berwick policeman. He hadn't imagined it this time; he'd definitely smiled. He stood up to leave, picked his cap up and tucked it under his arm.

"Excuse me, Sir."

It was the pathologist; he was addressing the coroner.

"Yes, Dr Morgan, what is it?"

"There is one other thing."

"Go on, Dr Morgan."

The pathologist coughed to clear his throat. Ashley looked at the Berwick policeman who all of a sudden didn't look so relaxed. The pathologist took a deep breath and spoke.

"The deceased had an unusual abrasion on the right side of his face, his cheekbone, Sir."

He waited for a signal from the coroner to continue. Thecoroner raised his eyebrows; the pathologist spoke again, this time a little louder.

"I'd describe it as a pattern or a symbol. About a quarter inch in diameter, the shape of a perfect circle with interlocking lines. A little like the Star of David, though it was difficult to make out every line. It would take a good geometrist or historian to figure out exactly what it was or what it means."

The coroner sat back down at the large desk, clearly interested in this latest development. He stroked his chin, pondered for a moment and looked the pathologist directly in the eye.

"And, Dr Morgan, in your opinion would you like to take a guess at what exactly caused this… erm… abrasion?"

The pathologist shook his head.

"I'm not in the professional habit of guessing, Sir."

The coroner smiled and removed his glasses again as if they were an imaginary barrier between him and the truth.

"I do apologise, Dr Morgan. Let me put it another way. In your professional opinion, what do you believe caused this abrasion?"

The pathologist stole a quick glance around the courtroom, making eye contact with Ashley and Kate for a split second, thenfocusing directly on the coroner.

"I'd be one hundred percent certain, Sir, that the abrasion and the bruise under the skin would have resulted from a heavy blow. Perhaps a punch from a person wearing a sovereign-type ring."

A collective gasp reverberated around the courtroom.

The voices grew louder. PC Renton leaned over and spoke directly with a uniformed colleague. Roddam did likewise with an uncomfortable-looking, middle-aged, overweight sergeant who shrugged his shoulders.

Ashley could now hear clearly the conversations and words springing from the courtroom, words like ‘attacked’ and ‘beaten’ and someone in the public gallery saying, ‘Poor boy’.

“Furthermore?”

The pathologist wanted to continue but could not be heard above the noise.

“Please continue, Dr Morgan,” the coroner boomed above the commotion.

Dr Morgan took another deep breath, then a hesitant yet confident look around the courtroom.

“I’d go further, Sir. I’d say that the injuries weren’t caused by a fall. I’d suggest that they were caused by a beating prior to the deceased drowning.”

Kate’s grip tightened. She couldn’t control her emotions any longer and broke down sobbing. Ashley put his arm around her as she trembled.

The coroner stole a quick glance in their direction and put two and two together. He held a hand up in the direction of the pathologist, opened his mouth to speak but the pathologist was now in full flow.

“The victim had bruising around his arms and shoulders, the type of bruising caused when someone is held against their will or forced somewhere.”

“Somewhere, Dr Morgan?”

The pathologist had now used up his fifteen minutes of fame. He was into uncharted territory.

“He was forced somewhere, you say? Isn’t that a bit like guessing… something you said earlier you didn’t do?”

The pathologist nodded at the coroner.

"Yes, Sir, I'm sorry. It's just that I'm reasonably certain some sort of altercation took place prior to this unfortunate young man ending up in the sea."

Kate buried her face in Ashley's chest; her dignity and composure left her as she cried like a baby. Ashley eased her to her feet and made for the exit with his arm wrapped tightly around her. The public gallery, court officials and the members of the press looked on sympathetically.

*Court adjourned* was the last thing Ashley heard as the door closed behind him.

"Why did no one think to get at that damned pathologist? I mean, we have the funds. Everyone can alter their train of thought if a little money changes hands."

"You think we should have bribed a pathologist, is that it? You think that's a wise move?"

"But look at what he said. That's never happened before. What if the coroner delivers an open verdict, worse, what if they reopen the case, what if—"

The elder of the gentleman didn't allow his colleague to finish his tirade.

"You're wrong. It has happened before and the Brothers always deal with it, always deal with the undesirables. The last time was just after the war."

The younger man listened intently, eager to learn even more of the organisation he'd devoted his life to. He thought he knew it all. He'd studied the history of the Keepers and the ancient ceremony that he participated in several times a year. In fact, he knew the hour-long ritual word for word. He had to know who to look at and which way to turn and what position to hold his head and the ceremonial sword. He needed to know the exact words of all his Brothers who took part in the ceremony too, as the Master would change it around routinely to test their knowledge. To make matters worse, a different ritual was performed several times a year and occasionally… thankfully… the punishment rite would be carried out.

The punishment rite. The most complicated of all.

Words he'd never heard of, generally an extra thirty minutesof actions and of course the violence and bloodletting. He was uncomfortable with the punishment ritual, especially when it was acted out for real, normally a small lamb or a goat, but just occasionally an unfortunate.

He would never forget his first one at the tender age of nineteen. Adultery. That was her crime. A brief sex-only fling with an outsider, an alien, who'd come on holiday to the island. Her husband was a member of the Brotherhood; word filtered back, walls have ears, and they'd been caught in a hotel bedroom in a passionate embrace.

The husband approached the High Council and insisted the ancient punishment ritual be performed on the two of them. Very rare. Two for the price of one.

He'd brushed up on the punishment rite the week before. Of course he'd studied it word for word; he knew the ceremony backwards and swore he'd recited it in his sleep.

So much study. "In 1950 it was. Spring."

His colleague's voice brought him back to the present.

"Of course, I can't remember it, but two or three of the older Brothers still can. You can imagine the euphoria after the war; by all accounts, it was a pretty special time. Soldiers still took pride in wearing the uniforms out and about. You can't think why. You'd think they'd have been glad to get into some nice civvies, but no."

He smiled, looked across at the younger man, listening intently. Something in his eyes beckoned him to continue.

"Some of them even thought that the uniform entitled them to free sex. The Americans were the worst of the lot. They were louder than everyone else and of course they had more money than the average Brit. I can't imagine what possessed two American soldiers to visit the island when Edinburgh and Newcastle were a stone's throw away, but they did.

"One of them was black, the first black person the islanders had ever seen in real life. They caused quite a stir. They'd been on the island for forty-eight hours when the trouble began. A seventeen-year-old island girl rushed into the Lindisfarne Hotel in a distressed state. She claimed that she'd agreed to go out on a boat trip with them over to the Farne Islands. They'd paid five pounds to one of the islanders for his boat for the day. It was more than a week's wages. How could he refuse?"

"They'd been on the boat for less than an hour when they came on to her. At first the girl explained it was gentle flirting, then a little stronger, sexual innuendo. The girl was a virgin and didn't know half the things they were suggesting. They anchored up in the bay about half a mile from shore and dragged her down into the galley. They stripped her and took turns to rape her. They made her perform the grossest acts of indecency you could ever imagine.

"The Brotherhood caught up with them halfway across the causeway. The fact they made such a hasty retreat proved their guilt. The Brotherhood dragged them back to the island and they were tortured for two days, then executed.

"They disposed of the bodies; they were too badly beaten to be left in the sea."

The younger man spoke. "But they'd be missed by their units."

"The islanders stuck together, just like they'd always done, just like they have done now. They denied all knowledge that the Americans had even arrived."

"But surely they must have told someone?"

The older man took a drink from an almost still lemonade that sat on the table between them. It had been nursed and fingered and pawed for twenty minutes.

"Of course they had. They had to inform the captain of the company where they were going every time they went on leave, but of course the Brotherhood claimed they'd never arrived."

"And?"

"And old Captain Yankee decided to pay a visit to the island. In fact, he brought a delegation with him and swore he wouldn't leave until they found out the truth. The Government in Whitehall got involved too. Even then the Government knelt down to the Yanks, gave them everything they wanted."

The older man laughed. "It seems that things haven't really changed. Whitehall ordered an enquiry, placed old Cap'n Yankee in charge, gave him the freedom of Northumberland, so to speak. The local constabulary at Berwick were instructed to cooperate without question, even flew two top detectives up from London. At one point, they were sure fucking Sherlock Holmes and Dr Watson would be crossing the causeway." Another laugh – another grin – another token sip at the now warm lemonade.

"The Brotherhood were worried; their darkest hour. Thirteen hundred years protecting the island from the undesirables, all hanging by a thread."

The young man sat captivated, taking in every detail, every fact and yet knowing the outcome of the tale would be a satisfactory one.

Satisfactory for the Brotherhood.

"The Brotherhood sent out a secret plea. Every banker, copper, politician, local dignitary, sleeping or otherwise was somehow notified of the consequences should the investigation continue."

He fixed a grin on his young colleague.

"And then someone came forward with just the information they were looking for. The American unit were stationed up at Lossiemouth in Scotland. A doctor seconded to the unit picked up the telephone. It appears Captain Yankee had contracted a dose of syphilis, after all too frequent encounters with the local whores. In fact it got even better. He'd been spending more on the whores than he had been receiving in monthly salary. A bank manager came forward too, confirmed he was deep in debt. I really honestly didn't think there were so many islanders dispersed so far and wide."

"So they blackmailed him?" The older man shook his head.

"Good heavens no, blackmail is dangerous. We much prefer a bribe, much safer. The Brotherhood hierarchy called a meeting. Called a meeting with an invitation to the captain. They said they had some important information. The captain turned up smoking a big fat cigar, waiting to hear the news of his missing troops.

"The Brotherhood explained how much they wanted to help the Americans and how grateful they were for their efforts in winning the war. The fat captain sat and absorbed the praise and then asked what the important news was. The Master of the Brotherhood said some important medical information had been forthcoming from the unit's doctor up at Lossiemouth. Both men had contracted syphilis. Both were in the secondary stages and had been very late in seeking medical attention."

"I don't understand, Sir. Syphilis isn't terminal, is it?"

"It can be, but that's not the point. The point was that both men were married with family back home in the States. The point was that they could not be cured; they would always carry the syphilis bacteria.

"The Brotherhood suggested a bizarre suicide pact and produced one of the men's dog tags that had been found snared on the causeway. The Brotherhood placed the ball firmly in the court of our fat captain. They asked if he wanted the doctor at Lossiemouth to come down to the island and help with the investigation; perhaps he might uncover some more information about the men and the unit. The captain turned ghostly white at the thought. Then they pounded in the final nail. They explained that the publicity was bad for the island. They wanted a quick conclusion to the matter and wanted to buildup the tourist industry that had been badly affected during the war. The Brothers offered the fat captain twenty-five thousand pounds in used five-pound notes that they suggested he could distribute as he saw fit for the benefit of the company and the men's families."

"Brilliant... absolutely brilliant, Sir. How could he refuse?"

"Exactly. Twenty-five thousand pounds was equivalent to ten years' wages in those days. How could our captain refuse?"

"That combined with a potential sex scandal."

The man drained the final dregs of his lemonade. His young colleague waited in anticipation for the conclusion of the story.

"The captain spouted on for a full five minutes about how the money would be directed to the soldiers' families in the US. He told the Brothers that the money would help to ease the pain and suffering and, the more he thought about it, the more a suicide pact was the likely outcome.

"The Brothers made it clear that the money would only be handed over if the captain exonerated the islanders and convinced all and sundry that the investigation had been concluded."

"He took the money?"

"You bet he took the fucking money. He took the money and ran. Only the poor families of the soldiers would never see a dime. Our bank manager confirmed that the captain's overdraft was cleared and the rest of the money changed into US dollars and transferred to his personal bank account in Oregon. The captain was as good as his word though. The missing soldiers were never mentioned again."

They sat in a small café two blocks away from the court buildings in Middlesbrough city centre.

"I'm frightened, Ashley. It's as if I've been wanting to find out the truth all along, but now someone official has actually said something untoward has happened. I'm not sure if I really want to know the details."

"You have to find out the truth Kate, you… we need to find out for Tom's sake, you heard what the coroner said: foul play. You'd suspected that from the outset."

Her tear-filled eyes had remained that way ever since the pathologist dropped his bombshell. Ashley had ordered two freshly baked tuna baguettes and two coffees. The coffees had been drained long ago, the two baguettes remained untouched. "What happens next, Ashley? You're the policeman."

Ashley raked his fingers through his hair.

"A policeman, Kate, not a lawyer. I really don't know what's going to happen when we get in there."

"But you must have an idea?"

"For what it's worth, I'd take a guess that the coroner is meeting with the Chief Superintendent of Northumbria and Cleveland police, though I might be wrong. I'd take a guess that the three of them are chatting the case over, discussing the pathologist's report and the coroner will be thinking about what verdict he's going to bring in and I think that these two guys can probably influence it."

"The verdict, Ashley." She smiled, and again the smile brushed Ashley's heart. "Take a guess. I won't hold it against you. What do you... guess the verdict will be?"

Ashley remembered back to the inquests he'd had to attend during his long police career. He'd had an uncanny knack of predicting all but one of the outcomes. Most were fairly straightforward. This case was heading for death by misadventure. The coroner would have no alternative. A respected pathologist had confirmed that Tom had been beaten before drowning. He all but suggested that the aggressors had thrown the body into the sea. The only thing that hadn't come out was where he'd been thrown in. Strange, he thought to himself, why no mention of the island?

Murder. Plain and simple.

The case would be reopened and the publicity surrounding the verdict would ensure that, at last, Tom's killers would be investigated thoroughly. Ashley took a deep breath and delivered his opinion to Kate, who sat ashen-faced and silent throughout. As they walked out of the café and into the gloomy,grey, smoggy Middlesbrough day, he reached for her hand offering the only gesture of support he could think of. She smiled a sad smile and slipped her hand in his, interlocking their fingers, the way lovers do.

Ashley looked around the court and in particular over to the throngs of people packed into the public gallery.

The Press!

Word had filtered through that this case was no longer the normal suicide or accidental death. The 'M' word had been whispered through countless mobile phones during the long recess. Colleagues and old pals had clogged up the grapevine and those that were working on the more mundane 'kitten up a tree' and 'Aunt Nelly reaches a hundred' had dropped everything to attend the final session at Number Two Court in Middlesbrough Crown Court, Albert Road.

Still holding Kate's hand, he studied the various members of the uniformed constabulary, the Berwick policemen, the Chief Constable and another uniform from Middlesbrough, but in particular Chief Superintendent Roddam.

Roddam looked slightly nervous. He fiddled with some notes and kept looking around the courtroom. At last, Ashley thought, perhaps now Holy John would take this seriously. This was Roddam's chance to speak out, to explain that Tom Wilkinson had definitely been on the island. He'd been beaten up on the island prior to being thrown into the sea. What more proof did they need to reopen up the case? Roddam had the written statement from Kate and the bank statement from Tom's flat. It was his duty to at least mention them.

Ashley glared at Roddam. He sat bolt upright, his uniform immaculate and each button polished for the occasion. His tie, freshly pressed that morning and hanging straight as a die with a gold and silver tie pin, the coat of arms of Northumbria Police.

He exuded confidence, a slight smile seemed etched permanently on to his face, and the look of his former boss made Ashley just a little uncomfortable.

The door on the far side of the courtroom eased open and a court official announced the coroner and then, "Court, stand." As instructed, everyone in the building stood. The coroner sat down and took thirty seconds or so to compile his notes. He didn't beat about the bush and called straight away for the Chief Constable of Middlesbrough.

After completing the formalities, he asked the high-ranking policeman various questions about where and when the body was found. He asked him to detail the enquiries made by his force and seemed satisfied with the policeman's replies. Finally, the policeman confirmed to the coroner that, in his opinion, given the condition of the body he was absolutely certain the deceased had been in the water a considerable time and therefore due to tidal patterns it was unlikely that the body had entered the sea where it was washed up.

"You may stand down, Chief Constable," the coroner commanded in his deep voice. He glanced at his notes again. "Could Chief Superintendent Roddam of Northumbria Police please take the stand?"

Roddam stood bold upright, gave a cursory nod in the direction of the coroner and, without losing a shred of composure, made his way to the stand. He confirmed his name and rank, swore on the Bible and faced the coroner solemnly.

"Chief Superintendent Roddam, I won't stand on ceremony," the coroner explained. He studied the large wad of paperwork on the desk in front of him. "It has been suggested on more than one occasion that the deceased's final hours were spent on Holy Island, which, as we know, is under the jurisdiction of Northumbria Police. Could you explain please what efforts your force has made to establish this fact? Given what the pathologist explained earlier today, it may be quite significant."

"Bingo," muttered Ashley under his breath, "wriggle out of that one."

"Yes, Sir," replied Roddam politely. "We investigated the possibility of the deceased visiting Holy Island prior to his disappearance. We investigated it not once but twice, at the insistence of the deceased's friends and family."

The coroner peered over his glasses. "Twice, Chief Superintendent Roddam?"

"Yes, Sir. On the first occasion, we sent an officer from Berwick-upon-Tweed. He knows the island and the islanders very well. He spent the best part of a week trying to ascertain whetherthe deceased had been on the island."

"And you found no evidence, Chief Superintendent Roddam. That's why you investigated a second time?"

"Correct, Sir."

"Why then, Chief Superintendent Roddam, did you investigate the matter again?"

Chief Superintendent Roddam looked at the notes he had made in a small black book. He looked back at the coroner. "Well, Sir, according to my notes, Detective Constable John Markham had liaised with friends and family of the deceased and had uncovered some more information that allegedly placed the deceased on Holy Island prior to his death." "Good old Holy John," Ashley muttered again.

"Let me get this right, Chief Superintendent Roddam," the coroner said again, "you investigated not once but twice."

"Yes, Sir," repeated Chief Superintendent Roddam.

The coroner glanced at the Chief Superintendent and then to the public gallery, looking at no one in particular.

"Very thorough, Chief Superintendent Roddam, if I may say so, and what conclusion did your force arrive at the second time of asking?"

Roddam's composure flickered for a second. A sickly cramp welled up in the pit of Ashley's stomach. He was aware that his lips had suddenly become very dry. Roddam looked down at his notes and he involuntarily wiped at the sweat on his brow, regretting his decision to knot his tie so tight.

"My officers checked every hotel on the island, interviewed more or less every adult living there. They checked out the pubs, the tourist information office and interviewed the owners of the pleasure boat cruises and fishing trips."

"And, Chief Superintendent Roddam?"

Chief Superintendent Roddam pawed nervously at his collar. "I'm afraid, Sir, we found nothing to suggest the late Thomas Wilkinson visited Holy Island prior to his death."

Ashley's instinctive reaction superseded any rational thinking as he leapt to his feet and blasted at Chief Superintendent Roddam.

"What do you mean, you found nothing? His mother took a call from him on the island. A bank statement shows he was—"

"How dare you speak to this inquest unannounced," the coroner shouted angrily. "I have not called any additional witnesses, nor do I intend to. Sit down immediately or I'll have you thrown out."

All at once, Ashley regretted his actions. This was no way to act in a coroner's court; he, of all people, should have been aware of that. He tried to rescue the situation.

"I apologise, Sir, but we have evidence that—"

"Silence!"

"But, Sir, I—"

"Quiet, do you hear? And sit down right this moment or I'll have you ejected."

Ashley groaned as two uniformed officers made their way into the courtroom. A young courtroom official pointed in his direction and he eased back into his seat. In the meantime, Chief Superintendent Roddam had approached the bench. No doubt the coroner would be told he was a bitter ex-member of the Northumbria Police Force and the chances of being able to address the court had been slashed to zero.

Kate placed her hand on his knee, gave him two or three pats, as if to say thanks. But he'd screwed up. He knew it. He'd screwed up big time.

Chief Superintendent Roddam continued where he'd left off. "As I was saying, Sir, before I was so rudely interrupted," he glowered at Ashley, "two investigations concluded nothing. We are fairly certain Thomas Wilkinson intended to go to the island but accept the fact that he never actually arrived. We also interviewed a very reliable individual at Whitburn near Sunderland who gave a very accurate description of a man that could have been Mr Wilkinson fall from the cliffs there. The localpolice and the coastguard carried out a search, but no body was ever recovered at the time."

The coroner flicked through the papers on his desk. “Ah yes, Tamara Shearing.”

“That’s her, Sir. I interviewed her myself; no reason to suspect she made the story up and a very detailed description right down to Mr Wilkinson’s black leather bomber jacket.” The coroner turned over the sheet of paper he was holding up. He held it at arm’s length, tilted his head slightly.

“And that was about three weeks prior to the body being washed up?”

“Yes, Sir.”

“Anyone else report the incident?”

“No, Sir.”

“And how old was this girl?”

“Fourteen, Sir.”

“Any evidence of any clothing found at the scene?”

“No, Sir.”

“And any bloodstains.”

“No, Sir, but then again, it was raining at the time.”

The coroner added one or two sentences to his pages full ofnotes and then looked up in the direction of the court officials. “I’d like to recall Dr Alex Morgan please.”

A man in a police uniform cursed under his breath.

The coroner took the pathologist through his earlier statements and the public gallery listened intently. He asked him to repeat the injuries and reaffirm his suspicions. Ashley never took his eyes from Chief Superintendent Roddam whom he hated more and more as each minute passed but couldn’t think why.

The pathologist was even more forthcoming, obviously more comfortable on stage, so to speak, this time around. At one point Ashley even thought he was about to deliver the death by misadventure verdict himself. A verdict that Ashley now thought was imminent.

One time Ashley wavered on an open verdict but, after the details of the fourteen-year-old's interview and the fact that no blood or clothing was found at the scene and the compelling evidence of Tom's injuries described by Dr Morgan misadventure was the only alternative open to the coroner.

A journalist in the public gallery doodled on his notepad, thinking up the headline for tomorrow's front page. *Murder!* He'd scrawled in big bold letters at the top of his report. Poetic licence, they call it in the trade, the right to exaggerate; after all, that's what sells the papers and it's what this pathologist was insinuating. *Beaten and pushed in the sea, murder victim washed up on Redcar beach,* he added in the margin on a page of his notepad.

The journalist chewed at his cheap Biro and just wished something positive had come from the Holy Island investigation. Now there really was a good headline: *Island of Horror* or *Holy Hell* he'd scrawled in oversized capitals on the bottom of his notes.

The coroner had heard enough. He dismissed the pathologist and thanked him politely.

"I'm calling a short recess," he announced. "I've heard all I need to hear. I'll return in thirty minutes with the verdict."

Ashley looked across at Kate; she gave a hesitant smile. Her eyes had lost that glazed over look. As much as Ashley had wanted the accidental death verdict so everyone could get their lives back together, Kate Wilkinson needed justice.

After what had been revealed in Number Two Court at Middlesbrough's Russell Street Crown Court building, he felt sure she would at least get the chance of a thorough investigation into her son's death. They would reopen the case, take it seriously this time, and possibly bring in a different constabulary to oversee the enquiry. He would present them with the evidence of the bank statement, Kate would tell them about Tom's phone calls from the island.

They hung around the corridor outside Number Two Court. An exhausted coffee machine spewed out yet another lukewarm Styrofoam cup of something that loosely resembled coffee. The drinker regretted the purchase as soon as it passed over their lips.

Sure enough, thirty-eight minutes after they'd left the courtroom, a court official announced to the overcrowded corridor that the coroner was ready. Without delay, the throng poured into the small courtroom.

The coroner looked organised and confident as he took his place at the large desk. Ashley thought perhaps he'd even taken a shower and changed his shirt, such was his demeanour.

He took a final look around the courtroom, placed a fisted hand over his mouth and cleared his throat.

"The evidence I have heard today, from both the pathologist Dr Alex Morgan and from the Northumbria and Cleveland Police Forces, has left me in no doubt as to the verdict I am about to deliver. A death is always hard to accept, particularly when the deceased is so very, very young, a man in the primeof his life.

My sympathies extend to the family and, in particular, the mother of Thomas Wilkinson.

"However, that misery and suffering is compounded when the cause and place of death is unknown or, indeed worse, if foul play is suspected. Dr Morgan is a highly respected and long-standing professional and indeed has been a great servant to the district of Cleveland for more years than I care toremember." He smiled. "I count him as a friend. He is convinced that Thomas Wilkinson was assaulted prior to his death." Ashley glanced at the pathologist. His expression didn't flicker, perhaps a look of mutual respect as he looked up at the coroner's desk, though Ashley wasn't sure. A low murmur hadstarted in the courtroom, an odd whisper. The coroner seemed to have paused for dramatic effect.

"However, I also need to take into account the investigation and personal interviews conducted by Northumbria and Cleveland Police and in particular those of Chief Superintendent Roddam, an officer with an exemplary police record, over twenty-five unblemished years. During the recess at lunchtime, I spoke at length with the members of the two forces and with Dr Morgan. I called Dr Morgan yet again in the final session, such is my respect for him."

Ashley became aware of a dry sensation in his mouth; he tongued at his palate searching for saliva, but found none. The hollow feeling was back in the pit of his stomach.

"But… try as I might, I cannot accept his claim that the injuries were consistent with a beating. That is, I am not one hundred percent convinced. I asked him if it were remotely possible that similar injuries could have been caused with a fall from a cliff or mountain where the body may have come into contact with a softer contact point, a grassy mound or compounded sand, for example. Dr Morgan thought it unlikely but conceded that it was possible.

"I have in my possession a report and photographs from Police Constable Dalton of Whitburn who has taken several pictures of the area where the young girl witnessed a young man fall. While I'm no expert on the geological make-up of a cliff, the photographs clearly show that the vast percentage of the area is covered in grass and fauna."

"No, no, no," Ashley whispered under his breath, "this can't be happening."

"By the powers vested in me by the Home Office, I therefore have no option but to deliver the only verdict open to me."

The coroner paused for a second, looked across in the direction of the uniformed police officers on the far side of the courtroom. He cleared his throat again and announced: "Accidental death."

# Chapter 13

The two colleagues climbed into the unmarked Northumbria Police squad car in Albert Road. The doors safely closed, their conversation now private.

"The Brothers got to the coroner, didn't they?"

The older man grinned, stayed silent, enjoying the ignorance of his colleague.

"How much did we pay him?"

"Pay him, constable! Pay him? I can assure you there was no need to pay Dr William Douglas, the highly respected coroner of Middlesbrough and Cleveland district."

The penny dropped with the young officer.

"Douglas… a Holy Island name… the coroner was an islander?"

The older man smiled, turned the ignition and shifted the automatic into drive. The car lurched forward, out of the city centre car park.

"Not exactly. He'd never ever lived on the island. His father moved down south just before he was born. But Dr Douglas's grandfather was a Keeper and handed down the teachings and principles of the order to his son and Dr Douglas's father passed them on to him.

"Pay him, no. In fact, Dr Douglas contributes five percent of his annual income to the order. So you see, he actually pays us." The older man laughed at the irony; his colleague grinned.

"Well I never."

"The order is probably more far-reaching than you would care to imagine, constable. Let me give you a history lesson. Back in the eighth century, when the Keepers were initially formed our numbers were just a few dozen, though strictly only thirteen in the temple at any one time. We carried on that way for a few hundred years and the Order moved with the times. We were a peaceful and charitable organisation confining the membership to the church-going men living on the island.

"We practised our rituals in secret, respectful and yet wary of the power of the Church. Occasionally a Brother did moveaway but consequently had to resign his position. Naturally, we took care of the wrongdoers; after all, that's the principle that the Order was founded under: the wrongdoers, the heretics and atheists."

*Protect the island and all those born under the star of St Cuthbert.*

"St Cuthbert gave us the ceremony and the ancient rites and symbols. And then came the inquisitions."

The car made its way to the outskirts of the city and the driverheaded out towards the A19 northbound. It was the best part of a minute before he spoke again. The passenger thought better of prompting him to continue and glanced across at hissuperior officer. He noticed his eyes glistening with every beam of light from the cars passing in the opposite direction. His cheeks remained dry as he spoke.

"Many of our members were persecuted and even burned at the stake during the medieval inquisitions. It nearly wiped us out. In fact, any organisation that even looked a little different to standard Catholicism was held to ridicule and yes…"

The man sighed, peered out into the gloom of the ever-darkening Cleveland late afternoon sky.

"… even cleansed by the Church. It was ironic; our very organisation was dishing out similar punishments to the non-believers and yet, just because we were a little different, had our own ceremony, the Church condemned us."

The driver indicated left and turned up onto the slip road signposted *Tyne Tunnel.*

"I suppose the church was frightened of our power, our principles, our strong beliefs."

He whistled out loud through gritted teeth.

"Power – that's a laugh. We didn't have any power then, not like we have today."

He continued.

"The island was too easy to find, and the priests and damned witch-hunters made frequent visits. In the early days, they were quite successful. I mean, it's not as if it's a big island, nowhere to hide. They found our temple and old relics and people were so frightened they told tales on their next-door neighbours and even members of their own families. It wasn't hard, everyone on the island knew who the Keepers were and, for the islanders, it was a case of accuse or be accused. The islanders were literally lining up to speak to the priest as the delegation crossed thecauseway.

"The tortures were horrific; most of the Keepers confessed to being a member as soon as they saw what lay in store for them. The nearest inquisition prison was in Berwick-upon-Tweed. The Keepers were generally racked."

"Racked, Sir, I don't understand."

"Racked, constable. One of the most notorious and successful pieces of torture apparatus of all time. The victim would be stripped near naked, male or female, it didn't make any difference, and tied onto a roughly constructed wooden- planked bedframe. At each end of the frame were pulleys and a roller to which the victim's ankles and wrists were secured. The clergy would always be present to put the questions to the terrified individual and the jailer would turn the handles of the rack if they gave an answer the priest wasn't happy with.

"The poor bastards were in a no-win situation, constable. Plead guilty to heresy and be imprisoned for life, maybe even burned at the stake, or beg innocence and be disabled for life. Torture doesn't drag out the truth; when will people begin to realise that? Torture delivers answers of desperation."

The sky seemed to darken as the driver gunned the pedal to the floor and a gentle rain began hitting the windscreen.

"Brother Michael Macnab, the Worshipful Master at the time, wrote an account of his experience on the rack when he was eventually returned to the island after seventeen years' imprisonment."

He turned to the passenger.

"Have you read it?"

"No, Sir, I don't believe I have."

"You should. You really should. He describes how one by one his wrist and ankles snapped as he continued to deny the accusations. He felt each bone bend like a piece of wet wood; the pain was like nothing he'd ever felt before. When the bone eventually snapped, it was almost a relief, he wrote.

"He even swore on the Bible, asked God to intervene and recited passages from the scriptures. The priest… this so-called man of God, the same God our Brother worshipped week in, week out, stood over Brother Michael and nodded his head towards the jailer. Brother Michael passed out as his hip dislocated and, mercifully, the punishment stopped.

"Under the ruling at the time, he couldn't be tortured again, but despite not confessing to anything, he still spent seventeen years in jail. For seventeen years the Order disbanded, partly because of fear, partly out of respect for Brother Michael, and it was only on Brother Michael's return was it resurrected. He made a vow. He vowed that the Order would be made stronger than it ever was.

"It would expand. A mass migration from the island. They were to create new Lodges in the borough and other parts of the country. The islanders would breed and educate their offspring like never before. Those with the biggest families would be helped financially. Before the end of the century, the children of that generation held lofty positions: judges, merchants, lawyers and teachers and, of course, policemen."

He turned and smiled at the passenger. "A lot of policemen. And of course the islanders looked after their own as you can imagine. Job interviews were foregone conclusions, court cases were decided before they ever came to court, and still they bred and expanded ever further. Some emigrated, founded new Lodges in America and Australia.

"At the same time, the five per cent income rule was introduced. Every islander that was part of the Brotherhood pledged five percent of his salary. That way we could educate our offspring and purchase land and property. We became better organised. We were ready for the inquisition when they eventually returned.

"Once again, our saviour was the good old tidal system of the North Sea. A Keeper on the mainland would notify the island that the delegation had arrived and more often than not they would time it badly and not be able to make it across thecauseway. They'd stop off at the local inns on route and of course the inns were owned or run by the Keepers. They'd be given the wrong tidal times or perhaps persuaded to stay a little longer by way of a free whisky or two."

The driver guffawed. "I don't know what it is with priests and fucking whisky, but they all seem to love a wee dram. They'll stand in their pulpits week in and week out preaching to the converted masses about the evils of drink and as soon as they smell the barmaid's apron they're first in the queue.

"And of course there was the Gatekeeper on the causeway, a Brother, always a Brother. He would be very persuasive advising them not to cross even when they would have made it quite comfortably."

"How would they notify the Brothers, Sir? I mean, there were no telephones back then."

"Good old fire, constable, a strategically placed pile of rubbish, old cobbles, fishing nets beyond repair, household waste, adjacent to the causeway on the sand, a permanent fixture. Fire and brimstone. It gave the Brothers time to hide the evidence and warn every islander what would become of them should they attempt to talk to the inquisitors.

"Eventually, the priests gave up and turned their attention to the towns and cities where easier pickings lay, richer pickings."

The passenger shook his head, let out a high-pitched whistle.

"And then, constable…" His hand slapped twice on the constable's thigh. "And then, constable… nothing… nothing would stand in our way."

They'd driven about forty minutes before a fully-fledged conversation took place.

"Tell me this afternoon wasn't a dream, Ashley."

"It wasn't."

"I stood and watched him shake his head as the verdict was announced. What's his name? Dr Morgan… the pathologist, that's it, Dr Morgan. He just sat there, shaking his head. Did you see him, Ashley?"

Ashley nodded. Despite the shadows getting longer and the darkness in the car, he nodded and then whispered gently, "I saw him, Kate."

It was a lie. A lie that Ashley could live with for the time being. Because Ashley hadn't seen him; his eyes had been fixed on his uniformed ex-colleagues. Ashley wanted their smiles to fade, fade into a different expression, a frown perhaps, maybe a look of sympathy, maybe even surprise at the coroner's verdict.

But no.

There were smiles. Definitely smiles and smiles that hadn't faded as they left the courtroom. At one point, Ashley even expected them to slap each other's back by way of a victory.And no surprise either, a look of confidence, especially Roddam. Roddam knew what the verdict would be, Ashley was sure of it.

Kate spoke, brought him back to the present.

"Where do we go from here, Ash?"

Ashley shrugged his shoulders.

"I don't know, Kate, I really don't know. Part of me wants to punch the whole damned lot of them. Part of me wants to get even."

"And just how do we do that?"

Ashley was thinking. *A good question. Just how do we get even*?

It was simple really; after all, he was a detective, shouldn't be too hard to work out. Someone on the island must have slipped up or would slip up if put under the right sort of pressure. Not from a cop, but from a visitor, a tourist asking some subtle questions.

He was already beginning to think up an undercover role, a birdwatcher or a photographer, maybe a researcher working on a book.

"We get even by proving that Tom Wilkinson was murdered on Holy Island."

"You're convinced, Ash?"

"I think everyone in that courtroom was convinced except for the coroner and…."

"And?"

"Maybe a few… maybe just a few other… sceptics."

"My offer's still on the table, Ashley."

"Your offer?"

"Yes. I'll pay you good money to take this case on."

"But—"

"But nothing, Ashley. I can afford it and you need a job." She placed a hand on his knee. "I want to get even too. Tell me you'll at least try."

He took his eyes from the road for a second and looked into her eyes. He breathed a sigh of relief as she removed her hand. "You can work from my office. I've a spare room that isn't used and I'll sort you a telephone and a computer out."

Ashley shook his head. She masked her disappointment well but needn't have worried.

"I'll work from one place and one place only… the island."

The two friends, an ex-policeman and the mother of his dead best friend, sat almost in silence for the rest of the journey back home to Newcastle. Ashley was thinking; he almost felt liketaking a notebook and pencil out but contented himself with the mental manuscript in his head. Ashley took the car down through the gearbox as he approached the Tyne Tunnel. Themobile rang, he pushed the earpiece in his ear and pressed the green button.

Holy John.

"I've just heard the verdict, Ash, I can't believe it."

"Me neither, John, me neither."

"You're not gonna let it lie, are you?"

"Damned right I'm not, John. I owe it to Tom."

He glanced across at Kate; she met his gaze, figured who it was on the other end of the phone.

Ashley spoke again. "Where do I go from here though, John? What happens now?"

"Where do we go from here, Ash?" He emphasised the 'we'. "I'm in it with you, remember? I want to get to the bottom of this as much as you do. It's tarnishing the island, my island."

Ashley breathed out slowly. "So you do believe he was there, John?"

"I'm fairly certain, Ash. I take it you're heading up there sooner or later."

"You're a mind-reader, Holy John."

"Copper's instinct, Ash, copper's instinct. Just keep me posted on your movements; whatever you find out, run it past me."

"I will, John, I will."

"One other thing, Ash."

"Yeah, what is it?"

"I don't think it would do any harm to have another meeting with the pathologist."

"Yeah, like he'll meet with me."

John Markham sounded hesitant. He paused, then sighed. "I'll see what I can do, Ash. Leave it with me."

"Fancy a drink, Ashley? I could do with one."

Kate's voice interrupted his thoughts; they took a few seconds to register.

"Well, Ashley, do you?"

"Erm yes… yes."

“Thank God for that, I thought you’d turned me down for asecond. It must be ten years since I asked a man out for a drink.”

Ashley smiled nervously. “Where did you have in mind? What about The Blackbird in Ponteland? It’s only a ten-minute walk from your house. I’ll get a taxi back over home afterwards.”

“Sounds good, Ash.”

Ashley signalled as he approached the entrance to Kate’s house, slowed up and stopped while Kate activated the remote control to the gates. The huge black lead gates groaned open slowly and Ashley drove through.

“Actually, Ashley, I think I’ve a cool bottle of Rioja in the fridge. Do you mind if we have that drink here? All of a sudden. I don’t think it’s worth the effort to go out.”

Ashley shrugged his shoulders. “I’m easy, Kate, whatever.”

The large house seemed cold, uninviting, lonely even. Ashley wondered why Kate, who’d been on her own for so long, needed such a big place. As in the office, the photos of Tom were everywhere. Kate dropped her handbag onto a seat in the hallway and walked through into the kitchen. Ashley followed her through, took a seat at the breakfast bar. Kate opened the fridge.

She raised a half-smile. “A 2002 Rioja, Ashley. Will you do the honours?”

She handed him the bottle and, a few seconds later, a bottle opener she’d retrieved from a kitchen drawer.

By the time he had opened the bottle, Kate had placed two heavy crystal glasses beside him. He poured the wine and Kate sat down opposite him. They took a mouthful at the same time, gazing over the tops of their glasses. Their faces were barely a foot apart. Ashley leaned a little forward. He could smell her sweet breath lightly perfumed by the Rioja. He took another sip, spoke gently, almost whispered. It was the wrong place and the wrong time to be feeling how he was feeling.

"I need to tell you something, Kate."

He wanted... needed to tell her about his fantasies as a sixteen-year-old, needed to tell her about his attraction to her, how unhealthy it all was and how he didn't think it was such agood idea to work so closely with each other. What would she say? What would she do? Laugh? Tell him he was being stupid and how she was old enough to be his mother. Is that what it was, a schoolboy fantasy that had never been realised?

And a new fantasy. Working in her office and the last two to leave in the evening and making love to her on her desk. "Well, Ash, what is it?"

Ashley opened his mouth, but the words wouldn't come. Kate set her glass down, leaned across and took Ashley's glass from his hand. She placed it next to hers and eased her backside from the seat, leaning ever nearer to him.

He froze as he gazed into those hypnotic eyes. He felt her lips on his, a gentle kiss, no movement, just barely touching. And his mouth opened wider and Kate responded. Ever close now, their lips moving in perfect synchronicity as if they'd perfected the art over many years. Joined together, Kate's tongue probed gently and erotically at his lips. She eased back slightly and traced her tongue along the surface. Ashley reached for her again, almost magnetically and the passion intensified.

# Chapter 14

John Markham was as good as his word. He sat in the pathologist's office in Redcar, Cleveland, three days after the inquest had been concluded. He'd explained that Northumbria Police were concerned that the investigation relating to the death of Thomas Wilkinson had not been investigated thoroughly enough.

The pathologist was only too happy to talk. It was as if he was pleased to get it off his chest. He spoke while John Markham listened intently.

"I wrote to Dr Douglas within a couple of hours of the inquest. I was furious."

"Angry?"

"Bloody livid. During the recess, I explained in detail the anomalies and he promised I'd be able to put them to the court."

John Markham waited for him to continue.

"It never happened, officer. He asked me to repeat my originalfindings then brought in this ridiculous idea about the deceased falling down a cliff."

"But why would that be so ridiculous?" John Markham asked.

"Officer Markham, I've been at more inquests than you've had hot dinners and I've been to at least twenty inquests where the deceased has fallen from a great height, down a cliff, a steep bank or a bridge, and the one thing that happens in every case in question is that the poor unfortunate snaps a few bones. It's inevitable. Imagine tumbling down a cliff; of course you're goingto break an ankle, an arm, a leg, a collar bone."

The pathologist stood. He was trembling visibly as he placed his hands on the desk and looked down at John Markham. "But not here, officer, not in this case. Not a broken rib or a finger or anything. Lacerations to the upper body. Explain that one to me. Explain how a body rolls one hundred and fifty feet down a cliff and only happens to injure the upper body and more particularly, the head and face."

He flopped back down in the chair and spoke in a whisper. "He was killed, officer. Beaten unconscious and deliberately thrown into the sea."

"You're positive?"

Dr Morgan nodded his head slowly. The two men sat in silence as the enormity of the statement sank in. The pathologist spoke.

"You need to reopen the inquest, officer. The police need to request a different coroner, one that will allow me to deliver my findings." He ran his fingers through his hair. "Douglas couldn't wait to get me off that stand."

John Markham sat motionless. "There was another anomaly, officer."

"There was?"

"Yes. Tom Wilkinson had slight abrasions around each wrist, the sort of abrasions you would normally find if someone has been handcuffed during a struggle."

"So what are you saying, Dr Morgan?"

Dr Morgan leaned forward, his face inches from John Markham's.

"I'm saying, officer, that you boys better get your house in order because something smells. Something stinks like a month-old haddock and somebody or some people aren't playing the game." His voice louder now. "I'm saying that if I don't hear that Tom Wilkinson's inquest is reopened by the end of the month I'm gonna throw so much shit at the fan that Northumbria and Cleveland Police won't know what day it is."

"Ash..."

"Yeah."

"John here, how are you?"

"Good, and you?"

John Markham dispensed with the niceties "I've been to see the pathologist in Cleveland."

"Yeah."

"Left him about an hour ago."

"Great. What did he say?"

"Are you sitting down, Ash? Cause you ain't gonna believe this."

"Jacob, it's me. I've some bad news." Silence.

"John Markham's been down to Cleveland to meet with the pathologist."

"Go on."

"The pathologist isn't happy; he wants the inquest reopened." John Roddam relayed the details to Jacob Moor who stood throughout the conversation, though he couldn't control the trembling in each leg.

A pause, a full minute's pause before Jacob announced, "The pathologist, John."

"Yes."

"He'll need to be taken care of."

The front of the office was a legitimate taxi office in the East End of Newcastle. Billy Graham had purchased the business at a token knock-down price after his bullies had engaged in a relentless twelve-month campaign that had effectively brought the business to its knees.

The owner had refused to bow down to the threats and intimidation and flatly refused to pay Billy Graham a single penny for monthly security.

It mattered not.

Graham had personally visited and threatened the man on at least half a dozen occasions and the sheer lack of respect the business man afforded him meant that Graham no longer wanted to enforce a monthly security service – he wanted the business – lock, stock and barrel.

Word would filter through the city. Don't fuck with Billy Graham.

The final straw came in the Christmas of 2002. His henchmen had disabled the entire fleet of cars over a twenty-four-hour period the weekend prior to Christmas Day.

It was the most lucrative weekend of the year for the drivers, the weekend's takings equivalent to a month's wages any other run-of-the-mill time of year.

It was the unofficial 'Christmas bonus' that would provide their families with gifts and presents and, in some cases, the summer holiday later on in the year.

The Newcastle punters were generous to a fault and a combination of excess alcohol and over-exuberant festivities ensured that the cab journeys were frequent and the tips were large.

The first car had been petrol-bombed outside the owner driver's council house in the Meadow Well Estate in North Shields.

He had been unlucky. Most cabs had just had their tyres slashed or a window or two broken, lights popped, the sort of inconvenience that would take a few days to put right.

It broke the resolve of many of the drivers, coming on top of the many months of intimidation and lost earnings they'd suffered.

John Balding, the owner of *Taxis 4U* received fourteen calls over that weekend from drivers apologising but reluctantly declaring they had no option but to hand in their notice.

He understood. It was finished.

The business he'd run successfully for twenty-seven years had breathed its last breath. It had given him a good living, it was time to admit defeat. His wife had begged him to sell up, accept William Graham's generous offer of one hundred and twenty-five thousand pounds for the industrial unit on Byker's Brough Park Industrial Estate. After all, she kept reminding him, he'd only paid twenty-eight thousand for it and the mortgage had been cleared years before.

She didn't understand.

He picked up the telephone and keyed in Billy Graham's personal mobile telephone number that he'd been told to call should he have a change of heart.

Billy Graham was pleased with his new acquisition, but he had slashed the original offer he'd made to the owner. Economic climate, he'd claimed. Times were tough, money tight, and anyway the goodwill of the business had been re-evaluated now that Mr Balding only had a handful of cars that were operational.

Graham was a good businessman, of that there was no doubt. He had smirked as he handed over the briefcase containing the cash.

He wandered through the small office at the front of the building, but not before he'd informed the two girls on the front desk that they were fired. The following week, he opened up the new office with Billy Graham's personally selected staff and embarked on a huge advertising campaign announcing that *Taxis 4U* were back in business.

He offered discounted cab journeys for the remainder of the month and made sure every client stepped from a *Taxis 4U* cab with their very own laminated plastic card, complete with telephone numbers.

And he wasted no time restructuring and reforming the building. John Balding had used the back of the premises as a small repair station for the cabs. He'd turned the far side of the building into a small lounge where the drivers relaxed or took a coffee or a beer or two at the end of a long shift or just relaxed between jobs.

Graham brought in his favourite architect who transformed it into his personal domain. Two full-sized snooker tables sat in the middle of the huge open-plan unit. A 48-inch plasma screen hung on each of the four walls and plush leather sofas sat on top of the ridiculously expensive, deep-pile carpet.

On the far side of the room where John Balding's makeshift bar had stood, Graham had commissioned a fully stocked optic bar together with draught bitter and Guinness and strong bottled beers from around the world.

It would be from here that he would plan his entire business operation.

In between the bar and the front office of the taxi company was Billy Graham's record office. He'd known he'd needed the office for a while now. His acquisition of the taxi premises had given him the impetus to set it up.

So many pies, he'd smiled to himself. How on earth do we keep check on everything? His own records system consisted of the odd scribble on the back of a fag packet and a glove compartment in his Jaguar XJS so full of paperwork that it could hardly close. It had to be replaced.

Margite was twenty-five, intelligent, a trained accountant and ambitious. Her father was German and therefore her planning and foresight were meticulous. She'd turned the whole operation around within a month.

She'd compiled Excel spreadsheets detailing the whore houses he ran and the protection rackets and legitimate businesses he used to front things up. She'd made sure the tax and NI contributions were in order and that the accounts were supplied to Companies' House on the very day they were due. She'd discovered discrepancies in the figures supplied by the dealers and madams and musclemen employed in Graham's empire. They'd all received a severe beating and told to get back in line.

Margite was brilliant. In all the years he'd been in business he had never really known what he was actually making. Now he knew to the penny and he was astounded. Margite received a brand-new BMW X5 as her reward for increasing the profits in every single division of his establishment. She'd been with the company three months and in the fourth month he was screwing her on the snooker tables and the leather sofas and across her very own office desk. Such was her stop-at-nothing attitude to succeed. (The X5 helped too.)

Margite's office, or rather her laptop, held a record of Graham's life.

Everything.

Every address, every dealer, every bouncer, every taxi driver, every shop they protected, every pound received and every penny spent. Margite positively glowed at their regular monthly financial meeting (her idea) as she demonstrated to Graham his wealth and the sheer magnitude of his operation.

Graham was on remand now and the first thing Margite did was to increase her monthly salary. Why not? If the very pillars of our society, our very own Members of Parliament, can determine their own pay rises, why shouldn't she?

She keyed in the change on the Excel sheet on her laptop and sent an explanatory e-mail to the bank.

His businesses would continue. She would make sure of that. He'd be going down for a long stretch, but they'd carry on. It was just that she would siphon so much off that she'd be a millionaire within five years. She smiled inwardly.

She had to hand it to Bulldog Graham. Thick as two short planks, yes, but he knew how to get what he wanted. She'd experienced that first-hand as she'd eventually given in to his sexual demands. She wasn't going to. Keep things strictly platonic had been her motto. But that night… she blamed too many wines and a silver-tongued cavalier with a hint of aggression and menace and a huge cock that brought a tear to her eyes as he thrust into her roughly with a fistful of her hair as she bent over the green baize.

Her world came crashing down at 8.05 on that fateful Monday morning. It was always quiet, Mondays always were.

She had never seen a warrant card before, but the police officer had been convincing and his shiny Northumbria Police badge housed in a battered old black leather wallet was obviously genuine. He'd advised her to remain quiet and read out her rights that she'd heard so many times before on the TV cop shows. And she sat in stunned silence as he loaded her records and CDs and cheque books and software into a large plastic box.

And she shook uncontrollably and chewed at her fingernails as he unplugged her laptop and placed it on top.

"Hello, could I speak to Rafi Patel, please?" "Rafi Patel speaking. How can I help you, Sir?" "Rafi, it's Robert Sinton, your solicitor."

"Good morning, Mr Sinton. How are you?"

"Good, Rafi… good… Rafi, we need to talk. There's been a development."

"A development, Mr Sinton, I don't understand."

"It's good news, Rafi. You're not going to believe it… they've dropped the charges against you."

"They have? You're sure?"

"Of course I'm sure, Rafi. I'm your bloody solicitor."

"What has happened?"

"I received a letter last week from one of the policemen who took your confession. Well, an ex-policeman anyway. He admitted that they'd abused you during the interviews, racially abused you, said you were terrified and would have admitted to anything."

"No," Rafi mouthed quietly into the telephone receiver.

"I contacted the Chief Superintendent at Market Street and he admitted that the policeman in question resigned a couple of weeks after your interview. When I pressed the Chief Superintendent he admitted there'd been an inquiry into racial abuse by this man. It was that policeman who interviewed you. Ashley Clarke, do you remember him?"

"Yes, I do, Mr Sinton."

"A copper who actually admitted to being a racist and was effectively drummed out the force. It's the last sort of thing Northumbria Police would want."

"So they dropped the charges?"

"Bloody right they did, Rafi. I said I'd be calling this Ashley Clarke as a witness. If he'd admitted it in writing there was no reason to suppose he wouldn't admit it in open court."

Rafi was speechless. He placed a hand on the shop counter to steady himself. His father looked up from the greetings card display stand. Rafi smiled; he wanted to scream to his father the good news.

"You're free, Rafi, free as a bird. You'll receive the letter in the post within the next few days. And my bill of course."

And, as he replaced the receiver, he recalled Ashley Clarke's words from what seemed like an eternity ago.

*I'm on your side and you're not going to prison.*

# Chapter 15

The UPS delivery vehicle collected the well-packaged box with the delivery address of Northumbria Police HQ at around lunchtime. The driver queried why there was no return address on the box, but Ashley had explained that the likelihood of no one being around to receive the box was nil.

The driver had huffed and puffed about rules and regulations, but a twenty-pound note had helped convince him to lift the box into the back of his van and get on with it.

"Rules are for the obedience of fools," Ashley had muttered as he drove off, "and for the guidance of wise men." And he smiled as the van containing the box with Billy Graham's world of illegitimate business dealings disappeared from view.

The drive to Holy Island took an hour and forty minutes. The traffic had been heavy, perfectly normal for a Friday, especially as a light drizzle had begun to fall from the grey city sky earlier that afternoon.

It always slowed the traffic up. People were suddenly afraid of their cars, hypnotised by the windscreen wipers, unsure how to demist the screens, paying attention to the local radio station advising them to '*drive carefully*'. So it's okay to drive dangerously when it's dry then? Go on chaps, it's perfect weather; hammer your foot to the floor.

He'd already confirmed a one-week holiday with The Ship Inn. They explained he'd managed to get the last single room in the hotel. But then they always say that, don't they?

He'd made his mind up to go when he uncovered yet more evidence that Tom Wilkinson had every intention of going to Holy Island. He'd awoken at four in the morning… the dream was vivid. He had been working on Tom's computer, on e-mails to be precise. Silly e-mails, the sort of silly things that happen in dreams, but the message was loud and clear.

He'd never even opened up Tom's computer since Kate had suggested he keep it all those weeks ago. He walked through to the lounge and removed the laptop from the bottom drawer of the television cabinet. He'd powered it up and, as expected, the machine was password-protected.

"Shit."

He was talking out loud to himself.

"What password would Tom have used? Numbers… letters. Numbers and letters. Jesus, it's impossible."

He punched a couple of words into the computer then Tom's date of birth. They were denied but he breathed a sigh of relief that the computer didn't limit his attempts.

"Girlfriends' names."

He remembered a few and typed them in. All denied. Then *password* and *qwerty* and each time the words *access denied* appearing on the screen.

He wandered through to the kitchen and clicked the kettle on. Perhaps a hot drink would stimulate his brain. He thought about his own passwords over the years: favourite places, Otterburn, Kielder, Ibiza, his nicknames at school.

He took his tea through to the lounge and placed it on the coffee table next to the laptop.

So many places Tom had been to in the world… impossible. As he took his first mouthful of tea, another password came to him. His favourite pet as a youngster: a big, soft, old boxer … Cassius.

"Pets' names. Tom's pets."

His finger hovered over the keyboard before he realised he didn't know any. He remembered an old tom cat and a mongrel dog that Tom had rescued from a gang that was beating it but couldn't remember any of their names.

"Is this some sort of joke, Ash?" Kate replied at the other end of the phone. "It's five in the morning, for Christ's sake, and you want to know the name of a pet dog?"

"Yes, Kate, can you tell me your pets' names… all of them."

"But, Ash, it's five o'clock. I was asleep. I—"

"Dogs and cats, not too worried about the goldfish and hamsters, don't think he'd use their names."

"Ash, I—"

"Passwords, Kate. I'm trying to access his laptop. I'm hoping he might have e-mailed the hotel about a booking."

The password was Blackie. Tom's old Labrador that Kate had bought him as he'd refused to walk away from a pet shop window on Heaton Road. He'd caused a scene outside theshop and, if truth be told, Kate had fallen in love with the pup too.

Tom had promised to walk it every morning before school and again at lunchtimes; Kate took the twilight shift. And he had been as good as his word and bonded in a special way with the dog and quite naturally it was a password he'd never forget.

The computer booted up and Ashley punched a fist into the air. Within a few minutes, he was in the e-mail inbox. Halfway down the third page was a reply from The Ship Inn on Holy Island.

*Further to your enquiry, I am pleased to advise that we have a single room vacancy for the dates you have requested. Please telephone the hotel at your earliest convenience in order that we may arrange to take a deposit.*

*Claire*

Not Clara, Claire.

"Claire. Good old Claire."

More proof that Tom had been to the island. Ashley looked again at the e-mail. Perhaps not proof that he'd actually been to the island, but certainly proof that he intended to go.

He saved the e-mail to his own memory stick, printed it off and telephoned John Markham.

It was late afternoon as Ashley climbed into the car. He drove carefully through the crowded Jesmond streets and headed towards the Great North Road.

Just over an hour later, he approached the small hamlet of Beal just off the main A1 dual carriageway between England and Scotland. He peered through the misty evening sky. Taking his foot off the accelerator, he almost glided through the village. Small cottages, small windows, the light straining to be seenfrom deep within. Almost like a Christmas card scene, but without the snow. He drove on through and a few minutes later, caught his first sight of the causeway. An uncontrollable shiver ran the length of his spine. He took a quick glance in his mirror. Nothing. His was the only car on the road and he pushed gently on the brake pedal as he eased to a stop. The tide had begun to surge in, the noise told him so as each wave crashed against the shore. He looked at his watch. No problem, thirty minutes to go before the official 'don't cross' sign would be posted. He closed the car door and walked up onto the causeway, pulling up his jacket collar to protect himself from the elements.

A faint orange glow glimmered in the distance. Holy Island.

He stood for a few minutes gazing out to sea and wondered what possessed people to live there. Okay, so it was pretty quaint, the tourists would say, and sure it was different, but why would anyone want to limit their lives to living on a small island that was cut off twice a day? No industry, no real career prospects unless you packed up and headed for the big cities. And yet, as he'd found out from Holy John, the islanders were fiercely proud and protective of their chosen place of residence. He turned and walked slowly back to the car, scratched at his beard and cursed. He was in disguise again, couldn't take the chance of being recognised. If there was anything untoward going on up there, John Markham would be made about as welcome as Saddam Hussein. No, Ashley would need to do it on his own; his pal could be called in at the last minute if necessary.

Ashley's hair had grown and the beard had thickened up the previous few weeks and he'd telephoned John Markham and arranged to meet him for a beer. John had seemed keen to see the e-mail from The Ship, said he actually knew the girl and would speak to her soon.

John had asked about Kate, about the inquest. Ash had informed him that Kate had put it behind her, buried her son and was getting on with life. Ashley had said she was a strong, determined woman with a successful business to run. While she felt a bit aggrieved at the verdict of the inquest, she wasn't going to let it ruin her life. John's last remark before the conversation ended was that it was for the best.

Ashley had arranged to meet John Markham in the Queen's Arms in Shieldfield at eight. He'd chosen the pub on purpose. It would be quiet, the regular punters turning in between nine and ten during the week. The weekend was different, a couple of quick ones in the Queen's about sevenish, then off to the city centre till closing time.

Ashley sat on a park bench directly opposite the Queen's. The beard hadn't quite covered his face yet, but it broke the shape of it. Essential undercover practice. His regular three-week haircut was now a month overdue and, bizarrely, he'd used a grey rinse on both his hair and his beard. With a small pair of round silver-rimmed glasses, he took on a kind of aging Richard Gere appearance. He wasn't at all displeased with the look. He'd visited Kate the previous day and she'd commented on how attractive it looked.

John Markham's car pulled into the car park ten minutes early.

He was speaking on the mobile as he climbed out. He looked directly at Ashley, police observation instinct kicking in. Ash looked up, gave a nod as if saying hello and Markham looked away.

A few minutes later, Ashley walked into the bar. John Markham sat at the table they'd shared during Ashley's drunken session after he'd been suspended. He was sitting nursing a bottle of Budweiser, fiddling with the bottle as if he didn't want to be there.

Ashley looked over, gave another nod and this time John Markham reciprocated, albeit a bit reluctantly, then looked over towards the door again. Ashley ordered a pint of bitter, felt it kind of went with the disguise. He looked around the bar and noticed two elderly gentlemen deep in conversation about Newcastle United and their latest dismal performance against Aston Villa and whether the manager was up to the job. They were the only other two in the bar.

Ashley took a long mouthful of the beer and winced as it hit his taste buds. He was not a real ale man whatever his appearance. John Markham looked at his watch: Ashley Clarke was never late. Ashley stared straight ahead, made small talk with the barmaid and became aware of John Markham staring. Was he studying the Richard Gere lookalike or perhaps the large-chested barmaid?

John Markham rose to his feet, approached the bar where he sat. Ashley tried to retain his composure… he'd been there a dozen times before in some tube station entrance or a seedypub in Soho. A criminal he'd arrested once upon a time or Mr Big of the drug world approaching him as he was undercover. The adrenalin kicking in as he convinced himself he'd been recognised and, at the very least, a fast trip to hospital.

But it had never happened. He'd always stood firm, always maintained his composure and confidence in his own ability. And again the adrenalin surged through him as his ex-partner directed a question at him.

"Have you got the right time, pal? I think my watch is fast."

Ashley froze as he made eye contact; surely Markham would see through the disguise from such a short distance. He held his breath, realised he hadn't even thought about an accent or a disguise for his voice. He was an expert, a natural, the team leader of the Crime Squad had said. Scouse, Cockney, Scots and, of course, Geordie, not to mention a Black Country droll he'd worked on whilst undercover in Wolverhampton several years ago. But he needed time, a little preparation to lose his natural tones. Preparation that he'd not undertaken as he opened his mouth to answer the question.

"Two minutes after eight," the barmaid replied.

"Thanks," replied John Markham, and smiled at the barmaid as he proceeded to alter the hands on his watch.

"Meeting a mate in here about now; shouldn't be too long." The barmaid returned his look, a flirtatious smile, not the sort of punter who normally frequented the Queen's Arms.

Markham checked his watch again, shook his wrist and looked back at Ashley.

"Thanks… enjoy your beer."

Ashley resumed breathing as Markham sat back down at his table. Two minutes later, without taking another mouthful of beer, Ashley got up and left.

*Sherlock Holmes, eat your heart out.*

He telephoned John Markham as he walked over the footbridge at Manors Station.

"A puncture, John. Can you bloody believe it?"

"No problem, Ash. Do you want any help? Can I come and get you?"

"No, John, no thanks, I'm up to my eyes in shit and tyre rubber and it stinks. Perhaps another time. I'm off back home for a shower."

"No probs, Ash, perhaps another time."

Ashley pressed end. John Markham sounded somewhat relieved that the meeting wouldn't take place.

He looked in the mirror and saw nothing but blackness, floored the clutch and pushed the gear stick forward. He eased onto the causeway and couldn't shake the feeling of dread. His car headlights on full beam as he made his way out into the North Sea, water lapping the causeway on both sides. Five miles an hour… no more. The escape tower up ahead, eerily painted a dirty white, neglected and windswept, silhouetted against the evening sky.

He started breathing normally again as he spotted the *Welcome to Holy Island* sign at the end of the causeway. He leaned forward, eased from his seat and pushed a hand up the back of his T-shirt, allowing the cool air conditioning to dry the sweat.

There were no signposts for a car park to The Ship Inn, and he pulled up directly in front of the residents' entrance. As he opened the door to the car, the wind howled up the street, cutting him in two. He shivered, reached over to the back seat for his Adidas sports bag. He took a final look in the mirror. He hated beards but there again had to agree that this week's growth of stubble suited him.

His hair had almost reverted to its normal colour and had grown another inch or so that it touched the back of his collar. Of course he had the mandatory glasses and an additional baseball cap that he intended to wear occasionally. If John Markham hadn't recognised him in the Queen's Arms from less than a foot away he had little chance of recognising him now, nor would anyone else.

He'd settled on a Home Counties accent, one he found relatively simple after his years in London, and decided he was coming to Holy Island to research a book, his latest novel.

He'd checked out a little-known American author who'd spent the majority of his youth in Surrey. The author's website had only one photograph taken from a distance and the author resembled the look he had adopted, complete with beard and glasses. He'd taken a little over three weeks to perfect his story, checking out masses of information and photographs on Google and had even read every one the author's published novels over an intensive ten day period.

He had to admit he'd enjoyed them and didn't mind playing the part of David Fox for the next few weeks. An author researching his next novel wouldn't arouse too much suspicion. He'd be expected to nose around asking questions of the locals, checking out the characters of the island and their traditions, scandals and hopefully even a murder or two. It was perfect. David Fox, best-selling author; in fact, he'd always thought he had a book in him.

"Mr Fox, I presume?"

"Yes… erm, how did you guess?" replied Ashley.

"I wouldn't say I'm a fan, but I've read a couple of your books, Sir."

"And you are?"

"Claire. Claire Macbeth. I'm the receptionist, come waitress, come barmaid, come everything. I've worked here since I left school. You could say I'm a bit of a fixture."

Claire from the e-mail; a good start, thought Ashley, attractive too. He guessed Claire to be in her late twenties, very tall and slim, with long auburn hair tied up in a ponytail at the back. She wore a pair of small, red-rimmed glasses that might have looked ridiculous on someone else but actually suited her to a T. She caught Ashley's look and removed them as she spoke.

"I need them for reading, Mr Fox, a necessary evil, I'm afraid." Ashley found himself back at school, in Kate's kitchen, as a fourteen-year-old.

"No honestly, they're great. They really suit you."

"Thanks, Mr Fox. I guess I'm a bit conscious of them. The optician convinced me to go with the red frame, but I've a black pair too, if you'd prefer me to wear them."

"Please… call me David and no, the red frames are just fine. Great, really nice."

Claire smiled, Ashley blushed. Thank God for the beard. Claire went through the formalities. Ashley said he'd be paying cash, didn't believe in credit cards and when asked for ID, handed over the forged passport he'd picked up from Kevin the Fixer at the North Heaton Sports Club the previous week. Kevin could get anything. Dodgy ID, forged licences, phoney tax discs, counterfeit money and even guns. He'd been a bit wary of Ashley, even though they'd known each other since they'd run together in the Ebor Street gang all those years ago. Kevin had a natural distrust of coppers, but over two pints, Ashley had managed to convince him he was genuine. Ashley said he'd be back in a month or two; there was something else he needed from Kevin.

"How long are you staying, David?"

Ashley didn't have a clue. Didn't even have a game plan. This was not normal policing, he couldn't go flashing a warrant card around, pressurise a witness or two. He couldn't do door to door, nor could he call on the assistance of any colleagues or access the police computer.

"To be honest, I'm not really sure."

He had a bank statement, the word of the deceased's mother and an e-mail suggesting he was about to make a booking. Nothing else. Jack shit. And unless someone or some persons on Holy

Island made an enormous gaffe, the killers would escape.

"You mentioned a week on the telephone, but to be really honest, we're quiet at the moment, so it shouldn't be a problem booking another week if you decide to stay longer."

Ashley nodded, smiled.

"Great, that's what I'll do." He reached in his pockets and pulled out a bundle of notes. "I'll pay in advance, a week at a time."

It was around nine o'clock when he made his way down to the bar. He was the only one there and was pleasantly surprised to see Claire standing behind the bar.

"You weren't kidding, Claire, barmaid too."

She'd dispensed with the glasses, changed into a loose-fitting white T-shirt and faded jeans. Ashley liked the look.

"Everything, David. I wasn't kidding. What will you have to drink?"

Ashley clawed at the growth on his chin, hoped whatever investigation he was going to undertake would finish fairly quickly so he could shave the damn thing off.

"Not really sure, just something light. Have you a bottle of Bud?"

"Coming up. Are you missing home already?"

"Sorry?"

"America. Budweiser. That's where you live… America, isn't it?"

Jesus, he was out of practice, almost slipped up within two minutes. Think, man, think. You're an

American author here on aresearch mission; you've set your next novel on a small English island.

"Yeah… Oregon, nice part of the world. Have you been?"

Claire shook her head as she bent down to the cold shelf to retrieve a bottle of Budweiser and a chilled ice-cold glass.

"No such luck, I'm afraid. I meant to go travelling and to Uni but just never got there. My grades were good enough at school, but my uncle got me a part-time job here and I suppose I liked it. I've been here ever since, nearly ten years."

"Where's this uncle of yours? He needs a good lecture, and what did your dad have to say about it?"

Claire's facial expression changed. He guessed he'd put his foot in it. She concentrated on opening the bottle, eye contact broken temporarily.

"My dad died when I was fourteen." Her eyes filled with sadness now. Ashley opened his mouth, but no words came. "It's okay, David, you weren't to know."

He reached across as he was handed the bottle.

"He was a good man." The voice came from behind him. Ashley turned around. A short elderly man dressed in an immaculate dinner suit and black tie spoke again.

"One of the best, George was."

Ashley nodded, "I'm sure he was," turned back to face Claire. "Sorry, Claire, I truly am."

Claire looked over Ashley's shoulder, made eye contact and proceeded to pour a pint of Guinness. The gentleman sidled upto the bar and sat in the seat next to Ashley.

"You must be the Yankee author, right?"

"Yes, David Fox, pleased to meet you."

He held out a hand. The elderly gentleman paused for a second, took a long lingering look at Ashley as if eyeing up a prize thoroughbred to see if it would make the grade and reluctantly shook his hand. It was fish-wet cold and, as the two men broke hands, Ashley placed his hand on his thigh and casually moved it a few inches to dry it. Ashley looked at the briefcase the man had placed on the floor.

"Frank Short, Mr Fox. Pleased to make your acquaintance."

"Off to the Lodge, Mr Short?"

The man took a long slow drink from the glass Claire hadplaced in front of him, wiped the froth from his top lip. "Familiar with the Freemasons, Mr Fox?"

Ashley thought back to the times he had been asked to join the Lodge, of the strange limp-like handshakes he'd been given overthe years by colleagues and senior officers. He wanted to tell the gentleman how many times he'd refused the invite to join and how certain individuals had changed their approach towards him which he thought was so wrong. He wanted to tell the gentleman that he thought the culture of preferential treatment for the Brothers amounted to an almost racist approach and, of course, as a confirmed atheist, it just wasn't possible to join an organisation founded on the belief of a Supreme Being.

"The Freemasons' organisation is very popular in America, Sir. I've a certain knowledge, though I'm not in the craft myself." Mr Short raised a glass.

"Me neither."

Claire interjected, “Frank belongs to the Brotherhood of the Island. The Keepers.”

“A spin-off of the Masons, right?” asked Ashley.

Claire shrugged her shoulders. The elderly man remained silent. Claire gave him a wry smile.

“Well, David, how would I know?” She held her arms open, took a step back so that Ashley could focus on her full form. “I’m hardly dressed for the occasion, am I?”

Ashley found himself staring at her for a little longer than necessary. The old man spoke.

“The Brotherhood has been in existence far longer than the Freemasons, Mr Fox. Some would say the Masons are a spin-off from the Brotherhood.”

Ashley’s jaw gaped.

“You mean you’re telling me that this small island gave birth to the Freemasons?”

The man took another long mouthful from his glass. Ashley was conscious of the door to the bar opening behind him and footsteps coming towards them on the ancient stone floor. The bar had changed little in a couple of hundred years.

“I’m telling you nothing, Mr Fox. Our organisation is unique, that’s all I’m saying, and other societies have latched on to our principles and ancient ceremonies. Of that there’s no doubt. Some of our Brothers have been asked to join the Masons over the years and have resigned in disgust almost immediately, blatant plagiarism, they say. We’ve managed to get a copy of the three degrees of the Masons’ ceremonies and some of the text is almost word for word.”

Ashley spoke in a hesitant whisper. "Might it have been the other way round, Mr Short? You know, the Brotherhood stealing from the Masons?"

The stranger, also dressed in an immaculate dinner suit and leaning against the bar, spoke with a soft lilt.

"Impossible, my friend. The Island Keepers date from Saint Cuthbert's time, our dearly beloved Saint actually drew up the constitution and the ancient ceremonies. We have the tomes in a bank safe in Edinburgh."

He held out a hand and Ashley took it.

"Jacob Moor by the way, pleased to meet you." "Likewise, David Fox."

Jacob Moor was a tall, dapper man, probably in his early forties. He had a confident demeanour and a cold, non- infectious smile.

"The first volume of the tome dates back to AD 687, ten years before St Cuthbert's death. It details the ancient ceremonies performed around that time and runs to over two hundred and ninety thousand handwritten words. It's quite incredible, Mr Fox. You, as an author, must appreciate that."

"Erm… quite."

Another three gentlemen, all suited and booted, walked into the bar and Claire proceeded to place a drink next to each of them without either asking or being told. Jacob Moor nodded as a glass of whisky was handed to him and threw back half the glass before he spoke again.

"Some people claim that the original Freemasons date back to biblical times and to King Solomon's Temple. This is not correct, Mr Fox, and there is no firm evidence to back it up. It is more likely that the

Freemasons we know today started in medieval times, evolving from stonemasons' guilds. The Grand Lodge of England, for example, didn't open until 1717. We have documentary evidence in Edinburgh that our Brotherhood was active a thousand years before."

Jacob Moor turned to his three Brothers assembled at the bar. "This is Mr Fox, gentlemen, an American author. He's here to research his next book and I'm giving him a little history lesson about the Brotherhood."

Ashley raised his glass in the direction of the assembled group. "I'd prefer to think of myself as half-British actually. My mother was born here and I spent nearly twenty years in Surrey. That's why I haven't got the accent. Thank Christ, eh?"

"I'd prefer if you wouldn't take the Lord's name in vain, Mr Fox," Jacob interjected. "Our friend Father Thompson may take offence."

Ashley noticed the dog collar of a stout, red-faced gentlemen at the end of the bar. He raised a hand in Ashley's direction. He'd been facing Claire and the collar hadn't been visible. "Sorry, Father, no offence I'd—"

"None taken, young man. It's something I have to live with these days. Better than all the cursing and effing and blinding on television, I suppose."

"Still, Father, I do apologise."

Father Thompson raised a glass, gave a smile and turned back to face Claire, apparently uninterested in the history lesson. Ashley focused on Claire, a smile and a sparkle in those beautiful green eyes every time she made eye contact with him. He quickly changed the subject.

"So I guess you guys don't like the Freemasons too much."

Jacob Moor shrugged his shoulders.

"Not at all. The Masons' principles mirror our own: good clean Christian living. We both believe that divine intelligence governs the working of the universe."

"God."

"Exactly, Mr Fox… God. Both organisations are founded on principles of morality, truthfulness and tolerance and a desire for self-improvement, looking after our fellow Brothers, especially in times of need."

Father Thompson spoke. "And every Freemason Lodge in England has a chaplain to ensure," he pointed at the ceiling, "we don't forget about the big man." Father Thompson laughed and the rest of the group joined in.

Another half a dozen men had joined the little entourage and two more were also walking through the door. Jacob Moor looked at his watch.

"Is everybody here, Father? We'd better be making our way downstairs soon."

"Everyone present and correct, Worshipful Master," the priest replied as he took a quick headcount. Jacob Moor threw back the rest of his whisky and Ashley took in the peaty aroma of his breath as he spoke.

"We'll be busy for a couple of hours, Mr Fox, but if you're still around, I'd be delighted to buy you a drink."

"Thanks, that would be good. We can carry on where we left off."

Ashley was feeling quite pleased with himself; he couldn't really have hoped to achieve any more than he had within the first hour of being on Holy Island. He'd arrived at the hotel where Tom Wilkinson had spent his last night, (he was convinced), worked his disguise very well, and it appeared that half the island knew of the author David Fox. He would poke around tomorrow without hesitation, safe in the knowledge that at least thirteen members of a secret society would be off home later in the evening to gossip to their wives and girlfriends about a certain American.

Ashley found himself alone with Claire and didn't mind in the slightest.

"So how come they know so much about me?" he asked. Claire blushed. "I'm sorry. I guess that's my fault. It's not often we get a famous American author staying at The Ship. I guess Imust have blabbed off a bit. You mentioned on the phone whenyou made your booking that you were researching a book andI'd read your second novel last summer. I slipped David Fox into a search engine and found you on a few dozen sites."

"But hardly famous."

She laughed. "Believe me, on Holy Island you're famous."

A few locals had begun to drift into the bar, they'd ordered drinks and slipped away into the dark recesses of the old inn.Ashley could picture the old sailors and fishermen of bygone years doing likewise. The old inn was steeped in history and intrigue; Ashley could smell it.

After Claire had served each customer, she returned to the spot where Ashley sat on a high bar stool. Over the next two hours they became well acquainted, Claire asking question after question about the author's books and what inspired him and Ashley thanking his lucky stars he'd taken time out to read Fox's books.

Ashley answered the questions, but each time tried to turn them around. He asked about the characters and especially the Brothers. Claire gossiped freely and, though he hated to admit it to himself, he flirted outrageously.

Just after ten, the small door opposite the entrance of the inn opened and the Brotherhood spilled into the bar area laughing and joking and slapping each other on the back. Father Thompson was the first to acknowledge Ashley as they all made their way to the bar area. No chance now of a private conversation with Claire.

"Quite taken with our Claire, are you, Mr Author?"

"David, Father, you can call me David, and, yes, Claire is good company."

Claire blushed, not for the first time, and Ashley became aware of a stare from Jacob Moor that he was none too comfortable with. The permanent almost plastic smile he'd worn earlier in the evening was gone and instead a grimace replaced it. Claire caught the look too, turned to Ashley, then quickly looked away. Ashley stared back at Jacob Moor determined not to be intimidated. It was a look he'd seen a hundred times before… jealousy.

Jacob Moor was jealous.

# Chapter 16

Ashley awoke as the first rays of the sun penetrated the small single bedroom above the street in Marygate. He pulled the curtain aside and looked out over the calm sea that was justvisible through the buildings opposite. Dawn had painted the sky a dusky shade of red.

He reached across to the bedside cabinet and strained his eyes to focus on the notes he'd written the night before.

There had been the odd murder on his patch in the West Endof London, normally alcohol or drug related, occasionally a gang revenge attack, but then the investigation was generally handed over to the murder squad. Ashley hadn't the experience, hadn't had the training, and looked down at the book to see what he had written.

It amounted to very little, but he'd noted in the corner of the page the look that Jacob Moor had given him. What on earth had that to do with anything? he thought to himself before taking a pencil and striking it out.

One thing gnawed at him: if it was murder, generally the police or whoever it was looking for the murderer would be looking for one person and one person only. Ninety-nine times out or a hundred, the victim would have been killed by one person. And even though the pathologist's statement suggested a savage beating, a savage beating could have been inflicted by one person.

But something told him that wasn't the case here. Why else would the islanders be covering up the fact that Tom had even visited the island? Why had The Ship Inn denied he'd ever been there, and why did two different policemen's enquiry draw a convenient blank each time?

He thought about confronting Claire about her e-mail but then that would cause the island to clam up even more. His disguise would be blown. No. He'd play it cool, act the part of a nosy American author and see what he could shake loose. Claire greeted him at reception, black glasses this time, a more subdued morning look and was he imagining it or had she applied just a little more make-up and lip gloss than she had yesterday? Her striking red hair hung loose around her shoulders, and just for a fleeting second, she bore an uncanny resemblance to Alexis. Then the moment passed.

"Morning, David," she said cheerfully. "Sleep well?"

"Wonderful, Claire, must be the sea air." It would have been even better with you lying naked beside me, he thought to himself, and realised that she was the last thing on his mind when he went to sleep and the first when he woke up.

She pointed. "Breakfast room's over there. Just help yourself. Bacon, egg, sausage, some black pudding if you like."

Ashley shook his head; the fry-up would lie uncomfortably in his stomach for most of the day. He had a knot there; it had mysteriously appeared the moment he set eyes on Claire, that smile, her hair, her ability to change the atmosphere of a room with a look.

"Sounds great but a little coffee and toast will do. I'm not used to these big English breakfasts."

Claire grinned. "Suit yourself. What are you up to today then, David?" she asked. "Where does your research take you? What is it you're looking for?"

He had prepared his answer meticulously, the same answer he would give to anyone on the island and a statement that would give him carte blanche to pry and quiz and question every islander he came into contact with, without arousing any suspicions… he hoped.

He took a deep breath, smiled at Claire as he replied.

"I'm looking to try to feel a part of this island, Claire. I wantto find out about the history of the place. I want to explore every nook and cranny. I want to know what it is that makes people live on a small island cut off from the outside world twice a day and I'm looking for some gossip."

"Gossip?" She grinned. "On Holy Island? Good luck to you. I hope you find what you're looking for."

"I want to know about the local characters; they might just find their way into the book. Under a different name, of course. Remember, I write fiction."

He held his breath, looked Claire in the eye. "And I'm looking for mystery, intrigue, maybe a murder or two from the past and legend, people disappearing from the island without trace."

Claire's expression never flickered as she burst out laughing. "You've been watching too many movies, David Fox. I think you'd need to travel back to the dark ages before you find the last killing on Holy Island."

"Ah... so you see, we do have a Holy Island murderer. Fantastic."

"A murderess, actually, but not exactly your average serial killer. She stabbed her husband in the chest in a fit of rage after he complained about the beef stew she'd cooked for him. She was hung in Berwick-upon-Tweed a month later. That's the last one, I'm afraid, not that mysterious really."

Ashley spied an opportunity, an opportunity for an island guide and perhaps a little romance.

"You seem to know a fair bit about the island, Claire. Care to give me a guided tour?"

He waited for the reaction, looked at her body language as she spoke. She ran her hand through her hair, the basic mating instinct of the animal kingdom... grooming.

"I'd love to, David." She looked at her watch. "I can only spare you a couple of hours though, say about ten."

Ashley looked at his watch. "Great... it's a date then."

He felt dizzy, light-headed even, as he made his way through to the dining room. He settled for a small helping of bacon and eggs after all. He returned to his room, grabbed a sweatshirt, his camera and the notebook. He made a point of turning over the page of the notes he'd written last night.

Claire had lost the receptionist look once more and had on a pair of Levi's tucked into a pair of black leather boots. She also wore a baggy black rollneck sweater and her hair was once again hanging freely. And that smile, that smile as she looked up and noticed him standing motionless a few feet from the reception desk. He only hoped he hadn't been standing there with his mouth wide open because that's what he felt like he'd been doing. Surely on this small island a girl as stunningly beautiful as Claire would have been snapped up long ago. He didn't think she was married, no ring, no engagement ring either, but surely Mr Lucky Bastard would turn up at some point over the next few hours. Jacob Moor… that look last night. Surely… no. Why not?

Claire broke his train of thought.

"I thought we'd start with the legend of Saint Cuthbert. You can't come to research the island and not know about our Saint."

Ashley shrugged his shoulders, held out his hands. "Fine. Where do we start?"

They walked for no longer than five minutes and stood outside the ruins of Lindisfarne Priory. Claire explained it was the spot of the original church that St Cuthbert spent his final years before sailing to Farne Island to die.

She continued. "He was Bishop of Lindisfarne and the monks brought him back home, so to speak, though his body is officially entombed in Durham Cathedral. Legend has it that the Island Keepers in fact switched the corpse and St Cuthbert's body is secretly hidden on Holy Island."

"Legend, Claire?"

"Yes, David. Legend states that his body is entombed in this church somewhere and the secret is handed down to only one Island Keeper from each generation."

"So one of our friends in the bar last night knows where the remains of Saint Cuthbert are?"

Claire beckoned him forward and they turned right towards the picturesque church in the grounds of the Priory. They walked towards the open door. Claire made the sign of the cross as she breached the threshold of the ancient church building. Ashley followed her, sniffed long and hard at the stale air inside. The church was steeped in history, soaked in sunlight and had been battered by the harsh elements of the North Sea for generations.

Claire turned and grinned, wagged a finger at Ashley. "Not remains, David, his body."

"I'm not with you." Ashley frowned.

"Legend has it that Saint Cuthbert's body never ever rottedaway. Ten years after his body was buried, his remains were to be moved, protecting him from the Viking invasions. The monks that opened his coffin found the body incorrupt."

"Incorrupt?"

"As fresh as the day he was buried, David."

Ashley wanted to laugh, but somehow the atmosphere of the old church stifled him.

"They sealed the coffin and fled. The monks of Lindisfarne wandered the north of England for seven years until they housed his body in a Durham church.

His body briefly returned to Lindisfarne. In 1104 it was decided his coffin would be moved once and for all to the new Durham Cathedral."

Claire was in full flow now, relating the tale she'd heard so often as a young girl. She was wrapped up in the legend from head to toe and enjoyed every moment, relaying the information like a museum curate. He watched her, mesmerised, not mesmerised by the information coming from her lips but by the way she delivered it. She turned and faced him as she continued. He could smell her sweet, intoxicating breath mingled with a delicate musky perfume. He took half a step forward just to be a little nearer.

"The monks and bishops and clergymen of the time had voted to inspect the body one last time. Thirteen monks entered the crypt on the 24th of August 688, over four hundred years after his death."

Thirteen men in the bar last night, thought Ashley, thirteen Island Keepers.

"The body was intact, David. Incorrupt. A miracle."

"Indeed, Claire, a miracle. A miracle that anybody believed it." Claire's facial expression changed. She'd been smiling, beaming as she delivered every word, assuming the listener would take as gospel the story her father had told to her as a small child, the words she'd read over and over again in countless books, the words Father Thompson had delivered in many a sermon around the anniversary of Saint Cuthbert's death.

"You don't believe it, David, you don't believe the legend of St Cuthbert. The monks, David, they saw it with their own eyes; religious men, educated men, men of God, why would they lie? What would be the point?"

"Men of religion have lied for centuries, Claire. Religion was founded to control the masses, to brainwash the less intelligent individual. Christianity, Hinduism, Islam, it's all the same, frighten the hell out of the small child early enough and you have them for life."

"No, David, you've got it wrong."

"Have I? Look at your own form of religion: Catholicism. Even today, the priest will pontificate from that pulpit over there of how you'll be sent to Hell and damnation forever and a day if you go against the Ten Commandments. Remember as a child being absolutely terrified to do anything because this all-hearing, all-seeing man in the clouds watched everything you did? Remember, Claire?"

"Yes, but?"

"But nothing, Claire. I was there too, I hid under the blankets as a five-, six- and seven-year-old and believed it too, I witnessed the so-called people of God, the priests and the nuns literally torture the children entrusted to their care."

"There's good and bad in all walks of life, David. You had a bad experience that's all. It happens."

"The good book, Claire. Have you read it?"

"Yes, of course I have. I?"

"I mean really read it, Claire. The Old Testament, it's positively evil. Murder, rape, child abuse, ethnic cleansing."

"You're mistaken, David. I don't believe it. You shouldn't be speaking like that, especially in here."

Ashley laughed. "What… in case he's listening, you mean? Believe me, Claire, I've tried the lot: meditation, hypnotherapy, psychoanalysis and religion is just about the barmiest of the lot." As Ashley opened his mouth again, a voice from behind him spoke.

"I'm afraid, Claire, the world is full of non-believers."

Father Thompson moved up alongside him like a ghostly apparition. Ashley noticed a door closing behind him. He was dressed in full cassock and the regulation dog collar.

"I would assume you're a non-believer, Mr Fox. Am I right?"

"Afraid so, Father. I find it difficult to believe there's a big man with a beard up there in the clouds that can see and hear everything and punishes us when we step out of line."

Father Thompson moved around behind Claire and placed two hands on her shoulders. Two versus one. She visiblyrelaxed. She closed her eyes as if in some sort of trance. Father Thompson spoke. Claire opened her eyes and smiled again. "Ye of little faith. I suppose you're a Darwinite, Mr Fox, a man that believes everything evolved from everything yet can'texplain what came first, the chicken or the egg."

"Can anyone, Father?"

Father Thompson massaged Claire's shoulders for a second or two, then released her, walked back round to face Ashley. He pointed at the roof of the Priory. Ashley looked up automatically, then cursed himself for doing so.

"The big man, as you so crudely put it, the man in the clouds, he's the only one who can explain it. And what, may I ask, are you doing in our Father's house if you don't believe?"

"I'm giving him a history lesson, Father," Claire interjected, "teaching him all about St Cuthbert."

"Quite," replied the priest in a sarcastic tone. "A history lesson last night and one this morning, Mr Fox. Quite the studious type."

"I'm researching a book, Father. I need to know everything about the island."

Father Thompson walked towards the door he'd appeared from and, as he reached for the handle, he turned round, paused as he glared at Ashley.

"Just make sure that's all you're here for, Mr Fox."

And before Ashley could reply, the priest had disappeared through the door. Ashley turned to Claire.

"What was that supposed to mean?"

Claire shrugged her shoulders. "You tell me." She reached for his hand and spun him around.

"C'mon, let's go. I think you've outstayed your welcome, can't be very nice for Father Thomson to have an atheist in his place of worship."

To Ashley's dismay, she broke the grip as soon as they walked outside. Ashley racked his brains for something to say, something delicate, something profound. Had he upset her? Had he insulted her intelligence? What was going through her mind? They walked in between the ancient tombstones. Ashley studied the names and dates. Huge conventional stone crosses, Celtic crosses, a sculptured pair of praying hands and the island names: Markham, Douglas, Drysdale and a name that stopped Ashley dead in his tracks.

“What is it, David? You look as if you’ve just seen a ghost.”

“Nothing, let’s get a coffee.” And as they headed out of the churchyard, Ashley made a mental note of the Freemason-type carvings adorning many of the stones. Squares and compasses, a Masonic-type apron, barely visible, finely carved into a tombstone two hundred years old. And he made a pledge to return to the ancient churchyard of St Mary the Virgin and spend a little more time there.

They walked along Fenkle Street and into St Cuthbert’s Square. Claire checked her watch on two occasions before eventually speaking.

“I’ll need to be heading back, David. I’ve things to do.”

The two hours she’d committed to had turned into forty-five minutes. Ashley decided to let it lie.

“Another time perhaps?”

“I’d like that, David, maybe Mass on Sunday.”

Ashley was about to object. “Only kidding, you idiot.” She punched him playfully in the stomach. He grabbed her wrist and held it tightly. Eye contact again, those eyes, those beautiful hypnotic eyes. Her hand relaxed, slipped to her side. Ashley released his grip. They stood motionless in the middle of the town square, a few locals going about their business. The tourists had begun to mingle, standing with their cameras and guidebooks, but they saw nobody; the square might as well have been deserted. Their lips, barely inches apart, that kiss, a beautiful tender moment, the taste, the warmth, the passion. Two lovers entwined, oblivious to the world around them.

The kiss that never came.

As she walked away quickly, she glanced back over her shoulder, mumbled some sort of apology, said she see him back at the hotel and a different look in her eyes now.

Fear.

Ashley sat in the coffee shop, the focal point right in the heart of St Cuthbert's Square. He sat with his notebook open and his pen poised. His strong, black, unsweetened coffee sat on the table untouched. He took a mouthful and swilled it around his mouth before tipping his head back and swallowing. The caffeine kicked in immediately like an electric shock to the brain. Hestarted writing.

On the first page:

*The pathologist's statement, the savage attack*

*The e-mail*

*Tom's telephone conversation with Kate*

*The*

*bank statement*

*Island Keepers*

*Masonic markings/tombstones*

*Roddam*

He would need a lot more before he felt the need to bring John Markham up to the island. John Markham's job came first. Roddam would have his balls if he knew that he was involved with Ashley on a case that was closed and Ashley had to protect him whatever. John didn't even know he was on the island, thought he was just digging around the libraries and newspaper archives of the North.

Bizarrely, during their last telephone conversation, John had warned him to be careful. An off-the-cuff remark perhaps, but nevertheless one that unnerved

Ashley and yet told him that Holy John too was more than uncomfortable with HIS island and the events that may or may not have taken place.

And underneath, right at the bottom, he'd written the words *cover up.*

Kate insisted that the islanders had done just that on her one and only visit to the island. How rational had Kate been on that occasion? Was she an anxious mother who had read too much into a desperate situation, maybe even imagined or subconsciously invented things. John Markham certainly hinted as much.

And now, his progress thus far and the characters he'd met in less than twenty-four hours.

Not a lot:

*Claire*

*Jacob Moor (Jealous look)*

*Father Thompson*

*The Island Keepers*

And scribbled at the bottom, the word *frustration.* Frustration at not being able to knock at doors and question the islanders. Frustration at not being able to show his warrant card, watch the blood drain from an individual's face and spotting the tell-tale signs of nervousness and blatant lies.

He didn't even know where to go or what to do next. He looked at his watch. The pubs and bars on the island would beopening up now; many an inspiration had been found lookinginto a beer glass. What harm would it do, perhaps he'd get a bit pissed up and rattle a few of the locals' cages, look for the lads who liked to roll around the floor a bit. It seemed as good an idea as any. Tom was able to handle himself; it would take one or two good men to incapacitate him.

He left two pound coins on the table, picked up his notebook and slipped it into his jacket pocket.

He walked across the road to a pub called The Crown and Anchor. He ordered a small beer and stood at the bar, ready to strike up a conversation with the barman. The barman took his money, then disappeared into another room at the back of the pub. Friendly sort, thought Ashley. Then Ashley spotted him. "It's Frank, isn't it?"

The old man looked up over his pint, wiped the froth from his top lip. "Well, well, if it isn't our American novelist."

"Mind if I take a seat, Frank?"

Frank Short shrugged his shoulders. "I'd rather you didn't. I was just enjoying the peace and quiet."

Blunt, thought Ashley, what do I say now? He looked at the barman who had returned; he smiled a knowing look and began pouring two beers.

"That's Frank, I'm afraid. Love him or hate him."

At this moment in time Ashley probably hated him. He waited until the barman had poured the drinks, handed him five pounds and told him to keep the change. He walked over to Frank's table and placed the two beers down. Frank reached across and took his glass.

"So, Mr Fox, how can I help you with your research? What is it you really want to know? I've lived here all my life," he took a generous mouthful of beer, "and in fact you couldn't be sitting in a better position to know everything and anything about the goings-on here on Holy Island."

Ashley drained his first drink slowly and deliberately, went for the jugular.

"Tell me about the Island Keepers, Frank. Tell me what it is that you guys get from meeting a couple a times a month and re-enacting an ancient ceremony. I mean, it can't be that much fun, can it?"

Ashley wanted a sign from the old man, a nervous laugh or twitch, perhaps a reaction, a defence of the organisation. He got nothing.The old man smiled.

"Fun, Mr Fox?" He sighed, rested his chin on his carved walking stick. "No fun, I can assure you. Not anymore." He paused, looked up at Ashley again.

"Why do you do it, Frank? What does it take for thirteen men to perform a little ancient ceremony week after week, month after month, year after year?"

The old man grimaced, took another mouthful of beer and Ashley waited for his reply.

"Mr Fox. Is that what you really think we're all about? An ancient ceremony?"

"Well, isn't it?"

Frank Short looked up at the barman, he looked a little uncomfortable, lowered his voice and suddenly lost his air ofconfidence. He sighed.

"You said last night you were familiar with the principles of the Freemasons." Ashley nodded. "The Keepers aren't any different really except…" The old man looked around the bar, pulled at his collar grateful of a little air. Suddenly the bar had become stuffy, almost claustrophobic.

"Except, Mr Short?"

"Except…"

The old man pushed his glass away, made to stand up."I have to get going, Mr Fox."

"Please, Mr Short, tell me, I promise it won't go any further." Frank Short laughed. "You're writing a book, Mr Fox. What do you mean it won't go any further? Why are you so interested in us anyway?"

"Curiosity, Frank, that's all."

Frank Short never elaborated any further. At one point Ashley thought he really wanted to, as if wanting to unburden himself, but it never happened. He was evasive about each question and gave no information of any significance.

Frank Short stood up, walked over to the bar and replaced his glass on the counter. He bid the barman good day and walked towards the door. As he passed their table, he stopped. "It used to be fun, Mr Fox, a noble organisation, only it's changed recently."

"Changed, Frank, in what way?"

The old man leaned forward, no more than a couple of inches from Ashley's face.

"You seem like a nice man, Mr Fox. Stop interfering in something that you don't know anything about. Leave the island, leave it for your own good and concentrate your research on that world wide web thingy."

"For my own good? What are you saying? Are you warning me off?"

Frank Short adjusted his flat cap, tightened his tie once more and placed a hand on Ashley's shoulder. He squeezed gently and let it linger for a moment. Ashley looked up and swore there was a tear in his eye.

"Good day, Mr Fox. I have to be going."

"Frank, no, please, wait."

The old man walked towards the door. The door opened then closed and Ashley sat on his own cursing his powers of persuasion.

Why was the old man so sheepish… it was as if they'd done something…wrong. As if they held some big secret. The ideals of the Masons: what were they exactly? He'd heard the rumours around the various stations he'd been assigned to. Look after each other, protect the family and look out for your Brother, fellow Masons. The Island Keepers, protect, protect the island. Protect it from what, exactly? Outsiders? No, he'd been made very welcome in the bar last night and what could be more outside than an American on a tiny island in the middleof the English North Sea.

He lifted his glass, took a mouthful. Suddenly, he wasn't so thirsty. He took out his notebook and turned to page two and alongside where he'd written *Island Keepers,* he scribbled Frank Short's name along with Jacob Moor and Father Thompson anda large question mark. It was time for some more internet research, this time on the Freemasons.

He made a point of wandering the streets of the island; thinking time. It took all of ten minutes and he found himself walking up Causeway Chare and looking out towards the sea which now covered the causeway. The early afternoon sun had polished the surface to a mirror-like sheen.

The island was cut off. He was stranded. A prisoner.

No way could he leave the island at this precise moment in time, whatever the reason.

A light sea fret had rolled in and the mainland had become obscured. He shivered, turned back to face the village and madehis way back to The Ship Inn. He was pleasantly surprised to see Claire serving behind the bar with several locals keeping her company. A few tourists were there too, sitting at tables, easy to spot in walking boots, cagoules and a guidebook or two or an information pamphlet about Lindisfarne Priory. And, of course, one or two obligatory sets of binoculars.

Not quite crowded, but the bar of The Ship had a pleasant ambience, a welcoming noise, different to last night. He looked over at the bar, gave Claire an awkward wave, which she ignored totally. He bit his lip and walked over. One spare seat strategically placed between two fit-looking young men: villagers... locals... probably fishermen.

"Is that anyone's seat?" Ashley asked politely.

"I'm afraid so, mate. There's a seat over there." The man pointed over to the far side of the room and grinned. Claire walked over, gave them a disapproving look.

"What are you having, David? I'll bring it over."

"Just a small beer, Claire, thanks."

The two young men glared at him and Ashley concentrated on staring straight ahead, not wishing to make eye contact. He turned and walked over to the table. A few minutes later Claire brought over the beer.

"Just ignore them, David. They'll be gone soon. Don't give them a chance to cause trouble."

Ashley took a sip from the glass and looked up at Claire with a puzzled look.

"I'm not with you, Claire... trouble... I don't understand." She sighed. "The seat is spare, David. He's winding you up, taking the piss. They do that with all the strangers. They think they're so damned macho. They're notorious for it. They've been barred from every pub on the island at some point, but then management always bows down and lets them back in again."

"Why?"

"Because they drink gallons, David, gallons and gallons every week. The average tourist has a few pints, then disappears after a couple of days. It's called profit, supply and demand; survival."

"So the seat's not taken?"

Claire shook her head. "Of course not."

The adrenalin surge. He'd experienced it a hundred times before. That boost just before you know trouble is going to break out. He'd made his mind up.

"Just stay there and keep out of their way. They'll be going on to the next pub shortly. The sooner the better."

"Friendly sorts, aren't they? Are there many more like them on the island?"

Claire shook her head. "They're the worst, if you ask me." Claire returned to the bar. Ashley was thinking. Could these be the scumbags that gave Tom a kicking before throwing him intothe sea? He waited a few minutes, his anger growing by the second. Don't lose your temper. He remembered his police training, remembered the self-defence moves, the restraining methods and the dozens and dozens of altercations over the years.

Claire had returned to the bar, busying herself washing a few glasses in the sink beneath. He walked across the bar, leaned over and spoke quietly to the man who had refused him the seat.

"Thought you said the seat was taken, my friend."

The man clenched his fists, his friend's body visibly stiffened. "It is... my feet are on it." His friend laughed out loud. He smiled and stared at Ashley.

It was a forced laugh, politicians on Question Time.

Ashley swiped gently at the man's calves and his feet fell to the floor.

Ashley whispered in his ear, "Not now they're not, motherfucker." The man leapt to his feet as his friend took hold of Ashley by his jacket. His accomplice pulled back his fist, ready to spring into action. Claire screamed as Ashley's forearm caught the man who held his jacket square in the Adam's apple and he fell gasping to the floor. His friend's fist was already propelling towards Ashley's face as he seemed to take hold of the arm in slow motion, deflected it and, in one perfectly executed movement, drove the man onto the floor with his thumb pressed deep into his wrist and his arm rigid behind his back. He placed his foot on the man's neck.

"I think you and your friend were just leaving, unless you'd care to finish this outside."

His friend lay red-faced on the floor, shaking his head furiously. Ashley looked at him.

"Looks like you're on your own, buddy."

"No," was all he could say. Ashley loosened his grip. The two men rose gingerly to their feet. The man holding his throat was coughing violently. For a split-second Ashley thought they were considering a second bite at the cherry but Ashley smiled confidently, puffed out his chest and took a half step towards them, making them all too aware he was up for it a second timearound.They backed away cautiously.

"It was a pleasure making your acquaintance, gentlemen. See you again, I hope."

The man who only seconds before had been pinned to the floor by his throat turned as he reached the open doorway. "Watch your back, stranger," he shouted. "Watch your back."

"I shall do just that, my friend," Ashley countered. "I'll do just that."

Ashley turned to face Claire with a cheeky smile. She stood open-mouthed, unable to speak, trembling gently.

"Pussycats really, Claire."

She shook her head. "Where on earth did you learn to do that? It was like something out of a Bruce Willis movie." She smiled.

"US Special Forces. Five and a half years, a little like your SAS, I think."

"They won't let it lie, David. They'll be back."

"How many?"

"I dunno, maybe another two or three."

"Should be a pretty fair fight then," he said as he claimed his prize of the lone wooden seat that sat at the bar. Claire handed him a bottle of Budweiser.

"That one's on me," she grinned.

But as she turned away, something gnawed at her. Something told her the incident that had occurred in front of her hadn't been real. Although she couldn't quite put her finger on exactly what it was.

# Chapter 17

He hadn't slept well that night, rose before it had even managed to break daylight and took a walk down Crooked Loaning to the opposite side of the island. No causeway here.

Nothing between Holy Island and Norway.

The North Sea was an awful grey-black colour, a light drizzle mixed with an early morning fret. He wondered what sort of day it had been when Tom Wilkinson met his death. He hoped he'd been unconscious when he entered the hostile world of the North Sea. Surely nothing could be worse.

Ashley zipped up his leather jacket and regretted his early morning wander as a gust of icy wind nearly knocked him off his feet. He turned round and headed back to the village. He'd enjoyed his little disagreement in the bar as always, but somehow didn't think those two bozos could be involved in Tom's tragedy.

Why was Tom killed? Was it a drunken brawl that went too far or something far more sinister?

He'd decided to cross the causeway today, take a trip up to Berwick-upon-Tweed, check the archives of the local newspaper, The Berwick Advertiser. He'd checked with Claire: the causeway was safe to cross just after ten. Berwick was atwenty-minute drive away.

Berwick was cold and grey; it hadn't changed much since his last visit as a twelve-year-old visiting some distant relation of his father's. It was stuck in a seventies seaside town time warp. That's how he remembered it.

He'd telephoned The Berwick Advertiser, put on his best Home Counties accent, intermingled with an odd Americanism and told them about the book and Holy Island and the necessary research needed to pen a novel. The newspaper had been only too pleased to assist David Fox, though insisted onan interview for the paper. Ashley was a little uncomfortable with that, but had promised to return later that week to fulfil his obligation.

He sat in the offices ofThe Berwick Advertiser on Main Streetat the lone desktop computer that had been reserved for him. An elderly lady, Dorothy fussed around him, explaining everything from the keyboard to the mouse and how to access the archives.

"We only go back forty-two years, Mr Fox," she explained in a beautiful Scottish border lilt. "It's a question of resources and time. But I'm sure you'll find more than enough to go on with. Now, can I get you a nice cup of tea?"

"A black coffee would be nice, Dorothy. Just a sprinkling of sugar."

Dorothy gave a smile and walked in the direction of a coffee machine over in the far corner of the room.

Ashley pulled out his notes with the key words underlined. He typed *missing persons* into the computer. Sixty-four results. Missing persons from Edinburgh, missing persons from Berwick and Newcastle, even a missing person from Carlisle on the west coast. Narrow the search. He keyed in *missing persons Holy Island.* Twelve results. Twelve missing persons from Holy Island, unusually high, he thought, given the size of the place but, then again, Edinburgh and Newcastle didn't have a causeway. He sighed and began reading the articles in detail.

The first three people were last heard of trying to cross the causeway, the next two likewise, but the sixth person was missing, presumed dead, fallen from a fishing boat a mile out to sea. Nothing unusual. The next one, 1990, washed from the causeway, presumed dead. His heart sank a little further after reading each piece. He wanted suspicion, doubt, a reason to carry on for the sake of Tom Wilkinson. He wanted the newspaper articles to cry foul. They didn't.

He typed in *murder Holy Island.* Nothing. He typed in *suspicious death Holy Island.* The same three words appeared in a box at the centre of the screen: *no results found.* His mood deepened as he read the next report and the next. *The causeway, foolish, drowned, swept away, presumed dead, in the hours of darkness.* He looked again at the last article, *in the hours of darkness.* It stuck out like a lighthouse beacon; were they crazy? What sort of fool would attempt a crossing in the dark? And then the tenth report: two young males, brothers, Bobby and David Copeland, again in the hours of darkness, a little after midnight, *coastguard alerted, too late.*

And then a flicker of recognition, the names… those names, the surname, same as the drummer from The Police. Then he remembered. A bad lot. They were two young drug dealers from Luton, apprentice gangsters, following in the footsteps of their father, Billy 'Mad Monk' Copeland. He was called Monk on account of his rapidly thinning hair on the back of his head, though no one dared call him that to his face. Mad because of his reputation in a fight. Ashley had crossed him once and it had taken four policemen to bring him down.

Mad Monk's boys… dead.

Ashley suppressed a smile. The world, and in particular Luton, would be a better place without them and he hoped their father was experiencing some of the hurt he'd dished out over the years. But what had happened? Ashley read on: A fishing trip, the archives said, and sure enough at the bottom of the article, the estate in Luton, Bedfordshire and a quote from their father: *Two wonderful sons, they'll be sorely missed.*

The date September 2003; he was still in London at the time. Strange how he hadn't heard of their demise, hadn't shared a few celebratory beers with the lads on the shift as they usually did when some low life that had terrorised and abused the general public received their comeuppance.

Another death in 2004 and 2005 and another in 2006.

His finger hovered over the keyboard. Twelve deaths in forty-two years, five deaths in the last five. He caught his breath, his hand above the keyboard trembled as he realised the enormity of what he'd just uncovered. Statistics. Incredible statistics.

What had happened to the law of averages? Why hadn't the paper questioned it? He typed in *Holy Island* again and the word *mystery... no results found.* He scrolled through the articles, looking for some sort of pattern. Young males. All young males, twenty-five to thirty-five years old, the two Luton brothers, Carlisle, Newcastle and Glasgow.

"Interesting?" a voice behind him questioned in a soft Irish accent.

Ashley looked round. "Erm, yes... sort of." He held out a hand.

"I'm David—"

"David Fox the American author, I know. The boss told me all about you, I'm to do your interview. I've been looking into your website. I know a fair bit about you already."

Suddenly, the interview seemed a little more appealing to Ashley.

"And you are?"

"Dearblah O'Hanlan. Most people call me Debbie. I don't mind, Dearblah's a bit of a mouthful."

She held out a hand. "I'm a journalist here at The Advertiser."

She bent slightly, straining to see the screen. She smiled.

"At least that's what my job description states, though it's not exactly what I had in mind when I took the job three years ago." She pointed at the screen.

"Those last three articles are my handiwork. Why are you interested in them? Hardly material for book research, is it?" Before Ashley had a chance to answer, she continued.

"Those jobs were interesting enough, but normally I get all the crap. Obituaries of the local cobbler, great Auntie Nell's 100th birthday bash, the village fete and summer fairs, but, hey, I'm told at least once a week I'm serving my time. Last week I had to interview an eight-year-old footballing superstar, Callum Douglas, who can keep the ball up two thousand times without dropping it. I mean, he was a nice kid and he gave me an incredible demonstration, but it's hardly the Yorkshire Ripper trial, is it?"

She stood up straight, her eyes fixed on Ashley.

Ashley took a deep breath, tried to compose himself, but her beautiful deep brown eyes drew him in like a black hole and her dark, silk-like mane of hair glistened and shone as the sun shimmered through the office window. And her accent. Her soft Belfast accent just made him melt.

"Tell me what you're looking for, Mr Fox. I'll try to help."

"I'm looking for mystery, Miss O'Hanlan. Intrigue… scandal. I'm trying to get a feel of the island, get into the heads and maybe under the skins of the locals. I want to be nosy. I want a story. I'm having a bit of writer's block. I need a stimulus to get moving again."

She spoke. "There's a story there alright."

Ashley sat up.

"Go on."

The young Irish girl paced slowly towards an open window looking onto the street. She took in a breath of air. Ashley's eyes surveyed the beautiful shape silhouetted against the brightness of the day. She walked back slowly to the computer. Ashley's gaze followed hers to the screen, and the gentle mix of expensive perfume and femininity intoxicated him.

"You're probably wondering about the five deaths in five years. A little unusual, you're thinking to yourself." Ashley nodded.

"It was the most exciting story that I'd come across in three years. Or at least I thought so. I'd covered a death story on the island back in 2005."

"A death?"

"A missing person initially but washed up on Berwick beach a few days later. I went to the island, interviewed the locals.

Apparently, he was a bit of a hoodlum from Glasgow. When the body was found he had three stolen credit cards on him. They belonged to the islanders. He was bad news, got what he deserved, they said, one of the locals from Marygate called him an undesirable, said he had no place on the island."

"An undesirable?"

"Yeah, that's what he said. The islander was a bit spooky, huge owl-like eyes, looked like Marty Feldman in Young Frankenstein, remember?" Ashley did remember. He recalled seeing the movie as a teenager.

"So we've stumbled on a horror movie, have we?"

Dearblah grinned. "Sorry, I get a little carried away sometimes. I've a vivid imagination, should've been a novelist like you. Anyway, he'd gotten into a fight with a couple of the locals and, as a result, got thrown out of his hotel late at night. He said he was leaving the island there and then. The locals warned him it was unsafe to cross and by all accounts they persuaded thelandlord to change his mind and let him stay the night."

"Where was he staying? What happened, Dearblah?"

"I'll tell you if you hold your tongue and remember, it's Debbie."

Ashley bit his lip. He was overkeen. Relax, he told himself. Remember your role: an author mildly curious about the island. "Sorry… Debbie."

"He was staying at The Ship Inn." He caught his breath.

"The Ship?"

"Yeah. Do you know it?"

"I'm staying there."

"Spooooky…" She laughed. "You'd better be careful, Mr Fox." She gave a wry smile, raised an eyebrow.

"Anyway he made his way to the causeway; a few people followed and tried to talk him out of it, said it was unsafe. He started jogging across the causeway, claiming he'd hitch a lift onthe A1. The thing is, the causeway can look so safe, but then the water rolls in faster than a man can run. It's lethal."

"And?"

"And the rest is history, Mr Fox."

"David."

"Okay… David. His body was discovered a few days later. That's what I reported in the article, nothing unusual, no foul play, just a drunken, argumentative, stubborn Glaswegian."

"And then more?"

"Yes. I'd read about the two brothers on a fishing trip. I thought it a bit of a coincidence, they were no angels either, by all accounts. But then two more in 2005 and 2006."

And Tom Wilkinson, Ashley wanted to reply as he bit his lip.

"So I'm sent back across to the island and I'm getting some really uncomfortable feelings."

She leaned across Ashley and took the mouse.

"I'd searched these archives too. They just didn't add up."

"So we have a bit of a mystery, Debbie?"

She shrugged her shoulders, bit into her bottom lip.

"I thought so, David. I went back to the island, started pokingaround, only this time the locals weren't so forthcoming."

"How come?"

"At first I wasn't sure, but then I fathomed it out. It was clear they didn't want to talk about anything that might affect business. I spoke to Jacob Moor. He runs the show on the island, head of tourism over there, a bit of a big shot, a lawyer and a magistrate here in Berwick." She laughed. "Apparently his wife Sheila is a fan of yours."

"Is she?"

"That's what Jacob has been saying; she's read most of your books."

"Jacob Moor, you say."

"Yes, do you know him?"

"Yeah, I've bumped into him. He's also the head of some local Freemason type group, the Keepers."

"That's him. He gives me the creeps, a real smoothie, thinks he's God's gift. He came on to me, I told him to fuck off." Ashley's mouth fell open, surprised that such a word could fall from such a perfectly formed mouth.

"I'd met Sheila on a previous visit, interviewed her over the disappearances. I wonder if she realises what a bastard he is?"

And Ashley could only think of the look Jacob Moor had given him when he'd become overly familiar with Claire in the bar, a look that said hands off, and he began to wonder.

"I questioned Jacob Moor. I asked him about the five deaths, asked if he thought it a bit unusual. For the first time, I was fulfilling my ambition and acting out the role of an investigative reporter."

"And?"

"He blamed the recent explosion in binge drinking. Said it was the scourge of modern society, over-strong lagers and vodka shots."

Ashley sighed. "He's probably right, I'm afraid."

"Maybe. And Jacob pointed to the pathologists' reports. They all confirmed an unusually high level of alcohol in each body."

Ashley turned in the swivel chair.

"So, he didn't think it unusual. Five young men dead in five years, all full of alcohol, washed up on a beach somewhere, stone dead?"

She shook her head. "Not at all. He laboured on the pathologists' reports and begged me not to write the feature." Ashley knew the answer to his next question.

"And what did you do?"

"I wrote the article. I spent many weeks on it, looked into the victims' backgrounds and visited the island several times. I interviewed those who would speak to me."

"I'm puzzled, Debbie. Some people wouldn't talk."

She shook her head. "Afraid so. Some refused point-blank. They just clammed up. And some…"

"Go on."

She stood up, stiff, uncomfortable even.

"Some of them, David, just seemed plain scared."

"Scared?"

"Terrified, when I think about it."

A shiver ran the length of Ashley's spine and he remembereda similar conversation he'd had with Kate Wilkinson.

"But that didn't stop me. I was loving it. Even the hours of research, the phone calls to pathologists, the coroners and the families of the victims. I wrote a damned good two-thousand-word article. I must have spent a week on it. My first piece as a real journalist and I realised at the time that I had in fact chosen the right profession and it was only a matter of time before I got the break I wanted with a daily tabloid or a broadsheet."

"And you felt this article could be the stepping stone, right?"

"Correct. I presented it to my editor with a huge grin. He read it there and then straight through. I stood trembling with excitement, watching his eyes absorb every line. It was the best story to come out of these offices for twenty years."

She flicked a strand of hair from her face and looked at Ashley. He glanced at his computer, shrugged his shoulders.

"So where's the story? It didn't come up in any of the searches."

He looked back at her and knew the answer to his question by the look on her face.

"They didn't print it, did they?"

She shook her head. "My first meeting with the boss seemed quite positive… and yet—"

Dearblah paused, looked out across the room towards the window that looked onto the street.

"Even then, I should have guessed. The signs were there. He came back to me the next day, said it was unfounded. I don't know. Perhaps he was right. Said it could ruin the tourist industry on the island. One or two people came forward with objections."

"Islanders?" She nodded.

"For the life of me, I just don't know how they knew."

"And?"

"It was clear he was being pressured. There was more than justhim behind the decision. He didn't listen to anything I said. I begged him to reconsider, pointed out the coincidences within the pathologists' reports."

"The coincidences?"

"Yeah. Three of the victims had lacerations and bruising around the head and face."

Ashley swore his heart skipped a beat as the words tumbled from the girl's mouth. He'd been hit by a sledgehammer, his flesh covered instantly in a hundred thousand goose pimples. He couldn't quite comprehend what he'd just heard.

"What did you say?"

"Lacerations, cuts and bruising on three of the victims. I'd suggested in my article that they'd been beaten before they'd fallen in the sea."

"You mean murdered."

Dearblah stalled, seemed to take a sharp intake of breath.

"I didn't exactly say that in the article."

"But reading between the lines you were sort of suggesting it?" Ashley stood up unable to get comfortable, he needed to pace the room, he needed to think about the next move. Walk and think. Before he could say anything else a tall thin young man walked into the room.

"Deb, you're wanted on the telephone. You can take it in office number three. Some lady with a great story for you, an eleven-year-old Stephanie Purvis has won the Border and Lothian under-fifteen cross country open race."

She acknowledged the man and looked back at Ashley.

"See what I mean? Looks like our meeting is coming to an end, David."

She held out a hand and Ashley took it. They lingered for a second or two before she broke the grip and walked towards the open door.

"Debbie."

She turned. "Yeah?"

"Can we meet up again?"

She smiled. "We're meeting up next week, remember? For the interview."

Ashley laughed. "Oh yeah, I'd forgotten… the interview."

As she left the room Ashley typed Tom Wilkinson into the computer.

One result, one story, penned by a fair Irish hand, but as he read through the article entitled *Newcastle Man Missing*, he realised something was wrong.

Something was very wrong indeed.

The article was written before Tom's body was washed up on the beach at Redcar and Ashley just couldn't tear his eyes from the fifth paragraph:

*Mr Wilkinson was a freelance IT consultant from Heaton in Newcastle upon Tyne. He was a popular member of the local community, a keen sportsman with a passion for travel.*

Two little words, but of great significance. Two words that should never have been written by Dearblah. And all of a sudden he didn't feel quite so sure about the attractive reporter from The Berwick Advertiser.

# Chapter 18

The reporter sat at the laptop, mildly frustrated. Everything stacked up. Perhaps she had been mistaken. Perhaps her normal suspicious nature had betrayed her on this occasion. She'd searched on *Yahoo* and *Google* and asked *Jeeves* all manner of questions about the American author David Fox, but so far had come up with a blank.

It was clear the man didn't like his picture taken. Even on his own website, the main picture had him sitting on the steps of what looked like the Vatican, wearing a pair of oversized sunglasses and the full body shot taken from fifty feet away. And if she was completely honest with herself, it did look like him. Nor had he tripped himself up. The neither here nor there English accent with an occasional American intonation seemed genuine enough. But then it would, wouldn't it; she'd never ever held a conversation with a half-American half-Brit before.

She went back to *Google*, keyed in *David Fox author* then scrolled up to images. She clicked on the icon. Fifty-seven different images, surely one would give a full mug shot with a decent pixel count.

She was out of luck.

"Shit," she cursed. Only two photographs taken reasonably close, but both of them blurred, grainy images.

A sudden burst of inspiration.

She keyed in *David Fox author* and then *awards*. The *Google* search results showed over five hundred results. Again, she clicked the images icon. Four results. The four results loaded instantly. She cursed again, no better, in fact, a damn sight worse. She took off her glasses and cast them aside, decided on a coffee. As she got up and arched her back her eyes focused on the video icon. She hadn't thought of that. There again, what chance was there to see a decent video clip when she couldn't even find a decent picture?

She clicked the mouse. One result.

One video of an award he'd received in London. She clicked play.

"Shit."

The footage looked as if it had been taken by a four-year-old at the back of the Royal Albert Hall. David Fox and his interviewer were like black and white vibrating pin men and still he had the nerve to keep his bloody sunglasses on. It's what celebrities do, she supposed. Victoria Beckham, Bono, Jack Nicholson, all parading around wherever they are like fecking flies under a microscope.

"Time for that coffee," she mumbled to herself and, as she made her way across the room, the audio of the video kicked in.

The clarity of the sound was perfect. A round of applause and then in a crystal clear voice, the interviewer asked what it meant to win the award. She rushed back to the computer and turned up the sound. David Fox paused for a second and smiled. He announced to the waiting press and selected audience how nice it was to be in England once again. In a carefully prepared short speech, he thanked the audience and the voting panel for awarding him the prize. He thanked his agent and publishing company and announced what a debt of gratitude he owed to his editor who turned a badly written yarn into a saleable commodity.

He thanked everybody and his dog in typical, slushy American fashion. He thanked them in a perfect American accent… There wasn't a trace of English in any word. Why should there be? David Fox was an apple pie, midtown American. His own website had mentioned he'd left England as a youth; he'd been in America for over twenty-five years.

So who was this impostor and just what was he doing on the island? And his questions, his curiosity about the island and the islanders. Just who was the man she was now so angry with? She picked up her mobile and located the name. It rang three times before he answered.

"Hi, it's me."

"Hi. How are you? Working hard?"

"Yeah, I'm fine, just been doing a little bit of research."

"So what can I do for you?"

"It's a case of what I can do for you."

"Go on."

She took a deep breath… stretched out the drama just a bit longer than was necessary. "Seems like we have an impostor on the island, Jacob."

It was ten in the evening before Ashley arrived back in the bar of The Ship Inn. There'd been an accident on the A1 at the entrance to Goswick Golf Club that had closed the road for two hours. He'd taken the opportunity to call Kate Wilkinson and give her an update on events as he'd sat in a lay-by. It had turned into a foul evening, the wind had picked up and the rain was coming down in torrents.

He reached the causeway. The tide was just beginning to drift in. The heavy rain made the causeway tricky and at times the slightly raised road almost blended with the sea. He took his time, no more than ten miles an hour. His hands loosened their grip on the wheel as he approached Causeway Chare that led into the village. He ran from the car and into the doorway of The Ship Inn trying to minimise the rain damage. He shook himself dry in the entrance porch. As he walked into the bar, Claire beamed at him. But it was different smile yet again. Claire Macbeth, the girl with a thousand faces.

"Hi, David, have a good day? Find what it was you were looking for?"

He shrugged his shoulders without answering the question, gave her a kind of not sure look that she seemed to understand. For some reason he felt uncomfortable. The seat he took at the bar seemed harder than normal and he found it difficult to find the right position. Without being asked, Claire placed a bottle of Budweiser on the bar.

"It's quiet tonight, David, hardly been a soul in all evening. With a little bit of luck, I'll get away to bed by midnight." She peered out of the window. "I can't see anyone venturing out now." Ashley looked at his watch. "I'm tired myself. Think I'll have this one and turn in too."

That smile again.

"Only two people all night. Frank Short for a couple of beers earlier on and then Jacob Moor about an hour ago."

Ashley looked around the bar and noticed he was the only customer in. No one sat in the darkened nooks and crannies of the old inn.

"Jacob was asking after you, wondered how the book was going, and wondered if he could help in any way. I said you were in Berwick researching some newspaper archives. Did you find out anything interesting?"

Ashley ignored the question, took his first mouthful of beer. It hit home. The effect was immediate.

"Jacob Moor… tell me about him, Claire. He's the big cheese around here, isn't he?" He took another mouthful, smacked his lips as the bottle left his mouth. "Bit of a smoothie, I hear, bit of a one for the ladies. You'd better take care of yourself, a pretty girl like you."

He wanted a reaction but got nothing.

"Are you likely to want another drink, David? I'll start and close up."

Ashley shook his head."Good."

Claire began turning the lights off around the bar area. Ashley looked on. There seemed to be a light switch for every damnbulb. As she turned off the lights to the main room, it cast a dull shadow across the whole bar area, and Ashley was plunged into a semi-darkness.

She stepped out from behind the counter and walked slowly towards the doorway and the darkened entrance, pushed the heavy door closed and secured the brass bolt at the top. She reached across to a shelf within the small enclosure, located a key, inserted it into the lock and turned it. She turned round to Ashley, then smiled. Claire Macbeth reached across for the light switches and the bar turned to pitch. Ashley became aware of the barmaid's intoxicating perfume as she breezed past him… and then it was gone.

# Chapter 19

Ashley Clarke skipped the magnificent Ship Inn breakfast, decided to grab a coffee and Danish pastry at the café by the harbour.

He crept quietly down the stairs a little before ten, sloped past the reception desk without meeting a soul and opened the door to the street, stepping out into the bright sunlight. He made his way down Marygate in the direction of the harbour. Claire watched him from the small kitchen window overlooking the street; her heart skipped a beat. After she had watched him disappear from sight, she walked slowly along the corridor towards reception. She peered into the dining room. Clear. The guests had all disappeared, out for the day exploring the Priory and visiting the craft and gift shops, maybe a trip to Berwick or even a train up to Edinburgh to visit the castle.

The telephone rang. She knew who it would be, same time every week, a phone call she dreaded and yet one she had to answer. She'd tried to ignore it in the past but it had never stopped him. He simply walked over to the hotel and had his fun in one of the empty bedrooms, always more violent, more experimental than he was in the confines of his own domain. She picked it up, took a quick look along the corridor as she read the familiar digits on the display.

"Hello."

"It's me. Okay to talk?"

"Yes."

"She took the 8.30 bus, won't be back till after four. It's time to play fucky, fucky, young lady; get your pretty little arse round here quick."

He grinned to himself and could swear a little more blood flowed into his ever-growing penis with each expletive. Jesus, if his wife could hear him speaking like this.

He was sure Claire loved it, loved every curse, the dirtier the better and what a performance she put in each time they met. He could count on two hands the amount of times his wife had allowed him to make love with the light on and, as for perversions as she called them, like oral sex, well… that was taboo, a strict no-no. It was for the animals. She'd grimaced, as he'd suggested it, two months into their twenty-year marriage. Not Claire. She'd sucked and fucked like a whore on heat ever since she was fourteen.

He'd trained her well. Anything went. She'd cried when he insisted they video their sordid performances, but she'd eventually succumbed. And the tears had flowed like a river as he had made her watch her online porn. He bought the standard sex toys and eventually, after getting a little bored, went a step further. Always a step further.

They'd had to tie her up the first time, knock her about a little, but eventually they'd succeeded and after a few sessions, they'd dispensed with the ropes.

"I'll get my coat."

"Good. It feels so long."

"But it was only last week, remember?"

He purred. "Yeah, how could I forget? See you in ten minutes then, okay? I'll leave the door open."

"See you soon."

"See you in ten."

Claire replaced the receiver and reached for her coat hanging on the back of her chair and wiped a tear from the corner of her eye.

Jacob Moor sniffed at his armpits and thought it wouldn't do any harm to use a little deodorant, maybe a squirt downstairs.

They lay in the Moor marital bed… spent. Their session had lasted a little over fifteen minutes, such was the expertise of his lover.

"A little too quick for my liking, Jacob," Kyle mocked.

"She shouldn't be so good. That tongue of hers is like a lizard. Give me ten minutes. The old fella will be standing to attention again."

Claire climbed from the bed and stepped into her black silk panties. She bent down and pulled them from the floor, up past her knees and over her hips.

"'Fraid not, I must go, Jacob. I need to prepare the lunches."

Claire reached onto the bed for her bra, and turned to face the bedroom door as she dressed as quickly as she could.

Jacob Moor hid his disappointment well, but realised she was right. After all, it was Jacob who owned the freehold to the Inn and he'd gradually turned it around over the last few years ever since he'd allowed Claire to manage everything.

She was almost like a slave; he paid her peanuts and abused her wherever and whenever he could and yet she'd still put heart and soul into it and gradually built up the profits. She tooka hand in everything: the food, reception, accommodation, the bar. She even cleaned the bloody toilets. He almost laughed out loud.

The only help she needed was a part-time barman and a dishwasher. Jesus, life was good, life was simple.

# Chapter 20

It was a relatively simple task to arrange a meeting with Sheila Moor. Ashley's suspicions, intuition, natural curious nature, whatever it was, drew him to the Island Keepers and Jacob Moor in particular. He couldn't explain why, but he felt sure the organisation was the key to the disappearances. What better way to get nearer to them than through the wife of the Worshipful Master? He would also talk to Jacob; after all, Claire had said he'd offered to help with the research.

It was as if Sheila Moor was glad of the company. Ashley had brought a copy of David Fox's latest novel to a small café by the harbour where he met the 'fan'. He'd perfected the American author's signature well and took great care inscribing the book to Sheila Moor.

Almost flirtatiously, Sheila Moor gazed into his eyes. She had gone to seed, past her sell-by date. She'd no make-up on, not even a smattering of lipstick and her wardrobe had seen better days. And yet Ashley could tell that Sheila Moor had been stunningly beautiful in her day, maybe not that long ago. Her fine features were smooth, hardly a wrinkle and she carried her slightly overweight figure elegantly. Nothing, Ashley thought, that couldn't be repaired with a few weeks in the gym, a lick of paint and a visit to the Metro Centre.

As she spoke, Ashley peered into the eyes of a troubled soul. He couldn't pinpoint how he knew or detail any mysterious body language or twitch of a facial muscle, but he knew. He'd seen those eyes a thousand times before, generally in a prison cell at the precise moment the criminal had thrown in the towel.

Sheila tried to appear enthusiastic, even talked about the plot of the novel she was holding, claimed she'd read the first few chapters when it was serialised in the Sunday Times magazine a few months ago.

"What is it that's troubling you, Sheila?" Ashley enquired. A minute's silence.

Sheila Moor feigned a smile. "It's that obvious, is it?" Ashley nodded his head, said nothing.

"You wouldn't believe it if I told you, Mr Fox."

"Try me."

Sheila Moor looked just for a split second as if she would talk, but then she composed herself and the moment passed. "You're a writer, not a listener, Mr Fox."

"What difference does that make? I can listen if there's something you want to get off your chest."

She paused, looked up and spoke. "Are you married?"

Ashley shook his head, prayed that the real David Fox wasn't either, though couldn't remember seeing anywhere on the internet about a Mrs David Fox.

"Then you wouldn't understand."

"Wouldn't understand what?"

Sheila Moor shook her head, smiled, looked around the table for something to fiddle with, settled on a small sachet of sugar. She twisted it between her fingers to the point of bursting. She spoke in a whisper.

"Imagine Mr Fox…" She leaned forward. "Imagine devoting and trusting your life to one person. Imagine you know everything and anything there is to know about a single individual. What makes them tick, what they like, what they don't like, how they smell. Imagine the feeling of producing a child together. Do you know how special that is? A son. A living, walking, talking image of his father and mother. His habits, my habits, little traits and the way he walks, how he shakes when he's nervous."

She laughed. "Just like his mother."

Ashley broke eye contact for a second, looked at the sugar sachet trembling between Sheila Moor's thumb and forefinger. She stood. "I must be going, Jacob will be home—"

Ashley reached for her hand. "No."

Their eyes met again and Sheila's gaze lingered for a second. In that glorious, oh so short period of time, Sheila Moor was ready. She opened her mouth to speak.

And then the unmistakable sound of her husband's voice shattered the silence.

"Good afternoon, dear. I just bumped into Father Thompson; he said I'd find you in here."

The sugar sachet split and tiny brown grains of sugar cascaded downwards, bounced onto the tablecloth as if in slow motion. Jacob stared into her eyes. "Helping our friend with a bit of his research, are we?"

Sheila held up the book. "He's gave me a signed copy, Jacob."

"Very kind of him, I'm sure."

Jacob turned to Ashley. "I should have mentioned, Mr Fox. My wife's quite a fan of yours. I really should have arranged a meeting earlier. Your eighth book now, I believe, is that correct?" Ashley nodded.

"I'll pick up where you left off, darling," Jacob announced. He looked at his wristwatch, never focused on a hand or a digit. "It's time for you to be getting home."

Without another word, Sheila Moor reached across the table,shook Ashley's hand and, before he could say anything, she was gone.

Jacob Moor sat smirking, a way too confident look on his face, and a strange cold shiver ran the length of Ashley's spine.

"I hear you had a good day in Berwick up at The Advertiser office, Mr Fox."

Ashley didn't answer; he considered the next course of his investigation. Why was Jacob so keen to get rid of his wife? He'd arranged the meeting with Sheila when Claire had told him Jacob Moor would be on council business all day. But he'd come back.

Someone had called him and he'd returned to the island just as fast as he could. Could it have been Father Thompson? Ashley had noticed him skulking outside the coffee shop as he waited for Sheila.

"I thought you were in Berwick today, Jacob. Did your meeting get cancelled?"

Jacob thought for a second, pawed nervously with his earlobe. "Yes, unfortunately." He grinned. "Or fortunately… depends which way you look at it. I hate the damn council business, but someone has to do it."

"That's right," replied Ashley glaring at the Worshipful Master, despising him more and more as each second lapsed. "Someone has to look after the island, isn't that so?"

"Quite, Mr Fox."

"Protect the island from the undesirables."

The word seemed to touch a raw nerve. Ashley grinned, lifted his coffee cup up as if to say cheers.

"Just something the Irish reporter said, Jacob, that's all. I take it you've heard of Dearblah O'Hanlan?"

"Just what is your purpose here, my friend?" Jacob asked Ashley politely, trying to gain a little composure, trying to turn the conversation round.

In for a penny, thought Ashley.

"Until I went up to the newspaper offices the other day, I thought I was researching a book."

Jacob remained attentive; it was as if both men knew that what was about to be said would turn both worlds upside down. "Now, Jacob, I'm not so sure."

"Go on."

"Now I feel I've stumbled upon something far greater than a three-hundred-page mystery novel."

Jacob laughed. "I'm intrigued, Mr Fox. Tell me more."

Ashley leaned back in his seat, placed his hands behind his head.

"Ask your Irish reporter, Jacob. I figure you and her are quite close; she'll tell you everything you need to know."

Ashley drained the cold dregs from his coffee cup as he stood to leave. Strangely enough, it tasted quite pleasant.

Ashley had put off the phone call for long enough. He wandered back down the main street and opened the door to the public payphone.

Not for the first time, he cursed the lack of reception on his mobile phone. Strangely, he could send and receive texts. He didn't relish the call to his ex-colleague in Strathclyde Police. He was going to ask him to break the rules, effectively put his job at risk. He was fairly sure Jordan Cameron would do just that; his favourite expression when he'd worked with him in the Met was, '*rules are for the obedience of fools and for the guidance of wise men.*'

Cameron continuously overstepped the mark during their time together in London. He'd think nothing of saying he had a warrant as he'd stormed into a house when, in fact, no such thing had been issued.

He'd bluffed it out; no one had ever asked to see the piece of paper normally issued by the local magistrate. Jordan hadn't taken any crap from the low life and was not averse to givingan unruly youth a slap.

Strangely enough, the decent parents had always seemed to approve. And lo-and-behold anybody who resisted arrest. Jordan would simply weigh in with his fists flying and take the consequences later; never his truncheon, only his fists.

Ashley remembered the only occasion where he'd lost his temper with a habitual serial offender, twenty-one years old, whose particular speciality was barging his way past old ladies as they'd answered his knock to their door.

Once inside, he'd rob them of anything and everything they had, but not before he'd punched and kicked them black and blue.

Jordan and Ashley had been lucky one night. The old lady had managed to pull at a distress cord as she lay battered on the ground. The two policemen had noticed the flashing red light above the front door as they'd passed in a patrol car. The door was ajar and they walked into a horrific sight in the passageway.The old lady's blood adorned the hallway and the beige carpet shimmered like a small crimson lake. She groaned but managed a faint smile as she witnessed the two officers walk through the door. Her knights in shining armour had arrived, the good old boys in blue. Her head returned back to the carpet and she closed her eyes.

As if on cue, her attacker walked from the lounge carrying a video recorder. He stopped dead in his tracks, stunned at what he was looking at, his exit now blocked. He held the recorder high above his head and hurled it in the direction of the policemen. The corner of the VCR hit Ashley square in the chest and he gasped as every breath of air was forced from his lungs. He fell to the floor as the pain from two broken ribs kicked in. The thug made a bolt in the opposite direction, desperately looking for another exit. Jordan Cameron caught up with him as he fumbled at the bolt of the back door. Jordan Cameron had remained cool, told him he was under arrest as he managed to release the bolt. He pulled at the door furiously, Jordan Cameron read him his rights. It was still locked, he turned his attention to the key protruding from the lock. Cameron swung a punch into his kidneys. The man yelped like a dog as he hit the floor. Cameron resisted the urge to kick his head in. He took him by the hair and hauled him to his feet. He remembered the sight of the helpless old lady who lay on the floor in the hallway and he hammered a fist into the bridge of the thug's nose.

The youth slumped to the floor again as his nose collapsed into his face and two jets of blood spiralled downwards from each nostril.

"Get up, you useless piece of dog shit."

The policemen aimed a heavy Doc Martens boot into his stomach. He pulled the groaning man to his feet again and that might have been the end of the beating if the thug hadn't grabbed at a kitchen knife as he was manhandled out of the kitchen. Jordan Cameron hadn't noticed the rack above the microwave. He should have been more alert, shouldn't have let his anger cloud his observations. The youth lunged for a knife and in one swift movement turned to face the policeman, the knife pointing just inches from the policeman's face. Cameron moved his hand down to his truncheon, a weapon he was proud never to have drawn. The youth was sweating profusely. He was nervous, twitchy, and he had the skinny, drawn face and shallow complexion of a user. Most of his teeth had rotted away or been knocked out as he followed his dangerous occupation. Nothing could come in the way of his next fix; it was all he lived for.

"I'll give you three seconds to put that knife down and, if you don't, you'll regret the decision for the rest of your life."

The knife didn't move; it hovered… suspended in mid-air. The youth was unsure of his next move; the fucking filth still blocked his exit and he was a big cunt.

"One."

Was the bastard wearing one of those stab proof vests? Maybe he should go for the thigh or a slash at the fucker's boat race. "Two."

The face, go for the fuckin' face, hit the cunt on three, then make a run for it.

Jordan Cameron never intended to count to three. *Two.* And in one swift, well-rehearsed, full-blooded movement, his truncheon smashed into the wrist of the knifeman. Before he could scream out in agony, a heavy fist crashed into his face, knocking his remaining front teeth into the back of his throat. Ashley managed to crawl through and pull the policeman off the unconscious youth, but not before he'd fractured his skull, right tibia, both forearms, a collar bone and several ribs.

The two policemen sat side by side in the kitchen, breathing heavily. Ashley reached for his radio.

"I suppose we'd better phone the poor twat an ambulance."

"You too, Ash, I think you need those ribs looked at." Jordan grinned. "And me too, I'll need a visit to the hospital."

Ashley looked him up and down. "You look okay to me, Haggisman, not a mark on you."

Jordan Cameron rose to his feet, held out two hands and Ashley reached out for them. He winced as the pain shot through his chest as Cameron carefully eased him to his feet. "Yeah, I look great, don't I? You'll need to do something about it."

The two ambulance men arrived within eight minutes. It was just enough time. They attended to the old lady first at the insistence of Officer Clarke. She would live… just. She would survive, maybe a week in hospital, though she would never spend another relaxed, trouble-free day for the remainder of her days.

Ashley insisted he was fine. A broken rib or two, that's all. He pointed at the video recorder on the floor and explained the story. He took the two paramedics through to the kitchen. "Officer Jordan Cameron." Ashley pointed at the officer in the corner.

"He's taken a bit of a beating, I'm afraid, but I think he's okay."

He gave a little wave. "Okay fellas… come to patch me up, have you?"

Jordan Cameron sat hunched in the corner, his face a bloodiedmess. Both eyes were closed and blackening by the second. A large flap of skin hung from the corner of his mouth and the freshly pressed white shirt he'd ironed pre-shift was stained scarlet.

Ashley picked up the phone, keyed in the number and waited. A female civilian answered politely. The phone call was directed through to DCI Cameron's mobile after Ashley explained he'd worked with him in the Met.

"Haggis man, how are you hanging?"

"Clarkey… is that you? Long time no hear. You must be after a favour."

Ashley sighed. Cameron was right, they'd been good friends. Why was it that nobody made the effort to pick up the phone, maybe arrange a long weekend, a reunion even? It just didn't ever happen.

Ashley outlined his problem, explained how Cameron could help him, though conveniently left out details of his undercover operation. He wanted to share the information with another policeman but at this very moment in time felt the need to be economical with the truth. Was it a trust thing? Just who could he confide in?

"Holy Island you say, Clarkey. I'm down in Galashiels tomorrow, interviewing a suspect in hospital. Holy Island can't be more than an hour away. Why don't we meet up?"

Ashley couldn't believe his luck.

"Great, Jordan, great. But not on Holy Island. I'll explain tomorrow. Let's meet halfway. I'll check the tides and get back to you, okay?"

Jordan Cameron and Ashley Clarke met in the Red Lion public house on the main thoroughfare through Melrose.

They'd spent a pleasant lunch together, caught up on old times and Ashley had delivered his request. The victim from Glasgow was well-known to Jordan Cameron, or rather his family was well-known. They were the hard men of the city, gangsters, they specialised in counterfeit goods, soft and hard drugs, and were suspected of running a few brothels on Glasgow's east side. And of course they were all thieves. The victim, Gordon or Gordy as he was known, was the youngest son of the head of the family, Tam Dalgleish. Gordon Dalgleish worked with stolen credit cards. That was his speciality. He had fourteen previous convictions.

Ashley's request was a simple one. He wanted to talk to Tam Dalgleish. Jordan pressed a little as to why, but when Ashley wasn't forthcoming, he took a step backwards. Good old haggis.

Four hours later, Ashley Clarke walked into the Nag's Head in Drumchapel, Glasgow. As instructed, he asked behind the bar for 'Big Tam' as he was known. The nervous-looking barman pointed over to the far side of the bar where an over large gentleman sat with similarly built friends in a cloud of cigarette smoke.

It seemed the Scottish smoking ban hadn't reached this particular area of Glasgow. Ashley introduced himself as a private detective. Why not? That was his occupation now. "Were you a copper then, son?" Big Tam asked.

He called me son… good start. Ashley thought about lying, looked around the bar at the men, big men, dangerous men with scarred faces, shaved heads and squashed noses, and felt just a bit intimidated.

"The Met, nearly twenty years."

"And where did you get my number?" Ashley searched for a lie, found none.

"Strathclyde Police, I have a contact there." Ashley smiled. "It seems you're quite well-known to them."

The big man's friends grinned, one of them laughed.

Tam Dalgleish scowled at them then at Ashley." And who would that be then?"

"I'm not telling you."

The silent atmosphere could have been cut with a knife. Big Tam took a long deliberate pull on his cigarette and announced loudly, "Get him a drink. I hate to see a man without a drink." Without being asked what he wanted, an associate of the big man quickly went to the bar. The barman had already started pouring the pint and it was unceremoniously dumped in front of Ashley, together with a whisky chaser. Tam looked around the table at the collection of misfits surrounding him.

Hangers-on, scroungers, the benefit brigade, men on his payroll.

Collectors and enforcers. And as soon as he paid them their dues, they'd piss it against the wall. No planning, no foresight, a little left over for wifey perhaps, as she emptied the pockets each evening.

Not Tam. He'd worked all his life, prided himself that he'd never pulled a penny from the Social and he'd sunk his investments into legitimate ventures. Well, half legitimate at least.

"Fuck off, the lot of ye!" He drained half a pint in one swallow. "This man has some information about Gordy."

Ashley took a mouthful from the pint glass, winced as it danced on his taste buds, but nevertheless was glad of the calming effect it gave him.

"Speak," the big man announced as the last of the drifters disappeared.

Speak, that's a laugh, Ashley thought to himself. He was hoping Gordon's father would be the one doing the talking, but saying he had some news about Gordy was the only way the big man would agree to a meet. Oh well, in for a penny. Just be a bit tactful, Ashley thought to himself.

"I have reason to believe Gordon was murdered."

Ashley waited for the table to be turned over. He waited for a punch or a kick or an attacker to hit him from behind. He waited for a reaction from the man who sat in front of him. The man who sat calmly, as if he hadn't even heard Ashley's dramatic statement.

Ashley arrived back on the island a little before nine o'clock. He walked back into the bar of The Ship Inn and set eyes on Claire Macbeth. Before they could strike up a conversation, the door flew open and Stephen Kyle stood panting and sweating in the doorway. He peered through the gloom, caught the familiar shape of the barmaid.

"Claire… it's Frank."

The rain had soaked his cheeks. Claire took his hands. "What is it, Steve? Slow down… tell me what's wrong."

He wiped a tear from his eye, moved his hand down and wiped the snot from his nose.

"It's Frank Short, Claire… he's dead. He's topped himself."

Ashley Clarke spent yet another evening on Holy Island unableto sleep, albeit the cause slightly different from the night before. The sight of Frank Short swinging from his own bedroom window with his own white linen bedsheets taut around his broken neck had unnerved him. If he'd wanted to kill himself, surely he could have found a more dignified, private way.

And the wind.

The wind itself had played a part in the macabre spectacle as the body swung slowly as if playing a tune on the breeze. He'd run up the street with Claire and Stephen Kyle, but before they'd got there a small army had amassed. The police had arrived within the hour and cut the old man's body down. A doctor had pronounced him dead at the scene.

He passed yet another policeman, a young ginger-haired lad no older than twenty-two or twenty-three years of age, an employee of Northumbria Police. He stood in a sentry-like position a few yards from the door of Frank Short's terraced house. Ashley breathed a sigh of relief as he failed to recognise him. He was aware immediately that someone was tugging at his jacket from behind. He turned round.

"Debbie… how nice to see you… what are you doing here?" She frowned. "You must have pulled that from the world bank of stupidest questions ever, David. I'm a reporter, remember? And a man has died under suspicious circumstances."

Ashley laughed. It *was* a stupid question, but it was the first thing that had come into his head.

"Suspicious, you say. What makes you think that?"

Dearblah took him gently by the sleeve. "Let's get a coffee. I haven't had one all day." She looked at her watch. "A world record for me."

They walked in the direction of the Priory.

"It's amazing what a big smile and a little flutter of the eyelidsachieve," she said as she peered over the top of the steaming cup.

I bet, Ashley thought to himself, I bet.

"The thing is, this young copper probably told me a little more than he was supposed to. I had my notebook out, pen at the ready and I'd flashed the press badge at him. Suicide, heannounced. Plain and simple."

Ashley didn't interrupt; Dearblah was in full flow, it was clear she had a story to tell.

"I could see in his eyes that he was hiding something. I asked him off the record, put my notebook in my pocket. He looked around, made sure no one was in earshot and leaned forward."

"And?"

She grinned. "He asked me for a date."

"A date?"

"A date. I told him to give me something and I'd give him my telephone number."

She sat back, grinning as Ashley pictured the scene in his head. "I'm a good flirt when I need to be, I have to admit," she announced, as she flicked her hair back from her face and looked upwards. "He told me there had been signs of a struggle. I pressed him. He said a vase had been broken and the detectives couldn't work out why he'd jumped through the glass window."

Ashley remembered the debris strewn across the pavement at the scene. He thought nothing of it at the time but sure… if you wanted to kill yourself, why not open the window insteadof throwing yourself through it? It didn't make any sense.

"Any more?"

"No. That was it, but Jesus, David, he was more or less saying that the poor old bugger was murdered."

Suddenly, the hot sweet tea in front of him had lost its appeal. "I think we should tell the police what we know about the young men's deaths," she blurted out. "I don't like it, David. I don't like it one little bit."

Ashley warmed his two hands on the cup, shrugged his shoulders.

"Tell them what, Debbie? Each death has been through a police investigation and a coroner's court. No suspicious circumstances whatsoever."

Dearblah spoke, but Ashley was miles away in his own thoughts. The police would arrive at the suicide version and the case would go to the coroner. And he was thinking that inevitably the coroner would come up with a verdict of suicide too.

He thought about his new found acquaintance in Glasgow, thought about *that* phone call. Thought how ironic it was after all the years he'd spent in the police that now a member of the underworld was helping him to solve his case.

Dearblah took her final mouthful of coffee, placed the cup on the saucer and pushed it into the centre of the table.

"You're not listening to me, are you?" She frowned.

"Not really, Debbie, no," he replied. "Let's go and get a proper drink."

And all he could think of was that article and whether the time was right to come clean, to push the reporter and ask the questions he knew he should. Whether the time was right to call John Markham and bring in the cavalry.

Sheila Moor sat in the office on Hyde Hill, Berwick-upon-Tweed, a tear or two welling up in her eyes, but her cheeks remained dry. She wasn't distraught, wasn't devastated or harbouring any hysterical feelings.

She'd known for some time their marriage was over, but nevertheless it saddened her. Where had it started to go wrong? She asked herself. She felt inadequate, let down. What had made her husband turn to another woman? Was it her fault? What would the islanders say?

The private detective breezed through the door. A young man by the name of Andrew Jackson, no more than thirty years old. What was he thinking? Was he thinking that Jacob Moor's middle-aged, slightly overweight wife was an old frump? Was he thinking she was past her sell-by date? Not a good screw these last few years, maybe a bit frigid.

"I have the tape, Mrs Moor." He paused. "Are you really sure you want to see it? It's a little graphic, I'm afraid."

Andrew Jackson had rigged up the camera in the bedroom of the detached house whilst Jacob Moor was on council business a week ago. He'd thought it a bit ironic how Jacob Moor had passed him on the A1 about breakfast time. He'd marvelled at the size of the small surveillance camera, the lens no bigger than a baby's fingernail. A smoke alarm in the middle of the ceiling had been the obvious place to hide it and the images would be relayed back to the offices in Berwick.

Sheila Moor's suspicions had been correct. Her weekly trip to Berwick on market day had been the ideal opportunity for her husband to engage in his extra marital activities. Sheila Moor had pressed the button on the remote control twenty minutes before she left.

Jackson had been waiting.

He had plenty of patience, but it wasn't called on today. Within ninety minutes, the door to the bedroom had opened and the two figures appeared. Jackson had pressed *record* on the small machine.

And the oversexed private detective had enjoyed every frame. It was as good as any porno he'd ever watched, made even more interesting as the characters were real, not actors. Sheila Moor sat at the table.

"Can I get you a cup of tea, Mrs Moor?"

Sheila Moor shook her head.

"Just get it over with, Mr Jackson. This isn't easy, you know."

"Yes, sure… I'm sorry."

Sheila Moor recognised the two figures as soon as they rounded the bed. She hadn't been a hundred percent certain as they'd appeared in the doorway, but as the focus automatically kicked in, the girl's image was crystal clear.

It figured. Everything fell into place now. Jacob had never been a pub man in the early years of their marriage; they'd hired a video or watched a soap. Coronation Street, occasionally Eastenders, and, of course, always Emmerdale. In the first few years of marriage, they'd hired a movie from the general dealers in the town and snuggled up with a bottle of wine, but now he never seemed to be away from the damn Ship Inn.

As her adulterous husband and his young lover… awfully young lover… embraced and began stripping off their clothes, she could take no more.

"I've seen enough, Mr Jackson. You can stop the tape."

"Sure, Mrs Moor, sure." Andrew Jackson was a little disappointed, but nevertheless complied with his client's wishes. After all, he was a consummate professional, he kept telling himself.

"You can prepare the bill. I won't be needing your services any longer."

Mrs Moor climbed from the seat and walked casually towards the door. Andrew Jackson couldn't help admiring her composure and the dignified way she held herself together as she left the room. As she left, he sighed and settled down into the padded leather seat, the seat he called his own.

He leered… stretched across the desk, reached for a box of tissues and pressed play. He thought perhaps it was just as well Mrs Moor hadn't seen the young man join the writhing couple on the bed five minutes into the video.

# Chapter 21

Sheila Moor had pressed her husband's shirt as usual. As usual, he'd thanked her politely, taken it from the coat hanger on the door and enjoyed the warm, starchy stiff feel of the cotton against his skin.

It felt good. Homely. Comforting. He looked at his wife and a momentary pang of guilt swept across him. But it was only fleeting. He cast his mind back to earlier that day.

Sheila was a good wife. He'd loved her once. Maybe he still did. He wasn't sure. What is love? Who really knows? He used to get goose bumps and tremble each time they met, each time they managed to sneak into a friend's bedroom or the back of his car, but then, as the meetings became more frequent, the feelings waned.

They did for everyone; it was just a sad fact of life. And now, as he gazed up at Sheila Moor, who'd taken another one of his shirts from the back of the door and spread it over the ironing board, he smiled. She looked at him as if sensing the intrusion but remained stoic.

He respected her. That was it.

He'd respected and cared for her for over twenty years, provided for her every need and seen that her personal bank account had been topped up every month. She wanted for nothing; he'd been a good husband, a good provider.

In turn, she'd raised their son well, had done a good job, and now he was studying hard for his Master's degree at Leeds University. Perhaps that was why she'd been a bit quiet lately. She missed Martin. A mother's bond is strong and she'd naturally found it difficult to adjust.

The Island Keepers had congregated in the bar. They'd begun arriving just after seven thirty. Ashley sat in a small alcove with Dearblah O'Hanlan. Claire had been cold, almost hostile, not so much as a smile.

Jacob Moor stood at the bar along with Stephen Kyle. Father Thompson was there too and a few others all dressed in the obligatory black suits and ties. They looked unhappy, sad; they were talking about old Frank, saying what a good man he was, how he'd shown no signs of suicidal tendencies.

It wasn't a normal Island Keepers' gathering; this wasn't a normal Lodge evening.

At ten minutes to eight, the crowd started to peel away, one by one. A young man replaced Claire behind the bar, who Ashley noticed had dressed in a calf-length black dress for the evening.

"Where are you off to tonight?" he asked.

She looked forlorn as she answered, "Downstairs to the meeting."

Ashley shrugged his shoulders. “I thought it was men only.” Jacob Moor took Claire by the shoulders. “She helps with the ceremony a few times each year.”

“Takes the part well,” Stephen Kyle interjected with a smile. Jacob walked towards the far side of the room with Stephen Kyle and Claire following on behind.

No sooner had the last man disappeared down the stairwell and the door clicked locked behind them than the main door to the bar opened and in walked Sheila Moor.

Something was amiss. Sheila Moor just didn’t come into The Ship Inn, or in fact any other hotels or bars on the island. She wasn’t a drinker, never had been. The barman verified the fact. “Hello, Sheila,” he responded. “Something wrong?”

Sheila took up a position on one of the barstools and shook her head. “Nothing wrong, Martin, nothing at all. I just fancied a drink. Perhaps I’ll catch up with my husband a little later on. How long will he be in the temple?”

Ashley and the journalist looked on.

“Sheila Moor,” Dearblah whispered, “Jacob’s wife.”

“Could be a couple of hours,” the young barman replied. “I believe they’ve a lot to get through tonight, what with Frank’s death and things.”

Sheila looked over to the doorway leading downstairs, then back to the barman.

“I’ll wait. Give me a large gin and tonic.”

The barman looked surprised. “Are you sure, Sheila? Are you sure you’re okay?”

Sheila Moor didn’t reply.

Dearblah turned to Ashley and, in the same whispered tone, said, "I interviewed her for the paper, remember?"

Ashley nodded. "Yeah… you said. I met up with her earlier today. She doesn't look happy, does she?"

"No, not really and just look how quickly she's gulping that gin." Sheila Moor had emptied half the glass without taking a breath. She placed the glass on the bar and looked around. She spotted Dearblah and Ashley, gave a little wave. She spoke to the barman again, placed a ten-pound note on the counter and stood up. She lifted the glass and emptied it in one long mouthful and picked up the refill. She walked over towards Dearblah.

"Mind if I join you, Miss O'Hanlan? And you, David?" Ashley stood up, pulled a chair out from the table.

"No, sure, Mrs Moor, by all means join us. You're more than welcome."

She held an outstretched arm towards Ashley as she stepped around the table. He took it gently and she lowered herself into the seat.

Sheila took another mouthful of gin and tonic. She'd slowed down a little, Ashley noticed, almost a delicate, ladylike sip. The first large one had obviously done the trick. She licked at her lips, then spoke.

"The story I nearly told you about today, Mr Fox, before my husband so rudely interrupted us."

Before Ashley could answer, she spoke. "A bit of scandal and gossip Jacob reckons you're seeking. Well, I just might just be the lady you're looking for because I've got the story from hell."

Ashley sat enthralled as Sheila Moor's amazing story began to unfold. By the time she'd reached the bottom of the second glass she was clearly drunk, but Ashley knew that what she was pouring out was the truth.

Ten minutes into the incredible revelations and accusations, Dearblah excused herself, said she had to make a phone call. She walked quickly to the telephone cubicle over the other side of the bar.

"She'll be on the phone to the paper," Sheila suggested. "Asking them to pull the front page."

Ashley wasn't so sure. He fumbled for the mobile phone in his pocket, accessed messages without taking his eyes from Sheila Moor. He keyed the 4 button twice, the 3 button twice, the 5 button three times and finally the 7 button once. He felt for the send button and pressed it twice, knowing that the text would be sent to the last person he had sent a text to… John Markham.

This was big, it was colossal. Sheila continued, her voice a little slurred now. Dearblah returned to the table, her face slightly flushed. Ashley half expected her to take out a pencil and notebook, but thankfully, she resisted the urge.

"Murdered poor old Frank Short, my husband and Stephen Kyle. I found Jacob's diaries just over two months ago. They were locked in the safe in our basement. They go back nearly thirty years and it took me nearly two weeks to read them. I found the key to the safe in the stupid little apron he wears for the meetings. It's attached by a little key ring and was hidden in a pocket. He was careless one night, came back half-pissed from the meeting and couldn't be bothered to put it away. I cleared up after him the next morning and as I picked it up, the key ring fell out. I racked my brain to figure out what the key was for.

"I was cleaning the basement when I noticed the old wall safe again. It had been there ever since we moved into the property over twenty years ago. Jacob had never let me see inside, said he didn't use it, said he didn't even know where the key was. I put two and two together and when he went out later that day I tried the key."

Dearblah sat quiet as a church mouse, fidgety and anxious, adrenalin coursing through her veins. This was a once in a lifetime story, a story most journalists would kill for – a story she had no intention of ever writing.

"At first I didn't pay much attention to them."

"The diaries?" Ashley asked.

"Yes. Jacob's diaries and every Keepers' meeting for the last four hundred and fifty years, every word detailed meticulously." She signalled to the barman. "Same again, Martin, a drink for our writer here and one for Debbie; one for yourself too." Dearblah leaned back in her chair. No real interest in the story, the story she already knew.

The barman raised a thumb in the direction of Sheila Moor and looked over to check the drinks on the table.

"At first I thought they were just manuals and the teachings of the Island Keepers. They seemed to detail the ceremonies, their beliefs and philosophies. All a bit boring, some dating back donkey's years. Then, as I flicked through them, I came to the present day. I noticed some names I recognised, the names of the wardens and, of course, Jacob was in there taking part in some of the ceremonies. I decided to start again and read them in chronological order from the beginning."

She acknowledged the barman as he placed the drinks on the table, waited until he was out of earshot before continuing. "And then every so often there was a heading."

"A heading?" asked Ashley.

"A heading," Sheila Moor repeated. She paused and looked up. "The Undesirables."

Ashley swore the blood in his veins froze as she spoke and almost instantly, the entire puzzle clicked into place.

"They might as well have changed the title to murder. At first I thought it was fantasy, it was like something out of the dark ages." She laughed, took a mouthful of gin. "I suppose it was the dark ages. Strangers. Always strangers. Strangers who'd somehow upset the equilibrium of the island or more importantly displeased one or two of the Keepers. It started over four hundred years back with a wife of one of the Keepers who'd been having an affair. The Keepers found out and reported back to the husband.

"They tarred and feathered the poor girl and paraded her through the streets near naked in a horse-drawn cart. She was humiliated and abused for nearly an hour; three times they took her around the island, a bigger crowd gathering each time as the news got around. Afterwards, her husband denounced her and told the jailers to do with her as they wished. They did just that. They weren't so explicit in those days. There were a lot of blanks in the diary, but it left little to the imagination what they did to the poor girl. The following day the husband accused her of being a witch and they took her out onto the causeway and hung her."

Sheila Moor's bottom lip trembled, but she bit hard and continued. Dearblah sat opposite. Ashley urged Sheila on mentally. He needn't have worried.

Jacob Moor's wife wanted this off her chest. She'd bottled it up for weeks, months, maybe longer, and as she'd read through his personal diaries, it had confirmed her suspicions that her husband had been taking his pleasure with another woman.

He'd always been highly sexed, but over the last few years his interest had waned. Or so she'd thought. She hadn't minded. Sex had always been a bit of a chore, even in the early days of their relationship and some of his requests had at times been unacceptable, she'd thought. But she'd done her duty on a regular basis.

"They murdered her. The Keepers banded together, plotted and accused and murdered her."

Sheila Moor took a deep breath, a tear rolled onto her cheek and she broke down, crying as she said, "And they haven't stopped killing since."

Dearblah stood up, went around the table and sat down beside Sheila. She placed an arm around her and Sheila Moor leaned into her and sobbed like a baby. The barman began to walk over, but Ashley waved him away.

Dearblah stroked her hair. Eventually, the sobbing subsided. Ashley sat motionless, unable to move, fearful of saying anything that would have Sheila Moor running from the room. They were treading on eggshells.

Ashley crossed his fingers under the table and spoke.

"Can you go on, Sheila? We need to know what happened, how many they have killed. You said they killed Frank. How did they kill him?"

Dearblah chipped in. "I think she's said enough. Let's—"

Ashley held up a hand, glared at the reporter.

Sheila Moor cleared her throat, reached for the glass of gin again and seemed to compose herself. She took a handkerchief from her handbag, dabbed at her eyes.

"I'm sorry. I know you must think I'm being stupid. After all it was four hundred years ago. I didn't even know the girl, but what she must have gone through was unimaginable."

She cleared her throat and spoke after a brief pause. "Humiliated in front of the town people, raped by two strangers, then publicly betrayed by her husband and killed. Heronly crime was to fall in love."

She blew her nose, looked across the table at Ashley. "The murders were few and far between, some fifty years apart. Nothing too unusual for those days. Life was cheap. Until that is—"

"Five years ago," Ashley interrupted, "when Jacob took over." Sheila Moor looked up at Ashley in astonishment. "You know about them?"

He looked across at Dearblah. "I suspected something wasn't right," he answered. "I scanned through the archives of the local rag. The statistics just didn't add up. But not until now did I have any real proof. Are the papers still in his safe?" Sheila Moor nodded.

"Five years ago, everything changed. Five years ago my husband became the all-powerful Worshipful Master of the Island Keepers and he's retained the position ever since." Ashley shook his head; the silence at the table was deafening. No wonder Jacob was so protective of his wife that day in thecafé. Did he suspect something? Had he discovered the diaries and papers had been disturbed?

"He hasn't a clue; he's down there poncing about in his finery."She laughed. "Jesus H Christ, if he only knew."

"Take me back five years," Ashley said. "Tell me what the diaries said."

Sheila Moor cleared her throat.

"Two brothers, first of all," she continued. "By all accounts, nasty characters. The writings suggested they'd got a hold of Claire Macbeth, tried to rape her but she'd escaped and managed to alert the Keepers. They were quite clever, really; they simply ran the two brothers out onto the causeway as the tide came in, made it look like an accident."

"But it was no accident, was it?" Sheila shook her head.

"No. The writings are very clear, the Keepers knew when they forced them across the causeway they would have no chance of survival. The Keepers are islanders. They know the tides like the back of their hand. And it happened the next year and the next, the crimes or so-called crimes getting pettier and pettier."

"Six murders in five years," Ashley stated. He looked across at Dearblah. "Isn't that right, Debbie? You wrote about the sixth murder, only he was just missing at the time. You knew all along; the poor bastard was washed up in Cleveland so it didn't make the papers here."

"But how should... how did I—"

"You knew when you penned the article he was dead. You slipped up, Debbie. You said he was a popular member of the community, said he was from Newcastle. Was, Debbie, not is. Your article said he was."

Sheila Moor glared at the reporter, all of a sudden regretting disclosing so much information. She reached into her handbag and pulled out a packet of cigarettes.

"A slip of the pen, David, that's all. It happens regularly to reporters."

Ashley wanted to tell her she was lying, have it out with her here and now and make the accusation he was so sure of. Sheila Moor spoke first. He decided to hold it for a little longer. "Do you mind?" she asked. "I gave up six years ago, but I simply had to buy a packet on the way here tonight."

Ashley shook his head. Sheila lit the cigarette and blew out a long, straight plume of smoke up towards the ceiling.

"He'd courted Claire, apparently got quite close to her and some of the Keepers objected. I mean, they would, wouldn't they? She takes part in the ceremonies. He'd made the mistake of telling someone in this very bar how much he thought of her. Another man in love, another crime in the eyes of the Keepers." Sheila flicked a long line of ash into the ashtray, continued with the story.

"They picked a fight with him. Two fishermen, not even Island Keepers. The Keepers plied them with beer and goaded them. The fracas spilled outside and the Keepers got involved. They battered the poor wretch and took him downstairs to the temple. It was then that Claire Macbeth rescued him."

"She did?" asked Ashley.

Sheila smiled, shook her head, took another drag on her cigarette and another mouthful of gin. She exhaled.

"It was a trap. She released him, helped him escape and persuaded the poor bastard he could run across the causeway in time."

No, thought Ashley, no. It couldn't be. That feeling again, the feeling Kate described as a teenager. The feeling of betrayal. He'd misjudged her. No, surely not.

"And then there was poor Frankie Short." She dabbed a tissue at the side of her eye, continued, "The poor old bugger had had enough, seen enough, he wanted out. He'd resigned his position only last week and threatened to go to the police."

Ashley thought back to his brief meeting with the old man. "It was in the diaries?"

Sheila nodded. "And more. Jacob and Stephen Kyle went to see him the night he was killed. They tried to assure him it was God's will. They went down the moral route, even re-enacted part of the ceremony there and then. Frank had said they'd gone too far with the last one. He was a good boy. Frank shared a few beers with him in the bar the night before he was killed." Ashley and Dearblah stared at Sheila Moor, unable to take their eyes from her. She looked up, blew another long plume of smoke high into the air.

"He told them to disband or he would go to the police. He insisted that the organisation cease right there and then. Jacob was the Master; he had the power to do it. It's written in the constitution."

She stubbed out the half-smoked cigarette in the ashtray. Her bottom lip trembled. "So, they killed him. They used his own bed sheets to tie around his neck, then pushed him through the window."

She breathed out long and hard.

"It's a bloody nightmare and what makes it worse is that my own husband seems to have been the major fucking influence." Her hand covered her mouth, she apologised. "I'm sorry. I don't think I've used that word in twenty years…"

She continued.

"It's there in black and white. At first, I thought it might be Jacob making it up but then I checked all the facts. It's true: my husband and his cronies are killers."

Sheila Moor talked on, smoked another three cigarettes. Ashley listened intently. Dearblah sat in silence. Just after 9.30, Sheila Moor explained her suspicions that her husband was having an affair and relayed the story about the private detective and the hidden camera.

A tear fell onto the table."I can't ever forgive him."

She took another tissue from her handbag and wiped at her eyes.

"What makes matters worse is that I know who he's been screwing and I've known the girl since childhood.

"Claire Macbeth," she whispered.

Ashley was speechless. An acrid, sour taste seeped into his mouth. No, he thought to himself. No.

Sheila Moor nodded. "We took her in as a fourteen-year-old when her father died. Gave her a roof over her head. I treated her no differently to my own son and this is how she repays me. I don't know what betrayal hurts me the most."

She stubbed out yet another barely smoked cigarette into the overladen ashtray.

"He's very persuasive though, my husband. Perhaps we shouldn't prejudge her. God knows what the poor bitch has gone through."

Just then, Ashley heard voices and the sounds of people climbing the stairs from the basement. A key rattled in the lock and the door opened. The Keepers made their way one by oneinto the almost deserted bar. Jacob Moor was the last to appear and Sheila Moor rose from the table. He walked across the room towards her… smiling.

Ashley was lost in his thoughts. He'd harboured feelings for Claire ever since he'd set eyes on her. Something had pulled at his heartstrings. She was beautiful, innocent-looking even, and mysterious. He thought this would end up so differently: he had contemplated an evening out or dinner somewhere. Now, once again, his love life, or rather lack of it, had crumbled like a child's sandcastle at high tide.

And now, in the cold light of day, Sheila Moor had revealed her for what she really was. So why, even now, could he not feel hatred for her? What was stopping him from despising this home-wrecker, this killer?

The story that had been relayed across the table that evening had been heart-stopping. A quite incredible almost unbelievable tale of an organisation playing judge, jury and executioner with people's lives. An organisation that went back centuries, an organisation all-powerful that had been killing for hundreds of years.

Sheila Moor had to be protected, and her evidence secured and handed over to the police. Would it stack up in a court of law? Every death had already been deemed accidental. What would it take to revive the investigations?

The diaries.

At least the diaries would reopen each case. And thoughts now of his worst nightmare. Tom had been killed. How would he break the news to Kate or would the news and conviction of Tom's tormentors bring final closure for her?

He was aware of Sheila Moor rising to her feet, taking a few steps towards her husband, who moved towards her with a slightly puzzled look on his face.

"Darling, what are you doing here? You don't normally—"

"I want a divorce, Jacob."

He stopped dead in his tracks. "You what… I don't—"

"A divorce, Jacob. It's simple enough. I'll spell it for you, shall I?" She had raised her voice a decibel or two. She looked around the room. She had everyone's attention, her husband was rooted to the spot.

"We'll start with adultery, shall we?" She forced a grin. "You've been screwing her." She pointed a finger at Claire Macbeth. "I have it on film. I hired a private detective to plant a surveillance camera in our bedroom."

Father Thompson stepped forward, took her by the arm. "I think you've said enough, Mrs Moor. There's a time and place, we really should—"

"Fuck you, Father, you're one of them."

Father Thompson's mouth fell to the floor. Before he could respond, she laid into them again.

"Murderers. You killed those poor boys. No matter whether or not you took a hand in the actual deaths. You all knew about every one of them."

Ashley couldn't speak. He didn't want to. He looked at Dearblah. Her cool, unemotional façade had slipped, her mouth had gaped open in shock at the spectacle she was witnessing.The congregated group of men stood shocked at the language pouring from the mouth of the wife of the Worshipful Master and not one of them had the nerve or the presence of mind to intervene.

And then Jacob Moor stepped forward. He took his right hand down to his left trouser pocket. Ashley thought the action strange. He looked his wife straight in the eye and, in a swift, well-timed movement, powered the back of his hand into her face, his ring connecting high on her cheekbone, splitting her face wide open. *His ring*, Ashley thought to himself, the mark on Tom Wilkinson's face, a *symbolic ring*.

She let out a muffled yelp and Ashley was momentarily aware of a spray of crimson liquid propelling across the room. As Sheila Moor hit the floor, Ashley leapt from his seat and sprang at Jacob Moor.

It was instinct. Pure and simple. He launched himself at the aggressor. It was for Tom Wilkinson, it was for Kate, it was for Sheila Moor who lay half-unconscious on the floor of the inn. But just as his clenched fist ranged within inches of Jacob Moor's face, the bodies were upon him. His head crashed into a table leg as the momentum of his attackers knocked him sideways. He lay gasping on the floor, his lungs crying out for oxygen, and he was aware of a deadweight sitting on top of him.

Claire Macbeth rushed forward, forcing herself between the gasping body on the floor and Jacob Moor.

"Leave him. Leave him," she cried out, joining the melee, scratching and kicking at the big man who was sitting on him. The man caught her leg in mid-air and yanked quickly, pulling her off balance. She crashed to the floor beside him, the air forced from her lungs.

"I'm sorry, David, really sorry, truly I am."

Ashley turned away, trying hard to hate the face he'd just looked at.

It was Sheila Moor who seized the moment, stunned the whole room into silence.

"I've called the police," she announced from the floor... almost in a whisper... but a whisper that deafened the wholeroom.

Her husband stuttered, "You've what?"

"The police, Jacob. I called them before I left the house. They'll be here within the hour."

"No," Jacob Moor begged. "No. Which police? Who, where?" She raised herself to her knees, the blood dripping from her nose onto the cold stone floor. The cavalry was coming. Ashley felt a warm glow building up inside. John Markham on his way and whoever it was, Sheila Moor had called.

"You're murderers."

She cast her eyes around the room that had fallen into a sinister silence. "Every single one of you."

She made eye contact with Claire Macbeth. "You too. You led them to their deaths, you tricked them."

Claire Macbeth shook her head, the tears rolling onto her cheeks, her mascara blending into a damp, blackening mire. And yet, each individual seemed to regain their composure at the mention of the police.

The big man who'd been sitting on Ashley stood up. He reached out an arm by way of an apology and lifted Ashley up. Ashley looked at his watch. The tide was clearing… not yet safe to cross, but within twenty minutes, it would be fine. It wasn't as if there was anywhere to run to. They'd meet the police crossing in the opposite direction. Their reaction made perfect sense.

Sheila Moor found her feet and flopped back into the seat, breathing hard. Jacob Moor walked towards the bar, waving away the concerns of his Brethren. Claire Macbeth was the last to regain her composure and, as she stood, she smoothed down her dress before making her way over to the toilet.

She returned within a few minutes, her eyes devoid of mascara but red and swollen. No one had uttered a word in her absence.

Jacob Moor had made a quick call on the public phone in a small cubicle between the entrance and the door to the kitchen. No one had heard what he'd said or who he'd called. He sat at the bar nursing a large whisky he'd poured himself. The young barman hadn't seemed to mind. It was the type of evening where money changing hands was irrelevant. Strangely, Jacob seemed to be smiling.

"It's over, Jacob," Claire said as she walked behind the bar. It was bizarre, Ashley thought to himself.

Even after everything that had happened, everything that had been said, Claire Macbeth returned almost zombie-like to her familiar position behind the bar. She looked at ease now; she looked different... at peace.

She began to pour a few drinks, placing them on the counter. They were quickly consumed. Gradually, the conversations resumed. Small pockets of conversations. The Island Keepers split into two or three groups. Claire Macbeth and Jacob Moor spoke together in whispers and Ashley consoled Sheila Moor, persuading her she'd done the right thing.

It was like a normal night at The Ship Inn on Holy Island. No one even considered leaving the premises.

The police arrived within half an hour, two uniforms and two suits. This event was big. It was huge for a small community like Holy Island. Ashley thought they could have spared a few more bodies.

He noticed the red-haired young policeman that had stood guard outside Frank Short's house. He gave him a nod as he made eye contact and the policeman reciprocated. Dearblah noticed him too, stood up and walked over to him.

The two suits made straight for Jacob Moor. Jacob engaged in conversation with them. Ashley watched and became aware of Jacob Moor pointing at certain individuals around the room: his wife, Dearblah and, if he wasn't mistaken, Ashley himself.

He began to feel claustrophobic, began to get a strange, uncomfortable feeling. Nevertheless, he felt compelled to talk tothe policemen; Jacob Moor had the gift of the gab, God knows what he was telling them.

Ashley would put his oar in, tell them what he knew, help them out a little with the beginning of their investigation.

Tam Dalgleish would help too and so would Holy John. It was time to make that call.

He stood up, made his apologies to Sheila Moor who still sat as if in a trance. He wasn't even sure if she'd heard what he'd said. He walked over to where Dearblah stood with the young policeman and the two suits.

Chief Inspector Roddam had received a phone call barely ten minutes after Berwick Police had received the call from Sheila Moor. The allegations she'd made were jaw-dropping. Roddam had gone to his garage immediately and, as he started the engine, he'd connected his hands-free mobile to the holder fixed onto the centre console.

He located John Markham's number and pressed call. "John, it's me."

John Markham had been enjoying a quiet beer in the police club at Market Street with one or two of his colleagues. Enjoying probably wasn't the right word but it was a quiet night, quiet because John Markham had hardly uttered a word all evening. He'd been that way ever since Roddam had delivered the news about Frank Short.

He'd known Frank Short for as long as he could remember. His mother's eldest brother had looked after young John Markham as if he'd been one of his own. The memories were long and sweet. He remembered the long hot days at the village bowling club where Frank was a member. The summers seemed so much better then and the old uncle and the young boy would sit for hours talking about anything and nothing.

He had never tired of Uncle Frank's stories about the war or his general take on life. As John Markham entered his teenage years his pals ridiculed him about the amount of hours he spent with *auld Frank.* They'd organise day trips to Newcastle or Berwick or fishing excursions to the Farne Isles and, of course, his pals had started to take an interest in the fairer sex. John Markham was as happy as Larry sitting at the bowling club with his uncle.

He couldn't explain it. Frank had an aura, he was a character. It was Frank who'd first introduced him to the philosophy of theIsland Keepers. He'd go on about what an honourable noble organisation it was, founded in ancient times with a strong religious background. He remembered the look of pride on Uncle Frank's face as he oversaw John Markham's initiation ceremony into the Island Keepers. He recalled the face he would never see again.

Only, in the last few years, Frank hadn't attended many meetings. One or two, perhaps an AGM. When John Markham pressed him, he'd simply said he was getting too old, but it was clear he'd become a little disillusioned. John Markham sighed. He was sure to get a good send-off next week. He laughed inwardly; the islanders always did like a good funeral, particularly the Brotherhood. The Brotherhood would do him proud.

Chief Superintendent Roddam interrupted his thoughts."There's been a bit of trouble on the island."

"I know. I got a text from Ashley Clarke. He's up there."

"I'll tell you all about it when I pick you up. We'll have to go. It needs sorting."

"We're going up there now?"

"Yes, where are you?"

John Markham took a long drink from his pint glass. Trouble, he thought. What could be happening up there now? Two days ago a suicide, his own dear uncle, now trouble. He drained his glass. Pretty big trouble, he thought to himself if Roddam had been summonsed.

Ashley stood opposite Dearblah. She spoke directly to the policeman.

"This is David Fox, Stuart, the American author." She reached for the policeman's hand. "This is my boyfriend, Stuart Mackie." Ashley frowned. She hadn't mentioned that when he'd been standing outside Frank Short's door yesterday.

"Your boyfriend… you never—"

"Mentioned it, no. I suppose I should have said." She smiled. "He's also an Island Keeper, Senior Deacon at the Berwick Lodge. Should have mentioned that too, I suppose."

Her smile said it all. Suddenly, it all fell into place.

Jacob Moor and Stephen Kyle walked across and stood on either side of the suits.

Dearblah continued.

"But then again, Mr Fox, you never mentioned that you were an impostor, did you."

For a second Ashley was stuck for words. He looked over the reporter's shoulder, caught the stare of Sheila Moor who was listening in to the conversation. He noticed the puzzled look on her face.

Jacob Moor didn't look at all confused as he spoke. Jacob Moor walked around the assembled group with an air of confidence. "We set you up with Debbie here." He placed a hand on the journalist's shoulder.

"She did a good job."

"Not that good," Ashley retorted. "I guessed she was in the mix too, somehow involved with the Keepers. I read her article about Tom Wilkinson's disappearance. She slipped up, not once, but twice in fact. I'm surprised the editor didn't pick up on it. At the time she penned the article, Tom had simply disappeared. No one knew he was dead at that moment in time except those that had killed him."

Dearblah tilted her head, waited for him to continue.

"Twice in the article, she referred to Tom in the past tense. He was from Newcastle upon Tyne she wrote, not is – was. And later on in the article, she did it again."

Jacob interrupted. "Now who's the detective, Mr Clarke?" He continued. "We needed to know how much you knew." He smiled confidently, looked around the room and placed a hand on Ashley's shoulder.

"Ladies and gentlemen, this is not an American author but a bitter and twisted ex-policeman called Ashley Clarke. An ex-policeman who intended to bring our noble organisation to its knees."

Not once in all the years undercover for the police had he ever been 'outed'. It was a feeling he didn't like. A feeling of impending doom washed over him, a feeling that rendered him speechless.

"When Debbie found out that the American author actually had an American accent, you were rumbled. Of course we had suspected as much with all the questions you'd been asking. It just didn't make any sense, didn't ring true. We took a photograph of you when you were poking around the village, blew it up on the computer and e-mailed it to one of our brethren in Northumbria Police. Your disguise was quite goodbut I'm afraid a good friend of yours in Newcastle studied it in detail and you were found out: John Roddam, an old colleague, Chief Superintendent Roddam."

Ashley cringed; that name on the headstone, an island name, it clicked somewhere in the dark recesses of his mind, Roddam, a Keeper. And it made sense: the inquest and the barriers he'd put up personally to stall the investigation.

Jacob grinned. "We have friends in high places, Mr Clarke… our Brothers are everywhere. God is good, the sun shines on the righteous. The Brotherhood comes before everything, Mr Clarke. The Good Lord always looks down on us; tonight has proved that yet again."

"Amen," said Father Thompson, his eyes raised upwards.

"It was me that took the phone call from Mrs Moor," one of the policeman explained. "The great architect of the universe put that call through to me, Mr Clarke… the big man… God… whatever you wish to call him. Of all the people that could have picked up the phone tonight, it was a Brother of the island that Mrs Moor blurted out her story to."

The policeman smiled. "The all-seeing eye, the supreme being." Jacob Moor laughed. "Ironic, isn't it?" He walked slowly over to his wife. "Why did you have to interfere, my dear?"

Sheila Moor was visibly trembling. Jacob Moor stood inches from her. He raised a hand and caressed his wife's swollen cheek. The mark from the ring was now clearly evident. A tear trickled down her face.

Sheila Moor hadn't wanted to believe what she'd found in her husband's safe. Even when she'd informed the police at Berwick exactly what she'd stumbled on, there was a part of her that sincerely believed it was all made up. And even when she'd blurted it out to Dearblah and the American author that was now actually an ex-policeman working undercover, she wasn't one hundred per cent convinced. She was confused. She had grasped at a tiny piece of something that told her it was too far-fetched to have ever happened.

But now she knew.

Her husband had always placed the Brotherhood first, always put an evening with the Keepers above all else: anniversaries, birthdays, whatever. Even their annual vacations twice yearly had to be arranged around his precious boys' club and of course, church, every Sunday, without fail and a special greeting and a dodgy handshake from Father Thompson.

Only it wasn't just a boys' club, was it. She knew that now. The policemen standing in the room. All Brothers. Dearblah O'Hanlan, one of them, it was clear that she'd been indoctrinated too.

She gazed at the barman, young Martin Dixon. His father, Godfrey, a Keeper, and his father before him. It was only a matter of time before young Martin came of age and followedin the family's traditional footsteps.

And Claire Macbeth. She'd even been down to the temple with them, taking part in the ancient ceremony, re-enacting the rape scene from three hundred years ago.

Jacob Moor pulled his hand away from his wife's cheek, turned to Ashley

"It's all true, Mr Clarke." He cast an arm out in front of him, moved it from left to right. "All Brothers." He turned to face Claire then Dearblah. "And not forgetting our wonderful Sisters too."

Ashley looked at the reporter. "The original story. It didn't ever exist, did it?"

"All made up, there wasn't one," she replied. "It's amazing what copy and paste can do on a computer keyboard. You took the hook like a starving mackerel and now I'm afraid the barb is well and truly stuck fast."

The policeman placed an arm around his fiancée and they both laughed at her analogy of Ashley's predicament.

# Chapter 22

Tam Dalgleish hadn't been surprised at the ex-policeman's revelation. Okay, so it had been a bit dramatic, but a surprise… no.

His youngest son had been working. Working at his chosen profession, and a couple of things just didn't add up.

Tam had tried knocking Gordon onto the straight and narrow, latterly by allowing him to manage a small engineering factory that Tam had invested in. It was merely a front, a way to turn dirty money into clean, and to pay a token amount of tax, *to be legitimate*. And yet, Tam had to admit he'd felt good taking half a dozen boys from the dole queue. They'd been boys like he had been all those years back, born on the wrong side of the tracks. He'd paid them a decent wage, no need to thieve and rob now and although one or two inevitably still would, Tam still felt a degree of pride in turning an insignificant number of lives around.

The factory had been losing over £5,000 per month before Gordy took over but it didn't matter as it would be propped up by one or two of Big Tam's more profitable businesses. Tam hadn't expected the factory to ever make money, that's not what it was there for, but, gradually, by accident, almost, Gordon had turned it around.

He remembered the day with clarity. He'd visited the factory as usual on the last day of the month. He noticed immediately, and for the first time, that every single machine had been in use and this time the kids weren't playing with bits of metal and steel. They were… working. Grafting like fuck they were, and the hairs on Big Tam's neck stood on end. Gordon had been in his office, on the phone to some company or other about an order. He'd thrown the monthly cash injection in an envelope onto his son's desk. It would replenish the bank account and help towards the wages.

Gordy had grinned. "Dinnae need it, Dad," he'd said. "The bank account is in credit." And then, "We've more orders than we can handle. I'll need two more lads and possibly someone to help me in the office."

Big Tam was astounded. He'd never given the boy any credit, thought he'd been successful by muscling his way around and living on his father's reputation. He was a businessman, a natural. For the first time in Big Tam's life, he felt a different kind of pride in one of his sons.

But thieving was in his blood. It had been bred into him. Every few weeks, he would take a phone call and be off. The phonecall that would ultimately end in his death had come from Newcastle. A bent shop assistant had kept the credit card from a particularly stressed woman in a Newcastle department store. He should have handed it back with her receipt but this time she only got the receipt. He picked the clientele carefully, always someone in a rush and if on the odd occasion they remembered and asked for the card, he'd slap his forehead and act dumb.

The shop assistant reckoned it would be at least two or three days before the lady noticed the card missing.

Two or three days for Gordy to fill his boots. And he'd done just that the whole day in Newcastle city centre, then over to the Metro Centre in Gateshead that evening.

He'd been tired as he noticed the signpost to Holy Island. He'd passed it a hundred times and always wanted to see what it was like. He telephoned his dad, said he would leave early the next morning, be in the factory about elevenish.

He'd booked in at The Ship Inn and thought it would be a nice way to end his lucrative little excursion. A small hotel's bedrooms were notoriously easy to get into; he may be able to pick up a little extra, a little icing on the cake.

Tam Dalgleish had killed him. He held himself responsible. He'd introduced him to thieving at six or seven years of age, his small son helping with the shoplifting trips. It was in his blood… it was in Big Tam's blood… and his father before him.

But for all that, Gordon was professional, never touched a drop of alcohol when he was *working*. It made no sense. The coroner's report said he had a high level of alcohol in his body. Not Gordy, he wouldn't do it. Nor would he have abandoned a car full of videos, DVD players, camcorders, iPods and power tools that the police found in the boot of the stolen car adjacent to The Ship Inn.

Big Tam picked up his mobile and the scrap of paper with the telephone number in Luton. He wiped a tear from his eye and began to key in the number.

They'd been led down the stairs and through the temple of the Island Keepers. In the centre of the room was a highly polished stone crypt four feet in height, surrounded by candles. Thirteen ornamental highly jewelled swords hung above it, suspended from a large silver square and compass attached by almost invisible wires from the ceiling. Jacob Moor stopped the entourage as they reached the centre of the room. He turnedto Ashley and to his visibly shaken wife.

"This is our temple, in case you haven't guessed. It's here where we carry out the ancient ceremonies, ceremonies devised from the teachings of the ancient Egyptians and the workings of King Solomon's temple."

"So why worship St Cuthbert? He didn't appear till much later. Why not worship the ancient Sphinx or a pyramid or the sun?"

Jacob Moor walked slowly around the crypt. His fellow Brothers stood in silence… in awe as he continued.

"We worship only one thing, Mr Clarke… the Supreme Being. St Cuthbert was a sign, a gesture by God to show how special the island was. We remember him for what he was, but we only worship the Supreme Being. God sent a saint to us, Mr Clarke, a saint. Can you imagine that?"

He nodded in the direction of Father Thompson. "An island the size of this and the Good Lord sent us a saint." Jacob Moor looked skywards and made the sign of the cross. He continued, "And on his death and years after, yet another sign. The incorrupt body."

Ashley recalled the lesson given by Claire Macbeth in the Priory.

Jacob Moor smiled. "The Brotherhood began shortly after St Cuthbert's death."

Jacob Moor stood directly in front of Ashley and Sheila Moor and spoke in a hushed tone. He spoke to his wife.

"You came close, dear. You came close to destroying an organisation that has survived for over a thousand years. We've survived the might of the Roman Catholic Church, the medieval inquisitions, the wars of independence and even the damn Vikings."

"Language, Mr Moor," retorted Father Thompson. "Remember where you are, Brother."

Jacob Moor doffed an imaginary cap towards Father Thompson.

"Sorry, Father. I do apologise." He stared at Ashley. "And you, Mr Clarke. Your little subterfuge as an American novelist didn't quite work, did it?"

"You're sure about that, Jacob, are you?"

Jacob bit back straightaway. "Of course I am. You've been caught out, captured by the Brotherhood, an organisation far more powerful than you can imagine."

"But what damage have I done, Jacob? Who else knows what I've been up to?"

Jacob Moor laughed, turned away and walked back towardsthe crypt "Oh, I see what you're trying to do,

Mr Clarke. You're trying to sow a seed of doubt in my head." He turned aroundand stared back at Ashley. "It won't work. You haven't been anywhere since my dear wife here delivered her dramatics. You haven't made so much as a phone call. There's only one person who knows you're here and she will be taken care of very soon."

Ashley froze. No. Not Kate Wilkinson. How could they know? "We managed to trace the number of the lady in Darras Hall, the mother of our last victim. We've been monitoring all your calls made from the public phone box, Mr Clarke. We have the most sophisticated equipment money can buy at our disposal and, of course, the help of our very own boys in blue on how to use it."

Jacob took a step forward. "You're working for her, aren't you."

"I'm working for no one. I wanted to find out what happened to her son. He was a friend."

Jacob ignored him. "Mrs Wilkinson will arrive here first thing tomorrow. We made a phone call, told her you'd been hurt in an accident and requested the pleasure of her company."

A sick nauseous feeling washed over Ashley. What a mess. Now Kate Wilkinson entering the lion's den. What would they do with her? What would they do with him, and what would Jacob Moor do with his wife, and what the hell was keeping John Markham?"

Jacob Moor answered his questions as if by some sort of divine intervention.

"You'll all have to die, of course." He looked at his wife who was vigorously shaking her head.

"Yes, dear… you too. You'll be pleased to know that Brother Kyle has recovered the contents of my safe. They've been placed somewhere else now, so you see, my dear, once you two and Mrs Wilkinson are taken out of the equation, the secret is buried once again."

"The police in Newcastle, they're aware of the killings on the island. If another three people disappear, they'll be here in a flash."

Jacob moved forward, his nose now inches from Ashley's face. "The police in Newcastle." He guffawed, a long, loud laugh almost like a cackle. His Brothers smiled too; Father Thompson broke out into a giggle.

"The police, Mr Clarke. I think I've a little surprise for you."

Roddam and Markham walked into The Ship Inn and were greeted by Jacob Moor.

"The Berwick lads telephoned. How bad is it?" asked Roddam.

Jacob Moor held up two hands. "Relax, Brothers, it's taken care of."

Roddam couldn't relax; he was thinking of the consequences had a non-Brother intercepted that call at Berwick. John Markham was still grieving. He was home now, home on the island, Uncle Frank's island.

Jacob Moor seemed to sense it. He stepped forward said how sorry he was about John's uncle and embraced him. John appreciated the gesture and hugged him tightly, trying hard to suppress the tears. Jacob's hand moved to the back of John Markham's head.

"He was a good man, John. One of the best."

They parted, Markham spoke. "But suicide, Jacob? I just couldn't believe it when I heard it was suicide."

Jacob nodded, then shook his head.

"I know, John, it's hard to believe. I know he'd been a bit depressed lately, but I just put it down to the bad weather. We've had a terrible time of it lately and of course the island always gets battered worse than the mainland."

"You thought he was depressed?"

"Yes. You must have noticed it too."

John Markham nodded. "A little, I suppose."

"Where's Clarke?" asked Roddam.

Jacob Moor frowned. "Down in the basement with Sheila." Roddam had been told that it had been Jacob's wife who'd made the call. Sheila Moor had nearly brought the ancient organisation down and for a second, he hated her. He almost hated Jacob Moor for failing to keep his own house in order. Roddam placed a hand on Jacob Moor's shoulder, squeezed gently.

"They'll both have to die, Jacob. You do realise that?"

Jacob Moor pulled a seat from the table and flopped down into it. He stroked at an eyebrow and massaged the side of his temple. He said nothing but looked up at Roddam and Markham.

"The Brotherhood comes before all else, Jacob. She could have brought us down."

It was only a slight nod, but a nod nevertheless. Roddam sighed inwardly with relief. Jacob Moor had been the mainstay of the Brotherhood in recent years. He'd devoted his life to it and had never shirked his responsibility when it came to important decisions.

He'd rooted out more undesirables in recent years and had covered the tracks of the Brotherhood well. There'd been a few murmurs of concern among the Brothers in recent years, but Jacobs's powerful and hypnotic oration had won the Brothers over, time and time again.

"I know, John, I know. The only thing that concerns me is how we do it."

John Markham joined in the conversation. "The causeway, surely, that's the only way."

"Almost like a tradition." Jacob Moor smiled.

The smile warmed Roddam's heart. He should never have doubted his Worshipful Master; all along he'd been planning the executions not debating whether or not they should take place.

John Markham spoke. "Two more deaths off the causeway might just raise a few eyebrows."

Jacob Moor was thinking about his wife's phobia of the sea. It seemed crazy that a woman who'd lived on an island all her life could be so terrified of something she looked at every single day of her life.

Roddam nodded. "You're right. We'll need to call an emergency meeting, get our heads together and work something out."

Jacob Moor laughed, looked at the two policeman. "We've six coppers here. I'm sure you lot can think of something."

John Markham looked Jacob Moor straight in the eyes, couldn't quite believe he could be so cold and calm when talking about the murder of his wife. What had happened to the family values preached by the Brotherhood for so long? Jacob Moor should be distraught, inconsolable; instead, he was sitting there smiling as if it was some sort of bizarre entertainment.

This couldn't be happening. Ashley sat on the cold floor, held around the wrists by two long rusty chains. Sheila Moor sat beside him. Her face was streaked with tears. God knows what was going on in her head.

In less than a week she'd found out her husband was an adulterer, a murderer and, worst of all, had given the command to his Brothers to chain his own wife up.

Ashley looked around as his eyes gradually grew accustomed to the poor light. Something reminded him of a Hammer House of Horror movie. The cell, or was it a dungeon, made to look exactly like that, a dungeon within the bowels of Dracula's castle? The only light came from two candles on top of two stone pillars in the centre of the cell.

The walls were adorned with painted symbols: globes, pyramids, squares, triangles, compasses and protractors. On the floor of the room, almost the entire length of the cell, lay a plush heavy-duty rug. It had been cut in the unmistakeable shape of a coffin with a set square, a mallet and a compass beautifully embroidered in gold thread. At the top of the coffin, where the deceased's head would lie, a skull and crossbones had been stitched in heavy black wool.

Sheila Moor hadn't spoken since her husband's address in the temple. Ashley looked across to where she sat. She stared into space, dejected, rejected… a defeated woman. He'd tried speaking to her a few times since they'd been chained up, but she'd simply stared ahead, zombie-like, looking into space.

It had been five minutes since his last attempt. She spoke in a whisper. "They won't get away with it, you know."

Ashley breathed a sigh of relief; she was still in the land of the living. Broken, yes, undoubtedly, but still there in spirit. Before Ashley could answer, she spoke again.

"They'll throw us into the sea like the rest of them. Take us away in a boat if necessary and concoct some lame story that the police and the coroner will accept. They'll accept it because they'll have chosen the professionals from within their own ranks."

Ashley was aware of exactly what Sheila Moor was saying. "The police are riddled with them and they have doctors and coroners and judges, magistrates, the lot. They'll cover it up just like they did with Frank's suicide."

Ashley was deep in thought. Those documents in the safe were dynamite if only Sheila Moor had hidden them or even put them in the post to someone in authority.

Sheila Moor looked across, smiled. Or was it a frown?

"I know what you're thinking, Ashley: if only we could get those papers off the island." She shook her head. "I'm sorry. A big mistake on my behalf, I admit, but you have to understand I just didn't think it were all possible." She continued, "It lists every Keepers' Lodge in the UK and every member. Thousands of them, maybe tens of thousands."

"So you're saying we're pretty well fucked then?"

Ashley and Sheila Moor laughed together. A much-needed injection of humour at an hour of desperation.

"They'll have moved the papers by now, though my guess is they'll still be on the island. They're funny that way: everything is here, the spiritual headquarters, so to speak."

"But it would be crazy to keep them here after everything that has—"

"But nobody knows what's happened," Sheila Moor interrupted. "The only two non-Brothers that know what's happened are you and me, Ashley, and we're pretty well fucked as you so eloquently put it. Look at us. We're shackled up like dogs in a locked dungeon twenty feet below ground. Who the hell's going to help us escape?"

Ashley had to admit it was looking fairly bleak. Where was John Markham? Surely he should be here by now. The evidence they now held between them and the pathologist and those papers: God knows where they were. Surely they could be located. The island wasn't that big. He was sure John would be here soon.

Sheila Moor was silent once more. She was contemplating… thinking.

She was thinking that there was no way on earth that they were going to get her into the sea. The thought terrified her. The phobia had kicked in as a five-year-old walking on the beach with her father one winter's day.

Sheila remembered they'd been collecting firewood and sea coal washed up on the beach. The young girl had been throwing sticks into the sea as the waves washed in and out. Running down to chase them as far as she dared, then racing back up the beach as they came in again. She'd tripped.

She fell face first onto the sand and been enveloped in a freezing cold blanket of salt water. She'd managed to scramble back to her feet, but the natural incline of the beach and the pull of the waves had tipped her backwards into deeper water. The icy cold water of the North Sea had filled her nostrils and lungs as she fought against the hundreds of hands that were dragging her out to sea. Her clothes were cold and heavy, her red Wellington boots filled with water weighing her down. She'd gasped for oxygen as her small head came out of the sea momentarily as she tumbled and rolled. Still the invisible hands clawed and dragged her down, further out to sea. She'd opened her eyes to get her bearings and the salty water bit into the soft tissue like a thousand red-hot needles.

It was no good. She couldn't fight the hands any longer… too many… so cold.

Her father ran in waist-deep and grabbed at an ankle as it thrust out of the water. He'd pulled the unconscious child from the water and luckily a district nurse out walking her dog was able to revive her.

Sheila Moor had never so much as paddled in the sea ever since.

And – she wouldn't give them the pleasure of an easy cover-up.

John Markham heard the commotion first. Faint, but nevertheless screaming. A man screaming.

"Listen," he shouted as Roddam and Jacob Moor looked up from the table they were sitting at with the policemen, plotting and scheming.

“There it is again.”

Jacob Moor cupped his hand to his ear. “It’s coming from the basement; it sounds like our prisoner.”

Roddam grinned. “He’s freaked out, an ex-copper in a cell, their worst nightmare, he’s lost his head.”

“No, not Ashley Clarke. Something’s wrong,” John Markham announced as he made for the door that led down to the temple.

Another scream, louder, the word *help* and Ashley Clarke’s unmistakable panic-stricken cries.

John Markham took the stairs three at a time, sprinted through the temple and over to the cell door. He stared through the barred opening. Ashley Clarke stood in the corner of the room, pulling furiously at his shackled wrists. The skin had broken on both wrists and blood streaked his arms. The focus of his desperate attention sat motionless, less than four feet away.

Markham pulled at the cell door. It was locked. He turned and ran back through the temple and was met halfway by Jacob Moor, Stephen Kyle and Father Thompson, behind them the policeman, and, at the back, John Roddam.

“The key to the cell!” he screamed. “Where’s the fucking key?”

“My briefcase,” replied Jacob. “Upstairs, my briefcase.” John Markham didn’t hang around; he barged past the startled group and ran up the stairs into the bar.

Jacob Moor peered into the cell and watched the last few seconds of his wife’s life ebb away. Father Thompson had collapsed and two of the policemen were trying to revive him. In less than a minute John Markham had located the briefcase, cursed as he realised it had a combination lock and dashed back down through the temple and over to the cell door.

He screamed in panic. "The combination, Jacob. What's the combination?"

Jacob Moor grabbed the case from John Markham and for a second his mind went blank. He stared up at John Markham, oblivious to all around him. John Markham slapped him in the face.

"The combination, man! The combination."

Jacob Moor shook his head slowly and John Markham grabbed the case from him. He smashed the case against the corner of the stone wall. The leather-covered plywood split open instantly.He took the case in two hands and pulled it apart like cardboard. The brass key fell to the floor and John Roddam lunged at it, inserting it into the lock. In an instant, the cell door was flung open.

Nobody made a move towards Sheila Moor's lifeless body. It was too late.

Everyone knew instinctively.

The heavy chain that had held her for the last few hours of her life suspended her body from her delicate neck, her backside three inches from the cell floor. Her face was swollen, blue in colour, her tongue bloated and protruding from her mouth, her eyes almost forced from their sockets, bloodshot and enlarged, having been starved of oxygen for so long.

"Oh, my God," cried John Markham, as he sank to his knees. Ashley spoke in between the tears. "John … thank fuck… where have you been, for Christ's sake?"

John Markham didn't answer, didn't meet his ex-partner's eyes,couldn't meet his eyes and at that very moment the terrible truth dawned on Ashley Clarke.

John Roddam was thinking. This time, the suicide was genuine. But two suicides on Holy Island in less than a week? Someone somewhere would want some questions answered, that was for sure. John Roddam had a horrible, sickly feeling that he just couldn't shake off.

It was déjà vu for Ashley Clarke.

Sheila Moor's death had brought it all back, nightmare after nightmare, throughout the hours of darkness. He thought he hadn't slept, but then again he must have; how else could his mind paint so vivid a picture?

The tramp outside the tube station waiting… wondering… questioning his judgement again and again.

July 7th 2005. The blasts were known as the 7/7 bombings, a series of coordinated terrorist bomb blasts that hit London's public transport system during the morning rush hour.

And Ashley might have prevented them.

Just before nine in the morning, the three bombs exploded within a minute of each other on three London Underground trains. Nearly an hour later, a fourth bomb on a bus in Tavistock Square.

Fifty-two commuters killed, seven hundred injured.

And the images, body parts strewn across the street… the Underground… and on buses. Lifeless corpses of young people… Always the young.

Students and young professionals with their life mapped out ahead of them. A life they would never see.

And the crystal-clear image of Sheila Moor wrapping the chain around her neck. He'd realised immediately what she was doing and he'd begged and pleaded with her to the point of tears for her to change her mind. She'd wrapped the chain around her neck twice, her right wrist barely able to move, as it seemed to be glued to the side of her face. She'd been propped up against the wall her legs bent, balancing on the balls of her feet. She snuggled her back flush against the wall then one by one stretched her legs out straight. She'd gasped as the chain pulled tight.

Ashley had screamed at her. He'd wanted to offer an alternative but couldn't think of any and as her brain was gradually starved of oxygen a ghostly smile crept across her face. Peaceful… at rest… no more deceit… lies… torture.

And as Ashley witnessed the gruesome spectacle, he wondered… just wondered if he could turn back the clock would he have done anything different… just like London.

A dream, Claire Macbeth with him in the hours of darkness talking softly and food and water and a glimmer of hope… explaining the facts, buckets of tears and begging forgiveness. A dream… only a dream.

John Markham sat in the cell as Ashley opened his eyes. It must be morning, he thought to himself, no natural light; he wasn't sure.

"Morning, Ash, sleep well?"

It was a stupid question. Ashley glared at his ex-colleague, his one-time friend.

"You too, Holy John, you're one of them."

John Markham sat on the far side of the twelve-foot by twelve-foot room as if wanting to maintain a safe distance between them. He nodded his head.

"Afraid so, Ashley, I'm afraid so. Initiated at twenty-one years of age, a family tradition."

"So you're a killer too."

John Markham sighed, raised himself up to his feet with an effort that suggested he'd been sitting in the same position for hours.

"I prefer to think of myself as an enforcer, Ashley, not so much a killer. I see nothing wrong with what we do ridding our island… his island… of the low lifes of this land. Society's gone too soft, Ashley. How many times have you done your job and got the bad guys to court only for a judge to give them a slap on the wrist and they're back on the streets before you can spit?"

Ashley's mouth was dry; he'd give anything for a hot drink and a toothbrush. He rolled his tongue round his mouth desperately trying to produce some saliva.

"We've evolved, John, we have a system. It may not be the best in the world but it works."

"No it doesn't, Ashley, it doesn't work. We've got murderers and child killers and paedophiles walking every street in every town in the land. It doesn't work."

"So your solution is to murder them, is that so?"

John Markham smiled. "An eye for an eye, a tooth for a tooth, the good book, Ashley, the greatest book ever written."

"Written by charlatans and fraudsters, John, thousands of years ago, just like the books on Greek mythology, Hinduism and Buddhism. It's all rubbish, John."

"No… it's not, Ashley."

"It is. Religion was an invention to control the people, keep them in check. The priests would tell them if they didn't follow the good book and the written word, they'd meet a fate worse than death. A good Catholic priest will instil the fear of the devil into a five-year-old child, tell him if he so much as farts on a Sunday, he'll end up in hell and be tortured with fire for eternity. The good book, John? Don't make me laugh."

"Don't listen to him, Brother."

Jacob Moor stood in the doorway of the cell, walked slowly towards John Markham. He placed an arm around his shoulders.

"Can't you see what he's trying to do, John? One voice in the wilderness, one man who claims he knows it all. Atheists, non- believers, John, the world is full of them."

"Thinkers, John," Ashley cried out. "People who take a look at religion and form their own viewpoint, people who view the scriptures for what they are… stories. They're no different from the stories about Norwegian trolls and flying horses and unicorns and fairies at the bottom of the garden, but you don't believe in them, do you?" Ashley continued. "But you believe that a figure in the image of a man with a big white beard sits on a cloud and sees everything that happens in the world and listens to every prayer that everyone utters in the world and grants their wishes. I spent fucking hours on my hands and knees, John, as a little kid petrified of the man."

"Ignore him, John. We know the truth, don't we?" Jacob squeezed hard. John Markham gazed childlike at him and smiled.

"Sounds too much like Santa Claus to me, John, a big man witha white beard giving the kids the presents they ask for, understanding every mother tongue of every land and every country in the world Do you still believe in Santa then, John? You sad bastard."

Jacob Moor took a step forward and aimed a kick in the ribsof Ashley Clarke. Ashley yelped like a stricken dog as the air was forced from his lungs.

"Blasphemer," Jacob screamed. "I'll not have that sort of thing under my roof."

Ashley broke out in a cold sweat, breathed in deeply several times.

John Markham stared at Jacob Moor, waited for him to continue. A pearl of wisdom… reassurance. This time Jacob Moor did not deliver a well-timed and thought-out reply. He did not deliver one of his marvellous hour-long speeches that John Markham had enjoyed so much over the years. Jacob Moor had the power to persuade.

Ashley took a deep breath, winced. "At least the ancient civilisations who worshipped the sun could actually see it every day. It actually existed. Tell me how many Christians have seen your god."

Jacob Moor turned to John Markham. "Ignore him, Brother. We have an emergency meeting in an hour's time at the temple." He looked at Ashley and smiled. "The main topic on the agenda is how we're going to dispose of him."

John Markham smiled almost hypnotic-like into the eyes of his Worshipful Master and the two Brothers left Ashley alone with his thoughts.

Everyone but everyone attended the most important meeting ever held in the temple of the Island Keepers in the basement of The Ship Inn. No apologies tonight. The thirteen current members of the council sat together quietly with the four Berwick policemen who had coordinated the cover-up.

They were welcomed without hesitation. They belonged to the Berwick and Tweedmouth branch of the Island Keepers and were attending as visitors. Jacob Moor would make a point of welcoming them at the beginning of his address.

The only person missing was Claire Macbeth. Jacob Moor had decided it wasn't necessary; he'd fill her in later on the decisions arrived at during the meeting.

This would be his most important performance ever. He'd worked on his speech through the long hours of darkness. The door to the Lodge closed quietly, a key turned and Jacob rose to his feet.

The chains biting into Ashley's wrists were unbearable. He'd convinced himself he'd torn the ligaments in both as he'd desperately tried to break free and stop Sheila Moor from hanging herself. He'd realised his task was hopeless, but the adrenalin had kicked in and he'd been unable to stop himself. He gazed down at the bruising beginning to discolour his hands either side of the chain and the congealed blood hardened around his palms and fingers.

A chorus of 'Things can only get better' played in his head.

Jacob motioned for Father Thompson to stand alongside him. Father Thompson stood nervously and walked around the perimeter of the floor. He positioned himself on the right-hand side of the Worshipful Master. *Unusual,* thought one or two of the Brothers as Father Thompson prepared to deliver his sermon.

"Brethren… I give you our chaplain, Father Thompson. Father Thompson will open the meeting in prayer."

Jacob Moor sat down and relaxed. It won't do any harm to warm the Brothers up with a little bit of God, he thought to himself as he concealed a smile behind the back of his steepled hands.

Father Thompson had been summoned to Jacob's house a little after two in the morning. He'd not long been sleeping but had got up and dressed without question and made the short walk from one side of the village to the other. He'd been honoured that the Worshipful Master had turned to him of all people in his hour of need. They'd prayed for a little while, then Jacob had explained what was needed in the emergency meeting later on in the day.

And Father Thompson had taken on board the enormity of what was happening and cherished his role in proceedings. He didn't let Jacob down. He delivered a passionate fifteen-minute address as instructed, tugging and tearing at the heartstrings of belief of every individual sitting before him.

He was in his element; why couldn't he feel so passionate in his normal Sunday address, an address that would be delivered almost parrot-fashion from the pulpit in the Priory? What was so different about today?

And as he delivered his final few words, it came to him. He was fighting for his religion. If necessary, he would be a martyr for the cause.

Jacob Moor had been proud of his chaplain and looked on with a strange respect as the man marched proudly around the perimeter of the room to a carefully orchestrated, dignified round of applause.

"Brothers… a history lesson," Jacob began. "Let me take you back to when our order was first founded. Founded in honour of a saint very dear to us, a saint sent by the Good Lord to look over us and honour us by choosing to reside in our very midst." It was a powerful start; Father Thompson had primed them well.

"We have been sent many challenges during our brief life on God's wonderful planet, but none as great as the one we have faced over the last few days. Brothers, the council assembled here today will go down in Island Keepers folklore… you will be written about for centuries to come."

John Markham sat in the temple, thinking to himself that perhaps Jacob's speeches were getting a little repetitive. He'd heard them since his first visit to the temple and never failed to have been stirred by Jacob's oration, his passion, and remembered many an occasion when the hairs on the back of his neck had stood on end.

"Last night was one of the bleakest I can remember in all the years I have dedicated to the cause." Jacob paused, took out a handkerchief and wiped at the corner of his eye.

"Last night, Brothers, I helped dig the grave of my very own dear wife." He pointed to the crypt. "Right there, Brothers, we moved the symbol of our dear saint and dug a hole with our own bare hands."

Jacob Moor seemed to teeter on the brink. He held out his hands and supported himself against the podium. "I could not shirk my responsibilities, Brethren. It had to be me." He seemed to steady himself a little. "But with the help of my fellow Brothers, we completed the grisly task."

He leaned forward. "I thank every one of my Brothers who helped me in the early hours of this morning." He wiped at another tear. "It was the hardest thing I have ever done in my life… but… Brothers… I did not evade my responsibilities. The Lord sent me a message in his infamous wisdom; he sent me a solution to the problem my dear wife posed."

He gazed around the room, slowly and deliberately, once more commanding the attention of the assembly.

"Brothers… I must ask you all to prepare to lie in the name of the Island Keepers. You are all aware how my dear wife met her death last night, not a death that can be easily explained away, a death that leaves too many loose ends."

He turned to the chaplain. They exchanged a smile before he continued.

"The dear Lord came to me last night in a dream. I was in torment, trying to snatch a few hours after…"

Jacob Moor gazed down at the crypt and the disturbed dust and dirt, swallowed hard and wiped at an imaginary tear before continuing.

"I hardly slept at all but, when I did awaken, the solution was clear as a bell. The Lord gave me that solution: the story which we must share with the island and the outside world." Another carefully orchestrated, deliberate pause as Jacob Moor reached for a glass of water. He took a mouthful, licked at his lips.

"From this moment in time, as far as everyone here is concerned, my wife has left me. You must spread the word in the village and the mainland." He reached into the inside pocket of his jacket, held an envelope aloft. "She was good enough to leave me a note, typed it on her very own computer."

He opened the envelope and pulled out a one-page document, gazed down towards it. "It's clear enough, Brethren. I've met someone else, she explains; do not try to find me, she writes. Brothers, I must live with the shame forever; it's theLord's will for the mistakes I've made along life's path, but I will do so to protect our ancient order."

The Brothers looked up in awe at their Worshipful Master. He had made the supreme sacrifice. John Markham knew what was coming next.

"I must ask you, Brothers, to do likewise and to be strong at this critical moment. None of us must shirk our responsibilities, grave as they might seem."

John Roddam was nodding his head; the chaplain's bottom lip trembled as he looked around, meeting the gaze of his fellow Brethren. They were united, united for the cause.

Ashley had heard the faint applause drift into his cell.

He heard a noise, looked up. Father Thompson opened the door to the cell, a personification of confidence. He locked the door behind him and slipped the key into his trouser pocket. He made the sign of the cross, looked upwards and took a step forward.

"How are you, my son?"

"Save your breath, Father. I'm no son of yours."

Father Thompson pulled out a chair from the far side of the cell and sat down.

"Be it so, friend, but I must do my duty."

"Your duty?"

"I've come to pray for you, Mr Clarke."

"Like I said, Father, save your breath."

Father Thompson bowed his head and sat in silence with his eyes closed. Ashley wished his chains could stretch the six-foot gap between him and the key in the chaplain's pocket. It was useless.

There was no escape from the chains and every time he was left alone, the heavy door to the cell was locked too. And he'd bet his last penny a Keepers' delegation stood guard in the bar upstairs. It was ironic: his only glimmer of hope lay with a Glasgow gangster and it was just that... a glimmer, a long shot. Oh, how he wished he'd confided in Jordan Cameron.

Ashley looked at the chaplain sitting in an almost trance-like state. Ashley smiled.

"FATHER!" he screamed at the top of his voice. Father Thompson almost jumped out of his skin, leapt a foot into the air as his seat spun out sideways and he landed in a heap on the cold floor. Ashley lay in a crumpled heap, laughing for all he was worth. The tears ran down the side of his face at the success of his prank.

"You stupid bastard," the chaplain sneered from the cell floor. "Whoooooaa… Father, be careful. Your big man won't approve of language like that."

"You're not normal, you're not. Just what do you get out of that, the predicament you're in? How on earth can you laugh and joke?"

"I always laugh, Father. Remember, the sun will still shine tomorrow."

Father Thompson raised himself to his feet, dusted down his cassock and looked daggers across the room.

"That may be so, Mr Clarke, but when it does, you won't be seeing it."

Father Thompson felt in control now as he stood above the prisoner of the Brotherhood. He was surprised but pleased how his words had ended the big joke.

"You're a condemned man, Mr Clarke, that's what I'm here to tell you. I've come to pray for your soul." He grinned. "So let's try to get serious."

Ashley despised the man of the cloth standing over him. "Let's get serious then, Father, shall we?" he growled. "Tell me about Claire Macbeth."

Father Thompson looked on. "In what way, Mr Clarke?"

"Tell me how she came to you as a fourteen-year-old and confessed that she'd shared in the pleasures of the flesh with Jacob Moor. She begged for help. Tell me, Father, what it was you did to help her."

Father Thompson counter-attacked quickly. "The confession box isn't about help, Mr Clarke, you should realise that. We have a duty to our Brothers and Sisters not to disclose anything—"

"Not Brothers and Sisters, Father, a child. A fourteen-year-old child raped by the man she called her uncle, a man she trusted, a man who abused her. Why didn't you stop it?"

"A priest has no power to stop such things, Mr Clarke, you know that. What's said in confession cannot be taken outside of the church."

Ashley raised himself to his feet, walked towards Father Thompson and cursed as his chains stopped him two feet from the nervous-looking chaplain.

"You mean to tell me, Father, your own sense of decency wouldn't allow you to talk to Jacob Moor, tell him you knew what was happening, tell him to stop, remind him of his morals, the code and ethics of your so-called noble organisation."

"I've told you, Mr Clarke, I—"

"A fourteen-year-old child, Father – raped and brutalised and you stood back and condoned it."

"No, I didn't, I couldn't, I—"

"You're a man of the cloth, Father, you're all powerful, a law unto yourself, and what about the murders? What did you do when she begged you to help her, begged you to stop what was happening, begged you to help her escape the hell that Jacob Moor and his cronies had imprisoned her in?"

Father Thompson stood motionless, shaking his head. "It wasn't like that."

"Wasn't like what, Father? You sat and watched in the temple as they paraded her around naked, re-enacting an event from three hundred years ago. She told me last night right here in the cell as she cried like a baby."

"I tried… I really did. I tried to tell them it was wrong."

"Tried, my arse, Father, you sat with your right hand twitching under your cassock while your Worshipful Master used and abused the poor girl."

Father Thompson fumbled in his pocket for the key to the cell door, desperate for a means of escape.

"I wanted to hold her, Father, but she wouldn't come near me, couldn't bear the touch of a man."

Father Thompson's hands were sweating.

"Murder, Father. Thou shalt not kill. What happened to that one, eh? Thou shalt not steal. You helped steal a young girl's innocence. Just how many commandments are you going to break? You use the commandments when it suits you; you're a bunch of hypocrites, the lot of you."

"Silence, do you hear? I won't listen to this."

"Thou shalt not kill, Father, thou shalt not kill."

"Undesirables." The chaplain bit back, raising his voice. "They were undesirables; the Bible mentions them more than once."

"Murderer, Father; you had a hand in the murder of all those people."

"Smite them. Kill the undesirables," the chaplain shouted as he walked towards the door.

"You killed innocents, Father; you killed my best friend."

"He was peddling evil."

"Liar, Father, you're a liar. He never touched a drug in his life. It was made up. Jacob Moor made it up, accused him, just to give you an excuse to get rid of him." Ashley smirked. "Not unlike Pontius Pilate with your beloved Lord, Father. He sanctioned Jesus's crucifixion; without just cause, you did the same. You're a murderer."

The chaplain covered his ears. "I won't listen. I won't listen to this."

"Then fuck off out of here then. Go on, fuck right off out of here, coming to pray for me as if somebody's given you the right to judge me. When will you be judged, Father, or has it already happened? My guess is you're fucked, Father. Murder, theft, child abuse, sodomy, rape: how many more crimes do you want me to list? How many crimes have you been a part of? You're going to Hell – you're a Judas, Father. You've betrayed a child, betrayed the young men that you helped send to their deaths… you're going to burn, Father… burn in Hell."

At last, Father Thompson located the key to the cell door. Breathing hard now, he turned away from his accuser. A tear fell onto his cheek. His palms were sweating. The key slipped from his grip and rattled onto the stone floor. The abuse behind him continued unabated. He fumbled for it again and gripped it firm, managed to insert it into the lock. As the door opened, he felt as if a wave of life-saving oxygen had washed over him.

Ashley had lost track of the time. There were no outside windows in the small cell and the hours of daylight and darkness had blended into one. Claire Macbeth had brought him some sandwiches and a hot drink but had said nothing as she placed the tray just within his reach. He'd noticed that her eyes were bloodshot and her cheeks streaked with tears. When had the tears started, he thought to himself, had she been crying for hours or had they started as she witnessed his plight? Had she any guilt at all? The steam had stopped rising from the plastic mug. He reached out for the now lukewarm cup of tea. No matter, it still tasted good. He devoured the sandwiches like a greedy dog. Nature's way, he needed the energy.

There was only one option available to the Island Keepers and they had made their decision. He had the information to bring their organisation to its knees, put the Brothers away for life. Roddam, Moor, the Father, even his one-time friend John Markham, and especially… Claire. They were all accessories to murder.

He heard voices. The cell door opened and a delegation of Island Keepers filled the small room. They were dressed in ceremonial aprons and blue-trimmed sashes that hung loosely across their chests. They each held an ornamental sword. Ashley's chains were opened and he squeezed at both wrists in turn.

Jacob Moor spoke as the delegation raised their swords, pointing towards Ashley. "The Brothers have instructions to kill you should you try anything silly, so please cooperate."

"Cooperate in what? Where are you taking me?"

John Markham answered. "You're to stand trial."

"Stand trial for what? It's a foregone conclusion, your chaplain said."

"Save your questions. You'll have plenty of time to speak," replied John Roddam. In a swift familiar movement, his old Chief Superintendent applied the Northumbria Police Force standard-issue plastic handcuffs to the wrists of the prisoner. Ashley winced as they bit into his wounds. A rough hand pushed him from behind as he was unceremoniously bundled from the cell.

The temple was almost in darkness save for a few candles flickering around the perimeter, and three on top of the stone crypt in the centre of the room. It was cold… oh, so cold.

The Brothers formed a makeshift guard of honour and Jacob Moor walked down the middle of them, occasionally nodding or exchanging a nervous smile.

He slow-marched around the crypt twice and climbed four stone steps and took his place at a high wooden throne-type chair decorated with jewels and ornate gold patterns.

He bowed his head and the Brothers took their place, four in slightly less elaborate wooden thrones in each corner of the room and the rest strategically placed in between. Again, Roddam pushed Ashley roughly towards the centre of the room. As he approached the crypt, a light was switched on and his eyes fell on two seats at opposite ends of the crypt. One was empty and obviously meant for Ashley, in the other sat a dishevelled Kate Wilkinson.

"Kate," he cried out.

"Oh, Ashley," she spoke as the tears begun to flow. "Thank God you're still alive. They told me you had had an accident, toldme I had to get here as soon as I could."

The sight of Kate Wilkinson sitting in the chair with her wrists tied to each arm plunged Ashley to new depths of despair. He could barely speak.

"They tricked you, Kate. I'm sorry, it's my fault. I should never have—"

"What's happening, Ashley? Is this some sort of sick joke? Who are these nutters? Why am I tied up?"

Ashley looked up at Jacob Moor, then gazed around the room. "These are the people who killed your son."

Kate Wilkinson's mouth fell wide open as she tightened her grip on the arms of the chair.

"Silence," ordered Roddam. "Sit."

He forced Ashley down into the seat.

Ashley raised his voice a decibel or two. "Every one of them had a hand in his death, Kate."

Roddam pushed Ashley forward, took a key from his pocket and undid the handcuffs.

"Don't go getting too comfortable." He grinned as he produced two pieces of gold-coloured rope. A chance, thought Ashley, at last a chance to do something – anything.

As if reading his mind, two of the biggest Brothers stepped forward, each one taking an arm as they forced each elbow down until they were parallel with the wooden arms of the chair. Roddam took great pleasure in applying the ropes a lot tighter than was necessary.

Jacob Moor began. "Chaplain, you may open the meeting." Father Thompson stood, walked over to the head of the crypt and held a copy of the Bible aloft. "Brothers," he began. "In the name of the grand architect of the universe and by the powers invested in me I will declare—"

"JUDAS!" roared Ashley.

"Judas, Judas, Judas," he began to chant. Father Thompson looked around for assistance; John Roddam strode forward and cuffed Ashley hard across the face.

"Silence!" he screamed. "How dare you? This is a place of worship." Ashley felt a trickle of blood run from his lip and down his chin. The pain danced across his face.

Task completed and the prisoner silenced, Roddam turned to Father Thompson.

"Please continue, chaplain."

Father Thompson, visibly shaking now, nodded at Roddam and prepared to speak again.

"Brothers, we, we…" he stuttered, glancing sideways at Ashleyas if expecting another interruption. "We are gathered here to… to… to… today to t… t… take?"

"Fucking murdering Judas Iscariot," Ashley screamed. He didn't want to disappoint.

"Murdering man of the cloth, child abuser, hypocr—"

A heavy fist propelled into his face and Ashley's world started spinning out of control.

When he came round he'd been gagged and his chair moved to face Jacob Moor from a corner at the front of the temple. His breathing was shallow and laboured.

Kate Wilkinson sat alongside Ashley, sniffing. Ashley turned to look. She was a quivering wreck, her tear-streaked faced blackened with mascara. She looked at Ashley, setting off another bout of crying.

"Oh, Ashley," she whimpered between the tears, "they're goingto kill us. We're on trial for our lives."

Jacob Moor appeared as if he was coming to the end of his address. Ashley didn't know how long he'd been speaking. He had no idea how long he'd been out.

“And therefore, Brothers, the decision you have to make today is a hard one. If you take the decision to spare their lives, then you must also take the decision to end our noble organisation and face the consequences. A trial… maybe evena prison sentence for some of us.”

Jacob looked down at Ashley.

“Ah, Mr Clarke, you’re in the land of the living again.” He signalled to a Brother over the far side of the room who, armed with a small dagger, walked towards Ashley and Kate.

“As promised, Mr Clarke, we always give our prisoners the right to reply.”

The Brother raised the dagger up to Ashley’s face and sliced through the rope gag that had prevented him from speaking. Jacob Moor continued. “Please try to avoid cursing and insulting us. Try to be a little constructive with your chosen vocabulary. It might just save your life.” Jacob suppressed a smile. He knew that whatever the prisoner said, it wouldn’t save his life. It was a forgone conclusion, it always was. Thirteen Brothers, thirteen votes and the majority count held court.

Thirteen black balls and thirteen white; a black ball meant death and a white one a reprieve. He wanted to smile, laugh out loud, but held his composure well. Never in the history of the Lodge since he’d been the Master had a white ball ever been cast. He was the Master of the Lodge, they were his men. He’d influenced every decision they’d ever taken. That’s what the Master was there for… it was his duty to control hisBrothers… Jacob’s men… and he was proud of every one of them.

He thought about the fourteenth member of the Lodge. He was pleased with what he'd created, pleased with the way he'd moulded her into what she was. As a young girl, she'd always been at the beck and call of her *Uncle Jacob*, always been obedient and trusting.

Ashley opened and closed his mouth several times. The saliva began to flow again.

"Brothers… our organisation has a long and proud history. It is your duty…" He paused and deliberately cast his eyes on every Brother gathered in the temple. They looked up at the Worshipful Master with their swords pointing at the floor. Jacob looked down at Ashley.

"The history books tell us, Mr Clarke, of the exploits of the Knights Templar and the Freemasons, the Illuminati and other secret societies based on the same principles and teachings as our own. At Bannockburn, the famous battle between England and Scotland in 1314, the historians write about a well-trained band of men fighting against the English side that turned the tide and won the battle for the Scots. The history books suggest those band of men were in fact the Knights Templar who'd made a base in Scotland after they'd been persecuted and harangued by the Catholic church. Those men were not the Knights Templar. They were Island Keepers. The Keepers had thrived in Scotland and we felt we owed a debt of gratitude to the country who allowed us a homeland. Nor could we forget the persecution we'd suffered in the early centuries at the hands of the English crown."

Ashley found his voice.

“You mean to tell me that a handful of men originating from Holy Island fought the might of the English army and won?”

“Not a handful, Mr Clarke, thousands of us.” Jacob smiled again. “I think now, Mr Clarke, you might just realise what sort of organisation you’ve infiltrated. We are proud men. Proud and determined to do what is right and just.”

A few of the Brothers were nodding in agreement. The first black balls were already being cast.

Ashley’s throat was dry; just how many Island Keepers were spread around the British Isles, how many Lodges were there and what power did they hold? The police at Berwick, Roddam and John Markham, men of power, men able to influence people’s lives. And then it dawned on him… the coroner at Tom’s inquest.

“Men of influence, Mr Clarke, men with the power to make decisions.”

“Like coroners?”

Jacob smiled. “Ah, you mean our friend Mr Douglas in Cleveland.” Jacob smiled and nodded, with a look that sickened Ashley to the pit of his stomach.

“You call yourself men of honour. You’re nothing of the sort. Cheats and frauds all of you.” He looked over to where Kate Wilkinson was sitting. “You robbed this lady of justice, murdered her son then covered it up. Your organisation is poison.”

“He was a drug dealer, he deserved to die. We have no place for people like that on the island. Society should do likewise.”

“He never touched a drug in his life; you invented it.”

"The island is sacred; it must be policed, protected at all times."

"Tom wouldn't touch a drug. He hated them. A few of us experimented just after we left school. Tom walked away, wouldn't have nothing to do with them," Ashley shouted at the Brothers. "Your Worshipful Master is a liar, gentlemen."

"Silence," screamed Jacob. "I won't have you accusing me in my own temple."

The lone voice that spoke was very quiet, barely above a whisper, but it commanded the attention of everybody in the room.

"I'm afraid you can't silence him, Worshipful Master." John Markham continued, "With the greatest respect, Worshipful Master, he is allowed to speak. The right to reply. Remember?" Jacob Moor paused for a second, unsure what to do or say. Ashley continued, "You have a chance, gentlemen, a chance to put right the wrongs of the past. You have an opportunity to give this lady justice. As we speak the father of one of your so-called undesirables is busy contacting the other victims' families. This won't go away, you can't sweep this under the carpet. They'll be knocking at your front door very soon. You won't be able to explain those deaths away so easily and if you get rid ofme and Tom's mother, you'll have another two to deal with."

"He's lying, Brothers, he's trying to frighten you."

"I'm lying Jacob, am I? Does the name Tam Dalgleish mean anything to you?"

Jacob Moor shook his head. Ashley glanced around the temple. The Brothers were looking at each other. He noticed a few reactions; a gentle murmur reverberated around the room. "He was the father of one of the boys you murdered. I spoke to him last week. He's a Glasgow villain and his son was too. You murdered his son and now he's on the warpath conducting his own investigation. He'll be here soon, gentlemen, with more questions. He's contacting the families of the other victims,your victims, gentlemen."

"He's lying, Brothers," Jacob snapped.

"No, I'm not," Ashley replied. "You're the liar. Tom would never take drugs."

John Markham raised a hand in the direction of Jacob Moor. "Worshipful Master, permission to address the Lodge."

Jacob Moor pulled at his collar, a bead of perspiration trickled down his spine. He looked across the void at John Markham and reluctantly nodded his head.

"A suggestion, Worshipful Master. With respect and not that I doubt your integrity, but why don't we get Sister Claire down here to clarify the situation? He offered her the drugs, didn't he? She can clear this accusation up straightaway."

John Markham raised an eyebrow towards the Worshipful Master.

Jacob Moor remained quiet, thoughtful. Surely Claire wouldn't let him down. Why would she change the story now? Claire, the girl he'd controlled since she was a child.

Ashley interrupted his thoughts. "Get her down here, Jacob. What have you got to hide?"

Jacob Moor looked up, a confident smile flicked across his face. He looked over at the Brother, his Brother, standing guard at the door of the temple and nodded just once. The Brother produced a key from his apron, inserted it in the lock and pulled at the heavy door. It creaked as it opened and the whole Lodge listened to the footsteps as they gradually disappeared. The Brothers sat in silence for the two minutes it took for Claire Macbeth to be brought downstairs.

Jacob explained the accusation to a nervous-looking Claire Macbeth who stood attention-like in front of his throne. Jacob liked the way she stood with respect. Respect for the temple, the Brotherhood, respect for her Master. That's what he was… her Master.

"Tell the truth, Claire," interrupted Ashley.

Jacob Moor frowned, nearly admonished the prisoner again, but remembered John Markham's words.

"All in good time, Mr Clarke, all in good time."

He turned to Claire again. "Do you remember that night clearly?"

Claire nodded her head. "Yes, Worshipful Master, clear as day."

"And do you remember calling me after you'd closed the bar?"

"I do, Worshipful Master."

He had her in his power. Yes, Sir, no, Sir, three bags full, Sir. "And can you tell the Brothers exactly what you told me that night?"

She wasn't sure exactly what was going on but her mind was racing. Jacob had been accused of setting up Tom Wilkinson. It was true. There were no drugs.

The enormity of the occasion slowly became apparent. Jacob hadn't killed an undesirable: the boy was innocent, weren't they all? She looked at Ashley

Clarke. He looked terrible and she yearned to take him in her arms, wash the blood from his face and cleanse his injuries. She wanted to bathe him, immerse his strong body in hot water and tell him she loved him with all her heart.

But she couldn't.

He hated her and who could blame him? She'd helped to kill his best friend. She was a murderess.

She looked at Tom Wilkinson's mother. Fear, anxiety. She looked into the soul of a broken woman.

Claire Macbeth could change it now, right this moment; shehad the power to bring the organisation to its knees, she had the power to break the man sitting above her. The man who had held her prisoner for fifteen years, the man who treated her like a slave, a plaything, the man who'd prevented her from even opening a bank account or learning to drive. He'd taken and organised every aspect of her life. He'd manipulated and oppressed her.

He spoke again, gently this time. His voice was soft… soothing. "What did you tell me that evening, Claire? What did the man do?"

She recalled the depraved acts Jacob had made her perform, and that first night as a fourteen-year-old when he robbed her of her innocence. She'd begged him to stop. It hurt so much, and he'd held his hand over her mouth as he grunted and groaned on top of her. It all came flooding back. He'd dominated her for as long as she could remember.

She'd tried to escape, get away from the hell she'd been living, but he'd always prevented it.

Once… only once had she managed it with some level of success. She'd ended up in a squat in Leeds, turned to prostitution just to survive. She had no money, didn't even have a national insurance number to claim benefits. She found she didn't exist when she'd applied for a position at the local job centre.

It took him only three weeks to find her. He'd used the *network,* as he called it. She would never forget that night. She'd been walking along a dimly lit street in the Chapeltown district of the city when a white transit van had slowed down beside her. Jacob sat smiling in the passenger seat and before she could turn and run, two men had jumped out of the back and bundled her in. The driver and her two abductors took it in turn to rape her throughout the night as Jacob looked on. Eventually, her body could take no more and she'd lapsed into unconsciousness.

When she'd woken she found herself back on the island in her very own comfortable bedroom, battered and bleeding. She was back home and knew at that very moment she would never escape her own private hell.

Jacob Moor acted as her nursemaid as she slowly recovered. Jacob Moor had helped her.

"Claire?"

She looked up at him, then again at Ashley. Ashley caught the look on her face and he smiled and nodded his head.

"The truth, Claire," he said.

She looked back at Jacob and opened her mouth."He offered me Ecstasy; put a packet in my hand."

Jacob Moor breathed an inward sigh of relief. Ashley turned to Claire and shook his head.

"And you, Claire." He sighed.

Claire looked in his eyes, the eyes which at that moment displayed surrender. She had been his last chance, his last throw of the dice and she'd let him down. Never before had she gazed into eyes like that: she expected to see hate and bitterness, but no. Just the eyes of a crushed man.

"Brothers." The Worshipful Master looked around his temple. "From the horse's mouth, so to speak. The undesirable offered our Sister drugs."

He turned to Ashley

"Mr Clarke, your friend was a peddler of filth. He was vermin." He turned to his congregation. "Gentlemen, this man has tried to drive a wedge between us. He tried but has not succeeded in destroying our organisation. He lied about the undesirable." He held two outstretched arms. "I am proud of you all, Brothers." He looked at Claire Macbeth and lowered his voice a little. "And you, Sister." He held out his right hand, pointed to a row of pews at the side of the room.

"You may take a seat, Sister. You are welcome to sit in on proceedings. It is now time to decide their fate."

What an end. What a result, thought Jacob Moor as he took his seat and waited for his senior warden to distribute the coloured balls. He had to admit to himself he had been a little concerned at the prisoner's outburst. His little speech had been quite convincing, a little too near the truth. And he'd been put on the spot. Markham had called his bluff. He had had no option but to call Claire Macbeth into the temple.

Claire Macbeth. Why did he doubt her? He gazed over to where she sat. How lucky was he to have this young lady pander to his every need? He reminded himself that it wasn't luck. Luck played no part.

Claire Macbeth sat over the far side of the room in torment. She could have stopped it right there and then. The look in Ashley Clarke's eyes. And had she witnessed the briefest of brief smiles? Why? Why had he smiled, why had he looked at her in a way she had seen portrayed on the silver screen as two lovers looked at each other? Or had she imagined it? Was it all a figment of her imagination, the look, the murders, this kangaroo court, Jacob Moor and his twelve apostles?

Father Thompson, one of them. She'd begged him to stop it and he'd done nothing. He'd stood and hid behind the cross, his beloved church. She hated him with all her heart.

It was a bad dream, a nightmare, and she could have stopped it right there and then and she'd done nothing. Nothing at all… and now the moment had passed.

The senior deacon stopped at Jacob Moor and handed him the two coloured wooden balls. Jacob met his stare, the deacon nodded and smiled. Jacob looked down at the two small balls in the palm of his hand as the Brother – his Brother – moved on to the next man.

Ashley glared across the room at Claire Macbeth. Never before had he so misjudged a human being. She'd had her chance. He'd been so sure as he'd met her eyes, so, so sure.

The senior deacon sat down, his bag was empty.

Ashley Clarke's and Kate Wilkinson's lives were hanging in the balance. The vote was about to commence.

It was an important part of the ceremony, a tradition that had spanned centuries. In the early days, the vote, if negative, had always resulted in death. Jacob was proud he'd resurrected that policy from the Brothers long ago. That's how it should be: an eye for an eye, a tooth for a tooth. Jacob cast his eyes upwards, mouthed a silent prayer as the senior deacon began his second trip around the temple collecting up the votes.

Jacob reached into the sack and pulled out the first ball. He held the black ball aloft. The Brothers nodded their approval. Another three black balls followed and any nerves or doubts that Jacob Moor harboured were quickly dispelled.

His Lodge… his Brothers.

Another black ball and another. One more required for a majority decision. Jacob Moor's hand trembled as he held the white ball upwards. One of his Brothers had let him down.

Jacob Moor, the Worshipful Master of the Lodge… betrayed. He reached inside and picked out another three white balls, knew at that very moment that the Lodge was split.

His hand shook as he reached into the bag again. A half-hearted ripple of applause echoed through the temple as Jacob Moor held the black ball aloft. The black ball that signalled death. But then, as Jacob Moor reached in his pocket for a black cap, he and his Brothers and Ashley Clarke and Kate Wilkinson became aware of a lone figure rising to her feet.

# Chapter 23

## Six months later

Stephen Kyle stood in the packed number three Newcastle upon Tyne Crown Court with his head held low. He had been charged with the murder of Frank Clarke and had been on remand in Durham prison since his arrest. He'd tried to blame it all on Jacob Moor.

That was the grounds of his defence, as it had been for all the other members of the Island Keepers. Dead men can't talk and nor could they defend themselves.

Four white balls, a divided Brotherhood, a vote of no confidence in the Worshipful Master.

Claire Macbeth had stood and spoken to the assembled Brothers. Her voice was quiet, barely above a whisper, racked with emotion, almost on the verge of tears. The Brothers had listened.

Jacob Moor wanted to shout her down, but somehow he kept quiet, somehow he realised the end had come.

She'd announced that there had, in fact, been no drugs and then turned to John Markham and disclosed that Jacob Moor and Stephen Kyle had murdered his beloved Uncle Frank.

Jacob Moor could have handled the situation if he'd just been given a chance. If he'd had the heart to speak out he would have convinced his Brothers including John Markham as he'd done many times before that Tom Wilkinson was a drug dealer and his Uncle Frank really had committed suicide. But then it had all gone horribly wrong.

Father Thompson fell to his knees crying as Claire sat back down and, as soon as Stephen Kyle looked into John Markham's eyes, the terrified Brother bolted towards the temple door, desperately trying to escape the clutches of the still grieving nephew.

John Markham caught him as he fumbled with the heavy lock. Stephen Kyle was a slight man and Markham dragged him kicking and screaming by the neck to the centre of the room. He held him up, legs dangling like a tortured ballerina as he propelled his heavy fist into the man's face. His nose popped like a balloon and a jet of blood splashed across the temple floor.

The unconscious man collapsed in a heap onto the temple floor and John Markham fell to his knees sobbing like a child. And the questions began. Roddam first, demanding answers from the Worshipful Master and then another Brother and another until a crowd had gathered around the throne. Jacob Moor had held up his hands and an eerie silence ensued.

His Brothers had turned against him.

Jacob Moor tore his crisp white cotton shirt to expose his left breast. He held the handle of the sword down to the floor and the tip rested on his nipple. It wasn't an unusual sight in the temple, the sword and exposure of the left breast part and parcel of the ceremony to initiate a new Keeper. The Brothers looked on, a little unsure of what part of the ceremony was being re-enacted. Markham looked up from the temple floor, knew what was about to happen, knew instinctively and could do nothing to prevent it, would do nothing to prevent it. Jacob Moor fell forward, gripping the sword with two hands. The handle of the sword powered into the stone floor and the weight of the Worshipful Master did the rest.

The sword travelled through his ribcage into his heart and out the other side of his body in a grotesque spectacle witnessed by everybody, blood bright red, arterial. He'd died instantly, the temple filled with the rich, cloying smell of congealing blood.

The trial hadn't gone well for Stephen Kyle and he knew before the guilty verdict came he'd be spending the best part of his life in a prison cell. The other Brothers had got off lightly; they'd stuck together and blamed Kyle, Jacob Moor and Claire Macbeth as the main instigators.

They'd taken a slap on the wrist and their lawyers had plea bargained for covering up the crime. The prosecutor had wanted the charge of accessory to murder, which carried a far lengthier sentence but had settled for a guilty plea to the lesser charge of concealment. They all got between three and five years. Roddam and John Markham had been forced from their positions in Northumbria Police as had the four Berwick policemen.

Their careers had been destroyed.

Big Tam Dalgleish was in court and noted the length of their sentences. He took notes and every single name. He'd be arranging his own little welcome home party for the Island Keepers when they were released, especially Father Thompson after Ashley had revealed he had been involved in his son's death.

Claire Macbeth stood trial two weeks later. Her solicitor Anne Haslam had begged her to allow her to introduce the abuse suffered at the hands of Jacob Moor and how she'd been forced from the age of fourteen to endure that abuse and the torture she'd suffered.

Claire Macbeth had refused. She might as well plead guilty, her solicitor had said at one point and even threatened to walk away from the case.

Claire Macbeth didn't fear prison. She had at first. She'd been terrified as the prison van had driven up to the gates of the female wing at HMP Durham, She Wing as it was known to the inmates.

The vilest women in history had been housed here: Myra Hindley and Rose West were two that came to mind. But then, as each day passed and the weeks turned into months, she realised that it was no worse than the hell she'd endured since fourteen years of age.

And so she should be punished; it was to be expected, deserved. She'd sent the poor boys out onto the causeway, coerced them, and persuaded them, never imagining that so many wouldn't make it.

She was giving them a chance to escape when she'd altered the clock in The Ship Inn by a few minutes. Jacob had his timing down to perfection, literally down to the second. He'd look at the clock and on the dot he'd order the prisoner to be brought before him. And Claire had watched Jacob's face as she'd persuaded the poor unfortunates to attempt the crossing.

Jacob was watching a game, he was watching a horse race with his stake firmly fixed on the favourite. Only she'd tampered with the odds on more than one occasion and begged Jacob, generally between the sheets, to give them just a squeak of a possibility; claimed it excited her.

Jacob didn't mind: it added to the power, added to the thrill of the chase, so to speak. So what if they escaped? They'd never return to their island. hell that was for sure.

Claire wiped a tear from her eye with a crisp white handkerchief as she sat at a table, looking out of her barred prison cell. But why so many and why Tom Wilkinson? Tom should have made it with time to spare. What went wrong?

She sat with Anne Haslam awaiting the van that would be taking her to Newcastle Crown Court.

"So what do you think my chances are, Anne?"

Anne shrugged her shoulders. "They'd be better if you let me—"

Claire held up a hand. "No, Anne, I've made my decision. I've lived these memories for too long and now, thank God, they're in the past. I've no intention of reliving them."

"They raped and tortured you, Claire, for heaven's sake. They abused you mentally and physically for years. You owe it at least to..."

The solicitor's voice tailed off as she looked over at Claire Macbeth shaking her head with her hands over her ears. She was blocking it out, refusing to even talk about it again.

Anne Haslam sat in amazement that incredible afternoon when her client had broken down in front of her. And she'd blurted it out between the tears and the sighs and the solicitor had sat and listened until eventually she'd shed tears as well. Only God knew what was going on inside the poor girl's head, but this was her way of dealing with it. She didn't deserve prison; she deserved a medal, an OBE or an MBE for the poor boys she'd saved from those bastards.

She'd been charged with murder and Anne Haslam had reasoned with the prosecuting lawyer that the charge of manslaughter on the grounds of diminished responsibility wasmore apt. The prosecutor agreed but, after meeting and assessing Claire Macbeth, quite rightly suggested she'd recovered from her ordeal well and, although a little withdrawn,would not fool a jury into thinking she was crazy.

But then again, she didn't want to. She had the right, the right to preserve the self-respect denied to her for so long.

The prison van pulled onto the quayside and was met by a frenzied media circus. It was the sixth day of the trial, the jury having been put up in an undisclosed hotel over the weekend. Television journalists and cameramen fought for the best vantage points and a line of police officers kept the pack at bay.The crowd was equally divided. To some she was a murderess,to others a victim. Word had gradually filtered from the island of the abuse she'd suffered at the hands of Jacob Moor and Stephen Kyle and a video had appeared on the internet which left little to the imagination. Jacob Moor had been the director and Stephen Kyle the willing participant carrying out the grossest acts imaginable on a terrified young girl.

It had been part of Jacob's private secret collection that had been taken in a burglary three days after his death. The person who'd posted the video had chosen the moment well.

As the prison van door opened, the appearance of Claire was met with a few cheers, a muted half attempt at a round of applause, and one or two jeers. A women's group stood in silentadmiration with placards held aloft that read *Free Her Now* and *Claire Is Innocent*.

Jamie Powell looked on and caught the briefest of glimpses of his one-time lover. He then turned and headed into the court building to meet Ashley Clarke.

Claire had been charged with three murders carrying the mandatory life sentence for each one. Her defence was a simple one: she'd never intended to send the young men to their deaths; she was helping them to escape. She was their only chance.

The prosecuting lawyer, a large red-faced man in his early sixties, was beginning to wear her down. He was asking the same questions again and again and was even beginning to annoy the judge. Claire looked at her watch. He'd taunted and accused her and goaded her for just under an hour. It was a game to him, a game.

“So, Ms Macbeth, if you say you were helping to save those poor unfortunates how come they all ended up in watery grave?”

Claire wanted to answer, wanted to tell him she didn’t know. Possibly alcohol, possibly something else. He didn’t give her a chance.

“Not a very good success rate, is it? Three young men you sent out onto an already flooded causeway and three bodies in the morgue.” He looked along the line of jurors and over to the packed gallery.

“Not very good odds, are they, ladies and gentlemen?”

“There were others, Sir,” Claire replied meekly.

The lawyer, Holmes, paused. “Others, you say?” He smiled at her and again at the jury. “Others, you say?” He leaned forward,rested his hand on his chin. “Then where are they, young lady?”

Anne Haslam couldn’t believe her luck. She removed her glasses and looked up from her notes. She stood up slowly, commanding the attention of the courtroom. It was a well-planned interruption, well-rehearsed. She just hadn’t expected her learned friend to open the door quite so early or easily. “Actually, Your Honour, I’d like to call an additional witness.” The judge looked down at his notes. “Name please, Ms Haslam.”

“Jamie Powell, Your Honour.”

Claire recalled the name, looked around the gallery. Her eyes focused on a man she vaguely recognised. He fidgeted in his seat, looked nervous.

“Objection,” yelled Holmes. “There’s no mention of a witness by that name in my briefing.”

She walked forward to the bench. "I do apologise, Your Honour," whispered Anne Haslam to the judge as she let out a sigh and fluttered her eyelashes in his direction. It worked everytime.

"He's literally only just been located this weekend; we've had a private detective on the case. I haven't had time to inform the court, though I did try to call you this morning."

"Objection, Your Honour."

The judge held up a hand, irritated by Holmes's voice.

"The lines don't open till nine, Miss Haslam."

Anne Haslam fired in the final nail. "The witness is critical to the case."

"And who is Jamie Powell, Ms Haslam?"

Anne Haslam paused… ignored the judge and her learned friend as well as the public gallery, aware all eyes were on her. She glanced at Claire Macbeth, then met every gaze of the twelve jury members before announcing.

"Jamie Powell is a young man Claire Macbeth helped to escape."

# Chapter 24

The Newcastle Evening Chronicle carried the dramatic news of Claire Macbeth's acquittal later that afternoon. Ashley had met up with Anne Haslam within an hour of the trial ending and the first editions of the newspaper had been placed on her desk. Ashley picked it up and surveyed the headlines.

"Incredible, Ashley," the lawyer said, shaking her head. "Who'd have thought this last week? I honestly thought we were dead and buried and the poor bugger was heading back to Durham."

"Yeah…" replied Ashley, "who'd have thought."

"It was the video, you know, the video that turned the tide, got the jury on her side. Whoever posted that video did us a huge favour."

Ashley nodded his head.

The break in at Jacob Moor's house was the easy bit. Viewing and posting that video on the internet was tough. It was the hardest thing he'd ever done in his life and it would remain his secret forever.

And to think at one point he thought that Claire was making it all up. He doubted her time and time again until he'd eventually managed to locate Jamie Powell alive and well in Wolverhampton.

"How is she, Anne?"

"She's good, Ashley... considering." The lawyer closed the newspaper, removed her glasses and spoke. "I'm sending her on a long holiday, Ashley. Do you know she's never ever been abroad."

Ashley shook his head.

"A local women's group started a fund and I've managed to locate the estate of her late father that Jacob Moor was looking after. She's not poor, Ashley, and a long holiday is just what she needs. The thing is, I don't know if she'll ever go back to the island."

"Memories."

"Bad memories, Ashley."

Ashley spoke. "Where does—" A loud rap on the door interrupted him and announced the arrival of Claire Macbeth. Ashley stood and was immediately aware of his legs letting him down. He'd experienced the same sensation as an eighteen-year-old in the boxing ring at training school in Hendon. The policemen showed her into the room, gave a cursory nod then left.

It was a reserved smile, a sad smile. Claire Macbeth looked at her hard-working and meticulous, clever lawyer and the man whose tireless detective work and sheer determination had freed her.

She broke down.

Anne Haslam took her client in her arms and the lawyer's pent-up emotion and stress of the trial broke her too. Ashley looked on as the two women sobbed their hearts out. It lasted a full two minutes before the lawyer was able to compose herself. During that time Ashley left quietly.

# Epilogue

## One month later

It was a love like Ashley Clarke had never experienced before. Alexis had never been far from his thoughts over the last year and had crept more and more into them during the trial. He'd blamed the job, not Alexis. Alexis had blamed him. It was time to exercise his demons. Alexis… always Alexis.

Everyone deserved a second chance. They'd agreed on a holiday, a week in Bermuda… not a bad place to start, he thought with a grin. The climate was nice at this time of the year, he'd been told.

After the holiday, they'd fly back to the UK and if they felt the same way about each other, possibly rent a place together for a while. It would take time, of that there was no doubt, but Ashley felt like he had all the time in the world for this girl.

She'd agreed to meet him at JFK airport in New York where they'd spend the evening and, as the wheels touched down on the runway, his stomach was turning cartwheels. He'd drunk too much red wine, an indication of his nervous disposition on an aeroplane and of course that first meeting.

As he descended the aircraft steps, he sobered up rapidly. He fumbled for a square of chewing gum to freshen his breath. He walked into the terminal and, after what seemed like an eternity, collected his suitcase from the baggage reclaim.

He'd heard America was security conscious these days, especially after the 9/11 bombings but, still, he was surprised at the fifteen-minute grilling he had at the hands of airport security. He'd answered their questions confidently though he had thought a few of them were rather peculiar. But the male and female officials had been pleasant enough and as they gave him permission to leave, they both made a point of wishing him a pleasant stay in their country. As he left the small claustrophobic cubicle and the door closed behind him, the female official beckoned through the glass window to another visitor to America to come forward from the lengthy queue. Security officer Clint McGregor watched as the latest interviewee walked across the wide expanse that led to the terminal exitand picked up the internal telephone.

"Ashley," she shouted.

He caught sight of her on the other side of the barrier, manned by two fully armed New York cops. She waved like an excited schoolgirl.

"Ashley… over here."

She looked different. He waited patiently as the sliding doors filtered the throng through one or two at a time. He expected a nervous meeting, perhaps a little cold even.

But no.

She rushed forward, her eyes pulled him in like a black hole and he took her in his arms and kissed her. He crushed her with a pressure that told her he never wanted to let her go and he knew… they knew… that it was right.

"Ashley, I've missed you so much, more than you could imagine."

"Me too… me too."

His hand caressed her face and he leaned forward to taste her again. His tongue pushed gently against her lips. It felt so good… so right, and he wanted to be in her hotel bedroom making love to her time and time again. He wanted to discover the parts of her body he had only imagined in the past.

He felt a hand gently push him in the back. He turned around to face the New York cop who was staring at him.

"Could you please move along, Sir? You're causing an obstruction." The cop was smiling.

Ashley blushed and took Claire's hand.

"C'mon, let's get out of here."

The cop's partner looked on. "Have a nice day, Sir," the cop shouted as they turned and walked away.

Claire Macbeth and Ashley Clarke left the terminal building and joined the queue for the yellow cabs.

The two cops watched them every step of the way until they took up their position in the cab rank.

The older cop, Gavin Anderson, turned to his young understudy, John Bonner.

Bonner raised his eyebrows. "Is that them, buddy?"

The older cop nodded his head. "That's them, John, our friends from across the pond… the undesirables."

Always a man of quotes, he placed a hand on John Bonner's shoulder.

"Put your trust in God, my friend, and keep your powder dry."

Ken Scott has also written or collaborated on the following books.

Race Against Me
This Heart Within Me Burns
Do The Birds Still Sing In Hell?
The Girl in the Pink Shoes
The Monster I Loved
Twenty Years a Stranger
Ghost of a Stranger
The World's my Oyster
Who The Hell is Alice?
A Million Would Be Nice
Jack of Hearts
Revenge is Sweeter than Flowing Honey
The Blue Door
Sherlock's Squadron
Fitted up but Fighting Back
Call Me Mistress
The Genesis Chamber
In Violet Sleep
The Gate That Cried Blood
The Devil Couldn't Break Me
The Survivor
The Girl With the Flower
Undercover in a Jihad Training Camp
And then the Penny Dropped
Not all Robbers Wear a Mask
Two Cops and a Robber
My Journey Through Hell
Soldier, Prisoner, Hunter Gatherer
The Five Amigos
The Psychiatrist
Heroes of Lamsdorf
Simply Fate
The War Within
Cycling the Camino de Santiago
Under a Spanish Sun
Don't Die Yet Dad
Death on the Haute Route

Printed in Great Britain
by Amazon

14918533R00212